RAVE REVIEWS FOR JOY NASH & *CELTIC FIRE*!

"Nash creates suspenseful, haunting and high-tension romance...a top-notch read."

—*RT BOOKclub*

"Joy Nash has created a lush world for senses of all kinds. ...This is a wonderfully fast-paced read full of romance, love and fantasy that will continue to burn in the hearts of readers after the last page is turned."

—Fresh Fiction

"Joy Nash is definitely one to be watched. She has great world-building skills, and her own personal magic with the pen is guaranteed to make hers a very strong name on the market in the not too distant future."

—Love Romances

"Wonderful! [*Celtic Fire*] contains everything one could want in a romance and even a touch of the paranormal. This book is truly a winner for all historical fans out there."

—A Romance Review

"Ms. Nash has added a liberal dose of historical detail on the early Britons and Roman military life…and embroidered a lively mystery around it. Readers of historical and paranormal romances alike will find great appeal in this offering from Ms. Nash."

—*Romance Reviews Today*

"Brimming with sexual tension and enhanced by a touch of humor, *Celtic Fire* is a good book."

—*Affaire de Coeur*

WORTH MORE THAN JEWELS

Barbarian. The thought rose sharply. She hadn't realized she'd sent the word into his mind until she saw his eyes narrow. Again, they were joined. And just like before, she had no clear idea how the union had come about.

His swift rage seared her. She withdrew as quickly as she could, heart pounding.

He rose and stepped toward her, causing her to tip her head back. He towered over her, his blue eyes glittering. "Keep to yourself, lass," he said evenly.

"I…I didn't mean to do it," she whispered. "I'll try not to let it happen again. Please. Let me go with you. I'll be no trouble."

He stared at her for what seemed a long time. Then his expression turned calculating. "Perhaps I'll take ye to the stones," he said, "if ye agree to give me something first."

Tiny wings fluttered in her belly. "Coin? Gold?"

"Nay. 'Tis something I've wanted since I first laid eyes on ye. Worth more, I am thinking, than all the jewels in your wee bag."

"What is it?" Clara whispered.

His gaze dropped to her mouth. "A kiss, lass. I would have a kiss."

Other *Love Spell* books by Joy Nash:

CELTIC FIRE

The GRAIL KING

JOY NASH

LOVE SPELL

NEW YORK CITY

LOVE SPELL®

August 2006

Published by

Dorchester Publishing Co., Inc.
200 Madison Avenue
New York, NY 10016

ISBN 0-505-52683-2

Printed in the United States of America.

This book is dedicated to all the members of Bucks County Romance Writers, whose constant encouragement and enthusiasm never cease to inspire. A special thanks goes to my critique partners, Donna Birdsell and Anita Nolan, and BCRW's goal-setting maven extraordinaire, Sally Stotter. This one's for you, guys!

Dear Reader,

There are, perhaps, more Holy Grail legends than can be counted. And yet so few follow the Grail in the early years, before Arthur and his knights set out to find the elusive magical cup.

The Grail King is the story of those early years.

Some of you may remember *The Grail King*'s Druid hero, Owein, from my previous Love Spell release, *Celtic Fire*. In the thirteen years that have passed between the stories, war and brutality have transformed Owein from troubled adolescent to embittered hermit. To read more about the experiences that have shaped him, visit my cyber home at www.joynash.com. You'll find three short stories—all free of charge—that tell of Owein's life in the years between.

Can Clara, the innocent daughter of Owein's hated enemy, help Owein release the pain of his past? The stakes, as you will see, are high.

For if Clara cannot prevail, a future king—Arthur—will never be born.

All the best,

Joy Nash

Chapter One

AD 130

Blood.

Why, in the name of all that was sacred, could he See naught but blood?

Pain exploded behind Owein's eyes, so vivid it sent him to his knees. By the might of the Horned God! The seasons had circled twice since last a vision had descended with such agony. Head bowed, he braced one rigid arm in the snow, waiting for the worst of the torture to pass. It was far better, he'd learned, to accept his gift than to fight it.

His breath formed a white shroud in the air before him. It lingered but a heartbeat before thinning into nothingness. He might have expected the Horned God's touch this day. Dawn winds had hurled sleet and snow into the mountains, unusual in Cambria, where the dark of the year passed more often in rain and fog. 'Twas a maelstrom born of magic.

A Druid's will drove the storm. Owein was certain of it. An intimate sense of the hidden one's power crackled in the air. Hope—as sweet as it was unfamiliar—constricted his chest. For years he'd thought himself the last of the Druids in the western mountains.

It seemed he was not.

Was the unknown Druid bound to Kernunnos, the great Horned God, as Owein was? Owein had little time to wonder as his vision came full upon him. He struggled upright, one knee buried in the snow, the heel of his hand pressed to his forehead.

After what seemed a bleak eternity, the solid hammering in his skull eased. With an effort he lifted his head, though its weight felt equal to a sack filled with stones. A vision wavered, vivid against the winter forest, yet at the same time distant, as if it belonged to a realm long vanished.

Blood.

A river of it. Thick and red, it streamed past his feet, a pulsing defilement of the virgin snow. Owein lurched upright and staggered along the crimson path, instinct driving him to its source.

The blood flowed from a woman.

A young woman, at that. The lass lay crumpled and pale, her long dark braids unpinned and tousled over the crystalline surface of the snow. Drifts claimed the lower portion of her body, wrapping her limbs and torso like a mantle of death. Blood—more than could possibly be contained in a score of human bodies—flowed from a jagged wound in her breast.

Owein's vision split. The image of the woman doubled and wavered. The ground seemed to fall from beneath him as a blinding spike of pain skewered his right eye. He gasped with the force of it, his knees crumpling. He went down hard, his hand scrabbling on a patch of ice.

He bowed his head and squeezed his eyelids shut, waiting. *Waiting.* The attack receded slowly, much as winter bowed to spring in the northern hills Owein had once called home.

His bunched muscles relaxed a bit. Though brutal, the

vision had been brief. The pain was bearable now—no more than a dull throb inside his skull. Fatigue dragged his limbs, as it always did when his Sight faded. That was the price he paid for his magic.

He murmured thanks to the Horned God for the favor of a vision. Then he muttered a second prayer—one of gratitude for a blessing so short-lived.

He eased back into a crouch, feeling normal save for a slight tingling on his scalp and the heavier weakness in his arms and legs. Both would be gone by dawn. For now, he was thankful enough that when he opened his eyes, the world would once again appear as it should. Gray sky overhead, white snow underfoot. There would be no woman. No blood.

He blinked, letting the dull light of the twilit sky filter into his vision. As he'd expected, the pristine snow on the path was marred only by his own footprints. The river of blood had vanished.

The woman had not.

Owein dragged a hand across his eyes, unwilling to lend full credence to his senses. But when he looked a second time, the figure lay as it had a moment before—pale and still as a corpse. This woman was no vision; she was real.

No mortal wound pierced her breast, but the snow falling on her pale face was itself a kiss of death. Ice had rendered her sable-lined cloak as stiff as an untanned hide. White frost dusted her braids and the ringlets framing her heart-shaped face. Blue tinged her lips. By contrast, her cheekbones and the tip of her straight nose were colored a raw, angry red.

Who could she be? Not one of his own kind. The last of the free Celts had been herded from the mountains by Roman spears. Resisters had been killed or taken as slaves, by order of the Second Legion's iron-fisted commander, Sextus Sempronius Gracchus. Those who'd surrendered had been resettled in the Roman fortress city of Isca.

Yet even if that grim history hadn't emptied the mountains of human activity, Owein would never have mistaken the unconscious woman for a hardy Celt lass. She was too delicately formed. Too dark. Too richly garbed.

She was Roman.

Amazement overtook his loathing. A young Roman woman, wandering alone in the mountains, more than a full day's journey from Isca? 'Twas pure insanity. He couldn't imagine one of her kind straying half so far from the fortress.

He reached out, his open hand hovering over her parted lips. Warm breath bathed his palm. Alive, then.

Something in his chest eased. He frowned. He hadn't even known he feared for the woman's life. Now an unexpected urgency flooded his veins. If she weren't warmed quickly, she would die.

Bending, he gathered her limp figure in his arms. His weakened muscles screamed in protest. Teeth gritted, he heaved her upward, scattering a shower of snow.

Shaking the stars from his vision, he shifted, distributing his burden more evenly. The lass started, then relaxed against his chest with a small sigh. As if Owein were a man to be trusted.

Slowly, he retraced his path, his breath laboring with each step. In normal circumstances the lass's small weight would have been as nothing. Now, in the aftermath of his vision, 'twas all he could do to place one foot before the other, trudging through lengthening shadows, whirlwinds of snow gusting before him. As he rounded a bend in the trail, the woman stirred in his arms. Her eyelids fluttered open.

Her gaze sought his. Her chapped lips parted, the tip of her tongue snaking between them. She drew a breath.

Instinctively, he dipped his head.

Her words came in Latin. It was a language Owein hadn't spoken willingly in many seasons, and it took him a moment to work out her meaning.

Ego inveni te. I have found you.

She blinked up at him. Pressed to describe her expression, Owein might have labeled it one of awe. He shook his head. She did not see him, not truly.

She lifted a hand to touch the bare patch of cheek above his beard. Her fingertip was a cool blessing on his heated skin.

She exhaled a whisper of misted breath. "You . . . are wreathed in light."

The reverence in her tone shook Owein to the core. Light? A harsh laugh stuck in his throat. Her words couldn't have struck the target farther from the truth.

He formed his reply carefully, the taste of the conquerors' language bitter on his tongue.

"Light? Nay, lady. Ye are mistaken. I live in darkness."

You are wreathed in light.

An odd utterance, and not fitting, in any case. Owein wondered at it, but feared he'd not have the chance to ask the Roman lass her meaning. Her eyes had swept closed and the blue tinge of her lips had deepened. Her breath came in uneven spurts, its rhythm marred by the shuddering of her body.

He tightened his arms around her. Was it his imagination, or did he detect the aroma of springtime?

With steps as quick as he could manage, he threaded his way through the broken bones of what had once been a village. A charred bit of stubble was all that remained of the settlement's encircling palisade wall. The cone roofs of the roundhouses, deprived of families to shelter, sagged like the faces of old women. In many cases, the thatching had scattered completely. Only one dwelling, on the fringe of the settlement, was not completely ruined.

He shoved open its plank door. Winter swirled into the hut, spiraling along the curved wall before settling with a sigh near the center hearth. He ducked inside, the door slamming crookedly behind him.

He'd left his fire smoldering. He'd meant to check his

traps before they were completely lost in the snow. A task, he thought belatedly, he'd left undone.

The Roman woman stirred in his arms, causing his weakened muscles to burn. Almost stumbling across the roundhouse's single room, he laid her not on the grass-stuffed pallet that was his bed, but on the bare dirt nearest the hearth. His muscles kinked as they released her weight. Bracing his arms on either side of her body, Owein closed his eyes and took a steadying breath. His strength was returning, but slowly.

Kneeling by the hearth, he used the last of his peat and deadwood to stoke a hot blaze. When he turned back to the Roman lass, the dust of ice crystals on her frozen cloak had already begun to melt. She'd soon be sopping wet if he left her wrapped in her icy garments. Gently, he lifted her shoulders and tugged at her cloak.

The garment was finely made, of long, soft wool lined with sable, the stitching so precise as to be invisible. The clasp was a gold pin with an ingenious guard designed to prevent the point from pricking the wearer.

She carried a small leather satchel. The front flap of the bag was decorated with the image of a prancing cat, of all things. He tried to ease it from her arms, only to find the strap threaded under her right arm and across her left shoulder. After a futile attempt to free the strap's frozen buckle, Owein simply drew his knife and cut a clean slice through the leather. He placed the bag on top of the cloak.

She wore a voluminous tunic of pale yellow wool with a geometric design embroidered in gold thread along the edges. Even wet, the garment was impossibly soft and fine. Unfortunately, it was also impossibly belted and pinned. The sleeves were fastened from shoulder to elbow with a series of tiny clasps. A gold-threaded girdle encircled her waist, cinching the tunic in multiple tiers of draped fabric at the bust and waist. Owein supposed the effect was meant to be alluring, and perhaps it might have been, if the dress were not wet, wrinkled, and spattered with mud.

He fumbled at the girdle's tiny clasps with blunt fingers, cursing under his breath. What idiocy prompted Roman women to bind their clothing so tightly? He managed to spring two buckles free, but the clasp of the third snapped in his hands. The sleeve pins were even smaller, and the lass's shivering didn't make his task any easier. Six pins on each sleeve; he broke three of the twelve.

He swept the small pile of gold aside. Obviously, this woman's family didn't lack for coin. Which made her presence in the high country near to impossible. Had she been traveling the Roman road along the coast? If so, how could she have strayed so far from her companions? A woman of her status might even have had a military escort. Owein didn't relish the thought of opening his door to a cohort of Sempronius Gracchus's Legionaries.

He lifted her small hand, chafing it in an effort to urge the blood to flow. She shivered, a small cry escaping her lips. He passed a hand over her brow, urging her expression to relax. Her lips parted again, and this time a softer, more feminine moan emerged.

It was not unlike the sound made by a woman while coupling.

Cursing under his breath, Owein pushed roughly to his feet. He was accustomed to solitude, not supple young lasses stretched before his hearth. The floral scent that clung to her skin was not an inducement to detachment. His body was responding, violently.

He dragged his pallet and winter furs to the hearth, positioning them as close to the flames as he dared. Straightening, he frowned down at the woman. He would have to finish the task of removing her wet clothes.

His loins stiffened further at the thought, even as his scowl deepened. How low he'd sunk, to lust after a Roman woman—and one not even conscious enough to curse him for it! But then, two twelvemonths had passed since he'd buried Eirwen. Perhaps the fact that his body could produce a cockstand this painful only proved he wasn't yet as dead as his wife.

Ignoring his discomfort, Owein crouched at the lass's feet and tugged off her frozen footwear. She wore boots crafted of thin leather, finely tooled and decorated with pearls at the ankles and toes. He shook his head in disgust. Hardly suitable for a Roman town house, let alone a trek through the mountains in winter. At least she'd had the sense to don woolen stockings beneath them. He peeled them off one by one. Her feet were like chunks of ice, and the tips of her toes were white.

Her dress came next. Lifting her torso, he stripped the wet wool from the lass's body. She wore a linen undertunic, devoid of decoration but so finely woven as to be translucent.

Owein stared, his eyes drifting to the puckered circles in the center of the lass's breasts, the dusky dark triangle between her thighs. Drawing a shaky breath, he crushed the hem of the undertunic in his fists. He drew the garment over slender legs. Her belly was flat, her hips slim, almost boyish. Her breasts were small enough to disappear into his hand.

He'd always preferred delicate lasses. His palms itched to touch her.

He resisted the impulse, easing the tunic over her shoulders with an efficient motion. Again, a heady floral scent teased his nostrils. In the dead of winter, this small Roman woman smelled of spring. A bead of perspiration slid between his shoulder blades. He wanted to look at all of her, drink her in, but he forced his gaze to her face as his arms slid beneath her naked body. For an instant she lay soft and yielding in his embrace. Then a shudder passed through her body.

The chill from her skin penetrated his overloaded senses. He transferred her quickly to his pallet and drew up the furs, swaddling her from neck to toe. A foray into his oaken chest yielded the remainder of his inventory of bedcoverings—

two thin woolen blankets. He covered her with those as well.

He lifted her sodden hair from her neck, fanning it toward the fire. The long braids were snarled and wet, but the color was dark and shining. Beautiful, her tresses would be, once dry and combed free.

Another tremor gripped her body. She moaned and clutched at her blankets, turning to one side, instinctively seeking the fire. Owein caught a glimpse of a small, rounded bottom as he adjusted the blankets. Easing to his feet, he watched the flickering light play across her face. Part of him wanted to reach out and run a finger along the outer curve of her cheek. The less foolish part of him wished he'd never laid eyes on her.

He knew well that the fire and blankets were not enough to prevent the corruption of her frozen toes. He dug in his mind for the remedy Rhiannon had used when he'd been a small lad. He'd wandered too far from the village during a snowfall. When he'd returned, he'd been unable to feel his fingers. He shut his eyes against the memory of his older sister alternately scolding and kissing as she'd wrapped his hands in warm, wet wool.

Rhiannon had been twelve years his elder, the only mother Owein had known. Even though his difficult entry to the world had orphaned them both, his sister had loved him fiercely. The memory of that love might have brought a smile to Owein's lips, had it not reminded him of all the Romans had stolen.

With precise motions, he set about the task of heating water. Hanging his cauldron on its tripod frame, he raked a portion of the fire into position beneath the vessel and filled it with snow from outside his door. While it melted, he rummaged again in the oaken chest. He emerged with several ragged lengths of wool, singed at the edges. Would his dead wife approve of his using her handiwork to give aid to a Roman woman? His chest felt hollow as he dipped the cloth into the warming water.

The lass drifted closer to consciousness. Her shivering was constant, though not as violent as before. A good sign, Owein thought—her body was seeking to warm itself. He crouched and wrapped her feet in the wet cloth, heating her skin, then drying it quickly.

He warmed her hands next, running the pad of his thumb over her palm and fingertips, searching for gray patches that indicated her skin had frozen past saving. He was relieved to find none. Experimentally, he circled one of her slight wrists with his thumb and forefinger. So delicate, and her palms, though red with cold, were soft and uncallused. The floral scent of her skin mingled with the musty odor of the wool.

She was a fragile blossom flung from a Roman garden into the wilderness. His brows drew together as he tucked the furs around her. Somehow, one of her hands remained in his, even after she'd been swaddled. As the night hours passed, he sat silently, chafing her soft skin with the roughened pads of his fingers. The chill of her body seeped into his soul, seeking his warmth.

It was not a welcome feeling.

Chapter Two

Clara came awake suddenly, gasping, her body shaking like a miller's sieve. Her hand was immersed in searing heat. She jerked back, to no avail. Something . . . no, *someone,* held her.

Someone was a man. A beast of a Celt—large, rough, and ruddy of complexion, with long red hair and a braided beard. Backlit by the flickering light, his mane glowed about his face like a halo of fire. A single thin plait hung from temple to shoulder, the end secured with a strip of leather. His eyes were a clear, brittle blue, like broken glass.

He had the look of a warrior about him. His broad chest stretched his buckskin shirt to the extremity of its rough seams. Despite the winter chill, the shirt had no sleeves, leaving Clara to stare at the corded muscles of his arms. He was in the prime of his manhood, sculpted like a statue of a god. The import of this observation settled over her like a blanket of frost.

He was not the man she sought.

She stirred, trying to lever herself upright. The fur coverlet slid across her skin. Her *bare* skin. Abruptly, she lay flat again, all but gagging on her panic. Straw poked through the coarse mattress, scratching her naked thighs and bottom. She was completely unclothed beneath the furs, and the wild man who must have removed her clothing was watching her closely.

He seemed to note the exact instant she recognized her vulnerability. One corner of his mouth twitched, and his gaze sharpened. The rough pad of his thumb scraped almost imperceptibly over her palm.

Clara was unprepared for the sensations the small movement brought. A pull deep in her belly, itching on the tips of her breasts. Something of it must have shown in her eyes, for his blue gaze flared, flicking downward, as if he *knew.* Though fur swaddled her body, revealing nothing, Clara's cheeks heated.

To her amazement, so did his.

Quickly, he dropped her hand and averted his eyes, busying himself with a fire that did not need tending. She watched as he prodded the blaze with a twisted stick. Flames leapt, but the heat seemed far away. She was chilled to her bones, to her very soul. She wondered if she would ever be warm again.

A dark sense of hopelessness assaulted her. Had she failed in her quest? She'd been sure the mountain she'd approached had been the Seer's. She'd followed Aiden's instructions exactly, but then the storm had struck, and she'd become disoriented. It was all too likely that she'd lost her way.

She wanted to sob her frustration. But she would not do that, here, before this wild stranger. There were scars encircling his wrists, as if he'd once been bound. Was he an escaped criminal? Keeping the blankets carefully wrapped about her body, she struggled into a sitting position, wincing as her tender palm scraped the dirt floor.

"My hands," she said, swallowing. "And . . . and my feet. They are afire."

The Celt's brow furrowed. "They are . . . frost." He

paused. "No. Frozen." He spoke the Latin haltingly, with a strong accent. His scowl deepened as he searched for his next words. "Will hurt . . . a while longer . . . but ye will not be scarred, I am thinking."

"Thank you for your kindness," she answered in Celtic, trying her best to imitate Aiden's mountain lilt. If she treated the barbarian like a civilized man, perhaps he would act the part.

A quick flash in his blue eyes betrayed his surprise. "Ye speak the language of the Celts?" he asked in his own tongue.

"Yes," she replied. "Though the pronunciation of some words eludes me. I learned from one of my father's . . ." Her voice trailed off.

He exhaled a sharp breath. "Slaves, ye mean to say."

The contempt in his voice rankled. His statement was an accusation, one she couldn't deny. "The lessons were freely given."

He snorted, the corners of his mouth drawing downward.

She studied him from beneath her lashes. Once again, the sheer size of him overwhelmed her. Again she found herself comparing him to a statue—larger and more perfectly formed than a common man. But he was not sleek and smooth like the statues that graced the forum in Isca. No, this man was rough and solid, with a dangerous look about him. His long red beard and mustache hid the nuances of his mood. With a sudden vengeance, she wished them gone.

She clenched her fists so tightly her fingernails bit into her palms. She hated that she was defenseless before him. Consciously, she straightened her spine. Father had always asserted it was the worst folly to show weakness before an enemy.

She cleared her throat. "I'm sorry to inconvenience you. I'll be on my way as soon as I might." She drew a breath and met his gaze. "What have you done with my clothes?"

He gestured to a heap on the floor. "They are wet."

"And my satchel?" she said in alarm. "Did you . . ."

"Your wee bundle is there as well," he said, eyeing her. "Nay, I didna paw through it."

She blushed. "I didn't mean . . ." But she had meant it, and his expression told her that he knew. He was no fool, this barbarian. The silence lengthened between them, growing thick and heavy until she could bear it no longer.

"I lost my way," she said. "It was stupid of me, I know, but the trail I was following ended, and then the storm began . . ." She drew a breath. "I'm seeking a wise man. A Druid."

At the Celt's scowl, she clutched the blanket more firmly to her breasts. "I was told he lived in this valley. Do you know of him? If you show me the path to his door, I'll be gone as soon as my clothes are dry."

He raised his brows. "Ye'll nay be going far, lass. Not chilled as ye are. Your feet willna bear even your slight weight, not for a day, at least."

As if to underscore his assessment, a shiver overtook her. Her body was ice cold, as if a winter storm still raged inside. She barely felt the fire, though beads of sweat stood out on her companion's forehead. The musk of his perspiration reached her nostrils. It was an intimate smell, one that caused her to shift away.

"The old Druid," she persisted. "He's a Seer. He can find things that are lost or stolen. Surely you know of him. Does he live nearby?"

To her surprise, the Celt stood abruptly and gave her his back. "There be few Druids left alive," he said without turning. "Your army has done a fine job of putting them to the sword."

Clara stared at the back of his head. Again he spoke the truth and again she had no answer. But she had no choice—she had to gain his cooperation. She *had* to find the Seer, and it was likely this man could lead her to him.

"I mean the Wise One no harm," she persisted. "Nor will I tell a soul of his hiding place."

"Ye are Roman," he said, as if that were an answer.

"Yes, of course," she replied to his broad shoulders.

Words began tumbling from her lips, as they always did when her blood pounded in her ears. "But I have no reason to alert the authorities. Just the opposite. I was directed to the Seer by an old Celt sla—friend," she amended hastily. "He told me the Wise One's heart is kind and true. I'm in sore need of his magic." She inhaled. "Please. Will you take me to him?"

The Celt was silent for several long heartbeats. Finally, he turned, eyeing her, clearly deciding whether she was worth the trouble of an honest answer. She resisted the urge to squirm under his scrutiny.

At last he spoke. "And who is this *friend*—" he said the word harshly, as if spitting out the uglier term she'd almost used—". . . who told ye tales of a Druid?"

"A Celt elder. An old man who lived in these hills, before . . ."

Her voice trailed off in the face of the Celt's scowl. She wondered, not for the first time, if she'd lost her wits completely to embark on this wild quest, even with Aiden's encouragement. A knot of fear tightened in her stomach. But then she thought of Father huddled in his sickbed.

She stiffened her spine. "He lived in these hills before he came to dwell in the city."

"Before Sempronius Gracchus and the Second Legion enslaved the last of the free Celts, ye mean."

Clara fought to control her expression as the Celt spat out her father's name. "Yes," she said.

"Where are your companions?" Venom laced his tone. "A wealthy woman such as ye would travel with an escort. Were there soldiers? Did ye lose them in the storm?"

"I came alone."

The Celt's piercing blue gaze bored into her. "If that be true, then ye are surely mad."

Her fingers twisted the edge of the fur blanket. "No doubt you're right. But I had no choice. Please. If you know the Wise One, take me to him."

A veil dropped over his eyes, blanking their expression.

She went still. "You know where he is."

He hesitated, and she thought perhaps he would deny it. But a moment later, he nodded once. "I ken the one ye speak of. But I wouldna name him wise. Nor kind."

"It matters not what you would call him. Only that you take me to him."

His gaze sought the fire, where it lingered moodily. Finally, he sighed. "Ye've found him already, lass."

"I don't understand."

He gave her a pointed look, brows lifted.

Several seconds passed before she grasped his meaning. When it did, her breath left her. *No.* It wasn't possible. She sought an old man. An elder.

Didn't she?

"You?"

The corner of his mouth lifted in a sardonic smile. "Ye look a bit green about the gills, lass. Am I nay what ye expected?"

A shiver saved her the embarrassment of a reply. She rubbed her arms, drawing up her knees to her chest. The scowl returned to the Celt's face as he poked the fire yet again. The flames leapt, giving off a shower of sparks.

Oh, gods. She'd imagined Aiden's Wise One as a barbarian Aristotle, wizened and ethereal. Never once had she considered the possibility he'd be a virile young male. But Aiden had assured her the Druid who had guided his clan was a gentle, holy man.

Clara tried to picture this burly, red-bearded Celt passing an hour of quiet contemplation. She couldn't summon the image. Surely he spent far more time chopping wood.

And yet . . . Her gaze drifted to the charred logs in the hearth. Didn't a wise man need warmth as much as a fool?

She examined the Celt from under her eyelashes. His body held more power than she could contemplate—and having lived her entire life in military fortresses, she was well suited to judging the strength of men. But perhaps his wild clothing, fashioned entirely from animal skins, influenced her perception. His shirt bore fur, turned to his skin. Rough hide *braccas* encased his powerful legs. His footwear was hardly more than skins bound to his feet and calves with a crisscross of thongs.

She caught his eye and he lifted his brows. Quickly she averted her gaze. The curved daub-and-wattle wall enclosed his simple circular dwelling. His furnishings were crudely made and haphazardly arranged. A chest, a table, a chair. His hearth wanted sweeping. Overhead, an untidy bundle of herbs hung from a smoke-blackened timber.

It was the dwelling of a man who didn't expect much from life. Had it always been thus for him?

"You are young," she said finally.

"Nay so young as you, lass." She thought she heard amusement in his voice, but when she searched his face, she saw no trace of it. "No Roman knows of my presence in these hills," he said. "And no Celt would dare speak of it to one such as ye. Who was this old man who sent ye to me?"

"A . . . servant in my father's household. He's called Aiden."

"Aiden?" Raw emotion lit his eyes, then was gone. He shook his head, his startled expression resolving into wry amusement. It made him seem almost human.

"Curse the old fool," he said. Then, tentatively, "He is well?"

"Yes," Clara said. Once again her fingers found the edges of the furs. "Though . . . his joints ache at times. He rubs his fingers with a salve I procured from a Celt healer—he would not abide by the leeches suggested by the Greek physician. But I don't think he truly wants to banish the pain. He claims the rhythm of the ache helps him predict the fall of the dice."

" 'Tis Aiden, to be sure. A more superstitious man ye'll nay encounter. The idiot sees signs in every turn of the wind, each squawk of the crow. Even the shape of his own spittle upon the ground."

"And you don't?"

The amused expression fell from his face. "True power ne'er comes so easily."

"But isn't magic a gift from the gods? To be used for the benefit of men?"

"Gods are capricious beings. They gift and curse with one stroke. They never grant power without demanding payment." He spat into the fire. " 'Tis a wise man who leaves the immortals to their own devices."

"And yet, if the need is great—"

"Whatever it is ye came for, dinna ask me to provide it."

Clara pursed her lips. He couldn't refuse her request. Her father's life depended on it. "I'll pay you well."

"I've no need of Roman coin."

"Then help me for Aiden's sake." She watched him closely. "He gave me a message for you."

The Seer grunted. "What message?"

"He said to tell you it wasn't your fault."

The Seer flinched as if he'd been struck. Rising abruptly, he strode to the wooden chest and jerked it open.

"If you would but listen . . ." Clara cried.

He extracted what looked like a garment from the chest. For a moment, he stood motionless, staring down at it. Then he tossed the fabric in her direction.

She caught it. "What—?"

"Put that on." Giving her his back, he headed for the door.

"Wait! Where are you—"

Too late. She saw a sliver of daylight through the open door; then he was gone.

"Oh!" Clara pounded the ground with her fist. Pain shot up her arm, but she welcomed the sting; it helped ground her anger. Rude barbarian! How dare he walk out on her when she'd traveled so far to find him? She scowled at the door, wishing she had something substantial to throw at it.

Unfortunately, she didn't. She had only his spare shirt. She shook it out. It wasn't like the crude one on his back, but a real garment, woven of linen, well worn and soft. She eyed her own clothing, crumpled in a sodden heap on the floor, her sleeve pins scattered in the dirt nearby. A hot surge of irritation flushed her cheeks. That embroidered wool had come all the way from Rome. How like a man, not to think to spread it to dry. The least he could have done was collect the pins into a pile.

Keeping one eye on the door, she let the fur blanket slide from her shoulders. She slipped the Seer's shirt over her head. The garment was far too large. The sleeves hung well past her fingertips and the hem trailed as far as her knees. Her breasts gaped through the open front. She rolled up the sleeves and tied the front laces as tightly as she could.

The shirt smelled of herbs, and of . . . *him.* Already she knew his scent—she suspected she would recognize it even blindfolded. It was a wild odor, not unpleasant, but not anything she'd encountered in Isca, or before that, Eburacum. Or before *that,* Londinium.

She clung to the memory of those places, because in them her father loomed large and strong, invincible in his Legionary armor. So different from how she'd last seen him—thin and wasted under his blankets, his face sunken and hollow. The Greek physician had proven useless and even Rhiannon, the Celt healer whose husband had once been an officer in the Legions, offered little hope.

Only Clara could save her father now—but only if the Druid lent her his aid.

Her gorge rose, but with her stomach empty, she tasted only bile. She clamped one hand over her mouth, praying she would not retch. The scent of the Seer's shirt, of all things, helped her nausea recede. The fabric smelled of pine and heather, mist and mystery. Magic and hope. When its owner returned, she would plead again for his assistance.

And if he refused?

"He cannot deny me," she said out loud, as if speech would make her pronouncement true. "He *will not.*" But she was not at all sure. Despite Aiden's assurance that the Seer was a good man, she sensed a darkness about him.

She attempted to stand, but, as the Seer had warned, her injured feet protested her weight. She could do no more than hobble. She gritted her teeth against the shooting pains and managed the few steps needed to reach her belongings.

She retrieved her clothing and shook it out. Dragging a low bench near the fire, she spread the garments across it. By the time she'd finished the task, her breath was shallow and labored. She fought back tears of frustration. She hated being weak.

Grasping her satchel, she returned to the pallet and sat cross-legged, facing the fire. As always, the image of the prancing cat made her smile. The bag had been a present from her father on the occasion of her twelfth birthday. Holding it comforted her, until she realized the shoulder strap had been severed by a sharp blade.

Annoyance heated her cheeks. Couldn't the brute have bothered to work the buckle loose?

Her reluctant host returned before long, carrying the skinned carcass of a winter hare in one hand and a pail of fresh snow in the other. She watched in silence as he spitted his kill, banking the fire beneath it. He dumped the snow into his cauldron. Taking a small box from a shelf, he threw a handful of something dark and crumbling into the vessel.

She considered the rigid line of his shoulders, the downward cant of his mouth. His surliness made no difference. She needed his magic. Needed him.

She took a breath. "Please hear me—"

He held up a long-handled wooden spoon. "Not now, lass." His dismissive tone raised her ire. He dipped the utensil into the brew and brought it to his lips.

"You don't understand," she said through gritted teeth. "There is no time to waste."

He shook his head as he ladled the mixture into a crude wooden cup. He offered it to her. "Drink."

She hadn't realized how great her thirst was until that moment. Her fingers brushed his as she accepted the cup. The small contact sent heat racing through her. She drew back quickly, cradling the cup in her palms.

"What is this?" she asked, peering doubtfully at the brown bits of debris floating on the surface of the brew.

"A potion of willow bark. Drink."

When she hesitated, he shook his head in exasperation. "Can ye nay take simple instruction, lass?"

She bent her head and took a sip. The brew was warm, not hot, and though it was bitter, it slid down her throat easily. He returned to his spit, rotating the hare's carcass slowly, searing it in the flame. Grease sizzled onto the fire, sending a savory aroma into the air. Clara blinked against a sudden light-headedness. How long since she'd eaten? A full day? More?

Her stomach sent up a rumble. She pressed her palm against it, mortified. A flash of real amusement lit the Seer's eyes. Just a spark, and only for a heartbeat, but it lifted Clara's hopes. Perhaps there was a touch of softness within him, despite his gruff ways. She sipped her bitter draught, watching as he tended the meat. Drawing a knife from a sheath on his belt, he cut a portion of seared flesh from the bone. He placed it on a thin slab of wood and offered it to her.

This time, she was careful not to let her fingers brush his as she accepted his offering. Keeping the blanket well over her bare legs, she perched the plate on her knees. Hunger overtook her and she ate with far less care than she'd been taught. The Seer watched her, a bemused expression on his rugged face, then rose and moved across the room. He returned to lay a hunk of stale bannock on her plate.

Clara eyed the barley bread with distaste. Only slaves and cattle ate barley. But hunger was a potent spice. She accepted the offering without complaint, using the hard bread to sop up the last bit of meat juices.

Where did the Seer come by his grain? Did he pilfer

from remote farm fields or cultivate his own small plot? She chewed thoughtfully, trying to imagine his solitary existence. She found she could not.

When she looked up, the Seer had seated himself in the dwelling's single chair. He leaned forward, forearms on his thighs, his big hands dangling between his legs. His fierce azure eyes unnerved her.

"Will you not eat?" she asked him. The Celt words were coming easier now. She was glad she'd practiced so often with Aiden.

"Nay. But ye may have as much as ye like. Though if ye've been without food for a while, 'tis best if ye dinna fill your stomach too quickly."

She put the empty plate aside. "I thank you, Wise—"

"Owein," he said sharply. "My name is Owein."

She hadn't known that. Aiden had called him only "The Seer," and "The Wise One," as if afraid to utter a given name.

"Owein," she repeated slowly, letting the Celt lilt of the vowels roll off her tongue. She matched the sound of it to his face. "Well met, Owein. I am called Clara."

Once again his gaze found her, but he said nothing. The corners of his mouth turned downward, and the lines of his face settled into a grim expression that even his beard couldn't hide. A quiver of fear rippled through her. Despite his youth, despite his reluctant kindnesses, she sensed he was a hard man, about as easily moved as a boulder. She worried the frayed edge of the blanket, an uncharacteristic reluctance to speak overtaking her.

"I've disturbed you," she said at last.

"Aye, lass, ye have."

"I wouldn't intrude on your solitude, except for the gravest of needs."

He said nothing.

"My father," Clara said. The last bite of the bannock turned to dust in her throat. "He's ill. Near death."

"I'm no healer."

"It's not healing I wish from you. There is . . . something that was stolen from me. A cup with healing power. If I can find it, I may have a chance to save my father's life." Perhaps at the cost of her own, she added silently. "Aiden was certain you could help me locate the thief. Please. I'll pay any price."

" 'Tis the gods who name the price of power. I guarantee the cost willna be to your liking. Far better to leave the immortal ones undisturbed and accept your sorrow. No man lives forever, nor should he wish it."

Clara twisted her fingers, glad for the pain the movement brought, for it helped distract her from the sickening roll of her stomach. "My father is my only relation, and he is not an old man. It's not yet his time to—"

" 'Tis nay my concern, lass."

"Are you saying you won't help me?"

"Aye, lass. 'Tis exactly what I'm saying."

Chapter Three

The merlin came into view before its owner did.

Marcus Ulpius Aquila's boots crunched the layer of snow dumped by the unexpected storm. Perhaps "owner" wasn't precisely the correct word, he mused. Rhys, a traveling musician and Marcus's good friend, didn't treat the small falcon like a pet; the Celt talked to the bird as if it were human. At times, Marcus swore Rhys listened to the animal as well.

An uneasy emotion snagged Marcus's gut. It was said the mysterious priests of the Celts—the Druids—spoke with animals, and could even compel the beasts to their bidding. A fantastic charge, one easily dismissed as superstition by an educated Roman. But Marcus considered such talents entirely plausible, for he'd seen far darker Druid magic with his own eyes.

He shivered. An icy chill hung in the air, sharp as a ringing bell. He drew to a halt on a rise of land devoid of trees. The road behind him was hidden by a dip in the hill, but to the south, the clear air afforded a rare view. The fortress city of Isca rose above a winding estuary of the river Usk, free of the fog that so often clung to her skirts. Flat, fertile farms spread out around her, like subjects bowing before a queen. In the distance, at the edge of a choppy sea, military ships jostled at the docks with ferries and merchant vessels. Beyond, across the Sabrina channel, the Mendip hills cast a jagged blue silhouette on the horizon.

The merlin circled above, wings spread, coasting skyward on an updraft left by yesterday's storm. Marcus had no doubt the bird belonged to Rhys—others of its kind had long since migrated to warmer climes. Sure enough, Rhys soon appeared at the bend in the road, his leather pack slung haphazardly over one shoulder.

Rhys might be of an age with Marcus, but to Marcus's mind the Celt had always seemed older. Perhaps it was because Rhys roamed Britannia, while Marcus never strayed far from his father's farm. Or perhaps it was because of Rhys himself. Taller and looser of limb than Marcus, the Celt was possessed of a thick shock of unusual silver-blond hair. His gray eyes echoed the valley mist. He kept his beard very short in the Roman fashion, but that in itself was another oddity. Most Celts had no use for a razor.

Rhys's long legs made quick work of the road as he advanced, waving a greeting. The movement caused the pack on his lanky shoulders to shift. He paused a moment to adjust it. He'd never allow the burden to fall, Marcus knew, for it held his livelihood—a Celtic harp.

Marcus strode to meet him. "Good day to ye, Rhys," he said, slipping easily into the Celt tongue he'd learned from his stepmother.

"Well met, Marcus Aquila." Rhys's voice was as clear as the air, a testament to his musical talent. He nodded to Marcus's soot-blackened hands. "Have ye just come from the forge, or are ye going to it?"

Marcus examined his palms with a rueful shake of his head. The last traces of black never disappeared from a smith's hands, no matter how vigorously he scrubbed.

"Neither," he said. "I've just made a delivery of hooks to

a neighboring farm, and I'm headed for home. And you? I'll wager you're bound for my stepmother's hearth."

"If Rhiannon will have me."

"You know she will," Marcus said with a smile. "But beware. Breena will have her fingers in your pack within the space of two heartbeats."

Rhys's gray eyes glinted. "The vixen will try to charm a trinket from me."

Marcus grinned. "True enough." At twelve years of age, his half sister possessed feminine wiles in abundance.

"The lass needn't fear I've forgotten her," Rhys said. But a strange note in his voice had Marcus examining him more closely.

"Is something amiss?"

It seemed Rhys made an effort to keep his answer light. "The world often looks gray when one's stomach is empty."

Marcus rubbed his chin, considering, but decided not to press the issue. "Rhiannon's table is a fine remedy for that particular sorrow." He clapped his friend on the shoulder. "We'll be especially glad of the company, as Father is away."

"Lucius Aquila is not at home?" Rhys seemed relieved by the news, which was odd, since Marcus's father had never failed to welcome the minstrel in his home.

"He's gone to Londinium to purchase seed for the spring. Egyptian wheat," Marcus said, puzzled. "But why—"

Rhys's merlin chose that moment to dive. With a shriek and a flutter of wings, it darted after an errant sparrow. Both men watched in silence as the falcon emerged from the brush.

Its talons were empty.

"Not every hunt is successful," Marcus observed.

"Nay," Rhys agreed.

"But I suppose each failure sharpens one's skills."

Rhys's gaze shifted to the distance. "Aye. One's skills—and one's need."

* * *

Clara's anger burned away the last vestiges of cold. A hot flush rose in her breast, crept up her neck, and fanned out across her cheeks. How dare the Seer—Owein—refuse her request? Suddenly, she couldn't bear to huddle on his pallet while he looked down on her from the chair. Gripping the edge of the bench, she hauled herself onto her tender feet, wrapping one of the woolen blankets about her body like a toga.

He said nothing, but his blue eyes were sharp and his expression set in stone. Why couldn't he be old and withered, as she'd expected? She hated his strength. It reminded her too keenly of her own vulnerability.

Show no fear. She'd often heard Father give that advice to one soldier or another, though he'd never uttered the words directly to Clara. Sextus Sempronius Gracchus was all too tolerant of his only child's weaknesses. No matter. She would follow Father's prescription anyway.

"A month past," she began, trying to sound as if Owein had already agreed to help her, "my father fell ill. He'd supped in a tavern. I think the meat must have been spoiled, though the tavern keeper claimed it was a fresh kill. Father said it was so heavily spiced that—" She drew up shortly, suddenly aware she'd veered off track. "The illness hit him hard. He took to his bed, unable to eat or even drink. His strength diminished rapidly. The Greek physician I summoned couldn't help him."

Owein regarded her in silence, his expression impassive. Still, he didn't get up and move away, or interrupt her story. She resolved to take that as an encouraging sign.

"I was afraid for his life. I had no choice but to bring out my mother's cup." Fear shot through her, so palpable she could almost touch it. Forcing a swallow, she went on. "Father had put it away after Mother's death. He said . . . it had caused her illness. She'd sickened after using the vessel to heal a dying child."

Owein's brows lifted.

Clara forged on. "The cup is wrought in silver and crystal, with strange markings. Father had forbidden me to touch it, but he was so ill. I had to try it. I gave him a little wine. The next morning, he rose and left the house."

Owein sat back, eyeing her. " 'Tis quite a tale."

"A true one. The cup holds great magic, but . . ."

"Its power claims a price." For a moment, he met her gaze. Clara felt a shimmer of understanding pass between them.

"What happened, lass?"

"I took to my bed. I felt as though I'd taken Father's illness into my own body. I was afraid I would die, like Mother, but the sickness didn't last. I was well by the next afternoon. That's when I discovered that while I was abed and Father gone from the house, the cup had been stolen."

Owein's attention sharpened. "By whom?"

She spread her hands. "If I knew that, I wouldn't be here. A petty thief, I suspect. I'd left my mother's cup in full view, and it wasn't the only item of value taken—several gold plates and goblets were also gone. The steward claimed he heard nothing, but then, the man is deaf as a stone. Two days later, Father's illness returned. He took to his bed. By evening, he could barely speak."

She fiddled with her sleeve. "This time, I had no cure to offer. At Aiden's insistence, I sent for the Celt healer, but she offered little hope. Father worsened. I was at my wits' end. Then Aiden told me of you. He said you could locate the cup with your Seer's magic." She drew a breath. "That's all I ask."

"And what then? Will ye walk into the thieves' lair and snatch it back?"

"Yes."

He snorted. "A wee lass like yourself?"

Clara squared her shoulders. "I'm not a 'wee lass.' And I am not without resources. I can hire someone to retrieve the cup."

Owein stroked his beard. The long red strands looked

silky, and not at all unkempt. But the braid at his temple was a potent reminder of his barbarian blood.

"Your father must be a rich man," he said.

She blinked. "Have you changed your mind about accepting payment for your aid?"

"Hardly. I only wonder how many soldiers are marching in search of ye."

"You needn't worry about that. I promised Aiden I would come alone to seek you. No one saw me leave the city."

"Unlikely as that is, I'll lay it to one side for a moment. What I am wondering is this—why did ye nay take the matter up with the Roman authorities? It's said Sempronius Gracchus commands Isca with an iron hand. Surely he could rout the thieves."

"No," Clara said, nearly choking. "I . . . you don't understand. The . . . commander can't help me in this."

"Why? Is your father Gracchus's enemy?"

Clara caught her bottom lip with her teeth. She could hardly reveal the truth—that her father *was* Sempronius Gracchus. The Seer would likely toss her into the snow.

"My father is no enemy of Commander Gracchus. He's . . . he's a merchant." The lie felt heavy on her tongue. "And in any case, the commander is . . . not at Isca this winter."

"Surely the Second Legion has nay been left unsupervised."

"Tribune Publius Aurelius Valgus commands in Gracchus's stead." That, at least, was the truth.

"Take your troubles to him, then."

"I can't. Valgus is . . ." She inhaled, seeking to calm the churning in her stomach that thoughts of Aurelius Valgus brought. "I don't trust Valgus, for all that my father seems to. But Father cares more for Valgus's bloodlines than anything else. The tribune will be Senator someday, perhaps even Consul. Father's promised me as his wife." She gave a bitter laugh. "*In manu.*"

Owein's brow creased. "What does that mean?"

"It's an old form of marriage, and the only one Valgus will accept. When a man takes a wife *in manu,* he gains absolute control of both her property and her person."

"Not a poor idea, I'm thinking. Ye want a keeper."

Clara sent him a disgusted look. "You speak as though you're of one mind with my father and Cicero. '. . . all women, because of their innate weakness, should be under the control of guardians.' Ha! I would rather put out an eye than marry a man like Valgus. But Father doesn't believe me capable of inheriting his property. In his eyes, I'm in need of protection."

"Ye think ye are not? I found ye half dead, dinna forget."

Clara crossed her arms. "I would have been fine if the storm hadn't arisen so abruptly."

"Ye might have died. Or worse, been discovered by brigands. They would not have nursed ye by the fire as I did, I can tell ye that. I've a mind to pummel old Aiden. I canna believe he would set any lass on such a dangerous path, let alone one such as ye."

"He knows how desperate I am."

His blue eyes frowned. "Ye canna escape your destiny, lass. My advice is to accept this Valgus as husband. Set about breeding sons for the glory of Rome."

"I won't. I can't." She took a step forward and dared to place a hand on his arm. She felt the taut muscle contract under her fingertips, but when she looked up at his face his eyes betrayed no hint of compassion.

"Aiden said you would help me. He said if you weren't willing, that I should tell you"—she let her eyes show her desperation—"to treat me as you would his granddaughter."

A sharp, foul expletive fell from Owein's lips. "He canna have told ye that."

"He did!"

"In that case . . ." Owein's attention drifted blatantly down Clara's body. "There is something ye can offer me."

Her stomach lurched. "You . . . wouldn't ask that."

Lust, pure and raw, darkened his eyes. "Why should I not?"

Panic beat in Clara's chest. At the same time, warmth spread from her belly to the tips of her breasts. From there it climbed steadily to her cheeks. "Aiden says you are a man of honor," she choked out.

"Honor is a cold comfort. Do ye know how long it's been since I had a woman? Since I've even seen one?"

Mutely, she shook her head.

"Two winters. Two winters since Sempronius Gracchus's men killed my wife with no mercy even for the babe in her womb."

His voice was flat, but Clara sensed his barely controlled violence. He'd lost a wife and child! Aiden hadn't told her that.

"I'm . . . sorry."

"Eirwen was killed fighting for our home. I wasna there to die at her side." He looked away. "That, lass, is how I treated Aiden's granddaughter."

Clara's breath left her. "Aiden's granddaughter was your wife? But he never . . ." She shuddered. How could Aiden have sent her to this man? Clearly, Owein despised her, and everything Roman. "I . . . didn't know," she finished lamely.

"There's much ye don't know. Go back to Isca, lass. Ye dinna belong here."

He stood. The sheer bulk of him overwhelmed her; she was forced to tilt her head to look up at his face. She fought her instinct to recoil, until a sudden movement of his body sent her stumbling backward. But he hadn't moved in her direction. On the contrary, he was the one in retreat. He strode to the door, nearly wrenching it from its pegged hinges. And then he was gone, absorbed by the snow-shrouded night.

Ill-mannered lout, she thought. But she trembled for the pain she'd seen in his eyes. She sank down on the chair he'd vacated. With a wife and child dead, he had a right to be bitter.

She was sick to her bones, thinking of the Second Legion's mountain purge. She knew Father had been disgusted when the reports of the botched village raids reached the fortress. Father hadn't wanted to resettle the free Celts in the first place—in his view, the scattered mountain villages posed little threat to Roman civilians. But after the governor's niece had fallen prey to Celt brigands on the road near Isca, the order had come from Londinium to clear the hills of all natives. Had Father not complied, he'd have been stripped of his command. Slaughter hadn't been his intent; he'd wanted a peaceful resettlement. But the Celts were a proud people. They hadn't surrendered.

Sighing, Clara rose and retrieved her tunic from the bench. It was still damp, but it hardly mattered. She couldn't remain dressed in Owein's shirt. She grasped the hem, battling a sudden reluctance to remove the garment. The linen imparted a measure of comfort. Had Owein's wife woven it? Had he worn it while he kissed her? She shook off the thought. With an efficient motion, she pulled the shirt over her head and laid it on the pallet.

Donning her own tunic was a challenge because of the damage Owein had done to her girdle and sleeve pins. She fastened them the best she could, then retrieved her boots, staring at them sadly. Ruined. Half the pearls were gone, and the leather was stained beyond repair. With a sigh, she slipped on her ugly wool stockings and slid her feet into the ruined boots. She took a step. Her soles were still tender; it was like walking on broken glass.

She'd no sooner dressed than the door scraped open. Owein appeared once more, his arms laden with deadwood. He glanced at her briefly, taking in the change in her attire, but said nothing. Depositing the wood near the hearth, he went down on one knee and set to the task of stacking it.

She hobbled past him and peered out the door. The sky was a startling blue. "The storm has lifted."

Owein grunted a reply. Clara limped across the room to the pallet. Bending, she scooped up his shirt and held it out to him, feeling for all the world as if she were taming a wild beast to her hand. "I thank you again for your kindness."

He rose and accepted the worn linen. "No kindness. I had little choice."

"You might have left me to die."

"Aye," he said. "I might have." He frowned at his shirt. Then he folded it carefully and stowed it in his oaken chest.

Clara forced herself to go to him, her hand hovering above his shoulder. "Owein. I need your help."

"I've given ye my answer."

"I won't accept it."

"Ye must. Your father will most likely die. 'Tis a hard thing to bear, but the sooner ye accept it, the better 'twill be. Marry the man he chose for ye, lass. Once ye have a passel of brats to care for, ye'll stop looking to the past."

Her hand descended onto his shoulder. The supple leather and soft fur of his shirt teased her fingertips, but couldn't disguise the muscle underneath. So much power, so much strength, and yet . . .

She moved in front of him, seeking his gaze. "What is it you fear?"

A slight widening of his eyes told him she'd hit her mark. He jerked free of her touch. "I fear nothing," he said. "Save that ye'll nay be gone soon enough."

"But—"

"Ye demand the use of my gift," he said roughly. "As if it were your right. It is not."

"Aiden thought it was."

"Aiden is a fool."

Clara was silent for a moment. Then, bending, she retrieved her satchel from the pallet and set it on the table.

"I told ye, lass. I have no need of coin."

"It's not coin I wish to show you." Her fingers, still raw and painful, trembled as she worked the buckled strap securing the satchel's flap. It refused to give way. The leather band had swollen with moisture during the storm, then tightened again as it dried. She tore at it, cursing under her breath.

A callused hand covered hers. "Let me do it if ye are so intent upon having it open."

She hesitated, then nodded and stepped aside.

His blunt fingers worked the buckle. The strap gave way. She thought he might examine the contents of the bag, but he did not. She upended it herself. A shower of coins and jewelry—all she could gather on short notice—spilled onto the scarred wood.

"I have no use for bangles," Owein muttered.

"No," Clara allowed. "But you may have something to say about this." She fished a small scroll tube from the glittering heap and held it out to him. Another offering for the beast. Perhaps this one would bring him close enough for the taming.

He took the tube. Frowning, he slid out the papyrus, spread it flat on the table.

And stared at Clara's secret.

Chapter Four

"Well met, Rhys," Breena said, catching her breath with a laugh. She'd run down the road to greet them, her long russet braid unraveling about her shoulders. Her blue eyes darted to Rhys's pack. Marcus could almost hear his half sister's unspoken demand: *What did you bring me?*

He suppressed a grin. Breena had begun to blossom into a woman, a process as bumpy as a cart ride over a rutted field. For the last sennight, she'd been so shrewish, Marcus had taken to eating his meals in the forge. But right now, the bright-eyed girl he loved had reasserted herself.

Rhys gave Breena a formal bow, as if he were about to partner her in a faire dance. "I greet ye, lady."

Marcus grinned. "Patience, Bree. At least allow poor Rhys to unshoulder his pack before you dive into it."

"I'm sure I don't know what you mean."

Marcus laughed aloud. Breena put her hands on her hips and stuck her tongue out at him. He made a good-natured grab for her, but she danced just out of reach. Despite Breena's newfound womanhood, there was still much of the child about her.

Breena turned to Rhys, giving Marcus her back. "Is Hefin with you? I don't see him overhead."

"He'll be off seeking his midday meal, but he'll soon return," Rhys said, offering Breena his arm. She flipped Marcus a triumphant smile as she placed a hand in the crook of the musician's elbow.

Marcus trailed the pair up the road toward his father's villa. A stone wall taller than a man enclosed the house and its generous yard, while the grain fields and workers' cottages lay outside. Behind the iron gates, the villa was fronted by a formal garden. Stables were near the entry gate, but the sheep and pig barns lay out of sight to the rear of the house, beyond the orchard and kitchen garden.

The main house was a rambling affair, with the stucco walls and tiled roof typical of Roman villas in Britannia. But Marcus's father, Lucius, a retired Legionary, had departed from convention on one important feature. At his Celt wife's insistence, he'd ordered the main receiving chamber enclosed with a graceful curved wall reminiscent of a Celt roundhouse. Despite the heated air circulating under the tiled floors, a hearth graced the center of the room. An odd marriage of elements, but such was the way of Marcus's family.

Rhiannon looked up from her cauldron as he entered. Gazing on his stepmother, Marcus saw a hint of the woman Breena would someday be. His half sister had inherited her mother's fair skin and russet hair. Her long, straight nose, however, matched Marcus's and her father's, a fact she strongly lamented.

Rhys sniffed the air appreciably. "Mutton stew," he declared. "And wheat bread."

Marcus grinned. Despite his lanky build, Rhys could consume enough food in one sitting to sustain a Roman plow horse.

"Rhys is here, Mama," Breena said.

"Aye, I can see the lad with my own eyes," Rhiannon said

with true affection. She treated the Celt like a second son. "The Great Mother's welcome to ye, Rhys."

"And to you, lady."

"Will ye stay long in Isca?"

"Please say you will," Breena said, forgetting her newfound maturity. Marcus only hoped her good mood would last. From the look Rhiannon sent her daughter, he guessed his stepmother shared his sentiments.

"We'll see," Rhys said, setting his pack on the tiled floor. Untying the top flap, he drew out a small pouch. "I've brought ye a gift," he said, his gray eyes suddenly serious.

He set the pouch in Breena's palm. She quickly loosed the knot. Rhys's gift was a pendant crafted in silver. Marcus leaned forward, captivated by its intricate artistry.

"Oh, Rhys!" Breena breathed. "It's beautiful."

Beautiful didn't begin to describe the piece. It was nothing short of miraculous, especially to the eye of a silversmith. Though practicality forced Marcus to work mainly with iron, he preferred silver. There was a delicacy and a challenge to the metal that absorbed him completely. But though Marcus could say without conceit that he was a fine silversmith, his skill was a mere child's hammering compared to that of the artist who'd created this treasure.

The pendant fit easily in Breena's palm. Marcus recognized the pattern, for Rhys's left breast was marked with the same sign. At its center, three silver spirals united as one, giving the impression of spinning movement. Encircling this pattern was a ring divided into quarters, entwined with two vines.

Rhiannon drew a sharp breath.

"Who smithed this piece?" Marcus asked. "I've never seen silvercraft so fine."

"Gwendolyn," Rhys said, a troubled expression flitting across his face.

"Your twin is a smith?" Marcus asked, raising his head. Rhys rarely spoke of his sister. He most certainly had never told Marcus she worked with silver.

"What do ye mean by bringing such a gift?" Rhiannon said. Her voice had gone taut, as it did when she was angry or frightened.

Marcus looked up in surprise.

"The time draws near, lady," Rhys said quietly.

Rhiannon shook her head. "Not yet."

"Have ye nay felt the truth of it?" Rhys's gaze slid to Breena. "I would wager your daughter has."

"Nay," Rhiannon said tightly."She is not ready."

Breena scowled, but held her tongue, a most uncharacteristic occurrence. Marcus divided his attention between Rhys and Rhiannon. They faced each other like warriors girded for battle. What in Jupiter's name was going on? Marcus had the distinct feeling he'd missed some vital fragment of their communication. He reviewed their words in his head, searching for some subtle nuance of the Celt tongue that might have eluded him. He came up empty.

During the long, heavy silence that ensued, Marcus became painfully aware he was the only one present whose veins were filled with pure Roman blood. Even Breena, child that she was, seemed to understand more than he.

"My grandfather senses Deep Magic abroad," Rhys said.

"As do I," whispered Breena.

Rhys watched Rhiannon. " 'Tis the storm. Can ye nay feel it?"

"Aye," Rhiannon whispered, looking away. "I can."

Marcus's brows drew together. Both Rhiannon and Breena had greeted the sudden snow with exceptional ill humor, as if the storm had blown in on some evil wind. He'd put it down to female tempers. He'd certainly felt nothing amiss.

Rhys held Rhiannon's gaze. "Then ye know as I do, lady, 'tis nay safe for Breena to dwell apart from her own kind. Even more because her blood cannot be denied. She's of the line of queens."

"How do you know that?" Marcus asked sharply. Rhiannon never spoke of her lineage, or of the throne she might have claimed if Britannia hadn't come under Roman rule.

"Breena's but a lass," Rhiannon said. "Surely—"

"Her woman's blood is upon her. She needs the protection of Avalon."

Avalon? Once again, Marcus had the frustrating sense he'd missed some important element of the conversation. He stepped forward, angling his body between Rhiannon and Rhys.

"Speak plainly." Marcus's voice reverberated sharply, his tone much more like his father's than his own. And just as if Lucius Aquila had spoken, all eyes turned to him.

Rhys's expression was grave. "Have ye never wondered, my friend, why I first came to this house?"

"It was nine years ago," Marcus said, bewildered. "You were fourteen, as I was. Barely more than a boy. You rang the gate bell and offered a song in exchange for lodging."

" 'Twas nay an accident of fortune I sought shelter here. My grandfather bade me come to the queen's daughter. Breena had touched Cyric with her dreams."

"Impossible. Breena's dreams mean nothing." Marcus's stomach twisted. His sister had been plagued with night terrors since before she could walk—she'd wake sobbing, but rarely remembered what had distressed her. "She'll outgrow them."

"Nay. As Breena becomes a woman, the dreams will only trouble her more. Her power is growing. She has the Sight, like Cyric. 'Tis nay an easy gift to bear."

Breena's eyes widened, and Marcus stared, aghast. "You speak of magic."

"Aye. 'Tis my task to search for those Celts touched by the magic and bring them to Avalon. All who dwell on the sacred isle possess the powers of the Old Ones."

Marcus's scalp crawled. "But that would mean . . ."

"Aye. We are Druids."

If Rhys had swung a forge hammer against the side of

Marcus's skull, Marcus couldn't have been any less stunned. But Rhiannon's expression was merely resigned.

Marcus turned on her. "You knew this?"

"Aye, Marcus, but—"

"And what of Father? Does he know his home has been defiled by a Druid? One who means to steal his daughter?"

Rhiannon's silence was answer enough. Marcus rounded on Rhys, his fingers curling into fists. With his smith's strength, he could easily throw the Celt out into the snow. Unless . . .

He forced a swallow down a throat dry as dust. Rhys was a Druid. The outlawed cult spilled the blood of men on their hidden altars, called ghosts and demons from the underworld, imprisoned enemy souls. Marcus's uncle had met just such a gruesome fate. Marcus's father, Lucius, had fought to free his brother's spirit, barely escaping with his own life. If Marcus dared attack a Druid, who knew what foul magic he might be struck with?

Marcus fingered the throwing knife at his belt, praying Rhys wouldn't see through his bluff. "Leave this house."

"Nay, Marcus." Breena's hand gripped his arm.

He threw her off. "No Druid is welcome here."

"Marcus, cease." Rhiannon's tone was pleading. "Rhys doesn't deserve your anger."

"You jest, Mother. He deserves far worse. This man has given me nothing but lies. And you—" He swallowed hard. "How could you keep such a thing from Father? From me?"

"Rhys is one of my own people. I didn't abandon my blood when I chose to marry a Roman, and I'll nay do so now."

"You know Father would never have allowed Rhys into his home had he known what he is."

Rarely had Marcus seen Rhiannon so distressed. "Aye. 'Tis why I did not tell him."

"And what now?" Marcus asked Rhiannon. Rhys made no move, nor did he speak. Could he cast a spell silently?

Marcus fervently hoped not. "Will this man spin a curse and bind us to his will? As your clan's Druid master once tried to bind Father?"

"The Druids of Avalon do not embrace the Dark," Rhiannon said.

Marcus eyed Rhys. "You cannot be sure of that."

"I am," Rhiannon replied quietly. "Marcus, any man may use power for ill purpose—a Druid as well as a Roman. But how can ye count Rhys among that number? There's no darkness in him. He's your friend."

"Friend?" Marcus spat out the word. "A friend doesn't present himself with deceit."

Rhys spoke at last. "Ye have the right of it, Marcus. I am sorry for that. I should have been truthful with ye from the start, no matter the cost. I ask your pardon."

A measure of Marcus's anger seeped away. Still, he gave no reply as he nodded to the pendant still nestled in Breena's palm. "What is this thing? This . . . circle. Is it enchanted?"

"Aye," Rhys said. " 'Tis a talisman of the Light. It's for Breena's protection."

"She's in danger?"

"Until she learns to control her gift, aye. An untrained power as great as hers may be used by one of stronger will." He paused, his gray eyes pained. "Cyric senses a Druid calling the Deep Magic, an act he has forbidden. Yesterday's storm—'twas but a hint of the power abroad."

"Who is this Druid?"

"Some in Avalon believe it is one of our own number."

"And you?"

Rhys's eyes were haunted. "I canna say."

Owein stared at the scrap of papyrus. On it, drawn in ink, was a symbol sacred to the Celts. A triple spiral, signifying the three faces of the Great Mother. But the mark didn't stand alone. A circle, divided in four equal parts and entwined with a pair of vines, encircled the spiral. The magic of the Old Ones, merged with another power. What did it mean?

He touched the Great Mother's spiral with the tip of his index finger. At once, a sacred Word sprang into his mind. A sound in the language of the Old Ones, the ancients who had raised great circles of stones and planted groves of sacred oaks. The silent acknowledgement of their power vibrated through Owein's body.

He spread his hand flat on the papyrus, covering the mark completely. His palm burned. The heat expanded, surging up his arm. The strange symbol seared his flesh. But when he opened his palm, his skin was unmarked.

"What is this?" he demanded.

"This mark is engraved on the cup I seek. Aiden bade me draw it on the papyrus to show you."

"*This* mark is on a Roman cup?"

"Once inside the bowl, and three times on the outside. But . . . I do not think the cup is Roman. Aiden said it was not."

Owein's brow furrowed. "Describe the vessel further, lass."

"It's . . . old," she said, hesitantly, as if the word were inadequate. "It's smithed in silver, inlaid with crystals. Tarnish darkens its surface, yet somehow the metal is no less radiant for the passing of time. The crystals are polished like glass, revealing a core of wood."

"And where did ye come by it?"

"I told you. It belonged to my mother."

"Aye, so ye've said. Did your merchant father trade for it?"

Clara's eyes swept down, and her cheeks flushed. "He . . . no. My mother received the cup from my grandmother. It's a family heirloom."

"Impossible. Some marauding ancestor of yours must have stolen it. No Roman could own such a treasure by right."

Clara bristled. "The mark holds magic, does it not? Celt magic? Aiden insisted it did."

"Aye, the old man spoke truly for once. Only a Druid Master could have smithed a grail such as ye describe."

"Grail?"

"A sacred vessel," Owein clarified. "Imbued with Deep Magic."

"Deep Magic," she repeated. "Aiden spoke of Deep Magic as well. But I don't understand."

"The Deep Magic is the power of the gods. A power that existed long before man, long before the Dark and the Light. It's a power a mortal cannot hope to control. And yet," he added softly, "many have tried."

Clara stared at him. "I think . . . I've felt it. Even as a young girl. My mother promised to tell me more of the cup when I became a woman, but she died suddenly, and Father locked it away. I know so little. I only know that when I touch the cup, I feel"—she paused, a crease lining her forehead—"more."

Owein watched her closely. "More what, lass?"

"I don't know. Just . . . more. There's no other way to describe it."

Owein shook his head. It was impossible that a Roman woman could claim a connection with the Deep Magic of a Druid grail. And yet, he could sense no deception in Clara. Still, there was no possibility the grail belonged to her family. No Roman had the right to hold a sacred Druid relic.

Suddenly, Aiden's intentions became clear. The old man had sent Clara to tell Owein of the grail's existence. Surely Aiden meant for Owein to claim the grail as his own.

Aware of Clara's eyes upon him, Owein lifted the papyrus and scrutinized the mark. Again a sacred Word reverberated in his mind, and this time, more gently, in his throat.

The papyrus vibrated in his palm. Power ran up his arm like a shock, to land sharply in his temple. He spread his palm on the table, trapping the mark beneath it. It burned, but he couldn't summon the strength to throw the scroll aside.

A vision formed. Owein braced rigid arms on the table, waiting for the pain he knew would come. It did not forsake him. It rushed like flame though his veins, struck like a sharpened spear behind his eyes. He gasped with the violence of it. Dimly, he was aware of Clara, her delicate hand at her throat, her dark eyes frightened. He had but a moment to feel shame that she would witness his weakness.

The vision overtook him. His legs crumpled beneath him, knees connecting with the hard ground. The edges of his dwelling blurred. His body felt heavy, then light, as if his flesh had suddenly evaporated from his bones. His spirit rose, traveling into a gray mist.

He stood in an otherworldly place, surrounded by fog, the grail resting in his hands. He gazed at the relic. The metalwork was exquisite, far finer than any he'd ever seen. The sign of the Old Ones gleamed. The quartered circle, entwined with vines, surrounded the triple spiral.

Owein knew magic, but never had he touched an object so potent as this. Even though he held the grail in spirit only, his fingers tingled with its power. The Druid who had smithed this cup had fashioned no less than a portal to the Deep Magic.

Some of that magic seeped into Owein's skin. The tingling in his fingertips intensified, igniting something akin to fire. The sensation raced like lightning through his veins. Every fiber of his being thrummed with it.

His blood stirred. This simple cup held power enough to defeat thousands. Power enough to drive the Second Legion from the western mountains.

But what human was strong enough to pay the price such power demanded? Owein's own Druid Master, Madog, had not been able to control the Deep Magic. The forces Madog had unleashed against the Romans had turned against him, killing him as surely as the Roman sword that had pierced his flesh. If Owein dared call the Deep Magic, would he fare any better?

But what of the Druid who had summoned the storm? It took vast power to control the elements of nature. The Deep Magic would respond to such power. Perhaps the Hidden One had strength enough to wield it.

He cupped the grail in his hands. The vessel was not large—indeed, the bowl almost disappeared between his palms. Its inner surface was smooth, save for the pattern in the center of the bowl. As Owein gazed at it, the triple spiral began to spin. Liquid bubbled into the cup, viscous and dark, deep red and shining.

Blood.

Its power drew him in, claimed a piece of his soul. Pain drove through him like a shard of white fire. An animal's cry tore from his throat, but some dark part of his mind welcomed the suffering. For gazing into the grail, Owein knew a fleeting glimpse of invulnerability. Of *immortality.* In the face of such power, what worth did one man's frail body hold?

A shaft of pain impaled his right eye. A bead of sweat dripped from his brow to mingle with the blood in the grail. An image appeared on the liquid's surface, indistinct and wavering. He reached for it with his mind, not willing to let it escape.

It was like grasping the fire-reddened tip of an iron rod. The pain of the embrace was too great. He flinched and his vision blurred. Mist surrounded him, blocking his Sight, as if the god of the grail had looked into Owein's dark soul and found him wanting.

His arms spasmed, causing his grip to falter. The grail slipped. He felt something drop from his fingers—no, not the cup, but the slip of papyrus bearing its mark. It tumbled into the fire and was lost. All at once, he felt someone's hands grasping his. The touch was cool, like healing water.

Clara filtered slowly into his vision. She crouched before him, her dark gaze probing. He had no idea what she sought, but her intimate scrutiny disturbed him. He tried to pull away.

"No!" Her grip was remarkably strong for such a delicate creature. The vision had weakened him. He couldn't shake free.

"Let me be."

"No. You're in pain. I . . ."

And then he felt it. The whisper of a presence in his mind, like a flicker of light at the edge of his vision. Another consciousness, seeking to merge with his own.

By the might of the Horned God!

He'd felt such a sensation once before. Then it had been Madog in his mind. But the woman kneeling before him was no Druid master. She was Roman! It was not possible she could touch him so.

And yet she had.

Her expression was dazed, her eyes wide. And yet awareness flickered there. She knew what she'd done. She'd slipped in through the pain. Through his weakness.

This small Roman lass was far more dangerous than he'd thought.

He could feel her inside his mind, trying to align his will more fully with hers. He sensed she was drawn to his memories. She wanted to dive from the surface of his soul into his darkness.

He could not allow it. He tried to wrest himself from her grasp. In his weakened state, he couldn't summon the will to break her hold.

Perhaps he could repel her another way. He filled his mind—and hers—with an image sure to repulse. In his mental picture, Clara was naked, standing with her breasts pressed against a wide tree trunk. Owein was behind her, his rigid cock stroking the cleft of her buttocks. One knee urged her legs to part, while his hands adjusted the angle of her hips. His hand snaked around the dream Clara's body to delve between her thighs.

The true Clara's eyes widened. She gasped, color flooding her face. A flash of her shock filled his mind—along with an unexpected flare of arousal.

Her reaction to his crude thoughts stunned him. He'd anticipated disgust. Revulsion. Not . . . curiosity.

His body responded instantly. The image in his mind shifted. Now the dream Clara lay beneath him, moaning and arching into his hand. A pleading whisper fell from her parted lips. Owein sensed the true Clara's surge of panic. Felt her control on her magic slip.

Her touch vanished from his mind.

Thank the Horned God! Owein crouched, one hand gripping the edge of the table, his chest heaving with relief. He didn't attempt speech for several moments, until he was sure his voice would be steady.

He looked up, and with an insolence he didn't feel, forced a challenge into his eyes. "Did ye enjoy what ye saw, lass?"

Her countenance flushed crimson.

He tried to rise, but his legs were unsteady. He lowered himself into the chair instead.

She regarded him warily. "What . . . happened between us?"

"Ye dinna know?"

She shook her head. "I think . . . was that magic? Aiden thought I had a talent for it. He said he saw a light around me."

"Let me tell ye about Aiden, lass. He once saw a light around a carp. He hung the dead fish in his house, until the stink brought the entire village to his door." He exhaled unsteadily. "But to answer your question—aye, ye have magic." *A master's talent.* But he didn't tell her that.

"Could you . . . teach me to use it?"

At the risk of baring his soul and his past to her scrutiny? He would offer himself at the fortress gates in Isca before he would allow that to happen. The ache behind his right eye intensified, blurring her in his vision.

"I'm no teacher," he said gruffly.

"But—"

"I told ye—no." The pain in his head pounded. His hands burned. He opened his fists and looked down.

His stomach lurched, his head spun. His fingers were red, as if they'd been dipped in blood.

He pitched forward. The ground rushed up to claim him.

Clara leapt as Owein's large body tumbled from the chair. But she could no more have stopped his fall than she could have halted the plunge of an oak. He fell hard, his head striking the ground near the hearth.

She put all her strength into rolling him away from the fire. By the time she succeeded in heaving him onto his back and out of harm's way, stars spun in her vision. His body was dead weight, solid and heavy with muscle. His face was deathly pale behind his beard. His eyes were closed and his breathing shallow.

Had the trance harmed him? It surely had frightened her—almost as much as the lewd image she'd seen in his mind. The thought of that scene filled her with shame, yet at the same time, it sparked a fire low in her belly. What kind of woman was she, to feel this way?

Tentatively, she picked up his hand. It was heavy and cold, and his skin was damp. How could the heat have gone out of him so suddenly? Was this the price of his magic?

How long before he recovered? *Would* he recover? Or would the darkness she'd sensed inside him rise? Panic clawed at her lungs. She'd been drawn to the black depths of his soul. For one frightening moment, she'd feared she would lose herself in his darkness. She might have, if she hadn't been so shocked by his lewd thoughts.

She shook his shoulder, trying not to let her desperation show. "Owein?"

If he heard her call, he gave no evidence of it. She hesitated, then gave his shoulders another shake. "Owein!"

He uttered a low moan. Beneath closed lids, his eyes

fluttered. She shook him again, and he moaned a second time. His arm flung out, nearly striking her in the face.

She jumped back. "Owein!"

He murmured something she couldn't make out. He rolled to his side, facing her. His countenance relaxed. Clara's breath slowed. In repose, he seemed much less formidable.

But in no way harmless. Her eye lingered on the muscles of his upper arm, then drifted across his powerful torso. When she caught herself staring at the bulge between his thighs, she jerked her gaze away. The dream image of him readying himself to thrust between her spread legs had been more than she could bear.

She shifted, trying to assuage a sudden ache between her thighs. Was this the feeling the kitchen girls giggled about when they thought she couldn't hear? She'd never understood their giddy talk. Certainly, she'd shuddered at the thought of abasing herself before Valgus that way. She'd never understood what appeal lay in opening one's legs to a sweating, grunting man.

Until now. For some reason, imagining herself yielding to Owein in that way didn't inspire the same disgust. Much to the contrary. It brought a curious warmth to her belly, and below.

Owein grimaced and opened his eyes, as if he'd felt the heat seeping into her belly. He stared at her for several seconds, then an amused light flitted through his blue eyes. Belatedly, Clara realized she'd snuck a glance at the bulge between his thighs.

Her face heated.

"If ye dinna mind straddling me," he said in a conversational tone, "I might try to accommodate ye."

Clara blinked. "What?"

He lifted his torso on his elbows, then groaned and lay flat again. With a rueful smile, he nodded at a point lower on his body. Clara couldn't help following his gaze. Her eyes widened. The bulge had grown considerably.

"One limb at least seems to be working," he said.

Her gaze snapped back to his face. Despite his obvious humor, he looked haggard and weak. "Is it always like this?"

He chuckled. "Generally, when I'm near a fair lass."

Clara's cheeks burned so hot, she wondered her skin didn't burst into flames. "I meant to say, are you always weak after a vision?"

His amusement died. "Aye. But it passes quickly." Rolling to his knees, he placed a hand on the overturned chair and heaved himself to his feet. He swayed slightly, then planted himself as firmly as an oak. Clara scrambled to her feet. She felt far less steady than Owein looked.

She needed his help, yet even at his weakest he was frightening. He put her in mind of a lion she'd once seen at the arena games. The beast had fought to the death. She'd been moved to pity, but her father had scoffed at her sentiment. "Given the chance," he'd told her, "that lion would tear you to shreds. Pity! Did Caesar show pity to Vercingetorix in Gaul? No. If he had, the Celt king would have destroyed him. One cannot coddle a lion."

Clara regarded Owein through narrowed eyes. Perhaps it was true one couldn't coddle a lion. But perhaps one could make use of its strength.

Owein righted the chair and sat. Clara seated herself on the bench opposite, studying him. Every line of his body was weary, yet she sensed his lingering magic.

"Did you See the grail in your vision?"

"Aye," he said after a moment.

A surge of hope washed through her. "Do you know where it is? Who took it?"

"Nay. The place in my vision—'twas not of this world."

Clara shut her eyes against a wash of disappointment. "Can you find out more?"

"I could seek a vision. Ask the Horned God for his aid." His hard tone indicated his reluctance to do such a thing.

"I would pay you well," she said. "I have gold and jewels

in my satchel, along with some coin. I gathered all that I could—"

He shook his head. "I want no payment for my trouble."

"But you will seek the vision? You'll help me?"

"Aye." His blue eyes shifted away. "For Aiden's sake."

"When?"

" 'Where' is the better question, lass."

"All right. Where?"

"Such an endeavor is best done in a place of power. A circle ordained by the Old Ones."

"A ring of stones, you mean."

"Aye."

An unpleasant shiver ran through her. She'd been raised on tales of bloodthirsty Druids and human sacrifices made within those stone circles. She pushed such thoughts aside. "When may we depart?"

"*I* depart on the morrow. Ye will stay here."

"Alone?" What if he didn't return? What if he decided to keep the grail for himself? Aiden had declared Owein a man of honor, but what if he were wrong? Her father would die. "No. I'll go with you."

He shook his head. " 'Twould be folly."

"I won't be a burden."

He gave a short laugh. "Ye would be a grinding stone hung from my neck! A mountain in winter is no place for a woman."

"Many women once lived in these hills."

"Aye," Owein said. "Celt women, not Roman ones. A Celt woman is strong and clever."

"Are you saying I'm weak and dull-witted?"

"I didna say it, lass."

"Clara," she muttered. "My name is Clara. Not 'lass.' "

He held her gaze for a moment, then snorted and looked away.

Clara's anger surged. She gathered her pride like a mantle around her, straightening her shoulders and drawing herself up to her full height. "I'll not be left behind. If you try to leave without me, I'll follow."

"If I were of a mind to lose ye, lass, 'twould be no challenge."

Her hands fisted in her lap. "You won't go without me."

His lips pursed. "I willna carry ye."

"You won't need to. I give my word on it."

"Ah, that's fine. The word of a Roman. Forgive me, lass, if I'm nay overwhelmed with joy."

Barbarian. The thought rose sharply. She hadn't realized she'd sent the word into his mind until she saw his eyes narrow. Again, they were joined. And just like before, she had no clear idea how the union had come about.

His swift rage seared her. She withdrew as quickly as she could, heart pounding.

He rose and stepped toward her, causing her to tip her head back. He towered over her, his blue eyes glittering. "Keep to yourself, lass," he said evenly.

"I . . . I didn't mean to do it," she whispered. "I'll try not to let it happen again. Please. Let me go with you. I'll be no trouble."

He stared at her for what seemed a long time. Then his expression turned calculating. "Perhaps I'll take ye to the stones," he said, "if ye agree to give me something first."

Tiny wings fluttered in her belly. "Coin? Gold?"

"Nay. 'Tis something I've wanted since I first laid eyes on ye. Worth more, I am thinking, than all the jewels in your wee bag."

"What is it?" Clara whispered.

His gaze dropped to her mouth. "A kiss, lass. I would have a kiss."

Chapter Five

"A . . . a kiss?"

Owein suppressed a snort of amusement. The expression on Clara's face—wary and curious at once—brought to mind a kitten exploring dangerous ground. His fingers itched to unravel her braids and spread her glossy tresses about her shoulders. She was unaware of it, but a pin on the sleeve of her tunic had come undone, baring a swatch of creamy skin. If only one or two more clasps would break, the yellow wool would surely slip far enough to reveal the curve of her breast.

He captured her gaze. "Aye. A kiss." He was crazed, perhaps. But it had been more than two years since he'd seen a woman, and he'd seen more of this Roman lass than he could bear. The strain of denying his desire had only grown. Just thinking of claiming Clara's lips had his body tightening in anticipation.

He'd wanted her the moment she'd blinked up into his eyes. But now that he'd discovered she wasn't so powerless as he'd first supposed, there was a more urgent purpose for his pursuit. He had to prevent her from dropping into that clear, calm state of mind that engendered magic. And there was no better way to achieve that end than to stir her emotions.

"I . . . cannot think why you would want to kiss me."

"Drop your gaze a bit, lass, and ye'll see why."

Her gaze darted downward, then snapped back to his face. She took a step back, her face flooding crimson. He didn't have to look into her mind to know that she was thinking of the rutting scene he'd planted there earlier.

She swiped her palms down the sides of her tunic. "Aiden said you were a man of honor."

"Is there so much dishonor in a kiss?"

"No. I suppose not." Her gaze moved to his mouth, as if drawn there by some invisible force. "But . . . you won't take more?"

"Only if ye ask."

Her eyes widened, as if such a possibility had never occurred to her. "I . . . I won't."

He laughed out loud. That startled him—he couldn't remember when he'd last uttered such a sound. "I felt your interest when our minds were joined. Ye canna deny it."

"No. It . . . it was disgust you felt."

His grin widened. "A kiss, lass. That's my price for taking ye with me to the stones. Otherwise, ye stay here."

Her breath caught. For a moment, he thought she would turn away, but then her shoulders sagged and she sighed. "Very well, if that's what it takes to gain your cooperation." She lifted her chin and squeezed her eyes shut. "Go ahead."

Owein crossed his arms over his chest. "Nay, lass. I didna ask if I could kiss ye. Ye must kiss *me.*"

Her eyes flew open. "I couldn't."

"Coward, are ye?"

"No."

"Repulsed by my barbarian stink?"

She scowled. "No. You seem clean enough. It's just . . ."

He spread his arms. "What? Surely ye've kissed a man before."

Her blush crept to the roots of her hair.

His cock, already hard, strained the seam of his *braccas*. "Ye mean to say ye haven't?"

She nodded.

He could scarcely believe it. "Are Roman men blind, then?"

She blushed harder. "No. It's because of my father. He's . . . formidable."

"And ye've never slipped his yoke to go behind a haystack with a lad? Not once?"

She shook her head. "There's one man I might have kissed, if he'd asked. But my father . . ." Her voice trailed off.

"Who was this timid lover, lass?"

"A young blacksmith. He's very handsome. I see him each week in the market, and sometimes he remarks on the weather."

Owein snorted.

Clara pursed her lips. "Once my maid dropped a basket of pears and he helped her retrieve them. So when he asked Father for my hand in marriage, I wasn't unwilling."

"So why are ye nay wed to this smith?"

"Because he *is* a smith. Father refused him."

Owein frowned. "Can a smith nay marry a merchant's daughter?"

"A merchant's—oh!" For some reason, Clara would not meet his gaze. "Of course she could. But Father wants me to marry a Senator, now that he's amassed enough property to secure such a match. He would never consider a tradesman for my husband."

"Ye are virgin, then?" Owein had difficulty anchoring that thought in his mind. No wonder the image of rutting he'd put in her mind had flustered her so. He throbbed at the thought of being the first to slip into her woman's passage.

He edged closer and tipped her chin with the knuckle of his forefinger. "One simple kiss, lass."

Her dark eyes searched his face. He wondered what she saw there. It had been a long time since he'd seen his reflection in another person's eyes.

Whatever she saw, it didn't seem to frighten her. Or at least, not enough to back off. Her lips firmed as she placed her hands on his shoulders. She rose on her toes, but the difference in their heights was too great. She couldn't reach his lips.

"Come." He moved to sit in his chair. Taking her hands in his, he re-anchored them on his shoulders. The new position put her head slightly above his. The flash of relief in her eyes told him she was grateful for the small illusion of control.

He opened his knees wide and pulled her firmly between his legs until he felt the press of her body on his arousal. Her eyes widened. She went still in his arms, but he could see her pulse fluttering in her throat.

She smelled of flowers.

"One kiss only," she whispered. "You won't force me to give more." It was half statement, half question.

"I prefer a willing woman, lass."

"Clara," she said, her voice rising. "My name is Clara."

"Aye, so ye've said."

He waited for her. She drew close, pulled back, then swayed forward again. Her breath whispered over his lips.

Anticipation stretched him taut, like a rope ready to snap. He couldn't remember when the promise of a kiss had consumed him so utterly. Perhaps it never had.

He closed his eyes. The next instant her lips brushed his, soft and hesitant. Cool, like a sip of water from a spring. Fire sprang up inside him but he kept the flames banked. He didn't wish to singe the kitten's fur.

"I . . . thought your beard would be coarse." He felt the words murmured against his lips.

"Nay," he said thickly. Her springtime scent surrounded him.

She pressed her mouth against his, inexpertly. He

moved his lips on hers, tasting. She caught her breath and tried to move away, but Owein shifted one hand to cup the back of her head.

"Dinna pull away, lass. Not yet."

He lifted her into his lap. She made a startled sound, then surprised him by going soft in his arms. Encouraged, he deepened their kiss, running his tongue along the seam of her lips.

She opened to him on a sigh, her arms entwining his neck. He plundered her mouth. She whimpered, her round bottom wriggling on his shaft as if seeking a more comfortable position. By the Horned God! This was more torture than any man could be expected to endure—and for a man who'd not bedded a woman in two years . . .

He set his hands on her hips and rocked her against him in a steady, sensual rhythm. "Lass, ye are so sweet."

To his misfortune, his whispered endearment brought her back to herself. She wrenched her lips from his, shoving against his chest with a cry of dismay. He released her reluctantly.

She scrambled off his lap and backed away, eyes wide, her hand at her throat. Her gaze flicked to his crotch, then quickly jerked to a point beyond his shoulder. "I . . . that's enough."

"Not nearly, to my thinking." He was sure his stones had turned blue. "Lie with me, lass."

"I cannot."

His gaze softened. "Dinna be afraid. I'll be gentle with ye."

"No," she said, backing up farther, until she stood almost in the hearth. "You don't understand. I can't dishonor my father. He believes a woman's value is in her purity."

"A woman's value lies in her strength. In the new life she brings to her husband and her clan." He folded his arms over his chest and frowned. "How many years have ye, lass?"

"Twenty."

"And ye havna the right to choose your own bed partner?" He shook his head. "I dinna pretend to understand the ways of the Romans, but it seems to me they treat their women like children. A Celt lass—"

Clara stiffened. "I am not a Celt woman. And what I do in my bedchamber is no business of yours. You've had your kiss. Our bargain is sealed. I will accompany you to the stone circle. Nothing like this will happen again."

But she didn't sound at all certain.

The door to the forge swung open.

A swath of sunlight flashed across the soot-covered floor of Marcus's workroom. Marcus blinked against the sudden brightness. Working more from habit than sight, he completed his task, maneuvering a set of long tongs to pluck a bloom of iron from the coals in the furnace. He transferred it to the anvil. Only then did he look up to see who had disturbed his sanctuary.

"Rhys."

The greeting had the weight of resignation about it. At Rhiannon's insistence, Marcus had allowed the Celt to remain a guest in their home. But the thought of sleeping under the same roof as a Druid sorcerer had left a knot in Marcus's stomach. He'd spent the night in the forge.

At least he was getting some work done.

Rhys shut the door, plunging the room into pleasant darkness once more. Unfortunately, Rhys remained inside.

"Good day to ye, Marcus."

"I didn't think you'd be about before noon," Marcus muttered. He'd heard Rhys ring the gate bell just before dawn, after providing song at the home of a wealthy Celt merchant.

"I've nay slept at all. The storm may have blown itself out, but I cannot help thinking the reprieve will be brief."

"I've no wish to hear of storms," Marcus said, inhaling the tang of hot metal and ash. He brought his hammer down on the raw iron, absorbing a satisfying jolt with his arm. "Nor do I wish to speak of my sister—" He turned the piece and hammered again, flattening the lumpy metal. "Nor your Druid clan, nor"—he slammed the iron with a solid blow—*"magic."*

Rhys drew up a stool and sat. "We'll speak of your work, then," he said. His eyes roamed the workshop and came to rest on a plank table shoved up against the wall. An odd collection of throwing knives and silver animal figurines—Marcus's two hobbies—littered the surface, interspersed with drawings done on wax tablets and scraps of papyrus.

In the center of the clutter lay a long wrapped parcel. "Ye have a sword ready for delivery?" Rhys asked.

"Yes." Marcus transferred the beaten iron back to the furnace, then moved to the bellows. He sent a long, steady stream of air across the coals, watching the flare of heat carefully. Too much, and the iron would soften more than he intended. Too little, and it would be brittle when it cooled.

A trickle of sweat rolled down the side of his face. His hair clung his scalp; his shirt to his torso. "The sword goes to Aurelius Valgus."

"The tribune? I didna ken ye had trade with the man."

"I don't," Marcus said sharply. He pulled the heated iron from the fire and folded the glowing metal on the surface of the anvil. "At least, I didn't before today. Sempronius Gracchus commissioned the sword. But now the commander is ill, and Valgus is in command. He's even moved into Gracchus's residence. The tribune demanded I deliver the sword to him."

"Ah," Rhys said. "Last night's feast was abuzz with the news that Valgus is to marry your fair Clara."

Marcus slammed his hammer on the anvil. "I cannot believe Gracchus would give her to that bastard rather than to me."

"Valgus is destined for the Roman Senate," Rhys said easily. "I've heard Gracchus wants nothing more than to be father-in-law to a Senator. You, my friend, are a backwater blacksmith."

"My blood is as patrician as Valgus's," Marcus muttered. "My own grandfather sat in the Senate."

"Aye, but your father renounced the seat to marry a barbarian," Rhys pointed out. "Now he tends wheat fields without the benefit of slaves. His sanity is suspect." He tipped his stool onto its rear legs and leaned against the wall. "Perhaps Clara asked for the match with Valgus. Does she appear willing?"

"I wouldn't know. She hasn't been at the market in days. That's one reason I agreed to deliver Gracchus's sword to Valgus. I'm hoping to catch a glimpse of her."

"To what purpose? It will only darken your mood. Choose another woman to woo. There are fair lasses aplenty in Isca."

"Perhaps," Marcus said, setting his hammer and tongs aside. He bent and adjusted the furnace vents. Rhys's advice, as always, had the ring of wisdom. His obsession was fruitless, and no one knew it so well as he. Why couldn't he put Clara out of his head?

Untying his apron, he hung it on an iron hook. "I'm to deliver the sword before noon," he said with a mild snort, "so as not to disturb Valgus's dinner." Belatedly, he realized he'd slipped into the familiar amity he and Rhys so often shared. He slanted the Celt a glance, conflicting emotions grappling in his chest. His best friend a Druid? The notion didn't seem real.

"Will you accompany me to the fortress?" he asked after an awkward pause.

"With pleasure," Rhys said smoothly, setting the front leg of the stool down with a bang. Rising, he strode to the worktable. "But first, I would inspect your handiwork."

Marcus was at the washbasin, scrubbing soot from his face and hands. He squinted into the polished bronze mirror. He should stop at the main house and change his clothes. He cared little if Valgus sneered at his blacksmith's garb, but if there was a chance he might encounter Clara . . .

Rhys caught Marcus's eye in the mirror. "Go on," Marcus told him. "Just be sure to wrap it again."

Rhys unrolled the oiled cloth to reveal a sheathed *gladius*. Intricate silver tracery decorated its crosspiece and pommel. The polished leather scabbard bore a matching silver edging and tip. Rhys slid the sword from its sheath and hefted it, checking its balance. He tested the shining edge with his thumb.

"A fine piece, Marcus, as usual. Ye are a true artist." He shook his head. "A fine joke that a man who loathes swordplay should produce such a beautiful weapon."

"Indeed," Marcus said wryly. It was the truth. He was far more captivated by the artistry of swords than by their use. Throwing knives, however, were another story. He had a fine hand with a dagger, especially those of his own design.

Rhys sheathed the blade and covered it with the oilcloth. " 'Tis close to midday now."

Marcus decided to forgo a change of clothing. He'd most likely not catch a glimpse of Clara, and if he did, what did it matter? She was beyond his reach.

They trudged the snowy lane to Isca in silence, Rhys squinting skyward repeatedly. *Searching for Hefin,* Marcus thought. But the merlin was nowhere to be seen. *Odd.*

Farmland gave way to the jumble of timbered cottages and thatched roofs that made up the city. The forum market lacked its usual bustle of customers, most likely because of the cold. The arena was busy, however, with men and slaves hurrying about.

"There's a slave auction on the Ides," Marcus told Rhys.

"You'll be there, I trust."

"Of course." Marcus attended every auction, buying what slaves the family finances could afford. And earning the contempt of the patrician Romans in Isca when he immediately granted their freedom. Another strike against Marcus as far as his offer for Clara was concerned. No doubt Sempronius Gracchus thought him mad.

Some of the slaves Marcus freed stayed on at the Aquila

farm, working for board and a small wage, but most did not. Financially and socially, the endeavor was a losing proposition. And yet Marcus's only regret was that he wasn't rich enough to free every slave brought to the auction stone. Men and women shouldn't be traded like cattle.

They approached the fortress. The massive gates stood open, as was common during daylight hours. Isca had been a secure city for two generations. The only threat the two soldiers at guard were likely to encounter was boredom.

"Marcus Ulpius Aquila, blacksmith," Marcus told the man who appeared the most alert. "I've a delivery for Tribune Valgus."

"And your friend?" the man asked, eyeing Rhys.

"My assistant."

The man made a note on a wax tablet and jerked his head, indicating they were free to pass. Inside the gates, the disorder of the village gave way to neat workshops, granaries, and stables. Commander Gracchus's legendary disclipline was evident everywhere. Soldiers went about their business with quiet purpose, streets were empty of debris, and the buildings were in such good repair that they might have been erected yesterday rather than fifty years earlier. Suddenly, Marcus regretted not changing his sooty clothes.

They approached Gracchus's residence, an impressive two-story house located in the center of the fortress. Marcus had barely rapped at the door when it swung open. An elderly porter wearing an expression of disdain took one look at the ragged pair on his doorstep and directed them to the servants' entrance.

Rhys chuckled. " 'Tis true enough, Marcus, ye could use a visit to the baths."

"As if you smelled like a rose," Marcus grumbled.

They followed an alley to the rear of the building. A kitchen slave directed them to an unroofed yard off the central court. Rows of amphorae, the rounded clay shipping containers favored for oil and wine, bordered one side of the space. In an opposite corner, freshly washed linen grew stiff in the cold air.

A portly Roman with shining white hair and an equally shining white tunic appeared. Marcus knew the man to be Gracchus's steward.

"How fares the commander?" Marcus asked.

The man nodded. "Of course, blacksmith."

Belatedly, Marcus remembered that the elderly steward was all but deaf. He repeated the question more loudly.

The steward's expression sobered. "Not well. The commander clings to life, but I fear it won't be long before he stands on the banks of the Styx."

"And his daughter? How is she?"

The question seemed to frighten the man. His gaze dropped to the floor. "As well as can be expected."

Marcus cleared his throat. "Yes. Well." He lifted the wrapped sword. "Tribune Valgus is expecting this delivery."

"He requests you await him in the main courtyard. He wishes to inspect the sword before extending payment."

"As the Tribune wishes," Marcus said. In an undertone, he added to Rhys, "Valgus had better part with the full amount."

"Don't count on it," Rhys murmured back to him as they followed the steward out of the work yard. "Gossip has it that he's in arrears all over town."

An interminable wait ensued. Female voices drifted from the kitchen. Marcus cocked his head, hoping to catch a glimpse of Clara on the upper-story balcony, but to no avail.

Valgus strode into the yard. Though only two years older than Marcus, the tribune already sported the thickened look of a man past thirty. He wore his haughty air with considerable pride. Many considered him a fine-looking man, and Marcus supposed he might have agreed, if it hadn't been for Valgus's eyes. Small and black, they had the unsettling habit of never resting in one place.

Marcus stepped forward. Forgoing a formal bow, he simply unfolded the oiled cloth and presented his sword.

Valgus accepted the blade, sliding it from its scabbard and testing the edge as Rhys had done. It was perhaps the finest *gladius* Marcus had ever made—with it, he'd hoped to gain Gracchus's favor, but that had been before Clara's betrothal. Now all he wished for was payment.

The tribune's expression betrayed nothing as he slashed a wide arc with the gleaming weapon. "It will do, I suppose."

The bastard had likely never held a finer sword. Marcus bit back a retort as Valgus flicked a finger toward the steward. The man stepped forward and placed a pouch in Marcus's hand.

Marcus made a quick count of the coins inside. "Nine *aurei?* This is but half the agreed price."

"It's more than the weapon is worth. Gracchus was far too generous in accepting your price."

"*I* will not accept this payment."

"You'll not have a *denarius* more."

"I'll take the sword back, then."

Valgus raised the tip of the weapon just enough to be threatening. "I invite you to try."

Marcus fingered the hilt of the throwing dagger at his belt. Rhys caught his eye, his expression clearly indicating caution. Valgus might be a pampered senator's son, with more conceit than true military experience, but he was still a trained swordsman. Marcus was a common blacksmith.

Though it rankled his pride, he stepped back and gave Valgus a curt nod. Depositing the meager pouch in his satchel, he turned to leave without waiting for a formal dismissal. It was a small act of disrespect, but at the moment, all Marcus could afford.

He strode toward the door to the work yard, Rhys close on his heels. As his hand reached for the latch, the door swung open. Marcus stood aside as an old slave pushed a small handcart loaded with two enormous amphorae over the threshold. An iron-rimmed wheel snagged on an uneven paving stone. The cart heaved. With a crack, the overloaded axle split.

The old man lunged for the amphorae, trying to halt their forward motion. It was no use. The wooden slats on the front of the cart splintered, sending the containers sliding to the ground. They crashed on the paving stones, shattering in a shower of clay. The aroma of olives filled the air as waves of green-gold liquid cascaded over the mosaic floor.

The slave went down hard on his knees. Marcus stretched out a hand, but before the old man could take the proffered aid, Valgus, new sword in hand, shoved Marcus aside.

"Worthless Celt swine."

The old man clutched the side of the cart, trying to heave himself upright. He didn't succeed. Valgus's booted foot connected with his ribs, sending him face first into the ruined oil.

"Ho, there!" Marcus said. If there was one thing Marcus hated above all else, it was the cruelty of the powerful to the weak. "There's no call—"

A second kick caught the slave in the head. The old man curled into a ball, moaning. Rhys darted forward. Heedless of the oil, he dropped to his knees beside the fallen man.

Valgus raised his sword arm. "Out of my way!"

Marcus grabbed Valgus's wrist, halting the weapon's downward arc. Out of the corner of his eye, he saw the commotion had brought several slaves out of the kitchen.

Valgus struggled to extract his arm from Marcus's grip, but a soft officer was no match for strength honed by daily labor in a forge. Marcus squeezed until he felt the grind of bones under his fingers. The tribune's face went scarlet. His grip loosened.

The *gladius* clattered to the ground, splashing oil.

Abruptly, Marcus released him. Valgus stifled a gasp. The shocked huddle of slaves scattered. Valgus lowered his arm, holding it in a natural position, but Marcus wasn't fooled. It would be some time before the tribune wielded his new sword.

"I'll have your word of honor," Marcus said quietly, "that you'll do this man no further harm."

"I give no such promise," Valgus muttered. "The useless cur isn't worth the price of his feed."

"I'll be content to undertake the burden of his care."

Valgus's expression turned calculating. "Ah, yes. I'd heard you collect vermin. What price do you offer?"

"None. You've declared him worthless."

"One man's garbage is another's gold. And even garbage has its uses. For example, I would take great pleasure in killing this slave. Surely that is worth a few coins." His gaze lit on Marcus's satchel. "Perhaps the exact amount of your purse?"

"That's preposterous."

"You would haggle over the price of a man's life?"

Marcus's anger flared. Valgus had turned the tables neatly, he realized. Seeing no other recourse—at least none that would not end in arrest—Marcus withdrew Valgus's pouch from his satchel and threw it on the ground. "Get the old man up and out of here," he said in Celtic to Rhys, not taking his eyes from the tribune.

Rhys looped one of the old man's arms around his shoulders and helped him rise. A low moan vibrated in the slave's throat. Marcus crouched, lending his aid. Under Valgus's glare, they carried the old man from the courtyard.

"Ye've made a powerful enemy," Rhys said once they'd reached the alley.

Marcus exhaled. "It couldn't be helped. I could hardly have left an old man to such a master."

"Valgus is nay my master," the old slave croaked. "I belong to Commander Gracchus's household."

Marcus passed a hand over his eyes. Not only had he lost all his coin, he'd paid it to the wrong man.

The old slave opened his mouth to say more, but a fit of coughing stole his words. Blood trickled from between his lips. He ended with a moan, his head lolling.

"We'll never get him home without a cart," Marcus muttered. "And now I've no money to hire one."

"I'll gain one with the promise of a song," Rhys said. "We've only to get past the fortress gates and into the city."

They carried the unconscious man past the guards, who eyed them but made little comment. No one cared much for an injured slave. Rhys begged a cart and pony from a tavern owner he knew well. Marcus eased the old man onto his back on a heap of straw.

Rhys bent over the cart. "I hope Rhiannon can help him."

"If she can't, there's little hope," Marcus replied.

The old man's eyelids opened. His eyes, blurred with pain, alighted on Rhys's face. "By all the gods in Annwyn," he breathed. "Ye are a Wise One."

Marcus stiffened.

Rhys gripped the old man's hand. "Aye, elder, your vision is true. Can ye tell me your name?"

The old man's eyes drifted shut. "I . . . I am called Aiden."

Chapter Six

So *this* was why a woman debased herself before a man.

Clara yanked her bone comb through her tangled hair, muttering under her breath. Yesterday's kiss had set her afire, as if someone had kindled a blaze in her belly. Her senses had magnified tenfold, all centered on Owein. She was aware of him as she'd never been of any man.

When he rummaged about, preparing for their journey to the stones, she felt his every movement. Each word he spoke echoed inside her skull. When his pine and heather scent teased her nostrils, her stomach pitched and tumbled.

He paused in his work, his gaze lingering far too long on the fall of her unbraided hair. An ache sprang up in her gut, but it was totally unlike the feeling one had after dining too heavily. No, the sensation was more akin to hunger.

Hastily, she gathered her hair at her nape and fashioned one long braid. She'd never worn such a plain style, but it was all she could manage without the help of her maids. She tied the plait with a ribbon from her satchel, aware of Owein's attention upon her. Her pulse fluttered and her breathing was shallow. Reaching deep in her satchel—

Owein had graciously repaired the severed shoulder strap—she searched past the coins and jewelry for her vial of rose oil. She drew out the bottle and uncorked it, breathing deeply.

At once her nerves calmed. Curiously, her actions seemed to have the opposite effect on Owein. He'd gone tense, his blue eyes sparking with unnerving intensity.

"What is that?" he asked gruffly.

She looked at him in surprise. "Why, it's nothing but rose oil." She dabbed a bit on her throat.

"Ye traipsed across the wilderness carrying a vial of scent?" His tone was angry, though she couldn't imagine why.

"It was hardly a burden," she said crossly, replacing the vial's stopper and stowing the bottle in her pack.

He shoved a bowl of stew into her hands. "Here," he all but barked. "Eat."

"I'm not hungry." She set it aside.

He grunted and settled beside her on the bench with his own meal. He was much too close for her peace of mind. Her eye lingered on the thin, primitive braid that hung from his temple. It sent a shiver down her spine. At least the hearth fire had been between them during the night. Even so, she'd lain awake for hours, listening to his steady breathing. And hoping. For what, she didn't know.

She watched him from under her lashes as he ate. He wasn't careless about his manners, as she might have expected a barbarian to be. Her gaze was drawn to his lips. They were firm and mobile, and very expressive. She wished his beard gone so she could examine them more thoroughly.

What would he look like clean-shaven? She traced the line of his jaw with her eyes, mentally removing his curly red mane. She would cut his hair as well—but perhaps not so short as a Roman man would wear it. She'd leave it curling over his ears and touching his shoulders. And then she would run her fingers through it . . .

"Lass."

Clara's gaze snapped to his. There was a knowing expression in his blue eyes. His attention dropped to her mouth. She lowered her eyes, her heart pounding. Would he try to kiss her again?

He didn't. He only retrieved her bowl and pressed it into her hands. His touch lingered—intentionally, she was sure. Heat flared in his blue eyes like the dark center of a flame. His finger stroked her thumb from base to tip, touching off a conflagration low in her belly.

He offered her a mug of *cervesia,* the barley beer favored by the Celts. It was a pungent beverage she'd never tasted. One whiff of it set her stomach churning.

His warm fingers closed on hers, anchoring her hand to the earthenware. "Drink. Ye need your strength for the journey."

Drink? How could she, when her heart was lodged in her throat? Her body tingled and her cheeks burned. She was shameless. What would Father think if he knew she was entertaining lustful thoughts of a wild barbarian? She could picture the censure in his eyes all too easily.

She brought the mug to her lips and forced a sip of the bitter brew. She had to get hold of her emotions. Surely one kiss from a man shouldn't reduce a woman's brain to gruel. She hated this helpless feeling.

The events of the last few days had been so far out of her experience, she could scarcely believe they had happened to her. Had she truly ducked through the fortress gates and into the mountains on the strength of her faith in an old man? Had she conversed with a barbarian Celt, slept in his dwelling, even allowed his kiss?

But perhaps most disturbing was when she had slipped into Owein's mind by magic. She didn't have a clear idea how it had happened. Perhaps Aiden had been right in insisting Clara held power in her own right. If only Owein would reconsider his refusal to teach her.

Perhaps she would ask him again.

* * *

They departed for the stones at dawn.

Clara wore new boots. They were a crude construction of fur and leather, fashioned by Owein's hand. She'd protested at first, reluctant to part with her own pearl-edged pair, damaged though they were. Owein had grunted and tossed them into the snow. She supposed he was right in deeming them unsuitable for a difficult mountain trek. But she couldn't help feeling that another bit of her old self had been tossed aside with them.

Now that she was actively searching for her mother's cup, she had difficulty taming her worry about her father. How did he fare? Did he even still live? Would she return in time to save him, buying herself time to convince him that Valgus wouldn't make her a suitable husband? Or would she return to find her father dead and Valgus livid over her disappearance?

She shuddered. At Father's death, Valgus would become her guardian, whether they were married yet or not. It was no secret that Father's fortune had induced the tribune to accept a soldier's daughter as wife—there were rumors that Valgus's own father was deeply in debt. Clara was certain the tribune would demand they marry quickly. As her husband, he would have full control of Father's vineyards in Gaul, his iron works in the south of Britannia, and the new villa and horse farm he was building near Isca. Not to mention the trunk of gold secured in the vault under the fortress temple.

Grim thoughts skittered through her mind as she followed Owein into terrain that grew increasingly more rugged. The wind was icy, but at least the sky was clear of clouds. A bright winter sun illuminated the bald tops of the mountains and cast shadows in the forested valleys between. Two days to reach the stones, Owein had said. When his vision came—if it came—they would decide their next move.

He'd spoken little since morning. He'd awakened

slowly, as if rising from a dream he didn't wish to lose. Once on the trail, he'd set a punishing pace. Or rather, his pace was punishing for Clara. For Owein, the trek was likely a leisurely stroll.

The descending trails were more treacherous than the ascending ones. Ice and snow slicked the ground. Clara suspected Owein kept to the forested trails because the footing was surer. Even so, she'd fallen thrice. The first time, she'd come down hard on her right hip, which ached still. After that, Owein stayed closer, to catch her before she hit the ground. Each time, his hands lingered as if reluctant to withdraw from her body.

His words, however, were anything but lusty.

"Can ye nay find your footing? I wish to reach the stones before summer."

"You might walk a bit slower," Clara muttered.

"A Celt woman would have little trouble keeping pace."

"I'm not a Celt woman."

"Aye, I ken that only too well, lass. 'Tis why I wished ye to remain in my roundhouse."

"My name is Clara," she ground out. She shook the wet snow from her hem. "Not *lass.* I'll thank you to remember that."

"I hadna forgotten, lass."

She scowled. He snorted—the closest sound to humor she'd heard him make since morning. She couldn't define his mood. She hefted her satchel, the only part of their provisions Owein had allowed her to carry. The rest—food, blankets, and a waterskin—were bound in a pack on his broad back. The bone hilt of a dagger protruded from a sheath attached to his belt.

Toward evening, they encountered a circular stone shelter, a smaller version of Owein's roundhouse. The thatch was missing in several places, and the small door was gone. It was clear from Owein's nod of satisfaction that he'd been looking for the place.

"A shepherd's sleeping hut. We'll make our beds here."

Clara peered through the doorway, a small flare of panic rising. "It doesn't look large enough for two." *Especially when one of the pair was as large as a bear.* "Surely you don't expect us to share such a small space."

Owein had bent to gather some scattered deadwood. He straightened, regarding Clara with brows raised. "Ye wish to sleep outside?"

"Not me," she said. "You."

He snorted. "I've no urge to freeze my stones."

Clara shivered inside her cloak. The sun had already dipped below the top of the mountain, leaving the valley dark and cold. "Promise not to touch me, then."

Owein piled more wood by the doorway. "I canna promise that. The shelter is far too small."

Clara closed her eyes against a sudden image of the two of them pressed into the small space. She bit her lip. "You promise you'll not force me to couple with you?"

The corners of his mouth turned down. "Barbarian I may be, but I dinna take unwilling women."

She watched as he shredded dry bark for tinder and sparked a blaze with the flint from his pack. Clara lowered her satchel to the ground and stretched out her frozen hands to the fire. The stone wall at her back was already warming.

She chewed the strip of dried venison Owein offered and washed it down with a sip from his waterskin. Her teeth and jaws ached with the effort of chewing—never in her life had she eaten such rough fare. From Owein's knowing glance, he guessed as much.

He kept the fire small, prowling at the edges of the light before settling down beside her. The night wind gusted, causing the flames to dim. Clara drew the edges of her cloak together, blessing its hood and its thick fur lining. By contrast, Owein's cloak was thin, ragged wool. But he didn't seem to notice.

"I'd give all the jewels in my satchel for a hot bath," Clara sighed.

Owein merely grunted.

"Could we build up the fire, at least?"

Owein raised his head. The meager flames glinted red-gold on his thick mane. "The deadwood I gathered must last us the night."

"Oh." Clara huddled in her cloak. "Of course."

Owein nodded toward the hut. " 'Twill be warmer inside." Retrieving the blanket from his pack, he crouched in the doorway and spread it over the dirt floor.

Clara was too cold and exhausted to protest the tight quarters. Drawing her cloak about her shoulders, she crawled past him. Some of the heat from the fire had found its way into the hut, but the wind whistling through the doorway and roof dispersed it quickly. It would be a long, cold night.

She curled up in her cloak as tightly as she could. Owein eased into the shelter beside her, placing his large body between her and the open door, blocking most of the wind. She lay on her side facing him, carefully avoiding contact. Unfortunately, that meant lying on her bruised hip.

He was as warm as a brazier filled with coals. Her shivering soon abated, but the sharp dart of pain in her hip prevented her from getting comfortable. She wriggled, shifting first to lie a bit more on her stomach, then more on her back.

She was startled when Owein's gruff voice reached out to her, almost in her ear. She hadn't realized his lips were so close. "Can ye nay be still, lass?"

"The ground is hard," Clara said crossly.

"My apologies for that. I neglected to pack a down-filled pallet for our journey."

"It would be no matter if I hadn't fallen on my hip."

"Turn over, then."

"And lose sight of you? I think not."

He snorted. "If I meant to seduce ye, I'd have done it by now."

She went still. "Are you saying you don't want to seduce

me?" She cursed herself as soon as the words left her tongue.

Owein muttered a rough Celt word—one that Aiden hadn't taught her. She heard a long sigh, then, a moment later, he reached for her. His hand closed on her upper arm. Before she could summon a word of protest, he turned her in his arms and tucked her against his body, her back pressed to his chest. One strong arm settled on her waist, pinning her firmly in place.

She gasped. "Let me go."

"Nay. Ye wriggle too much. Go to sleep."

"With your hands on me? Impossible."

He chuckled and drew her even closer, until she felt the length of his phallus hardening against the cleft of her bottom.

She went still, her heart pounding against her chest so wildly she couldn't fill her lungs. Owein shifted, his arm brushing the underside of her breasts. His hot breath bathed her neck. His touch had her melting like beeswax in the summer sun. She waited, both dreading and longing for his next move.

It never came. His arm grew heavy and his breath deepened to a soft snore.

He'd fallen asleep.

Chapter Seven

"Shouldn't he be coming around?" Marcus peered over Rhiannon's shoulder at the ugly mark Valgus's boot had made on Aiden's temple. "It's been hours."

"He needs time," Rhiannon murmured. She probed the bruise, then moved her fingers to the back of Aiden's head, pressing his scalp in various places.

Breena sat on the opposite side of the bed. "His response depends on the cruelty of the trauma," she told Marcus. "When the head receives a blow, it must heal in stillness. The more severe the blow, the deeper the stillness it seeks."

Marcus sent his sister an incredulous look. "How do you know that?"

"I've been reading Hippocrates," she said with a note of defensiveness.

"In the original Greek, no doubt," Marcus grumbled. He hated Greek.

"Of course," Breena replied airily. "Too much is lost with translation." At Rhiannon's nod, she dipped a length of linen in a bowl of wine and daubed a raw scrape on

Aiden's elbow. She was the picture of competence, her hair tamed in a thick braid.

Marcus shook his head. Rhys seemed bemused by the changes in Breena as well. The Celt stood leaning against the wall, his gaze fixed on her hands.

Marcus scowled. Surely his eyes were playing tricks on him. Rhys had twenty-two years to Breena's twelve. He thought of her as Marcus did—as a sister.

"Come," he said abruptly, turning. "Let's leave the women to their work."

He started for the door, only to hear a low moan from the bed. He turned back in time to see Aiden's bleary eyes fall on Rhiannon, then travel to Breena.

"So much Light," he said in wonder. "But . . . where is the one who saved me?"

"Here," Marcus said, stepping forward.

The old man's head turned. He blinked once, then his awed expression turned surly. "Nay," he said impatiently. "Not this one. He has no magic. No Light." He struggled to rise on one elbow.

" 'Tis I ye seek, elder," Rhys said.

"Aye, there ye are, Wise One. Shining green I see behind ye. Ye are strong in the magic of the forest."

Rhys's gray eyes registered his surprise. "Ye can see this?"

"Aye," Aiden said. "That and more." He reached a trembling hand to Rhiannon. "Your Light is gentle. A soft glow."

"My magic is slight," Rhiannon said, tilting a cup of wine to Aiden's lips.

The old man's scrawny neck bulged as he swallowed. It reminded Marcus of a chicken. He flexed his fingers.

"But ye, lass." Aiden's bony hand descended on Breena's forearm. "Ye are shining white. Ye are a Seer. Like *him.*"

"Like who?" Rhys said sharply.

Aiden's shriveled shoulders started to shake, and a tear leaked out of his eyes. "He is from my life . . . before. Before the soldiers came. Like a son he was to me. They didna take him, though. He is alive. Hiding." His gaze darted to Breena. "This lass's magic is strong, like his."

Marcus's stomach turned. He could do without all this talk of magic.

"My power is not so great, elder," Breena murmured.

"Dinna deny your strength, lass, as he did." He licked dry lips. "Ye favor him in other ways as well. Ye have the same hair . . . same eyes. He's young, though nay so young as ye. The Romans brought him from the northlands as a slave. I saved him, ye know, after they flogged him nearly to death."

Rhiannon gave a small cry. Her hands, usually so steady, shook. Wine sloshed over the edge of the cup she held. Marcus stepped forward and took it. He steadied her with one hand on her shoulder, but she didn't seem to notice his quiet support.

"This Seer," she whispered. "Where is he?"

"Alone," Aiden said sadly. " 'Tis not a good thing for a man to be alone. 'Tis why I sent Clara to him."

Marcus's jaw went slack. *"What?"*

"Clara has the Light about her, too. It glows like the sun. Aye, she is Roman, but her link to the Deep Magic is strong. She bears the Lost Grail. The cup fashioned by the Daughters of the Lady."

It was Rhys's turn to gape. "Nay. That cannot be."

Aiden's voice was fading. "I assure ye it is. I held the grail in my own hands. It bore the mark of Avalon—the triple spiral of the Great Mother and the four-quarter circle of the Prophet. Gracchus was all but dead, but Clara held the grail and called him back to life." He lay back with a wheeze. "The grail is gone now. Stolen. But the Seer will find it."

Rhiannon leaned forward and clasped Aiden's hand. "This Seer, elder. What is his name?"

Aiden looked confused. "Ye dinna know?"

"Nay. I do not."

The old man lay back on the cushions, his breath wheezing from his lungs in a long sigh. "But of course, ye dinna know Owein. He came from the northlands."

Marcus's gaze darted to Rhiannon. The color had drained from her face.

"Owein," she whispered. "My brother."

"You think Rhiannon's Druid brother conjured the storm?" Marcus asked.

Rhys paced the width of the forge. As always, Marcus seemed as calm and steady as the anvil he leaned on. But Rhys knew his friend too well to think he was unmoved. Color rose on Marcus's neck and ears.

"It is possible," Rhys said.

"Owein's no stranger to dark magic," Marcus muttered.

Rhys stopped pacing. "Ye know him?"

Marcus studied a pair of tongs. "I've seen him. It was thirteen years ago. I was a boy of ten. Owein's Druid master, Madog, slaughtered my uncle and cast a dark spell on his soul. When Madog died trying to imprison my father in the same way, Owein tried to complete what his master began." He passed a hand over his eyes. "If Owein has grown in power since that time . . . by Pollux! I don't know what's worse—thinking Clara lost in the hills, or believing that she has found Owein."

"If what you say is true, then Owein could very well be the Druid who called the storm." A curious sense of relief washed through Rhys. As much as he loved Rhiannon, contemplating Owein's guilt was far preferable to believing what was whispered by the Druids of Avalon—that Rhys's twin, Gwendolyn, was the rogue Druid.

"If Owein is calling the Deep Magic, I need to learn his purpose. I have to find him," Rhys said.

"Rhiannon begged Father to locate Owein after the fighting died down in the north. Father put out some inquiries, but nothing came of them. It will cause my stepmother much pain if Owein has once again aligned himself with dark magic."

"Rhiannon is a strong woman."

"She loves too deeply."

"And ye do not? What of Clara?"

Marcus scowled. Pacing to his workbench, he plucked a dagger from the clutter. Rhys eased to one side, away from the slab of wood that Marcus used for a practice target. For all Marcus's unflappable good nature, Rhys knew his friend could turn deadly when sufficiently provoked.

"I should have pressed Clara more." He grimaced. "Spoken to her of something other than the weather. If I had, she might have come to me in her distress, rather than taking the counsel of a senile old man."

"I dinna think Aiden has lost his wits."

Marcus brought his arm forward with a sudden motion. His dagger sliced the air, rotating once before thudding into the center of the target. "What kind of man would send a delicate Roman woman into the mountains to seek a wild Celt?" he demanded.

"What kind of Roman woman would act on his advice?"

"A desperate one," Marcus said. "A grieving one. Rhiannon's been to Gracchus's bedside. If she couldn't cure him, the man is all but dead." He expelled a rough breath. "If Clara succeeds in finding Owein, he's likely to hold her for ransom, if he does not kill her outright. By Pollux, her father commands the Second Legion! Owein will hardly be moved to help her retrieve a magic cup."

"If the cup Clara's looking for is truly the Lost Grail of Avalon, I have no doubt that he will help her," Rhys replied. "He will want the grail for himself."

Marcus looked ill. "What is this vessel? What power does it hold?"

Rhys shifted uncomfortably, sweat trickling down his neck. He could hardly reveal the secrets of the Lost Grail to Marcus, but he sensed his friend wouldn't accept silence for an answer.

"Many years ago," he began carefully, "before the Roman army marched on the west country, a ship from the east was wrecked on the shores of Avalon. The only survivor was a woman, heavy with child. In her arms, she cradled a plain wooden cup. She spoke of a carpenter prophet from the East, who followed the way of the Light. She gave no name, so the Druids called her simply 'The Lady.' "

Rhys shifted his stance. "The Lady birthed twin daughters. Soon after, she disappeared into the swamps. The Druids succored her babes. Before many years passed, they discovered the twins were bound to the Deep Magic."

"What is this Deep Magic? Is it good? Or evil?"

"Neither. Or both. The Deep Magic existed long before the Dark parted from the Light. For those able to call it, Deep Magic can take either form."

He paced toward the furnace, despite the heat. "The twins were taught the Ways of the Old Ones. They learned the craft of silver and the magic of crystals. As young women, they combined their powers to create a silver and crystal casing for their mother's wooden cup, in which they had discovered great healing power." *Among other powers,* he added silently.

"This cup was lost?"

"Aye. When the Legions marched on the west. Druidry was declared outlawed. The Druids fled Avalon. Many were captured and put to the sword; others went into hiding. The grail was lost."

"And you believe Clara's cup is this grail?"

"If Aiden's description is accurate, it can be nothing else. It bears the mark of Avalon. I must find it."

"The cup can go to Hades," Marcus said. "It's Clara's safety I care about." He slammed his open palm on his worktable. "But how can I leave Isca to search for her with Father gone? My first duty is to Rhiannon and Breena. Even if I do go into the hills, where would I look?"

Rhys could have solved that problem easily enough with Hefin's help, though he dared not reveal that fact to Marcus. But the merlin had been absent for more than a day. Rhys's concern for the bird was growing. Hefin rarely strayed.

The door to the forge opened, admitting Rhiannon, her face pale and weary. Marcus went to her at once. Putting an arm about her shoulders, he guided her into the room.

"How is Aiden?" he asked.

"A bit improved. Breena sits with him now. But he is old. I canna be sure—"

"You can't blame yourself if he dies," Marcus told her. "The fault is Valgus's alone. That bastard—"

A sharp crack of wood on stone nearly caused Rhys to jump out of his skin. A gust had blown the forge door inward, slamming it against the wall. Rhys moved to close it, only to be knocked backward by a flurry of wings.

He only just managed not to lose his footing on the ash-strewn floor. "Hefin!"

The merlin executed a tight circle of the forge before landing on Rhys's raised arm. Rhys was stunned—to his knowledge, the bird had never before entered a building. A glance at Marcus's face told him his friend recognized how significant this behavior was. For a Roman without magic, Marcus Aquila had uncanny perception.

Marcus, in his typical stoic manner, said nothing. Rhys ran a hand over Hefin's back. Something was amiss. Not an injury; a quick survey of breast and wings told him the animal was healthy. No, he sensed the bird had a message, one Rhys would not like.

"What is it, friend?" he murmured.

Hefin cocked his head, regarding Rhys with an unwavering eye. There was a glint of urgency in the animal's gaze. The realization unnerved Rhys; at times, Hefin seemed almost human. He sent a soothing thought to the bird. He couldn't converse with the animal here—he needed solitude and the magic of the forest.

He turned to find Rhiannon and Marcus watching him closely—Rhiannon, with an expression of understanding; Marcus with a look of horror. A muscle ticked in his friend's jaw. Marcus's fingers flexed, as if itching for one of his daggers.

Rhys felt his cheeks grow warm. The weight of the deception he'd foisted on Marcus weighed more heavily now that the truth had come out. He'd handled the situation badly—had he transformed friend to enemy? How many times had Cyric told him that the purpose of the Light was just the opposite—to turn his enemies from the path of hatred?

He all but fled the forge. The chasm between Cyric's teaching and Rhys's fulfillment of his duty was wide and deep. How could Rhys hope to lead Avalon after Cyric's death? For that was his birthright, the one promise that made all his years of wandering bearable. And yet . . . sometimes he could not help wondering if Gwendolyn would be better suited to the task.

Gwendolyn, with her quick laughter and daring ways. Her loving heart and her unflagging energy. She was the younger, but she'd ever possessed the stronger will. Even so, their differences had struck a perfect balance. Together, they'd been invincible.

They had even shared one mind, their thoughts passing between them as easily as spoken conversation. But now? Now Rhys could barely remember what it was like to have Gwen speak to his soul.

He passed through the gates enclosing the villa grounds, Hefin circling above him. He felt his estrangement from his twin in the deepest part of his being. The rift had begun nine years ago, when Cyric had presented them with differing tasks. Rhys was to wander Britannia, searching for those with latent Druid power. Gwen was to remain in Avalon, tending the needs of the clan and teaching the initiates Rhys brought to her.

Their duties had been the opposite of their desires. Gwen envied Rhys's wandering; Rhys envied Gwen's home on the sacred isle. Why had Cyric set them on such conflicting paths?

Rhys clenched his jaw. The estrangement was more Gwen's doing than his. He'd come to peace with Cyric's command. For nine years, since he'd been little more than a lad, Rhys had traveled in Roman towns, never passing more than a fortnight in one bed. He sought those linked to the Deep Magic.

By contrast, Gwen had railed against her duty. Whenever Rhys made a brief visit to Avalon, he heard the accusations. Gwen was forever disappearing into the swamps and forests, telling no one of her purpose. When she returned, she gave no explanation. For some reason, Cyric refused to curb her insolence. The clan had been tolerant at first, then impatient, and finally, angry. But no one, least of all Rhys, could discover how Gwen passed her time away from Avalon. Like Rhys, Gwen was strong in the magic of the forest. She was adept at covering her trail.

Then, a fortnight ago, the first ill winds had risen, and Cyric had fallen sick. Gwen had not been present.

Rhys's breathing ran shallow. Mared, Avalon's healer, had declared Cyric's malady magical in nature. Avalon had buzzed with suspicion. Rhys couldn't believe what they'd whispered—that Gwen's absence proved she was responsible for her grandfather's malady. Surely, *surely,* Rhys's twin could not have embraced the Dark. Surely Gwen was back in Avalon now, assisting Mared in nursing Cyric back to health.

Snow crunched under Rhys's boots as he traversed the stubbled field and ducked into the forest beyond. Once surrounded by trees, he halted and looked up. Hefin perched on a high branch, running his long wing feathers, one by one, through his beak.

"Just get on with it. Tell me what's happened."

Hefin settled his wings. A moment later, a thought formed in Rhys's brain. Or not a thought, precisely, for the language of animals was different from that of humans. Image. Instinct. A series of sensations, a deep knowing. Rhys closed his eyes and let his human mind merge with that of his companion. For an instant, he became the merlin.

In that instant, he learned more than he wished to know.

He broke the connection with a gasp. The magic had weakened him; he staggered forward, grasping a limb to stop his fall.

He bowed his head, fighting tears. His grandfather's illness had worsened. Avalon's healer had given up hope of his recovery.

With his last breath, Cyric was calling Rhys home.

Chapter Eight

Clara woke slowly, sleep seeping from her mind as did wine from a cracked cask. Her dreams had been warm and pleasant, like sunshine. The sensation of a summer garden lingered. High walls surrounded a profusion of blooms in every color; an azure sky arched over head. A sky, she thought, that reminded her of someone's eyes.

She snuggled into her covers, desperate to steal a few last moments of sleep before Father's voice boomed through the courtyard. Father's habit was to rise before dawn, and Clara always rose early to greet him.

But perhaps she would remain abed today . . .

A warm stream of air tickled the back of her neck. She wriggled and shifted, but for some reason couldn't manage to roll onto her back. Something solid and uncomfortable prodded her bottom. What was a big stone pestle doing in her bed?

The last echoes of her father's voice faded. Reality asserted itself in the form of a heavy arm pinning her torso. A large hand lingered dangerously close to her breast. A bearded chin tickled the sensitive place just below her ear.

Her back was pressed up against Owein's chest. His thighs cradled her lower body. And that stone pestle pressing against her buttocks? Her body went rigid, her chest no longer able to send air into her lungs. That was no pestle!

She tried, gingerly, to shift away. Owein started, his sudden gasp of breath rasping her ear. He murmured a soft word and drew her closer. His hand found her breast. Squeezed.

Flames licked her belly, and lower. Panic clogged her throat—panic and breathless anticipation, wrapped together in one inextricable Gordian knot. Owein murmured again. A soft kiss brushed her shoulder. His hand left her breast to travel a slow torturous path down her stomach, across her hip, along her outer thigh. Catching the hem of her undertunic, his warm fingers delved beneath, stroking upward on bare skin. Her tunic rode up around her waist, baring her lower body. Clara pressed her legs together, dreading, wanting . . .

The heel of his hand pressed the triangle of curls that guarded her sex. There was an exquisitely sensitive bit of flesh there, and he sought it out, rocking and shifting his hand against it. The movement sent a spiral of heat through Clara's limbs. A soft moan escaped her lips. Instinctively, she moved her hips, mimicking his rhythm.

"Aye, Eirwen, like that," he murmured, nuzzling her ear.

Clara froze. Eirwen? Owein's *wife?*

His fingers stroked, teased. Her unruly body ignored the panic in her brain, opening to accommodate him, her legs parting as if of their own accord. His fingers slipped between, into slick wetness.

His next stroke was more intimate than she could bear. It was as if he'd touched the very center of her soul. A soft sob escaped her lips. Moisture gathered in her eyes.

"Eirwen," he murmured again.

She closed her eyes. Oh gods. She didn't want him touching her this way—not when he thought she was another woman.

She shrank back, trying to evade his probing fingers. The movement only served to press his phallus more firmly against her bottom. His *braccas* were undone, she realized with a sickening start. His hard flesh pressed like a hot brand on her skin. His hands drifted to her hips, lifting her slightly as his erection probed between her legs. The tip of his shaft pressed against her slickness.

By Jupiter! He could take her this way! It would be like the image he'd sent into her mind.

It was all she could do to haul enough air into her lungs to speak. "Owein!" Another breath. "Stop!"

"Hush," he said, planting a wet kiss on her ear. "Let me love ye. There'll be little enough chance after the babe is born."

Hot tears gathered in her eyes. Behind her, Owein's phallus withdrew slightly. His hands positioned her hips for the joining thrust.

"No!" Taking advantage of the slight space between their bodies, she twisted her torso hard, rolling toward him. His surging shaft jabbed her hip.

She wrenched one arm free. Planting her hand on his shoulder, she shoved with all her strength. "Owein. It's Clara. Stop this."

"What—?" He blinked and jerked back as far as he could manage in the close quarters of the hut. Pushing himself up on one elbow, he stared at her, his expression blank. His *braccas* hung open, revealing the shadow of a huge erect phallus.

Clara wrenched her eyes from *that*. She shrank back against the opposite wall, hastily pushing her tunic over her legs. Dawn light streamed through the door and the gaps in the thatch ceiling, creating a haze inside the shelter. A patch of light landed on Owein's chest, drawing her eye. A sprinkling of russet curls were visible through the loose lacing of hide shirt.

Clara reached for her cloak, pulling it across her lap. Scant armor, but all she had. Owein's gaze flicked over her, then down at his phallus. A sheepish expression crept over his face. He did up his laces.

"You were having a dream," Clara said shakily. "You thought you were with your wife."

Owein's eyes turned hard and his mouth went down at the corners. Clara's hand crept to her throat. A Legionary had killed Owein's wife. One of her father's men. What would Owein do if he discovered Clara's lie?

She should tell him the truth. Confess her identity and be done with it. But if she did, would he abandon the quest for the grail? She couldn't take that chance.

Owein shook his head and sighed, seeming to force himself from his bleak memories. " 'Tis sorry I am if I frightened ye."

Clara sat up and attempted a smile. "Think nothing of it." After a brief silence, she added, "It's morning. We'd best go."

"We have time yet." His eyes did not waver from her face. The blue of his irises appeared almost black. " 'Tis best if we wait for the morning sun to soften the ice on the paths. Meanwhile, 'tis warm enough in this shelter for even a pampered Roman lass." His voice grew husky. "I could warm ye even more, if ye wish."

Clara stiffened. "I don't wish it."

He chuckled. "Ye do. Or at least your body does. I was nay so deeply caught in sleep that I didna feel the welcome between your thighs."

Her cheeks burned with shame. "You're mistaken if you think I welcomed your attentions. I . . . I was caught in my own dream. My eagerness was meant for another."

He raised his brows. "Your blacksmith?"

Clara grasped at the suggestion. "Exactly so. It was Marcus Aquila I dreamed of."

Owein's amusement abruptly vanished. "Marcus Aquila. Commander Lucius Aquila's son?"

"Yes," Clara said, startled. "How did you know?"

His expression was grim. "I once encountered Lucius Aquila in battle."

"Oh. Well. Lucius Aquila is no longer in the Legions. He's a farmer, and he has a Celt wife. She's the healer who visited my father."

"Rhiannon." Owein had gone so still, Clara wondered if he breathed.

"Yes. Do you know her?"

"I did." His tone clearly indicated the matter was closed. He levered his large body into a crouch and ducked out the door.

Clara stared after him. Owein had met Lucius Aquila in battle? Perhaps he harbored a grudge against him. Had she endangered Marcus's family by making their whereabouts known? She rubbed her arms, suddenly chilled.

She left the hut and ventured into a thick copse to take care of her personal needs, after which she scrubbed her face and hands vigorously with a handful of snow. Owein shattered the thin coating of ice on a stream and filled his waterskin.

They broke their fast with more strips of dried venison. Clara tore off a piece with her front teeth and chewed until her jaw ached. She would have had less trouble gnawing her satchel's leather strap.

Owein, apparently, had teeth made of stone, for he devoured his portion easily. To her relief, the shadow that had passed over him at the mention of Lucius Aquila had lifted. He watched her eat, the amusement returning to his eyes.

" 'Tis not the soft fare ye are accustomed to, I am guessing."

Clara swallowed a mouthful of what tasted like burnt wood shavings. "It's fine." She took a swig from the water skin, wishing it held wine. She grimaced, then scowled when Owein's amusement deepened.

"I suppose a merchant's daughter spends her life within easy reach of every luxury," he said.

Clara studied her clasped hands. "I suppose that's true."

"No wonder ye have such little sense."

Her head jerked up. "I have sense!"

"Oh, aye. Sensible Roman lasses often wander the hills in winter seeking outlawed Druids."

"I had no choice about that," Clara said quietly. "Not with my father lying ill."

"The danger was too great."

"I had to find you. I'm sorry I disturbed your home, but—"

" 'Twas nay much of a home, lass, in case ye hadn't noticed." He sighed. "But I was content there, for a time."

She hesitated. "Until the Second Legion came?"

"Aye." Bitter hatred crept into his voice. "Until Gracchus's men arrived."

"I . . . I've heard Commander Gracchus is respected by Romans and Celts alike in Isca. He's known as a hard man, but a fair one. I . . . I also heard that the raid on the hills was ordered by the governor in Londinium. Perhaps . . . perhaps Commander Gracchus regretted what he had to do."

"A fine notion, lass, but one I canna credit. Ye may not have noticed, safe in your merchant father's house, but to the Legions Celts are no more than beasts. Best killed, or at the least herded to the city and fenced."

"Many Celts in Isca are free. In the city, they have comforts they could only have dreamed of in the mountains."

"Glass cups and deep cushions. Aye, a fine trade for the home of one's fathers." He shook his head in disgust. "Comfort. It leads only to weakness."

"Romans are not weak."

"Are ye so sure? Aye, ye have armies and fortresses. Fine weapons. Standing together, surrounded by walls, ye are strong enough. But alone? One Roman alone is as weak as a babe." He stood and started assembling his pack. "Especially a woman."

Clara pushed to her feet. "That isn't true!"

"Nay? Could you defend yourself if the need came upon you? Could ye use a knife on a man in a fight?"

She blinked. "Me? You jest. No woman could best a man."

"Ah, but I say ye could, if that merchant father of yours had looked up from his money long enough to teach ye how to wield a knife. No Celt father would do less than give his daughter the means by which to defend herself."

"A Celt father teaches his daughter to handle a blade?" Clara couldn't believe it.

"Aye." He unsheathed the dagger at his waist and pressed it into Clara's hand. Her fingers closed on the hilt. Bemused, she looked down at it.

"Not like that." His hand covered hers, adjusting her grip. "You're a slight lass. Nay tall enough to hack into a man's chest."

Hack into a man's chest?

If Owein noted Clara's revulsion, he ignored it. "Even if ye had strength enough in your arm . . ." He lifted her hand and brought it down in an arc. "See? Ye couldn't stab down at such a high target. But that doesn't mean ye canna hit your mark." He reversed her grip on the knife, so the blade pointed upward.

"But—"

"What ye must learn to do is to use your size to your advantage. Attack from below." He made a fist and demonstrated with an imaginary knife. "Slice upward into the stomach. Or better yet, stab between the legs."

The dry venison Clara had swallowed threatened to make a reappearance. "I couldn't." She tried to loosen her grip on the dagger. His hand covered hers, preventing it.

"This is ludicrous," she said. "I could never kill a man. Or even wound one."

"Do ye know how many men wouldn't hesitate to use your body and slit your throat after?"

"Hundreds, I'm sure," Clara said dryly.

" 'Tis nay a jest I'm making, lass."

"But I'm traveling with you," Clara protested. "That's protection enough from any brigand."

"I canna be at your side always," he said, his voice tight.

Clara met his gaze, still holding the knife between them. "Is this . . . because of what happened to your wife?"

His jaw clenched. "Eirwen was a tall, strong woman."

"But she was heavy with your child."

"Aye." He released her hand and stepped away, grief and sorrow warring in his eyes. With an effort, he mastered both emotions, turning brusque. "The first thing ye must remember is that surprise is the greatest advantage a woman brings to a fight. Ye must be quick—wound your attacker, then make your escape." He illustrated an attack with an imaginary dagger. "Try it."

Clara sighed. She didn't see the point in the exercise, but there seemed to be no recourse but to humor him. "All right." She mimicked the thrust, jabbing upward into empty air.

"Put some passion into it, lass."

"My name is Clara," she muttered. "If you can't remember that, I've a mind to sink this blade into *your* gut." She thrust upward again, venting her frustration. Would he perish if he pronounced her name just once?

"Aye, that's better," Owein said, intent on her form. "But put your whole weight behind the thrust."

Clara tightened her grip and gave another sharp jab.

Owein nodded his approval. "Twist the blade at the end of the motion, when it's buried in your enemy's flesh."

Ugh. Clara considered dropping the weapon right then and there. But one look at Owein's expression told her that wasn't an option. Bending, he produced a second dagger from a sheath hidden beneath the leg of his *braccas*. She blinked. She hadn't known he carried another blade.

"Fall into a crouch and dip one shoulder, like this . . ." He executed the move. " 'Twill give ye better leverage."

She imitated the best she could.

"Ye can do better." He resheathed his blade and spread his arms wide. "Take me for a target."

Clara was aghast. "Attack you? I couldn't!"

"Afraid?"

"No."

"Weak, then."

"No! I . . . just don't wish to hurt you."

His blue eyes glinted. "Abandon your denials, lass. Your weak Roman blood tells."

"Oh! You—" She swung.

He jumped aside, laughing.

"Are"—she slashed again, her blade meeting nothing but air. Abandoning all restraint, she flung herself at him. "—a"—*slash*—"barbarian"—*slash*—"brute!"

His arm shot out, snagging her wrist and lifting her blade over her head. Caught by her forward momentum, Clara stumbled into his chest. With an efficient motion, he divested her of her weapon. Laughter reigned in his eyes. Clara inhaled a sharp breath. Had he staged this futile lesson just to humiliate her?

If so, he'd not had his fill of amusement. He gave a mock bow and extended the dagger, hilt first. "Another try, lass."

She looked from the blade to his face. "What?"

"Again," he said, exasperation plain in his voice. "Perhaps this time, ye'll trouble yourself to remember my instruction. Dip and come up. Use your weight to your advantage. Ye'll never best a man trying to overpower him from above."

"You mean . . . you truly want me to learn how to fight?"

"Of course. What do ye think?" He extended the blade.

Clara took it. "But . . . why?"

"The road can be a dangerous place. I don't know where my vision at the stones will lead us, but wherever it is, I canna watch ye every second of the way. I'll rest easier knowing ye can at least defend yourself until I come to your aid."

"No. I meant . . . why do you care?"

He stared at her, the blue of his eyes as intense as the sky above. Two spots of color showed on the high ridge of cheekbone above his beard.

"Again," he said gruffly.

"No. My arm aches."

"I dinna care. Again."

Clara sighed as she adjusted her grip. Owein spread his stance. "Have at me, lass."

"Clara," she said through gritted teeth. She slashed upward, but he danced away. How was it a man so large could be so light on his feet?

With a blur of movement, he grabbed for her. She ducked under his arm and jumped aside, using her lack of height to her advantage. What other advantage might she draw upon? A sudden thought sparked. She eyed him, noting the position of his feet and the shift of his weight. When he lunged for her a second time, she was ready. Her shoulder dipped, drawing him forward. Then, with a sudden movement, she shifted the blade from her right hand to her left, reversing the pivot of her torso. She thrust her left arm upward, the entire weight of her body behind it.

He deflected the move with a grunt and a curse. She'd done him no damage—he was far too swift for that, and he'd been expecting her attack, after all. But the flash of respect in his eyes told her that she'd succeeded in taking him by surprise.

The small victory left her flushed with pride. She met his raised brows with a sweet smile.

"Ye favor your left hand?" he asked curiously. "I hadna noticed." He gave his head a small shake, as if not able to believe he'd been so unobservant.

"I favor the left, but my tutor insisted I hold my pen with the right. Now I can do most tasks as well with either."

Owein nodded approvingly. " 'Tis a fine advantage in a fight." Reaching for her shoulders, he pivoted her and pulled her into his body, pressing her against his chest. Heat skittered down her spine and snaked into her belly.

His lips whispered close to her ear. "Try it like this, lass . . ." Taking her left hand in his, he drew her into a low crouch, then guided her arm in a sharp upward thrust.

"In a fight ye may only have the opportunity for one good blow. Ye must make the most of it."

He released her. Deprived of his support, she swayed, trying to regain her equilibrium. It was a difficult task.

Owein hefted a short, stout branch in both hands and held it before him like a shield. "Again."

"Again? But what of the element of surprise?"

" 'Tis the motion you're practicing. When danger comes, ye must fight without thinking." He revealed a flash of white, even teeth. "Or is your Roman blood too weak?"

Clara's grip tightened on the dagger's hilt.

Owein's smile broadened. "That's it."

He egged her on, urging her to sink the blade. He watched each movement with a critical eye, directing her to spin right or left as circumstances warranted. Each blow sent a jolt up her arm.

Her shoulders burned with fire, but she gritted her teeth and said nothing. She spun and slashed again and again. Finally, when the sun had succeeded in hoisting itself over the upper edge of the mountain, Owein lowered the branch and called an end to the lesson. Clara blinked into the sunlight.

Owein inspected the gouges she'd inflicted on the wood like a sculptor appraising the work of an apprentice.

" 'Twill do," he pronounced at last, tossing the branch aside. Facing her, he grinned. "Until the next lesson, at least."

Chapter Nine

The stone stood on a rise of snow beneath a cerulean sky. It was not so large as Clara had imagined, nor so broad. It was but a single weathered lump of rock, a far cry from the massive ring of smooth-hewn pillars and lintels Clara had once seen on the southern plains near the old Celt fortress of Sarum.

"Are you sure this is the place?" She wasn't inclined to be generous, not when Owein had left the shelter of the valleys to trek over treeless, ice-covered mountaintops. The wind bit through her cloak. Her thighs ached with climbing and she could no longer feel her toes inside her boots.

"I thought we were looking for a circle," she complained. "That's but one stone."

"The smaller stones lie hidden in the snow."

"Wonderful." Clara let out a long sigh as she trudged in the white furrow left by Owein's long legs.

Owein glanced back. "Wishing for a fire? Or a hot bath?"

"You know that I am." She caught a glimpse of his grin before he turned.

"Ye should have stayed—"

"Don't say it," Clara warned, drawing her hood tightly about her ears to block both the wind and Owein's taunting. She'd wished a thousand times over that she'd stayed behind. But the earth would shake to pieces before she'd admit it.

Owein's mood sobered with each step toward the stone. It took longer than Clara had hoped to traverse the downward sweep of snow-covered hillside. Distances in the high mountains were deceiving—more than once she'd thought a landmark near only to watch it recede as they approached. The rock did the same. By the time they reached the stone—which Clara was surprised to realize stood taller than Owein—the sun had sunk behind the hills.

Clara swallowed her dismay. The wind was frigid on the exposed slope. With a sigh, she resigned herself to a night spent huddled in her cloak. Owein lowered his pack to the ground. Clara rubbed her hands, trying to work the life back into them.

His gaze swung toward her. In two great strides, he closed the distance between them. Large, warm hands enveloped hers and took over the task of making her blood flow.

"I've pushed ye too hard."

"I'm fine."

He gave a half snort and continued rubbing. Gradually, her fingers warmed. Other parts of her body heated as well. The places he'd stroked before—while he dreamed of his wife—came to life. Her stomach, her shoulder. The sensitive place just below her earlobe. The tips of her breasts . . .

She stepped away, pulling her hands free. He let her go, but his eyes remained watchful.

"How long will this take?" she asked, unnerved.

"The Horned God keeps his own time, lass."

He turned and paced a few steps from the great stone, then bent to clear away an armful of snow. A smaller stone appeared, lumpy and gray like its sire. Wholly unremarkable, and yet . . . when Clara closed her eyes she imagined she felt a faraway tingling.

Owein paced a wide arc, exposing about twenty stones in all. Then he retreated a good distance from the stones and fashioned a crude shelter with snow walls. He transferred the pack inside it. Unfastening his cloak, he spread it on the ground and indicated Clara should sit. "You'll await me here, lass."

"My cloak is warm enough," she said. "You'll need yours."

He gave a tight smile. "Nay."

She plucked the well-worn garment from the ground and offered it to him. He took and spread it again inside the makeshift walls.

"Be biddable just this once. Sit."

"But—"

"Now."

With an aggrieved sigh, she obeyed. In truth, it was a relief to be off her feet. And the snow walls did break most of the wind.

He paced a circle around her, his lips moving silently, his head bowed. Clara felt a subtle force rise in his wake—with a start, she realized he was enclosing her in a ring of magic. When he returned to his starting place, he lifted his gaze. "No matter what happens, what ye see or hear, ye must stay in this circle."

"You mean to cage me?"

"I mean to protect ye."

"The two are one and the same."

"I willna argue. In this ye will obey me." His tone was harsh.

Clara hesitated, then nodded.

"I'll have your word."

"I will stay."

He gave her one last look, as if gauging the honor of her pledge, then turned and strode toward the circle. He made a circuit of the stones, touching each one and standing before it for a time in silence. When he reached the headstone, he stepped past it into the center of the circle.

Owein lifted his arms. A Word emerged from his lips. The power of the syllable struck Clara's mind like a mallet. Around her, the night fell silent. Even the wind ceased its howling.

Owein stood motionless half the night, waiting. But when the vision finally came, it took him by surprise.

First, there was darkness. No vision at all, but blackness so thick and dry that it took all his effort to breathe. Gradually, his eyes picked out flat, hard shadows.

He was inside walls. A Roman chamber, to be sure, for the enclosure was small, square, and airless. A line of light spilled from beneath a closed door. Owein willed it to grow, expanding the illumination until he could see his surroundings.

The chamber appeared to be half-completed. It was empty of furnishings, with a single door and no windows. An unfinished mural wrapped three sides of the space. Pots of pigment and brushes lay scattered on the floor, atop an oiled cloth, as if the artist had stepped out for a breath of air. No doubt he needed one—his painting was not for the faint of heart. It depicted a city under siege. Flames consumed the town's timber walls; bloody bodies, some with limbs and heads hacked off, lay in heaps. In the foreground, soldiers streamed from the belly of what looked like a giant wooden horse.

Owein's gaze scanned the room, alighting on a sack he'd not seen earlier. It lay half open, its contents spilling across the mosaic floor. Plates and goblets of gold and silver tumbled atop each other like bright children's toys.

One goblet caught his eye. It was wrought in silver and crystal. The intricate ornamentation upon it matched Clara's drawing. A triple spiral encircled by a circle woven with vines.

He reached for it, though he knew that his spirit-hand would not be able to touch it. All the same, his disappointment was keen when the familiar mist swirled into his vision. When the fog cleared, he found himself within the stones.

He bowed his head and braced himself for the pain.

Clara gasped as Owein's body jerked, his back arching as if someone had lain a lash across it. His powerful legs crumpled. Pain battered the edges of Clara's mind—just a shadow of what Owein's agony must be, but still she flinched from the savagery of it.

Was this what Owein endured each time his god sent a vision? How in Jupiter's name did he bear it?

The urge to go to him was fierce. She wavered within the protection of the circle he'd made for her, watching as he struggled to his feet. She felt the pain wash over him; with a start, she realized their minds were joined. She was a specter hovering on the edge of his consciousness. Did he even realize she bore witness to his suffering? If so, he gave no indication.

Her breath hung motionless in her lungs. Owein swayed on his feet; attempted a single step. Even such a small task was beyond him. Once again, his large body collapsed in the snow.

"No!" Clara leaped over the wall of her makeshift shelter. A pulse of energy resisted her progress. She pushed through it. The sensation was like passing through fire, but she hardly registered the discomfort. In a heartbeat she was free and running.

She dropped to her knees at his side, her heart pounding, panic twisting like snakes in her belly. "Owein?"

He stirred within her mind. A moment later, he heaved himself up on one knee, his arms trembling with the effort. His face had gone pale beneath the red of his beard.

She cradled the side of his face, his temple plait brushing the back of her hand. Raw, blistering pain bubbled into her mind. Emotions far too violent for her to grasp. Sorrow, anguish, hatred—the searing darkness of Owein's memories struck her like a physical blow, sending her sprawling backward into the snow.

How could he bear such agony alone? Tentatively, she made her way to him and placed her palm on his forehead. This time she expected the pain. She sucked in a breath as the memory of a day long past flashed from Owein's mind to hers.

Flames licked like red tongues along the slope of the thatched roofs. A Legionary's helmet flashed in the sunlight. Soldiers advanced, swords drawn. There were so many. More than Owein could count.

The attackers had hacked through the front line of Celts. As the youngest of the warriors, Owein had been left in charge of the village. But he hadn't stayed at his post; he'd run ahead to the fighting.

He'd not expected the Romans to slip in behind and attack the children and elders.

Owein had managed to stay alive during the battle, though not without cost. He'd lost his sword when a Roman blade sliced his upper arm. The limb dragged, bleeding freely as he ran toward the screams. He felt no pain. At least, not yet.

A child's shrill cry assaulted his ears. Moira—Enid's little lass. He lurched toward the sound, not willing to believe he couldn't save her.

A rough hand halted his progress, spinning him about. "By the gods, lad, ye canna mean to go back."

With difficulty, he focused on the speaker. His kinsman, Cormac. "I have to," he gasped out. "It's my duty."

"Ye must count it lost, then," Cormac said, all but dragging Owein from the slaughter. "There's naught ye can do."

Darkness rushed the edges of Owein vision. He swayed on his feet. "Nay. Nay—"

"Nay," he moaned. "Nay."

"Owein?" He trembled under her touch. Shifted, and

cried out again. She felt the exact moment he became aware of her crouching by his side. His body tensed.

Anger flared along the thread of their mental connection.

"Nay." He tried to shake her off. "Let me be."

"I want to help you. I . . . I see a village burning . . ."

"Nay." With a burst of scorching power, he snapped the connection between them. The pain and horror of his home's destruction vanished from her mind. His big, powerful body slipped from her arms and slumped on the ground. His eyes fluttered closed.

"Owein?" She shook him, hands on his shoulders, but her strongest effort barely stirred him. She framed his face in her hands, fingers threading through his mane of red curls. Climbing half atop him, she shook him again.

"Owein! Answer me!"

Nothing. She pressed her thumbs to the side of his neck, seeking the pulse of his life's blood. It was weak and uneven. "No," she whispered. She pressed her face into the crook of his neck. Was he dying? Because of her? Tears squeezed from her eyes. She aligned her body with his, shifting to lie atop his torso. Slowly, his arms crept around her.

"Lass," he rasped. "Could ye kindly climb from my chest before ye squeeze the last bit of breath from my lungs?"

But his arms didn't relax. If anything, they closed more tightly around her. One large hand covered her bottom.

Clara went still. Her hands framed his face. Her breasts were squashed against his chest. Their hearts pounded together in one uneven rhythm. She lowered her forehead into the crook of his neck and breathed his scent deeply. Pine and heather, and rough-cured leather. Her leg—oh gods!—her leg had somehow become wedged between his. His hard phallus pressed against her thigh.

"Lass . . ."

She struggled to produce an answer from a throat gone as dry as an old well. Her fingers curled on his shoulders. His hands found their way to her waist.

Instinctively, she rocked her hips against his hardness.

He gave a weak chuckle. "Have ye changed your mind, then, about coupling with me?"

Clara lifted her head and stared. "You cannot even stand! How can you think of . . . of *that?*"

His phallus hardened even more, and his eyes, when she looked into them, glittered like polished gems. "There's hardly any time when a man canna think of coupling," he said.

One large hand covered her breast, squeezing softly. Her breath came in a gasp. The last connection she had with her magic fled. Fear and anticipation rose, entwined as one.

Two women warred in her brain. One, shameless and wild, wanted to open for him. The other, dutiful and civilized, clung desperately to her father's instruction. His face rose in her mind. Father hadn't considered a Roman blacksmith worthy of her. What thoughts would he have concerning a wild Celt?

Shame washed through her. "No," she whispered. "Owein, please. No."

His hand stilled on her breast. "I can give ye pleasure."

"I'm . . . sure that's true. But please, I want to stop."

Did the slight tensing of his muscles mean she'd hurt him by her rejection? But, no, that couldn't be. He was toying with her. He'd been so long without a woman—any female bold enough to straddle him would serve.

She stifled a hysterical laugh and shoved herself off him. He let her go. He pushed himself up, wincing at the effort.

"You're still weak," she said, alarmed.

He leaned on one arm, his breathing heavy. " 'Twill pass soon enough."

She eyed the circle of stones, wanting very much to be outside them. "Can you walk?"

"Not yet."

"But you wanted to couple?"

"I told ye, a man always wants to couple."

"Not all men," Clara said seriously. "My father and mother . . . they kept separate rooms. Mother nearly died birthing me and I think Father couldn't bear the thought of risking her life for another child. After she was gone, I thought he might take another wife, but he didn't. He said he hadn't the heart."

"He loved her too deeply, perhaps, to seek another."

"Yes, I think that's true." She hesitated. "But you . . . you didn't . . ." She looked down.

"Love my wife so deeply, ye mean?"

She nodded.

Silence stretched between them. Finally, Owein sighed. "Eirwen was a fine woman. Tall, strong, and brave, and pleasing to the eye as well. She . . ." His voice drifted off.

"Tell me."

He sighed. "When my clan in the north was conquered by the Romans, it was many years before I . . . before I found a new home. Aiden—he helped me when I . . ." He swallowed. "I owed him my life. His granddaughter nursed me, and when she wanted me for a husband, he was pleased. So I joined hands with her. She was a dutiful wife. She never gave cause for complaint." His tone told her he would say no more.

He pushed unsteadily to his feet. When it became apparent he wouldn't be able to walk unaided, Clara fit herself into the crook of his arm. Together they passed out of the stone circle.

"Ye gave me your word ye'd stay within the protection I conjured for ye."

"I couldn't. Not when I knew you needed me."

He stared at her for a long moment before lowering himself to the ground inside the snow shelter. Clara reached for his pack. "Do you wish for food? Water?"

He shook his head, then winced and pressed two fingers to the center of his forehead.

She eyed him with concern. "Does it hurt?"

"Aye. 'Tis the Horned God's payment."

"Then . . . your request was answered? Your god sent you a vision?"

He nodded.

"Was it . . . did you See the grail?"

"Aye."

Hope leapt in her breast. "Where is it?"

"That I dinna know." He paused, looking inward. "The room had no window. I saw only a sack of gold and silver plates and goblets. The grail you described was among them. 'Twas a small chamber, with a mural on the wall." He shook his head. "I dinna pretend to understand Roman sensibilities, lass. The scene was a battle, running with blood. Even half-done, it was a horror. Who would want to look upon such a thing?"

Clara's head came up. *It couldn't be.* "An unfinished battle scene? What did it look like?"

" 'Twas a city under siege, its attackers pouring from the belly of a giant horse."

"The siege of Troy by the Spartans," she whispered. "My father was especially fond of that battle."

Owein gave her an odd look. "It seems a strange favorite for a merchant."

Clara swallowed. "Yes. But Father commissioned an artist to paint it nonetheless."

Owein eyed her. "Ye know the room I saw in my vision?"

Clara stifled a hysterical laugh. She'd trekked halfway across the mountains only to discover her mother's cup had been within arm's reach. "The chamber you describe is in my father's new country villa. But how did the grail get there?"

"Perhaps your father brought it there."

"He couldn't have. He never left the fortress the day that the cup was stolen." He eyes widened. "But Tribune Valgus did. I heard the steward mention it. He'd been in the house the night before, asking after Father's health. Valgus had been assisting Father with the villa. He could have taken the cup and the other treasures there."

"Why would he do such a thing?"

"My guess is that he wants to sell them. It's no secret

Valgus's father is in debt. That's why the tribune agreed to our betrothal—and why he insisted on a marriage *in manu.* Father has no heir but me. Valgus wants control of Father's property."

Her jaw tightened. "He couldn't even wait until the wedding to begin his thievery."

The last rays of the evening sun set the swamps afire.

Rhys poled his raft through the reed-choked channel. From a distance, the sacred isle of Avalon formed the aspect of the Great Mother. The tallest of Avalon's two rounded hills formed her breast; the smaller mound, where the apple trees spread their branches, was her pregnant belly. A long, gentle ridge formed her outstretched thigh.

Rhys guided his craft to the hidden dock. Above, Hefin spiraled in tight circles. A wisp of smoke rose from the village. He started up the path, his footsteps sluggish. In some childlike recess of his mind he half-believed his haste would create the tragedy he dreaded.

The palisade gate was barred. A small, squat figure loitered before it, a Roman sword at his belt. Rhys's gaze narrowed. Cormac was not of Avalon. Why had he been allowed to act as sentinel?

Rhys greeted the northern Celt with an abrupt nod. "What brings ye to Avalon?"

Cormac drew himself up to his full height, which was no higher than Rhys's chest. The rough warrior had a man's torso, but his fleshy limbs hadn't grown past the length of a child's. His head was large and bulbous, his features coarse. The dwarf roamed Britannia, as Rhys did, but with baser purpose. He gathered information and offered it for coin.

Cormac sheathed his *gladius.* "I arrived yesterday, with news of Legionaries scouting in the Mendips."

This brought Rhys up short. "Will their route bring them close to Avalon?"

"Nay. They remain at least a half day's march from the isle. They're poking about some old silver mines."

Rhys's shoulders eased. "No trouble for us, then." But Cormac, no doubt, would still want payment. Why did Cyric allow this man in Avalon? If it were up to Rhys, he would kick the dwarf back to the northlands.

"Your grandfather worsens," Cormac informed him.

Rhys sobered. "Aye, I know. Give the signal for the gates."

Cormac placed two fingers in his mouth and gave a series of sharp whistles. The palisade gate swung open almost at once.

In less time than it took to string a bow, Rhys was surrounded by friends. Hushed greetings sounded in his ears; arm after arm pulled him into an embrace. Smiling, he unshouldered the pack that held his harp and returned their greetings.

Very few of the clan were Rhys's true kin—the connection they shared was born of magic. He'd plucked most of them from dim lives in Roman towns. All were dear to him.

He searched the gathering for Gwen as tall, balding Trevor related news of Cyric. Two days before, Rhys's grandfather had slipped into a steep decline. Mared, the healer, and Rhys's uncle, Padrig, had carried the Druid Master to the high slope of the sacred isle. Cyric lay in a healing hut near the white stone that guarded the entrance to the Lost Land, the vestibule to the Celtic Otherworld, Annwyn.

Rhys drew Trevor aside, out of hearing of the rest. The older man nurtured a tender feeling for Gwen, and was one of the few who still believed her innocent of calling dark magic.

"Is my sister on the high slope with Cyric?" Rhys asked.

Trevor's habitually serious expression grew even more sober. Silently, he shook his head.

"Gwen left when ye did, a fortnight past. She hasna returned." It was Rhys's cousin, Blodwen, who spoke. Rhys greeted her with a quick embrace. Their mothers had been sisters, and he harbored a deep affection for her. As always, Blodwen's face was shadowed by her cloak's deep hood.

"I canna believe Gwen would be so neglectful," Rhys said.

Blodwen's fingertips grazed his forearm in sympathy. Rhys covered her hand with his own. Together they left Trevor and crossed the village yard, halting near the small stone building that housed Gwen's forge.

"I am glad ye are here, Rhys."

"I came as quickly as I could," he told her.

Her gray gaze touched his, then skittered away. Familiar pity tugged at Rhys's heart. His cousin never looked at anyone for long, as if by averting her eyes she could hide the long, hideous scars on her face. Though she was only two years his elder, she seemed far older. Her hair had prematurely turned gray and her shoulders were as hunched and bent as an elder's.

Yet if Rhys looked hard, he caught an echo of the beauty Blodwen had once possessed, before two Roman soldiers slaked their lust on her body and sharpened their daggers on her skin. That had been eleven winters ago, when Blodwen was a girl of fourteen. The promise of magic had been strong within her, but after the attack it had vanished. She was a gentle soul, the only one of the Druid clan barren of magic.

"All will be well now that ye've returned, cousin."

Rhys shook his head. "If Mared and your father canna drive off the evil that sickens Cyric, I surely cannot."

"Ye can if ye find Gwen. Surely she will listen to ye. Make her put a halt to this!"

"My sister has nothing to do with Cyric's illness," Rhys said sharply.

Blodwen's bit her lower lip. "Just last summer, ye worried Gwen sought magic deeper than her talent. Is our grandfather's illness not proof of it?"

"I canna believe Gwen would do Cyric harm."

"They quarreled before she left the last time."

Rhys stilled. "What of?"

Blodwen darted a glance toward Trevor. "What do ye

think? Cyric urged her to clasp hands with Trevor—or with any man of Avalon. Gwen refused. Her defiance troubled Cyric deeply. He wants her to wed."

"Gwen and Cyric have had words on that subject many times. There's no reason to believe she would call the Dark against Cyric because of it."

Blodwen's pitying expression was worse than any argument. "I love Gwen as ye do, Rhys. But I ask ye: if Gwen hasna cast this evil, then who?"

"I may have the answer to that," Rhys said. "I've learned of a Druid living in the mountains of Cambria. Owein, of the line of Queen Cartimandua."

Blodwen's eyes widened. "A Druid and a king as well?"

"Aye. Owein is a Seer, like Cyric. But where Cyric serves the Great Mother, Owein is bound to the Horned God."

"The Horned God's power is vast," Blodwen said in a hushed voice. "And easily turned to darkness."

"There is more. Owein seeks a magic grail. The cup has been in the possession of a Roman family in Isca, but was recently stolen. I believe the vessel is the Lost Grail of Avalon."

For several seconds, Blodwen only stared. She licked her lips. "The . . . the Lost Grail has been found?"

"Aye, it would seem. Found and lost again. I mean to search it out and bring it home." He shifted his pack to the ground. "But right now, Blodwen, I need to see Cyric."

"Of course."

He turned toward the village gate. Cormac jumped aside, clearing a path. Rhys stared at the dwarf. By the Great Mother, had the meddling spy heard every word he'd spoken? Rhys sent the misshapen brute a scowl.

He strode through the palisade gate, Blodwen at his heels. "Please, Rhys. Take me with ye."

Rhys halted. "Ye know it is forbidden."

A tear rolled from her eye, catching on the ridge of a long scar. She dashed it away with the back of her hand. "I would be with our grandfather when he draws his last breath. My own father is there! Am I nay as much kin to him as ye and Padrig?"

"Of course," Rhys said, his tone gentle. He reached out and cradled her scarred cheek in his palm. "But I canna bring ye to the high slope. One's magic must be strong to venture so close to the Lost Lands."

"I dinna care."

Rhys let his hand fall. "Ye are needed in the village."

He felt her eyes upon him as he departed. The urge to relent was strong. Blodwen was right; she should be at Cyric's side. But it had been Cyric himself who had enchanted the high slope against those with no magic.

Rhys forced his steps along the winding trail to the summit, resisting the temptation to plow straight up the incline. To cut the spiral path short was an insult to the Great Mother.

When he reached the peak, he spied Padrig sitting before the entrance to Mared's healing hut, a fire crackling beside him. The elder Druid's arms rested on his knees; his dark head was bowed. He looked up at Rhys's approach, and for a scant moment, his weary expression relaxed.

"Rhys," he said, rising to envelop the younger man in an embrace. "Nephew. Ye are here at last."

"Aye," Rhys said simply. He inclined his head toward the shelter. "May I . . ."

"Of course. 'Twill do Cyric good to see ye." The lines of exhaustion returned to Padrig's face. "If he wakes long enough to know ye."

The numbing tones of Mared's death chant seeped around the edges of the hide-draped doorway. Was Cyric's end truly so close? Steeling himself, Rhys drew aside the skin and entered.

Billowing heat and cloying herbs assailed him. A blazing fire gave rise to a haze of smoke; the only illumination came from the coals in the crude hearth, visible between the soaked packets of herbs. Rhys swallowed the urge to cough, his breath exploding in a violent wheeze.

Shadows blurred in a sudden wash of tears. Rhys blinked back his grief and the shapes resolved themselves. Cyric lay on a straw mat, a woolen blanket covering his frail body. Mared knelt by his side. She nodded, never wavering in her song.

If not for the spread of the snow-white beard across the blanket, Rhys mightn't have recognized Cyric at all. He'd been ailing a fortnight ago when Rhys had left Avalon, but the change that had been wrought by fourteen days was frightening. The Druid master's lanky frame had shriveled to a thin, sunken shell. Red rimmed his eyes; his skin was the texture of mottled papyrus.

Rhys knelt at Cyric's side and took his frail hand in his own. There was yet a glimmer of warmth, and Rhys found himself nurturing a frail hope.

"Rhys."

"I am here, Grandfather."

Cyric's eyes blinked open. "Ye spend far too much time away from Avalon, my son."

Rhys all but choked on his grief. He'd become a nomad at Cyric's order—was he now to be berated for his obedience? Or had his grandfather's mind already drifted into the mist?

" 'Tis true," he said simply. "I've been too long away."

"I am sorry for that," Cyric said. "I"—he paused to draw a rattling breath—"have felt your absence in my heart."

Tears stung Rhys's eyes. "I have missed ye as well."

Cyric stirred, as if trying to rouse himself. "Listen closely, Rhys. 'Tis an urgent task I give ye. Ye must gather the blessed, so they may learn the way of the Light. Away from Avalon, the Dark may touch them first." A cough scraped his throat. "An ill wind rises. Ye canna let it destroy the clan."

"I will fight by your side, Grandfather."

"Nay. I willna fight. My path is one of acceptance."

Rhys bowed his head and pressed his grandfather's

shaking hand to his forehead. "There are other paths," he whispered.

"I willna do battle with evil as my spear, Rhys. And yet . . . it seems the Light inside me is nay shield enough for the Dark that oppresses me."

"Light ever conquers Dark, as the sun ever rises," Rhys said. "Ye taught me that even before I had words enough to understand."

Cyric's eyes were gentle. "Lean close." His words were so weak they were naught but a pale whisper.

With a sick heart, Rhys obeyed Cyric's request. He was surprised to feel a soft laugh against his ear.

"Tell Mared to take her unending dirge outside. Her chants scrape sparks on my soul like a blade on a honing wheel."

Rhys found himself blinking back a new wash of tears. He straightened and turned to Mared. "Please," he said, with a nod to the door. "I would be alone with Cyric."

Mared's chin jerked down and the notes of her healing song roughened. Clearly, she disapproved of Rhys's request. When Rhys didn't look away, she nodded once and retreated.

"At last," Cyric said, his relief evident. "Help me sit, Rhys. And bring water. My throat is dust."

Rhys slipped his arm behind his grandfather and raised him against the backrest. His aged body seemed naught but a bundle of bones covered with sagging skin. Rhys's heart squeezed painfully. In his mind, Cyric still loomed tall and powerful. Nine years earlier, he'd gathered what was left of his family. Defying Roman law, he'd returned to the sacred isle to practice the magic of the Old Ones and the ways of the Lady of the Grail. How could a man so strong in the Light be brought low by darkness?

He tipped water to his grandfather's lips. For all his thirst, Cyric drank but a sip before motioning for Rhys to take the cup away. "I . . ." A wet cough shook him. "I ask for Gwen, but Mared refuses to bring her."

Rhys's throat went dry. " 'Tis nay Mared's choice. Gwen is . . . gone."

"Gone? Gone where?"

"I dinna know."

"Ye should." Cyric's quiet statement rang like an accusation.

Rhys felt ashamed. " 'Tis true, that."

A tremor passed through Cyric's body. " 'Tis so cold. Can ye nay build up the fire?"

If the fire were any hotter, the walls of Mared's hut would surely melt. But Rhys only nodded and added another block of peat to the coals.

"Gwen is strong in the Light. Strong enough to stand against the Dark. If ye stand behind her."

"Gwen has left Avalon." Anger colored his words. How could his twin have abandoned her grandfather? Could it be that Gwen truly had conjured Cyric's illness? Rhys didn't want to believe it, and yet . . .

"Rhys." Cyric's eyes lost their focus. His brow contracted.

Rhys's breath stalled in his throat. A vision? Now, when the veil between Cyric's life and death was drawn so thin? The stress of the magic could kill him.

Cyric's eyes drifted to a point above Rhys's right shoulder. His head cocked to one side, his expression intent. A subtle light illuminated his face—not the red glow of the hearth, but a white light that seemed to come from within.

The air was thick with smoke from the peat Rhys had added to Mared's blaze. Rhys struggled to breathe, but curiously, Cyric's breath grew stronger. His eyes focused, but Rhys knew whatever scene he viewed was not of this world.

Cyric's voice rang true. "A new line forms. A line of a Future King, who will unite Britannia in Light. He will be born of the line of the Lost Grail, a vessel wrought by blood and filled with tears. Cloaked in magic and silver by the Daughters."

Blindly, Cyric put out a hand. Rhys caught it. A tingle

like lightning raced through him, pure power that belied the weakness in Cyric's body.

"The grail of the Daughters must return to Avalon. When it does, the gates of the Lost Land will open. A Daughter of the Lady will enter."

"Grandfather—"

Cyric's hand tightened like a claw on Rhys's arm. "Gwen is a Daughter of the Lady. She must marry and bear a daughter if her line is to continue. Ye must—" A fit of coughing broke his words. "—bring your sister home, to await the grail's coming. If ye fail . . . I See a bleak future. The King will not be born. Britannia will fall to darkness. Please, Rhys, find her. Promise me."

"Ye have my word," Rhys whispered. "I will find Gwendolyn."

Another fit of coughing broke over Cyric. Wordlessly, Rhys slipped onto the pallet next to his grandfather and held him until the spasm passed. The hide at the door lifted, admitting a stream of sunlight. Rhys blinked against the intrusion.

Mared entered, with Padrig close behind. "Ye've tired him," she said, accusation clear in her voice.

"I've done no more than listen."

Cyric lifted his hand. "Padrig. Come to me."

Padrig knelt by Cyric's pallet.

"I will soon sail to the land beyond the west."

"Nay, Cyric! We can fight this curse upon ye! If ye would but allow the clan to call the Deep Magic—"

"Nay." Cyric's eyes closed briefly. "No mortal can control the Deep Magic. I willna risk the Dark. I would have only Light."

Padrig's jaw set. "Light fades."

"Ye are wrong, uncle," Rhys said.

Padrig's lips pressed into a thin line, but he said nothing.

Cyric's voice trembled. "Death is near. Come close—I would name the one who will guide the clan after my passing."

The air expanded in Rhys's lungs. To lead in Cyric's

stead was a burden he would shoulder with a heavy heart. And yet—he'd always understood this was his life's purpose. In truth, he welcomed the duty. Finally, he would be allowed to set roots in the fertile soil of the sacred isle.

He felt the weight of Cyric's gaze upon him. Lightheaded, he drew a deep breath, but the air, thick with peat smoke and herbs, only made his mind spin faster.

"To lead the clan is the path of duty," Cyric whispered. "Avalon's master must tread this path with wisdom and courage."

Rhys bowed his head, felt his grandfather's hand come down upon it. Cyric said a Word in the language of the Old Ones, sealing his word as law. Mared and Rhys, and, after a brief hesitation, Padrig, murmured their assent.

Stillness descended. Cyric drew a breath, and then his frail voice dropped into the silence like a stone tossed on the silver-still surface of a meadow pool.

"Gwendolyn," he said. "Gwendolyn will rule in Avalon. Rhys will bring her home."

Chapter Ten

A day after his ordeal within the stones, Owein had recovered enough to insist that Clara practice a full hour with the dagger before retiring for the night. Clara endured his goading with poor grace, grumbling as she thudded the blade over and over into the stout pine branch he held in his hands. By the end of the lesson, she would have been more than pleased to sink the knife into his thigh.

She guessed he knew it well enough, too.

They'd descended from the high country, but the terrain was still rocky. As the sun disappeared over the ridge of the mountain to the west, Owein called a halt to their exercise. He examined the knife for nicks, then pulled a flat stone from his pack and honed the edges. When the blade was sharpened to his satisfaction, he surprised Clara by removing his leg-sheath and presenting it to her.

"Ye'd best be armed at all times," he said, watching as she reluctantly fastened the sheath to her calf. He handed her the sharpened dagger. "But I must warn ye—there's scant advantage to possessing a weapon if ye dinna mean to use it."

"I'm not sure I'd be able to. I'm not very strong."

He tapped his finger on her head. "This is where your strength lies. Are ye a woman grown? Or a pampered child, trained to weakness?"

Clara flexed her fingers on the dagger. In an odd way, she'd grown accustomed to its feel in her hand. She slid the weapon into its scabbard. The weight on her calf felt strange.

"Thank you," she said quietly.

She moved to the mouth of the shallow cave where Owein had made their camp. Every muscle in her body ached. She rubbed her upper arm, wincing when she probed the muscle too deeply. Armed or no, she was exhausted. At least the nook was relatively dry and blessedly free from the wind. Beyond that, the accommodations left much to be desired.

Sighing, she sat on the ground and opened her satchel. Extracting her vial of rose oil, she dabbed the scent on her throat. For a moment, she closed her eyes and imagined herself in the bathing room in her father's house. When she opened her eyes again, it was to find Owein watching her, his expression as sharp as her newly honed blade.

Abruptly, she straightened, clearing her throat while she stoppered the vial and put it away. She cast about for something to say. "How close are we to the sea?"

"A half-day's journey, no more."

"Then we're near the road! The last miles to Isca will go quickly." She hugged herself. "We can rest tomorrow night in a *mansio!*"

Owein gave a noncommittal grunt. "Dinna raise your hopes. There may not be an inn to be found."

"Oh, but I'm sure there is. And I have coin enough in my satchel." She frowned, looking at Owein with new eyes. She'd grown accustomed to his wild appearance, but if they were to travel on the Roman road, something would have to be done about his wild mane and uncivilized garb. There was no merit in asking for a fight.

"I think," she said cautiously, "if we are to travel the road, you should cut your hair and remove your beard."

Owein's hands, bearing flint and dagger, paused in the air. Clara's gaze skimmed his strong jaw, her imagination shearing away its red fur. Her heartbeat quickened at the prospect of seeing him without it.

He eyed her. "Only Romans clip their beards."

"And free Celts who wish to advertise their wealth."

He gave a swift shake of his head. "I'm nay one of those."

"But you must shave! We're sure to meet other travelers. What will they think of us? A Roman woman would never travel in the company of a wild Celt."

"And yet," he mused. "Here ye are."

She sent him a scowl. "This is not a jesting matter. The first military complement we meet will detain you."

Flint and blade connected with a crack, showering sparks. "A wealthy Roman woman wouldn't travel alone with any man."

"She would travel with her husband."

"On foot? With no slaves to trail behind? Who would lift her hem across the puddles?" He struck the flint a second time, only to have the sparks die on the damp tinder. He muttered a curse.

"The wife of a free Celt would not be expected to travel in luxury."

He shot her a look she couldn't interpret. "Put that scheme out of your mind. I'm nay of a mind to travel the road. We'll take a forest trail."

"Traveling in snow and mud will take twice as long as making use of the road. What will you do when we draw close to the city? You won't be able to avoid notice then." When he made no comment, she gave an exasperated huff. "You look like a wild beast. You're likely to end in a pen at the arena. The beard must go."

"Nay."

She planted her hands on her hips. "*Aye,*" she said, mimicking his Celt accent. "It must. You're far too wild to be my husband."

He sat back on his heels and raised his brows. His gaze dropped to her breasts, and lower. "Is that an invitation, lass?"

"*Clara,*" she said irritably. "And don't try to change the subject. The beard must go."

"I'm a man, not a smooth-faced lad."

"I've not noticed that facial hair contributes to or detracts from manliness. It's only a matter of custom."

"I told ye nay."

"But why not? What's so important about a chin covered with hair? Unless . . ." She smirked. "Perhaps you have some disfigurement? Maybe you wear your beard to cover some flaw."

Owein shot her a withering glance. "If ye canna be silent, I've a mind to find a gag."

"Will you bind my hands and feet as well? And carry me slung over your shoulders like a trussed deer? I've heard tell of wild Celts who find wives in that manner."

His blue eyes sparked. "Have a care, lass. Ye have no idea how appealing that notion sounds."

He struck the flint again, and this time the fire caught. He bent close to the tinder, his breath nurturing the flames. Clara imagined him doing the same to her—blowing gently across her body, kindling a fire within.

A dart of flame shot along the edge of a twig. Her belly tingled. She squelched the sensation and returned to the subject at hand. "You know I'm right about this."

"I know ye are like a dog with a bone." He fed the fire with twigs and peat, then bits of larger wood. "We'll travel the forest trails by night. When we reach your father's villa, I'll enter alone, in case Valgus is there. Then I'll bring the grail to your father's city dwelling."

"But that would be imposs—" She swallowed the words.

Owein believed her to be a merchant's daughter, with a home in the outer city. Not the daughter of the fortress commander, whose residence was within the fortress walls.

She swallowed. Did her father still live? If he did, she couldn't waste precious time struggling through the forest by night, not when a dry, paved road would allow her to reach him so much more swiftly. "I'll not travel in the forest," she said. "We must pose as husband and wife. So you *must* shave your beard."

He was silent a moment; then his expression shifted. A mischievous gleam sprang into his eye. Clara's gaze narrowed. She didn't trust that look at all.

"Perhaps," he said slowly, "I can be won over to your plan, if ye do a bit more to persuade me."

"And what would that be?" she asked warily.

"Ye wish to act the part of my wife. If ye took on the role in all aspects, that would be a powerful inducement indeed."

Clara's belly flooded with heat. When he gave her a leering grin, she pursed her lips and looked away.

"You are a churlish lout," she informed him, trying to keep her voice steady. She cast about for the words most likely to set him back. "Now that I think on it, you needn't agree to be my husband. There's another possibility. You could be my slave."

Owein's smile abruptly vanished. "Nay."

"Then you have to remove your beard."

"There's a third option," Owein said, busying himself with the fire. "Ye could travel as a lad."

Clara gaped at him. "No one would believe that."

He appraised her frankly. "They will, with no trouble. Ye are small in the hips and bosom."

He thought she had a boy's body? Clara's cheeks burned. "But . . . my clothes are a woman's."

"I can steal ye a shirt and *braccas* from the first farm we pass. All that's left is for ye to take a blade to your hair."

"Cut my hair? Are you mad? I can't return to Isca with a shorn head! If my father yet lives, the sight would surely finish him off!"

"Ah, so ye wish me to cut my hair, but ye are nay willing to do the same?"

"It's not the same thing at all! Men wear their hair short. Women do not."

Owein fed the last of the deadwood into the fire. It flared hotly. Clara extended her hands toward it with a sigh. She couldn't think of anything more blissful, except perhaps a hot bath. And a meal of soft wheat bread, fruit, and fresh meat.

"Attend your cloak, lass," Owein said sharply. "It's about to go up in flames."

"Oh!" Hastily, Clara beat out the sparks that had settled on the wool, then surveyed both the cloak and her tunic with a sad shake of her head. Never in her life had she worn garments so ragged. And her scalp . . . she longed to feel the teeth of her comb. She pulled the leather thong free and started unraveling what was left of her braid.

" 'Twould be a shame to lose those shining strands," Owein's voice sounded strained.

Clara looked up. Coming around the fire, he crouched before her. With a solemn reverence at odds with his usual taunting manner, he speared his fingers through her hair, spreading the locks like a cloak over her shoulders.

He captured her gaze. Time seemed to cease; the air between them shimmered. It was only the heat from the fire, Clara told herself.

" 'Twould be a rare joy, I am thinking, to see ye clothed in naught but the mantle of your hair."

Clara felt as if the point of an exquisite, burning blade had sunk into her belly. "Even with my boy's body?" she managed.

The teasing light returned to his blue eyes. "Aye, even so." His voice came low and rasping. Her body softened in response.

He let out an unsteady breath. "I'll shave my beard, lass. And cut my hair to my shoulders."

"You . . . you will?"

"Aye. And take the part of your husband."

"For appearance's sake only. I'll not couple with you."

"I wouldna force myself on ye. Ye know that. But I will claim one concession from ye."

She licked her dry lips. "What is that?"

"Lie with me this night. Accept my hands upon your body."

"But you just said—"

"My hands, lass. Only my hands."

The dark place between her thighs tingled. "No. I can't allow it."

He made a show of settling himself against the back wall of the cave, his hands behind his head and his legs stretched toward the fire. "Then the beard stays. And we keep to the forest path."

"*You* may do what you wish. *I* intend to take the road. I'm going to rest in a proper bed tomorrow night."

"A lone Roman woman, afoot, with no servants or baggage? The innkeeper will take ye for a whore."

Clara hadn't considered that. Likely, it was true.

"Would it be such a hardship to lie by my side?"

The wistful vulnerability in his tone weakened her resolve. "All right," she heard herself say. "I'll lie with you. Only . . . not for the whole of the night."

A smile played at the corners of his mouth. "Ah," he said. "Now we're down to the haggling. Not the whole night, then. How long?"

"Until . . . until moonrise."

He laughed. "The moon is full this night. She'll rise as the sun sets, and the light of day is already waning. 'Tis nay nearly long enough."

His quiet certainty sent a shiver of anticipation down Clara's spine. "From twilight until full dark, then."

"From sunset until the moon shines overhead."

"But—"

" 'Tis my final offer, lass."

She sighed. "All right. Half the night."

He gazed at her. "And ye'll accept my hands on your body."

She bit her lip and closed her eyes. "You may touch me if you keep your hands atop my clothing. I'll not undress for you." Surely that restriction would keep her honor intact.

The corner of his mouth crooked. "Any more rules?"

"You'll shave first. I'll not lie with a bearded Celt."

She couldn't tease out the mix of emotions in the swift glance he sent her. Humor, yes, and desire, but she had seen both before. Now another emotion simmered beneath those, half-hidden. Not anger, precisely. Wariness? But why should that be? He had nothing to fear from her. Just the opposite.

"Sit beside me, lass," Owein said softly. After a slight hesitation, Clara obeyed. Her heart kicked up a beat when he placed a hand on her calf. Even through the layers of linen and wool, his touch felt warm.

She sat, motionless, barely daring to breathe as she watched his strong fingers dip beneath the hem of her tunic. His rough fingertips skated over her bare skin. Her lips parted on a small intake of air. She heard his soft chuckle. Fire flooded her cheeks, but somehow she couldn't move, or even look away.

"We agreed you would keep your hands atop my tunic," she said breathlessly.

"Aye, so we did." His fingers slid higher, encountering the leather sheath he'd given her. With a deft movement, he slipped the dagger free and withdrew his hand.

Hastily, Clara tugged her hem down to her ankles. Owein tested the blade with his thumb, then, to her surprise, offered it to her. When she didn't take it, he grasped her left hand and closed her fingers around the hilt.

"Get on with it, then," he said gruffly, releasing her. "Cut my hair as ye like. Just try not to take my head with it." He shifted, giving her his back.

Understanding dawned. "You want me to do it?"

"If ye will."

"All right." She knelt behind him, her legs slightly splayed, her breasts nearly touching his body. It was an intimate pose, but, she realized, one that signified his trust. No man turned his back on an enemy wielding a blade.

"I'm waiting, lass."

"Clara," she said, annoyed. "My name is Clara. Why can you not say it?"

He grunted.

Her hand trembled as she lifted his hair from his neck. Thick and curly, the ends were a mass of snarls, but the russet strands were silky-soft. She fingered the long braid at his temple. It was, perhaps, the most primitive thing about him.

"Dinna cut the plait, lass." His tone brooked no argument.

"As you say," she said, draping the braid over his shoulder. She gathered the rest of his hair at his nape.

The blade sliced cleanly. Clara cut away the tangled sections of Owein's hair, leaving shorter lengths free to curl over at his nape. She had the oddest urge to lean forward and kiss his bared skin. The thought caused heat to rise.

Ye'll accept my hands on your body.

Her breasts tightened and her belly went into a free fall. Her hands trembled—suddenly, she didn't trust herself to wield the dagger. She set it aside and tried to cover her unease by running her fingers through Owein's curls. His scalp was warm.

He went cat-still. Clara's strokes faltered.

He cleared his throat. "The beard next, lass. Before the light of day fades completely."

"Yes." Clara took up the knife and inhaled deeply, willing her nerves to calm. He turned about, returning to his original position reclining against the wall of the cave. She eyed his long, muscular legs, bent at the knee and splayed open.

She would have to kneel between them to execute her barber's task. From the amused look in his eye, it was what he'd intended.

She pursed her lips. "Remember, I have a blade in hand."

"Aye, I ken that well enough." He settled more comfortably against his rocky cushion, his eyelids half-closed.

The sensual, lazy look about him flooded Clara's belly with twisting heat. She scooted as far forward between his legs as she could without touching him. Unfortunately, he was leaning slightly back; when she reached for his chin she would pitch forward.

"This isn't going to work," she muttered.

"I'll keep ye steady." His hands went to her hips, then slid upward. "Ye are so slender," he said, bemused. "I can span your waist with my hands."

She glanced down, then wished she hadn't. His big thumbs touched just above her navel; his fingers flexed at the small of her back. His palms were so warm they all but burned her hips through her clothing.

His voice, husky and low, fell on her ear like a caress. "If ye go about your barbering any slower, the moon will be overhead before ye are done. In that case, ye'll lie with me until dawn." He gave a self-satisfied smile. "Perhaps longer."

She stiffened. "I . . . I don't want to cut you."

His hands tightened on her waist. "Just be done with it."

"All right." She raised the blade. Gripping the knife with her left hand, she slid the edge down his right cheek. A tuft of red hair fell over her hand.

She cast about for some subject to steady her nerves. "Do you know," she said, "the great Alexander of Macedonia commanded his men to shave their beards."

He opened one eye. "And how do ye know that?"

"Father told me. He said Alexander gave the order after he observed that bearded men were at a disadvantage in battle. Oftentimes, the enemy would grasp a man by the beard so as to hold him steady while planting a spear in his chest."

Owein gave a noncommittal grunt.

Clara transferred the knife to her right hand and began scraping the hair on Owein's left cheek. His braid brushed the back of her hand. "The Macedonians were stronger for their shorn chins. Don't you think Alexander was clever to command his soldiers to shave?"

"What I am thinking is no Celt war chief would live long after issuing such an order." He shifted, causing Clara to jerk the blade back lest she slice his skin. "A Celt cuts his hair only in disgrace."

Clara's gaze flew to Owein's face. "You believe I mean you insult?"

"Nay, lass. What I believe is that my beard frightens ye."

Perhaps that was true, Clara thought, as more of the unruly mane fell away. Owein was far less forbidding without his facial hair. She drank in the sight of him. His straight jaw. His strong cheekbones. His chin was firm, almost regal.

She reversed the blade and scraped it from the base of his neck to his chin. All the while she was aware of his fingers flexing on her waist, keeping her steady. And pulling her closer. Her knees collided with the inside of his thighs. His thumbs moved on her hip bones.

She traced the curve of his exposed upper lip with her finger, mesmerized. It was so soft, and yet so masculine. His tongue darted out and licked the pad of her thumb. Desire sliced through her.

Her trembling fingers slipped on the dagger's hilt. "Oh!" She stared down at the drop of blood welling from the fleshy base of her thumb.

Owein's hand closed over hers. "Let me see, lass."

He examined the cut, then carried her injured hand to his mouth and suckled the wound. His lips pulled; his tongue soothed.

Flames leaped in her belly and spread lower, to the dark place between her thighs. She stared at him, her lips parting. She couldn't take her eyes from his newly exposed chin. With his beard gone, he was beautiful.

She'd not been the most skillful of barbers. Stubble clung to his skin, and a red scrape marred his neck. Even so, Clara could hardly grasp the magnitude of the change she'd wrought. How young he looked! And how . . . civilized. He might have been a man she'd seen haggling in the forum market, or a young officer at one of her father's military receptions. But for the long, primitive plait dangling from his temple, he resembled a citizen of Rome.

Hesitantly, she put out a hand and traced the arch of one cheekbone. He went instantly still, his breath catching. The sound gave her courage. She drew her finger down the line of his jaw, letting it trail off the tip of his bare chin.

He spoke, his voice low and vibrant, sending a shiver along her spine. "Well, lass. What do ye think of your handiwork?"

"You look . . . very fine. Noble, even."

His eyes never left her. "My grandmother was a queen."

She blinked at him. "Truly?"

"Aye. She was Cartimandua of the Brigantes." His gaze flicked away. "The Romans took her throne."

Clara had no reply for that.

His eyes flicked to a point beyond her shoulder. "The moon has risen."

She started, glancing behind her. Sure enough, a golden disk had appeared, a shining orb above the mountaintops.

Ye'll accept my hands on your body.

Her mouth went suddenly dry. "So it has."

His strong hands skimmed over her shoulders and arms. Shivering, she hugged her torso. She felt fragile, like glass.

Owein seemed to sense this. Gently, he retrieved their discarded cloaks. He spread his ragged garment on the ground and urged her to sit upon it. He spread her fine one over her lap.

His hands lingered. "May I lie under your cloak, lass?"

She looked into his eyes and nodded.

Chapter Eleven

Cormac sighed in pleasure.

A long fall of silver hair brushed his hip. Bountiful breasts, soft and full, pressed against his thighs. The wench knew her way around a cock. A fine joke, that. What would the Druids of Avalon do if they knew what their Daughter was about?

His large palm covered her crown, holding her head steady while her clever tongue and teeth worked his shaft. 'Twas hard labor indeed, for his manhood was long and thick—the gods' compensation, perhaps, for his stunted limbs. Wenches recoiled at the sight of his grotesque form, until they saw what hung between his thighs. Then they lifted their skirts readily enough.

This lass had been a fine conquest. 'Twas nay often that he was the first to bring a woman to bliss. She made a gurgling sound as the tip of his blunt spear touched the back of her throat. He closed his eyes as his pleasure expanded, tugging her silver-blond tresses taut. She responded with a muffled groan.

Her nimble fingers found his stones and squeezed. His

hips bucked. By the Horned God! He'd taught her well. Despite the cold seeping through the sparse walls of her crude forest shelter, sweat trickled down his temple to his ear. Her tongue slid along his length and he hardened unbearably. In another heartbeat . . .

The lass lifted her head and slid from his grasp, as elusive as a running stream.

No! Cool air struck his cock, causing it to twitch. "By the gods," he roared, reaching for her. "Finish me, woman."

"Not that way." An arrogant smile touched her pouty lips. Cormac's erection lost some of its urgency. She never missed an opportunity to show him who held the upper hand.

"I want to feel ye, Cormac, deep inside. Like the first time." Gracefully, she arranged herself on the fur blanket and parted her legs. "Dinna finish too quickly."

For a moment, he considered walking away. Rising, tying the laces on his *braccas,* and leaving her wanting. As she'd done so many times to him.

Her eyes glinted silver. "Dinna consider it." Her hands slid up her body, cupping her breasts. She squeezed them in offering.

Cormac wasn't fooled. 'Twas a command, not a gift.

A command he dared not disobey. He rolled himself between her spread thighs and entered her with one brutal thrust.

"Oh, aye," she gasped. "Harder."

He began to work her, surging and retreating in response to her demands, cursing himself for a fool. He'd thought he could handle any woman—but a Druidess? He'd been a fool to attempt it. Now he was a hapless fly caught in her web.

A web of pleasure, to be sure. The lass's inner muscles were like nothing he'd ever felt, and he'd had more women than he could count. She was alive inside. Legs clamped around his hips, she milked his cock until his brain stuttered. But he knew better than to allow himself release too soon. He'd paid the price for that indiscretion only once. His wrists and ankles bore the scars to prove it.

He closed his eyes, slowed his thrusts, and endured the blissful torture. The wave built like thunderclouds, darkening until he could endure it no longer. His fingers bit into her skin. He plunged deeply, violently, ramming her womb.

An animal cry tore from her throat as she broke. Cormac's own release followed. He shuddered, pumping his seed into her body. Rolling to one side, he lay panting.

He'd never swived a wench like this one. Never.

His breathing had hardly slowed when she spoke. "Tell me all ye know of the Lost Grail."

Cormac opened one eye and groaned. "Can it nay wait until morning?"

She sat up, her silver hair flowing over her shoulders. The power of their joining crackled around her. When he squinted, he fancied he could see the faint outline of her magic.

"How could the Lost Grail of Avalon have rested so quietly all these years in Roman hands?" she asked angrily.

Cormac dragged a hand across his eyes. "I dinna know. Rhys brought the news. Why do ye nay ask him?"

"Ye know I canna do that."

He felt her displeasure shimmering around him like a threat. He sat up, shaking himself awake. He had no desire for his beard to fall out, or worse, to have his ankle broken in a fox hole. "Perhaps the grail awaits its true keeper."

"A Daughter of the Lady," she murmured, her lips curving in a self-satisfied smile. *"Me."* She laughed, her gaze drifting downward.

Cormac forced a swallow down his dry throat. She was eyeing his cock again. Under her scrutiny, it was growing for the fourth time that night. He repressed a groan. The lass's magic was going to kill him.

At least he would die in bliss.

She rose and paced the narrow confines of her lean-to. 'Twas no more than a collection of boughs spread across a cleft in the rock, here on the low side of the sacred isle. From the outside, the shelter appeared to be nothing more than a tangle of vegetation. Bold she was, to taunt the Druids of Avalon within reach of their power.

She turned to him. He took a moment to enjoy the sight. Her legs were long and shapely, her waist trim, her breasts full. Gray eyes tipped with dusky lashes; skin so smooth he never tired of touching it. Long silver-blond hair curled enticingly at her hips, framing a matching thatch between her thighs. She was far too fine for a man of his age and temperament. That made coupling with her all the more exhilarating.

"Why did ye nay bring me news of the Lost Grail afore now?" she demanded. "I should have known of it before Rhys."

"I didna know. I've only recently come from Londinium."

She halted at the darkest part of the shelter, beside the stone. Tall as a man it was, milky white and wedged in the black soil. She'd found it buried, covered with dirt and vines. Cormac couldn't even touch the thing, so vast was its power. But she could wrap her arms around it with no thought of harm.

"And the Druid king," she said petulantly. "I should have known of him."

Aye, the king. Owein, Cormac's own kinsman from the north. A fair shock that had been. He'd thought the lad long dead.

Her gray eyes turned accusing. "Ye were late in coming to me. Did ye nay hear my call?"

"Nay, lass." 'Twas a lie, of course. He'd felt her summoning spell clearly. He'd resisted it as long as he could before returning to the swamps. It never did to let a woman think she owned a man, even if it were true.

"I had a job in Londinium. By the gods, how the land is beaten and tamed there. I canna see how any Celt can bear it."

"Many have grown soft with Roman pleasures," she

said scornfully. "They are no better than the pigs they call masters."

" 'Tis true." On this subject, at least, they were in agreement.

"When the Lost Grail is in my hands, I will make certain the Romans never venture near the sacred isle."

Cormac's lips twisted. "The Romans defeated the Druids once before, despite the power of the Masters and the Words of the Old Ones. What makes ye think one lass can stand against them?"

"Ye doubt me?"

"Nay. But I canna help wondering why ye hide yer magic from the others. Surely Avalon should stand united against Rome."

Too late he saw the menace in her eyes. "Ye dare question my judgment?"

"Nay," he hastened, alarmed. "Nay. I only—"

"Fool." She lifted a hand, palm turned upward.

The burning sensation started in Cormac's toes, then quickly spread up his legs, to his groin, his belly, his chest. He lurched to his feet, stumbling away. "Nay. Please—"

Phantom fire engulfed his head, seared his lungs. He bent double, gasping for air. 'Twas an illusion, he knew, but that only made the agony worse. It could go on forever if she wished.

Pain ripped through his body. He stumbled and fell, sprawling on his arse.

She lowered her hand and the pain stopped. Cormac's heart pounded.

"Bitch," he muttered. Lunging, he grabbed her ankle and gave a savage yank. She fell hard atop him. With a deft movement he rolled her onto her belly and pressed her cheek to the cold floor of the hut. Leaving her no time to catch her breath, he lifted her hips and slammed his cock into her.

She pushed herself up on rigid arms, arching her back like a cat. "Aye, Cormac, aye. Like that."

Her magic glowed around them as they rutted, sparking brighter with each thrust. She needed him for that; 'twas the reason she would never let him go. Her full power had been unleashed by his lovemaking.

He thrust hard, offering her all his strength.

"The Lost Grail," she panted. "Ye must bring it to me."

Cormac groaned. Reaching as far as he could with his stunted arm, he entwined his fingers in her hair. Ruthlessly, he tugged her head back. "I'll need payment, wench. Gold and silver. I know Cyric has a cache of Druid treasure."

She flexed her inner muscles, tearing a growl from deep in his throat. "Ye'll have payment when the grail is in my hands."

He jerked his hips and she moaned. "What would Rhys say if he saw ye rutting like a whore?" he taunted.

"No doubt he'd say ye taught me well." She rocked against him, her magic crackling around their joined bodies. "How I've missed ye, Cormac." Her tone turned plaintive. "How many women have ye had since last I saw ye?"

He thrust and grunted, emptying what was left of his soul inside her. "None like you, lassie. None like you."

Owein stretched out beside Clara, drawing her fine cloak over both of them. His heart pounded like a galloping war pony. Hours of darkness stretched before him, hours when he would explore every dip and angle of her lithe body. His loins firmed almost beyond bearing. Why did this Roman lass affect him so deeply? By rights, he should scorn her. But he did not. On the contrary, he'd never been so entranced.

Rolling onto his side, he reached out and gently covered her breast with his palm. Her body stiffened. He made a soothing sound with his tongue, as if calming a frightened kitten.

"Relax, lass. I would never hurt ye."

"I know."

He circled her nipples through the soft wool of her tunic.

They peaked to tight beads under his touch. Her small breasts felt full and heavy. She squeezed her eyes shut, her breath coming quicker. Her body was opening for him—he could smell the musk of her arousal mingling with the scent of roses.

He stifled a groan. He was painfully hard, but he tried his best to ignore his clamoring needs. He wanted her pleasure so much more than his own.

"Owein . . ."

"Aye, love?" He tugged at her nipples through her tunic.

A mewling sound emerged from Clara's lips. Immediately, her body went rigid, as if appalled she'd uttered such a noise. By the Horned God! How was he to survive this half-night of love play?

He murmured softly, rubbing her shoulders until she relaxed again. Her gaze clung to his. The trust and silent entreaty he saw there nearly undid him. He didn't deserve her faith. But he was selfish enough to accept it.

He plucked at her breasts, rolling the peaks between his fingers.

She gripped his arm. "Owein, no, I . . . stop."

He stilled. "Ye would go back on your word?"

She hesitated, then let out a long sigh. "No."

A chill breeze gusted into the cave, causing the fire to waver. Clara shivered. If Owein could have conjured the hot bath she longed for, he would have done it in that instant. The memory of Clara half-frozen and covered with snow was still fresh in his mind.

He propped himself on his elbow and looked down at her. She was not pale and cold now—her cheeks were flushed, her lips pink and welcoming. A warm feeling expanded in Owein's chest.

Wide dark eyes blinked up at him. She was frightened, aye, but aching for his touch just the same. Passion ran deep inside her. Deeper, likely, than she knew.

Anticipation pulsed in his veins, settled heavily in his loins. He placed his hand, fingers splayed, on her belly. For a time, he forced himself to do no more than watch his hand rise and fall with her breath.

When her trembling faded, he moved his hand lower, until his thumb brushed her woman's mound. Her breathing quickened. If he were to lift her skirt and search beneath, would he find her virgin passage soft and ready? He longed to test the notion, but he'd promised not to delve beneath her tunic.

At least not until she removed it for him.

She could never be his in truth. He understood that, accepted it. No wealthy Roman woman would entrust her life to a barbarian outlaw. And as for himself, he would never be free of the dark hatred he held for every part of her world.

But here, in the wilderness, all that seemed very far away.

He cupped Clara's sex. Her hips came off the ground and her legs parted. Her defenses were melting, her body opening. If he'd been hard before, now he was rigid beyond bearing. He set a steady rhythm, rubbing the fabric of her tunic across the bud where her pleasure centered.

"Owein, I . . ."

"Relax, lass. Do ye enjoy my touch?"

She pulled in an unsteady breath. "I think you know that I do."

"Tell me how ye feel."

"As though . . . I'm engulfed in flames."

He quickened his rhythm and she writhed, gasping his name. He shifted atop her, anchoring her splayed legs with his lower body, his gaze never leaving her face. He wanted to watch her eyes as the pleasure broke over her. In the soft glow of the full moon and the dying fire, they shone like two unfathomable pools.

She spread her arms, gathering handfuls of his cloak. "I feel like I'm dying."

" 'Tis a sweet death, to be sure."

She arched into his touch. "Don't let me face it alone."

"I'm here, lass."

She clutched his arms, her fingernails gouging his flesh. She was close to her release, but she fought her ultimate pleasure. Her reluctance to yield would not last, however. A fierce triumph rose in Owein's breast. He, a barbarian Celt, would be the first man to demand Clara's surrender.

"Let it go, lass," he whispered. "Take your pleasure."

Her passion broke. His fingers moved on her, sharpening her pleasure. A sob tore from her throat. Her body convulsed as she gasped his name.

The sound echoed in his soul. It caught him and pulled him with her. Sensations expanded, until he could no longer keep them within. His pleasure exploded, shattering what was left of his emotions. The door to his heart splintered.

And suddenly, he felt her there, inside him.

Her Light flooded his mind. It probed the deepest corners, seeking to illuminate places best left in dismal darkness.

Her touch laid his memories bare. A white fog enveloped him, carrying him into the past.

A war cry tore from Owein's throat. His victim's dark eyes went wide. The slash of a blade, a spurt of blood. The body thudded to the ground. Owein yanked his weapon free. His head jerking up, he sought his next adversary.

Battle calm descended. The grunts and screams of his companions and enemies floated like mist. Owein's own cries seemed to ring far from his ears. His sword clanged dully against a Roman gladius.

His armor combined with his hatred to form an invincible shield. His opponent's snarls and curses did not touch him. Pain, fear, and defeat—they were words with no meaning.

He would not rest until every Roman was dead. He swung his sword low, cutting his opponent's legs from under him. The soldier fell. Triumph flashed through Owein, as fierce and sexual as an orgasm. He spun about, ready for more.

Only to see Nia with a gladius *sunk in her belly. Her own sword was limp in her fingers.*

For an instant, Owein hung suspended. An image from the night before flashed through his brain—Nia arching against him, calling his name as pleasure overcame her. Then the memory snapped, shattered by the exultant cry of her murderer.

The Roman gave his sword a savage twist, his elbow jerking backward. His blade emerged from Nia's stomach covered with blood, trailing a rope of gut. The woman whom Owein called friend and lover stared down, uncomprehending. Her lips parted.

She looked up, into Owein's eyes.

"Nay . . ." he whispered. He took a step forward, meaning to catch her in his arms.

Hot, boiling rage bubbled from a bottomless well of anguish. He opened his mouth, an animal's cry in his throat. The sound never emerged. A blow came down on Owein's skull, sending him careening into darkness.

"Nay." Owein shoved himself up on shaking arms. Black memories buzzed like a swarm of midges. He shook his head, trying to clear it.

Clara lay beneath him, staring up with wide, shimmering eyes. Shame and anger shot through him. He didn't want her pity. Couldn't bear her sympathy.

"Owein . . ."

She moved against him, unconsciously stroking his sex, rigid again. His cock throbbed. He wanted nothing so much as to thrust into her core and forget the past. But he knew, with the unerring instinct that told a man his own death approached, that if he surrendered himself to Clara, he would not be able to hide. She would be inside his mind, probing every dark secret, shedding Light on every humiliation.

Please, Owein. Let me in.

The words echoed inside his brain. He stared down at her, aghast. Only the strongest of Druids could speak within another's mind. Abruptly, he heaved himself off her. He felt her reaction, a single suspended note of hurt and confusion. Summoning all his magic, he snapped their bond.

He rolled, panting. He had to escape. Had to get away.

"Owien, wait. What—?"

He couldn't answer. Heaving himself to his feet, he lurched beyond the ring of firelight. Clara's cry echoed in his ear as he stumbled into the night.

Glancing up, he saw the moon had reached its zenith.

Chapter Twelve

He sat on a stool by a hearth mending a plow pony's harness. The low light of a banked fire illuminated his task. Owein looked down at the leather strap in his hand, bemused. He owned no pony, had no fields to tend. This life, this home, could not be his.

Yet he knew, with the certainty of a man existing within a dream, that it was.

A vision. He rubbed the faint ache in his forehead. A bowl of barley dough graced the table near his elbow. Near it rested a mug of cervesia, *fragrant and fresh-brewed. He lifted it to his lips and sipped.*

He'd never tasted such a fine beer.

There were other hints of a woman's touch. Overhead, neat bundles of herbs hung from the rafters. His shirt and braccas *were woven from wool—and indeed, there was a loom against the door, displaying a half-finished blanket.*

Owein nearly dropped his mug. Beside the loom was a pallet. Two small bodies nestled there like sleeping pups. A lad and a lass, their bodies entwined beneath the furs. The lass's curly hair was red, like Owein's. The lad's crown was silver-blond.

Owein's heart contracted. These were his children. He knew it beyond a doubt. A wishful dream—or a vision of the future?

"Owein?"

Clara struggled upright, sleep clinging to her brain like a dirty rag. She wiped a hand across her eyes. They burned. She'd cried herself to sleep after Owein had left her.

The fire's heat was long gone. The air had warmed somewhat, however—she could hear the drip of melting snow. Mist-gray clouds piled on the horizon. Another snow? She shuddered at the thought.

Her stomach was sour; her limbs tingled with the after-effects of magic. The union she'd shared with Owein hadn't been accidental this time. When his pleasure had exploded, she'd seen the path into his mind and had taken it. She'd plunged into the dark of his soul before he'd even had a chance to realize she was there.

Her stomach lurched again. Images of war were etched behind her eyelids. The gasp of a dying woman—Owein's first lover—echoed in her ears. But the worst had been Owein's rage. It had rushed through her own veins, hot, terrifying, and endless.

She called his name again. No answer. But surely he couldn't have gone far. His cloak was spread beneath her and his pack lay open.

Shakily, she gained her feet. The aftermath of the magic caused her to stumble. Joining with Owein in that way had been beyond frightening. And yet—she longed to touch him again. She wished with all her heart that she could offer the Light within her to soothe his darkness. If she could ease his anger and pain, she wouldn't count the cost.

She drew a steadying breath. Was the tight emotion in her chest love? The notion wouldn't dislodge itself from her mind. Love Owein? It was laughable. They could share no future. It would be pure folly to love him.

If only she had a choice.

She retrieved her cloak, shaking out the filthy thing and settling it over her shoulders. Her tunic was little better. The wool clung to her skin, making her itch. How she longed for a warm bath! With a sigh, she retrieved her satchel and tried to content herself with the last dab of her rose oil.

Not satisfied, she moved from the camp, following the downward slope of the land. At least she could wash her face and hands in the stream while waiting for Owein to return. Stepping lightly, she made her way down the hill and parted the low brush guarding the water's edge.

And discovered that Owein shared her desire for a bath.

He stood in the center of the rushing stream, facing the opposite bank, completely unclothed despite the chill air. His hair was slick and gleaming with moisture, his shoulders broad and strong against the light of day. His powerful legs and bare buttocks dripped water.

But his back . . . Clara swallowed a gasp. By Jupiter! His back was a hideous mass of scars. His skin bore long ridges punctuated with deep, round gouges. Such marks could only have been caused by a Roman flagellum—a slaver's whip fashioned of multiple leather thongs embedded with bits of sharp metal.

Clara's gorge rose. The wounds were old, but what agony they must have caused. She'd caught glimpses of public slave floggings in Isca and had never failed to lose whatever food was in her stomach. Had Owein struggled against his bonds as the lash flayed skin from muscle? Had he tried to avoid the cruel blows? Cried out, begging for mercy? Or had he prayed only for a swift death?

For it was surely a death sentence he'd cheated.

Her breath came hard. She wanted nothing so much as to kiss his scarred flesh, let her lips absorb the memory of the lash.

A thin beam of sunshine freed itself from the clouds. With a quick motion, Owein bent and sluiced an armful of water over his head. Drops of water sparkled as they fell, like a thousand gems of light. They bounced on his neck and shoulders, splashed over the broad expanse of his back, painting every lash and pucker with a sheen of wetness. She drew in quick breath.

He went still.

She should have whirled and fled up the trail, but somehow, she couldn't move, couldn't take her eyes from him. He turned and looked at her, his expression inscrutable.

He stood before her, a figure of wild perfection. Despite his shaved chin, his body did not evoke the Roman ideal of masculinity. He was far too powerfully built. His form lacked the languid grace of Apollo or the supple swiftness of Mercury. Nor did he embody the dominance of Jupiter or the arrogance of Mars.

Even a statue she'd once seen of the great Hercules fell short. Perhaps because Hercules had been wrought in marble, while Owein was wrought in flesh.

He was brawny and rough. Red-gold hair, glistening with droplets, curled on his chest. The hair darkened to copper over the rippling muscles of his stomach. Her gaze dropped. A nest of auburn framed a phallus that was growing before her eyes.

She jerked her gaze upward.

She might have thought he would utter a mocking word, but his habitual humor—even the darker aspects of it—was absent.

"You were meant to die under the lash," Clara said evenly.

"Aye."

"What was your crime?"

"Rape. Of my master's wife."

"You were a slave?"

"Aye."

She searched his eyes. "The charge was a lie."

He paced to within arm's reach. "Ye canna be sure of that."

"I can. You would never force yourself on a woman."

"How can ye say that, lass? After last night?"

"I . . . I welcomed your touch. I wanted more. You were the one who drew back, because of—" She inhaled. "I shouldn't have slipped into your mind. I am sorry."

His fingers curled. "Ye dabble with forces ye dinna understand."

"Then teach me to understand them."

" 'Tis nay knowledge for a Roman."

"But what of the bond between us?"

"We share no bond. Between our people, there is only war."

"That's not true," Clara said. "Perhaps in the north there is war, but here in the south there's been peace for years. Celts and Romans have joined their lives. Why, you once met Lucius Aquila in battle, but now he's married to a Celt healer. They—"

"Silence."

"—they have a daughter—"

"Silence, I said."

Owein's vehemence startled Clara into obedience. He ran a hand over his face and looked at the treetops. A quick peek told Clara his arousal had faded.

"Does . . . do your wounds pain you still?"

He looked back at her. "Nay. Most times I forget they are there."

"And other times?"

"Other times I regret I didna commit the crime for which I paid."

She inhaled a shaky breath. "How did you come to be a slave?"

For a moment, she thought he wouldn't speak. Then the answer came, carefully devoid of emotion.

"I was taken in battle and sold as spoils. My master transported me to a quarry in Cambria. For nearly two years, I tried to escape. Each time I was caught my punishment was worse than the one before."

"And the last?"

"My master's wife accused me. She was a garish, painted woman who whored with her husband's slaves. She wished to add me to her stable. In truth, I would have cut off my cock rather than pleasure her with it. I told her as much. By that time I didn't care if I lived or died. Until I saw the flagellum."

"How did you survive the flogging?"

"I hardly know. I managed to crawl into the forest. I'm nay sure how much time passed before Aiden found me."

"You were fortunate he did."

"Fortunate?" His laugh was harsh. "Aye, I suppose, if ye consider how unfortunate I'd been to have my home overrun by Romans. How unfortunate to be knocked senseless in battle and deprived of the opportunity to fall on my sword. How unfortunate I was to have been sold like a beast."

"I . . . I'm sorry."

"Ye needn't be. Ye didna wield the sword, nor the whip."

"Still—"

His expression shuttered. "Toss me my clothes, lass."

Clara started at the reminder of Owein's nakedness. Cheeks heating, she retrieved his *braccas* and shirt, which lay drying on the bank. Moving to the water's edge, she held them out to him. He climbed from the stream, the chilled water already transforming to heat on his skin. How did the fires burn so intensely within him? Clara hugged her arms to her body and stepped back.

To her surprise he didn't don the garments, only threw them over his arm. Stepping into his boots, he walked naked back to the camp. Once there, he sifted through his pack and drew out wool *braccas* and the white linen shirt Clara had worn while her clothes dried.

"Did your wife make those?"

He shrugged into the shirt. "Aye."

He shoved his long legs into the *braccas,* but paused before he did up the laces. She looked up to find him watching her, the amused expression she knew so well back on his face. With a start, she realized her attention had been fixed between his legs. Her face reddened.

He laughed softly. She wasn't aware she'd moved until her back hit the wall of the cave. " 'Tis no crime to look, lass."

"I wasn't—"

"There's no crime in wanting, either."

"I don't want you."

"Ye did last night," he taunted softly. "Ye opened your thighs for me."

"But . . . you were the one who ran. You're afraid of me. Of us. Of the connection we have."

He stiffened. " 'Twas nay my fear ye felt."

"I think it was. You've seen cruelty and evil, Owein. Darkness lingers inside your mind. It's crippling you. I . . . I think I can help, if you'd only let me. Please—"

He gave a swift shake of his head. "Ye don't know what ye are asking."

She lifted her chin. "I do, and I'm not afraid."

He regarded her with sober eyes. "Perhaps ye should be."

" 'Tis an outrage! A disgrace." Padrig's strident voice sliced through the air. His long limbs jerked as he paced before the fire. The Druid elder looked like a toy Rhys had once seen in the hands of a Roman child—a jointed ivory man mounted on a stick.

Mared lifted a hand. "Have a care what ye say in this place. The Great Mother listens."

"I'll nay shrink before the Great Mother," Padrig snapped. He came to a halt. "And I'll nay accept the rantings of a possessed man as law. Of course Cyric would name Gwen as his successor. He is caught in her Dark enchantment."

"Ye canna know that," Rhys said sharply.

"We must discern the will of the Great Mother," Mared said.

"The Mother remains silent," Padrig muttered.

Rhys barely heard their bickering. Cyric had denied him his birthright! The shock of his grandfather's pronouncement darted through his chest with every breath. His limbs felt almost detached from his body. He looked up at the sky and imagined lifting his arms and becoming lost in the clouds.

Hefin's silhouette swooped toward him, a black blur against the lightening sky. Rhys held a forearm aloft. The merlin settled on it, ruffling and folding its wings. Rhys took comfort in the bird's familiar weight.

Padrig's dour gaze drew him back to the earth. "Ye must lead Avalon when Cyric passes, Rhys. 'Tis your right and your duty."

"Nay," Rhys said quietly.

"Ye canna accept an old man's witless ramblings!"

"There is nothing wrong with Cyric's wits. I sensed no darkness in his words." Rhys took a deep breath and ignored the ache in his heart. "If Cyric has declared my sister leader of Avalon, I must abide by his will."

"But ye are her elder," Mared protested.

"Gwen's power is greater. It has always been so."

Mared frowned. " 'Tis a power without discipline."

"Then my sister will learn patience."

"And what of the clan?" Padrig put in. "Our people want ye at their head, Rhys. Not Gwen. She's angered many. Ye've nay been here to witness it."

"She shirks her duties," Mared said. "She disappears into the swamps, sometimes for an entire moon."

"Avalon has seen even less of me," Rhys said.

"They see your obedience to Cyric's will." Mared advanced to lay one wrinkled hand on Rhys's arm. "They see ye gathering the blessed from the Roman towns and bringing them to a new life. Most of them came to us through ye."

" 'Twas Cyric's vision that brought the Druids back to Avalon," Rhys said. "Would ye have me defy his last command?"

Padrig's eyes were grave. "For the good of the clan."

Rhys shook his head. Hefin startled at the movement. "Cyric's Sight is bound to the Great Mother. Perhaps the Goddess has shown him some truth the rest of us are blind to. Nay, I willna go against Cyric, no matter my own wishes. Gwen must lead Avalon."

"She must be present for that," Padrig muttered. "And she is not."

"Surely she's not far."

"Cormac searched the swamps and the surrounding hillsides. He found no sign of her."

"Cormac is nay of Avalon," Rhys said sharply. "I dinna trust him." He jerked his arm, sending Hefin skyward. "I will search for Gwen, as I promised Cyric. I will find my sister and bring her home to face her duty."

"Or her judgment," Padrig said darkly.

Rhys nodded. "Or her judgment."

Chapter Thirteen

The *mansio* smelled of rotten fish.

The inn was a dingy two-story structure surrounded by a high wall. Clara hadn't even reached the gates leading into the yard when the rank odor of decayed seafood—and worse—assaulted her. Apparently, the establishment's isolated location was sufficient guarantee of prosperity. Its owner certainly didn't aspire to cleanliness.

She bent her head into the icy wind and forced her feet forward. If the place were warm, she could ignore all else. Sleet stung her face like a thousand needles. Worse, the storm's vague, sparkling undercurrent set her senses on edge. Was this the Deep Magic? She frowned, trying to grasp what she didn't understand.

Owein surveyed the *mansio* with distaste. "I'd sooner sleep on the open moor than pass a night in this Roman privy."

If not for the frost on her nose and chin, Clara might have agreed with him. "It looked better from afar, didn't it?"

"Lass, a man couldna back up far enough to make this hovel look good."

A blast of frigid air flung the words from Owein's mouth. Clara huddled in her cloak, trying to warm her fingers in the fur lining. She wore Owein's cloak atop her own, though she'd protested when he'd settled it on her shoulders. He'd ignored her, pausing only long enough to don his hide shirt over his linen one, his one concession to the cold.

She slid a glance toward him. He might hide it well, but she sensed he was suffering as much as she. Not from the cold—after all, he carried a furnace within. No, she suspected it was the storm's magic that troubled him. His mouth had settled in a grim line that would not be broken.

"Are you well?" she asked.

He rubbed his right temple. "Aye," he said, casting a dark glance through the hostelry's iron gate. The yard was barren save for clumps of garbage, a heap of empty wine amphorae, and a pile of broken furniture. White mist emanated from a ramshackle privy.

A large rat scurried across the yard. Clara fought a surge of nausea. "Perhaps there's a better place farther on."

"None we'll reach before dark."

Clara curled her fingers, but her hands were so numb she couldn't feel the press of her nails on her palms. "I hope the food is edible, at least." She reached toward the gate bell.

"Wait. Give me your satchel."

She paused. "Why?"

"It contains your coin. The innkeeper will expect me to carry our purse."

"Best let me keep it. You'll find it difficult to match the coins to the price."

He snorted. "I'm no idiot, lass."

"I didn't mean to imply you were. I only meant that you aren't familiar with Roman coins. It will look odd if you hand over too little or too much."

" 'Twill look odder still if I stand aside and let my wife do the counting. This is your world, nay mine. Give me your satchel."

To argue would only delay Clara's entrance into a heated room. "All right."

The satchel's strap was across her shoulders. She would have to remove both Owein's cloak and her own in order to hand it to him. But her fingers were too stiff to do much more than fumble with the cloak pins.

"Let me."

Owein's hands were so hot that she hissed when they enveloped her fingers. She savored the warm abrasion of his calluses until they raised tendrils of pain on her skin.

His gaze narrowed. "Ye should have told me ye suffered."

And have him comment again on her weakness? "I hadn't noticed until now," she lied. She tugged her hands from his grasp. "Please. Just ring the bell."

"I'll have that satchel first." He unfastened the cloak pins, his fingers brushing her throat. Darts of tingling warmth accompanied his touch. All too soon, the satchel was slung over his broad shoulders and the cloaks refastened.

"One more bit of advice. Hard as it may be for ye, keep silent while we're in this place."

"You can't be serious."

"I assure ye, I am." He reached out and gave the rope a strong tug, setting the bell clanging.

Clara jumped and covered her ears. Owein chuckled.

The door to the inn swung open. A large man appeared in the doorway. He peered across the yard, seeming reluctant to brave the driving sleet for even the brief journey to the gate.

"Salve," Owein called. "Have ye supper and a bed for my wife and me?" His Latin was rough, but serviceable. It was odd to hear him speak her language.

"I take only coin," the man shouted. "No barter."

"You're in luck, friend. I have silver."

"Silver?" The man stepped into the yard. His large form plowed a path over the sleet-crusted ground.

The innkeeper had the swagger of a military man, though his enormous belly indicated it had been some years since he'd left the Legions. His beard was short and scraggly, his neck thick. His round nose crooked to the left.

His attention lingered on Clara a fraction longer than politeness allowed before shifting to Owein.

"One room, you say, and supper?"

"Aye. For my wife and me."

"Six *denari.* Not a *sestertius* less."

"Six *denari?*" Clara cried. "I could buy wine to last three months for that amount. You cannot be—"

Owein placed a warning hand on her shoulder. "Remember what I told ye."

"But this man means to rob us blind! Six *denari?* Why—"

His grip tightened. "Silence, woman. Or ye'll feel my open palm on your arse."

Clara bristled. She opened her mouth, a hot retort burning her tongue.

"Think hard before ye speak," Owein warned in a low voice—but not low enough that the innkeeper couldn't hear. "Remember how ye squealed at the last beating. And remember what happened when it was done, after your squirming turned my cock to stone."

Clara nearly choked.

The innkeeper threw back his head and let out a bark of laughter. "Good going, friend," he said, chuckling. He took a key ring from his belt and fitted it into the gate's lock. "Though to my mind, it does no harm to let a shrew scold once in a while, for the joy of punishing her later."

"I'll keep your advice in mind," Owein said, propelling Clara through the open gate. His hand slipped down her back and gave her bottom a quick slap. The innkeeper chuckled.

Clara's face flared so hot she was sure if she laid her palms on her cheeks her skin would be seared. She stepped close to Owein and landed a sharp, discreet jab in his ribs. His brisk intake of air provided a small satisfaction.

He leaned close, his lips brushing her ear. "Dinna think I wouldn't enjoy spanking your arse," he whispered. "Speak again, and I might try it." She could hear the laughter in his voice.

She pursed her lips and held her tongue.

The wind shifted, the sleet abruptly becoming enormous white flakes. They followed the innkeeper across the yard, tracing the crusty path he'd made, which was already beginning to fill with snow.

The hostelry was a medley of heat, sweat, and laughter underscored by the odor of cheap wine and *cervesia*. Fortunately, the aromas of roasted meat and fresh-baked bread were also present. Clara's stomach rumbled. She would settle for any meal that didn't consist of dry, stringy venison.

Owein thrust Clara behind him as they entered the main room of the tavern. "Stay close," he muttered. "And keep your hood up."

"I'll take that payment now, if you please." The innkeeper's tone was pleasant but firm, accented by a hand on his dagger.

"Of course," Owein said, his fingertips brushing the hilt of his own weapon. He unbuckled the flap on Clara's satchel. "For the price ye named, the bed linens must be clean and a pitcher of hot water provided." He paused to consider. "And we must have a chamber pot."

The man's eyes flicked to Owein's dagger, then back to his face. "As you say."

Owein counted out the coin with the air of a man who completed such transactions often. Clara raised her brows—perhaps she'd been hasty in assuming his ignorance. She dared a glance around the tavern. The place was lit with cheap tallow tapers that left a haze of smoke in the air. The innkeeper's patrons numbered about twenty men, a mix of lower-class Romans and free Celts, clustered around heavy plank tables. A pair of females circulated among them, laden with trays of food and drink.

The younger barmaid was amply blessed by Venus. Her breasts were fully as large as wine jugs and her rounded hips swayed with every step. Men tossed lewd compliments and coin whenever she made a show of leaning across a table to deliver a mug.

The buzz of conversation dipped a notch as Owein and Clara entered. Several men eyed Clara with undisguised interest. One man actually licked his chops. She eased close to Owein, glad that his bulk matched even the largest of the inn's patrons.

The innkeeper waved them to two empty seats at the end of a table. They were not too near the hearth, but Clara hardly minded. The atmosphere in the room was close; already she could feel her fingers and toes thawing. Owein removed his pack and dropped it on the floor near his feet, but kept Clara's satchel on his body. He slid onto the bench, facing the door. Clara took the opposite seat, easing her hood back to allow a quick perusal of the room.

Owein's posture relaxed—deceptively, Clara thought. His gaze roamed, never settling for long. The buxom barmaid arrived. Owein ordered wine for Clara and *cervesia* for himself.

A blond, bearded man with mottled skin was seated on the bench to Clara's right. His small eyes flicked over her, then shifted to Owein, whose gaze was elsewhere. A leering grin spread over his face. His hand disappeared under the table. He gave Clara a wink as his arm began moving with a jerking motion.

Clara's jaw went slack. Was he milking his rod? Here, in the common room of the tavern? She ripped her eyes away, heart pounding. Suddenly, a bed in a snowbank seemed like a fine idea.

She scooted as far to the end of the bench as she could without tumbling onto the ground. "Owein," she said in a strangled whisper. He sent her a questioning glance. "This was a mistake. Perhaps we should move on."

Owein glanced at the pock-faced man. Despite the taut weariness about his eyes, he seemed more amused than disgusted. "Fainthearted?"

The pock-faced man stiffened. He squeezed his eyes

shut and gave a low moan. An instant later he relaxed, caught Clara's eye, and winked.

Clara half-rose from the table, her gut twisting with revulsion. The air in the room was too thick. She couldn't get it into her lungs. "I cannot stay in this place."

Owein's hand closed on her wrist. "Lass. I gave nearly all your coin to that brigand of an innkeeper. Now ye wish to leave? Ye'd freeze yourself to death over a man polishing his sword? And what of our meal?"

"But—"

"Sit."

Reluctantly, she let him pull her back into her seat. He was right. "I'm sorry. Of course we must stay."

His gaze softened. "None will harm ye. Not with me here."

The buxom barmaid brought their drink, bending low in front of Owein. It seemed to Clara she took far longer to deliver his mug than was necessary. Owein's gaze lingered on the girl's generous globes. When he pressed the last of Clara's coins into her palm, he was rewarded with a wide smile.

Clara scowled and looked down into her wine. Owein tipped his mug to his lips. Clara took a sip from her cup, then immediately regretted it. The wine was little better than vinegar.

"Not fine enough for ye, lass?"

She forced another gulp. "It will do."

He regarded her in silence for a moment, then hailed the barmaid. She appeared at his side within a heartbeat. "Two more mugs of *cervesia,*" he said, offering up his empty cup.

"As you wish, sir," the girl purred. She brushed her breasts against his upper arm as she turned away.

"Perhaps we should take two rooms for the night," Clara said darkly.

Owein lifted a brow. "Why would that be?"

"So you can be alone with that . . . that whore."

He grinned and tapped Clara's satchel. "The coin is

gone. Do ye think she'd accept one of your necklaces as payment?"

Clara's retort was interrupted by the girl's return. Two new mugs, two bowls of stew, and a generous hunk of bread appeared before them. The barmaid lingered, her hand on Owein's arm.

"My *wife* and I thank ye," Owein said with a meaningful glance at Clara.

The girl's gaze flicked to Clara's face, then her bosom. With a huff and a roll of her eyes, she flounced off. Owein chuckled. Clara didn't know whether to be amused or outraged.

The tavern might be plebian and the wine sour, but the fare the girl had brought looked edible enough—in fact, it looked far more palatable than the pock-faced man's meal. The stew was thick with beef and the bread recently baked. Perhaps the extra coin Owein had pressed on the barmaid had not been money ill spent.

She broke off a piece of bread and fished a large chunk of meat from the bowl. Owein made short work of his own portion. He ate with a deftness of movement, his head down, but even so, Clara could tell he kept watch on the room. Whatever curiosity their presence had attracted had waned, however. Only the pock-faced man seemed to pay them any attention.

"We'll retire soon," Owein said after a time.

To one bed, Clara thought abruptly. She watched as Owein signaled the barmaid for yet another mug of *cervesia*. Was that his fourth? His fifth?

"Do you mean to render yourself insensible?"

Owein snorted. "Have ye nay seen a man take refreshment?"

"My father drank sparingly. He—" She broke off as Owein's face contorted. His skin had gone suddenly pallid. "Owein, what is it?"

He lowered his head and pinched the bridge of his nose.

"Owein," she repeated urgently.

He looked up. His left eye was unfocused, wandering to the left while his right eye stared straight ahead. A vein pulsed in his temple, bulging blue against the fairness of his skin. She grasped his arm across the table and felt a spark of energy. *Oh gods.* Not a vision. Not here, in this crowded room.

"Owein. Can you hear me?"

His hand tightened on his mug. The clay cracked and collapsed inward, spilling dark liquid across scarred wood. The pock-faced man looked toward them, his eyes narrowing.

Clara leaned across the table, her voice lowering to a desperate whisper. "Owein. What should I do?"

"A vision approaches." He shook himself. "I canna be inside these walls when it comes."

Dread squeezed Clara's throat. "Then we shall leave." She started to stand.

"Aye." Owein planted his palms on the table and heaved his large frame upright. For a moment he remained motionless, staring straight ahead.

Clara hurried around the table and tugged on his arm. "The door is this way."

He wouldn't be moved. He stood, eyes fixed on some scene only he could see. Curious glances darted his way. Clara pulled on his arm with all her might. "Owein—"

He threw back his head.

"Blood!" he shouted.

All conversation died. Heads turned.

"Blood shall flow! Roman blood!"

Clara yanked desperately. "Owein! Be silent."

He shook her off. "The winds of power rise."

Muttering erupted from all corners of the room.

"Madman . . ." "Witless lout . . ." "Get the bastard out of here."

Owein's body jerked, as if some unseen force had punched him full in the gut. He staggered backward, slamming into the table behind him.

"By Pollux!" A Roman with a wild dark beard leaped to

his feet and shoved Owein backward. "Keep back, you barbarian swine."

Owein turned a baleful eye on him. "Beware, Roman. Your days on the isle of the Celts are dwindling. By the stones and the sky, I vow it will be so!"

Clara grabbed a fistful of his cloak. "Owein. We must leave this place. Now." But he would not be dislodged, no matter how hard she tried.

"Drunken idiot," someone muttered.

The pock-faced man rose to his feet. "No." His voice rang through the room. "Not an idiot. A Druid."

A deadly silence fell. Owein pivoted slowly, his arm outstretched. "Aye. I am Druid. Did ye think us gone? I tell ye, we are not. We will rise again."

The dark-bearded Roman touched the hilt of his sword. "Only to fall harder than before."

Owein fixed a hard stare on the man. Dancing light from the tapers glinted on his red hair. His lips parted.

A single rasping syllable emerged from his throat.

All at once, every flame in the tavern flickered. *By Owein's command?* Clara wondered wildly.

"The Druid casts a curse!" a man shouted. The buxom barmaid screamed. Terror rippled through the room. For a moment, time hung suspended.

The reprieve would not last. They had to get out.

The door was not far and no one had yet thought to block it. Clara angled her shoulder into Owein's side, trying to shove him toward the exit. She might have more readily moved a mountain.

The bearded Roman stepped forward. "Celt scum. I'd wager Commander Gracchus would like to admire you in chains." He spat at Owein's feet. "Perhaps I'll make him a present of you."

The pock-faced man shifted uneasily. "Have a care," he muttered. "A Druid curse can wither a man's cock."

Owein's gaze focused on the Roman, his expression one of pure disgust. "Roman dog."

He advanced a step. Benches scraped on the stone floor. Men shifted away, apparently unwilling to come to the aid of their rash comrade. But the bearded Roman stood his ground.

Owein stared at the man, unblinking. "Ye will die within a year," he pronounced. "Drowned in the sea."

The bearded man drew his sword and angled the tip at Owein's belly. "Then I'll be safe enough killing you now."

Clara screamed as the Roman lunged.

The sound seemed to pierce Owein's trance. In a single motion, he shoved Clara aside and spun in the opposite direction. The Roman's blade thudded harmlessly into the table between them.

Clara recovered, gaining her feet. "The door's behind you. We must get out, quickly." Owein's pack and cloak remained under the table, but there was little she could do about that. She only prayed he stayed lucid long enough for them to make their escape.

It was not to be. The Roman surged, blocking the path to the door. His blade flashed.

A bloom of red appeared on the sleeve of Owein's linen shirt. He stared at it, his eyes once again losing focus.

"Blood," he whispered.

"Watch out!" Clara cried.

The Roman thrust. Owein sprang away, his dagger appearing in his hand. He dropped to a crouch, his body coiled like a warrior-god of legend. His fierce blue eyes never wavered from his opponent, but Clara sensed he wasn't free of his trance. The otherworld lingered—helping or hindering, she couldn't tell.

His brows drew together tightly and the muscles in his neck bulged like cords of iron. His breath came hard. It was clear he was in pain, and not only from his wounded arm. She remembered how weak he'd been each time a vision faded. How long before he faltered?

The battle shifted, placing the door to the yard at Owein's back. If he could manage to strike a quelling blow, they might be able to make a run for the gates. But it wouldn't be an easy task. Clara eased close to the fight, crouching low. Her own dagger was strapped to her calf. She'd endured Owein's instruction, but did she have the stomach to use a blade in a real fight?

Easing up her tunic's hem, she groped for the weapon. Her hood slipped from her shoulders. An instant later, her head jerked backward, her neck wrenching painfully. The pock-faced man! He'd grabbed hold of her braid and was using it as a tether. Clara's fingers skittered over the dagger's hilt as he gave a savage jerk. She ended flat on her back, gasping for air.

His grotesque visage leered down at her. His scabbed lips parted, revealing a rotten, gap-toothed grin.

"Yer man's havin' some trouble, lassie." His rough words slurred together. "Best come with me."

"No." Clara struck out blindly, her fist connecting with his shoulder.

The weak blow seemed to boost his spirits. "So ye like it rough, aye? Well, dinna fear." He jerked her braid, snapping her chin to her chest. "I prefer a feisty wench."

He yanked Clara to her feet. From the corner of her eye she saw Owein and his opponent grappling for the single sword. The Roman threw Owein off.

The pock-faced man snapped the braid down, forcing Clara's gaze toward the ground. "Better than a lead on a dog," he chuckled. Wrapping the length of hair firmly around his fist, he started for an empty corner of the room.

"No!" choked Clara. She tried to twist away, but the movement only afforded the man an opportunity to shorten her tether.

"Ah, come on, lassie, what's the fuss? Ye've taken one Celt sword between yer legs. What's another?"

Clara stumbled, bent nearly double. Frantically, she groped for her dagger. All her strength was nothing against this man. Could she fend him off? Or would an attack only enrage him?

As the dagger slipped from its sheath, a desperate idea sparked. With a quick motion she slashed not her attacker, but her plait, severing it cleanly.

Deprived of the tether's leverage, her captor stumbled, cursing. He recovered quickly from his surprise, however, lunging at Clara and catching her cloak before she could scramble away.

"Bitch," he spat. "Ye willna best me."

Clara slashed at him with her knife, using the underhanded motion that Owein had taught her. It was for naught. Her attacker's hand clamped like a manacle on her wrist. His grip tightened painfully, grinding muscle and bone. Her hand spasmed and the dagger loosened from her fingers.

Anger surged. She would *not* be taken by a lout who dumped his seed beneath a tavern table! Swiftly, she caught the dagger in her left hand. With a deft motion born of Owein's relentless coaching, she dipped her shoulders and let her weight drop. The pock-faced man stumbled.

She thrust the blade upward, directly into his groin.

Her attacker let loose a bloodcurdling shriek, his hands wrapped around the hilt of Clara's knife. The dagger looked like nothing so much as a blood-soaked phallus. Clara recoiled, her stomach heaving. The pock-faced man crumpled to the ground.

She wanted to fall to her knees and retch—and perhaps she would, later. At that moment, an instinct for survival she hadn't known she possessed kept her on her feet. They had to escape.

She whirled about. Owein and the Roman were grappling hand to hand, both weapons lost. Onlookers shouted jeers and encouragement. Owein's arm dripped blood and his gaze was unfocused. Did he even see his opponent? Or did he struggle with some creature from the otherworld of his gods?

He battled like a man possessed, but Clara could feel his strain. Taking advantage of his weakness, she slipped into his mind. Could their union help her to urge him from the tavern?

She eased along the perimeter of the room, inching toward the door. The portal was blocked by the rotund form of the innkeeper. He had sword in hand, but made no move to enter the fray. His bulk quivered as he shouted encouragement to Owein's opponent.

The gate key jiggled at his belt. Clara drew up short. Without the key, there would be no escape. Hardly daring to breathe, she approached. The innkeeper was so intent on the fight that he took no notice of Clara's trembling fingers. She unhooked the key from his belt. Gripping it like a weapon, she pressed her spine against the wall.

Closing her eyes briefly, she concentrated on strengthening her mental connection with Owein. The hot flames of his rage seared her. She struggled to remain calm in the face of his darkness. Instinctively she soothed him, letting the light and coolness of her own spirit flow toward his.

She felt his awareness first, followed swiftly by surprise, then anger. His mind recoiled, trying to wrest free of her invasion.

She held firm. They'd shared a thought before. If she sent him a suggestion now, would he heed it? She could but try.

Owein. Move toward the door.

To her surprise, he shifted immediately, pivoting to afford himself a view of both his opponent and the door. Had she compelled him with magic? Or had his trance made him biddable, like a person walking in sleep?

The innkeeper was their first hurdle to freedom. Hiding the gate key under her cloak, Clara drew herself up to her full height. "You will stand aside and let us pass." Her tone was that of a patrician lady to a slave.

He grunted. "Why should I?

"Surely you don't wish a Druid curse upon your head?"

"Curse?" He snorted. "Mumbled nonsense, more like." But he didn't look so certain. "I'm of a mind to keep your husband. There's a fine reward for delivering a brigand to the fortress."

"You'll be lucky to escape with your life if you try to hold him. Didn't you see the tapers flicker at his command?"

The innkeeper's gaze darted to Owein. "A coincidence. I'd just opened the door. A gust must have entered."

"Are you sure? Because it seems quite a chance to take with your life. If I told you some of the things I've seen him do . . ." She shuddered. "You'd not be so glib."

She sent a thought toward Owein. *The tapers. Make them flicker.*

She felt a Word in her mind, and a stabbing pain at the base of her neck.

The flames surged, then died, plunging the room into darkness.

"By Pollux!" The innkeeper's voice nearly failed him.

Clara felt his bulk shift, freeing the door. An instant later, Owein was at her side. Clara lifted the latch and wrenched the door open. Owein thrust her before him into the yard.

The world was a blurring swirl of white.

"Go, lass."

Owein's hand closed on Clara's upper arm. Her shoulder was nearly ripped from its socket as he dragged her across the yard toward the gate. The snow had fallen thickly while they'd been in the *mansio.* It rose in white waves to cling to her tunic.

With shaking hands, Clara fitted the key in the gate. She could hear shouts from the doorway—would any be so bold as to follow? The iron bars creaked open. Owein slammed it behind him and started for the road.

"Wait," she said.

"Lass—" She could feel his desperation, his fear that his legs wouldn't hold him upright much longer. His vision had passed and the strength was seeping from his bones. Her stomach rolled and her hands trembled. The magic was affecting her, too, though not, it seemed, so much as he.

"I'll not have any of them following us." She inserted the

key in the lock and turned it. Only then did she allow Owein to drag her across the road and into the shelter of the trees.

He managed only a few steps before pitching headfirst to the ground. His fatigue lapped like an ebbing tide at Clara's spirit.

He struggled to support himself on one arm. "Do they follow?"

She peered through the trees. "No. At least, I think not."

"Good." He sank into the snow, his breathing labored. Instinctively, Clara reached for him with her mind, wanting to give him her strength.

He mustered enough will to block her.

"No," she said. "Please—"

"I'll not be led about like a dog."

"Did . . . did I do that?"

He gave her a level look. "Aye."

"I . . . I wasn't sure."

"Ye gave your word ye would keep out of my mind."

"You needed me. If not for my aid, you'd still be in that tavern, trying to best a sword with a dagger."

"I dinna need your help," he muttered. Leaning heavily against a stout tree, he heaved himself to his feet. His legs protested his weight. They buckled, sending him back to his knees in the snow.

"It would seem you do need my help," she said quietly.

"I need but time."

A shout came from the direction of the inn. "Time is something we don't have," Clara said tersely. Crouching at his side, she draped his arm over his shoulders. "Can you stand if I take some of your weight?"

He hesitated. "Aye, I think so."

They made their way farther into the forest, sloughing through drifts of powdery snow that hid dangerous patches of ice. They fell twice, and each time it was harder than the last to regain their footing. At least the storm was lifting, Clara thought. The snow came more sparsely, lit by the light of a hazy moon. The wind gusted, sending a wild froth of snow careening into her face. Overhead, the black limbs of the trees groaned.

"We need shelter," she said, more to herself than to Owein. Indeed, she wondered if he could even hear her. He'd sunk back into his trance. His erratic gait caused her to misstep more than once, and his shallow breathing told her the pain hadn't abated.

Their forward progress was slow. Toward what? Clara couldn't guess, but Owein, in his otherworldly state, seemed to have a purpose. Did a second vision guide him?

She concentrated on putting one foot in front of the other, scanning the darkness for any formation that might provide shelter. But they'd left the high country behind; in this wood she could see no cave, no fortuitous overhang of rock. Only black trees, white snow, and the otherworldly glimmer of moonlight.

They stumbled along. Gradually, Clara became aware that the trees seemed to have pulled back from their path, and the ground was no longer uneven under her feet. They followed a narrow road—perhaps an unpaved cart path.

She looked up at Owein. His expression seemed more purposeful—or was the dim light playing tricks on her eyes? "Are you guiding us somewhere?" she asked cautiously.

He leaned heavily on her shoulders, his breath harsh. "I . . . I think so."

"You're not sure?"

He didn't answer. Tentatively, she extended her mind to him, only to feel his instant recoil. "Do not, lass."

"Let me," she murmured. "Please. Let me give you some of my strength."

"It willna come without cost to yourself."

"I know," she said. "I don't care. You cannot go on much farther alone."

He drew a breath. An instant later, she felt his mind open. His surrender, though she'd urged it, terrified her. He must truly be weak to accept her aid.

Icy fingers crept along her spine. Owein was so hale, so

vibrant. His spirit shone like a living flame. But when the visions came upon him, that light dimmed to ashes.

It was her fault he suffered. She'd come begging at his door, ignorant of the terrible favor she asked. She wondered that he'd agreed to help her at all, despite Aiden's entreaty. For he'd surely known the cost.

She slipped into his mind, wanting nothing but to give him the strength he'd expended on her behalf. She felt a rush of elation when he didn't resist her touch. This time, she held herself loosely on the surface of his spirit, avoiding the darkened corners that held memories and feelings she knew he didn't wish to share.

The task didn't come easily. Owein's darkness beckoned. She wanted to submerge herself within it. Burn it away with her Light.

His pain pounded as a dull ache behind her eyes. Nausea surged. Her head felt as though the top of her skull had been lifted into the air. But Owein's steps grew surer, his breathing less labored.

The moon emerged from the clouds at full light, sharpening the shadows, just as the wood gave way to a bluff overlooking the sea. A small building was visible, nestled at the treeline. Clara blinked, not quite willing to believe it was real.

It was an old army watch station. "Did you know this was here?" Clara asked.

"Nay. Kernunnos led me to this place. The Horned God takes care of his own." He let out a breath. "When it suits his purposes."

"Your god is a hard master," Clara murmured, turning her attention to the structure. A single story, squat, square, and unimaginative, constructed of stone. The door was damaged and a corner of the slate roof was missing.

Clara peered into the dim interior. A stone ledge built into one wall would have accommodated two narrow bunks. A table and two chairs, mostly undamaged, stood in a corner, with a hand lamp atop. But the most welcome sight was the iron brazier and the pile of charcoal and tinder, with a weathered flint box nearby.

"This is wonderful," Clara murmured.

"Your lofty Roman standards have fallen mightily, lass."

The faint humor in Owein's tone made her smile. "I suppose they have."

He slumped heavily against the door frame. Alarmed, Clara reached for him with her mind, only to have her overture firmly rebuked. "I failed ye in that tavern," he said bluntly. "And now . . . 'tis a poor protector who canna even keep his feet."

"You led us to this haven."

He slipped the strap of her satchel over his head and nodded at the flint box. "Will ye make a fire? I fear I haven't the strength."

Clara lit the hand lamp first, then knelt and heaped charcoal in the brazier. The tinder sparked, and the coals settled into a glow. She extended her hands over the warmth. Owein sank to the floor, his back propped against the wall. A frown creased his forehead.

Clara eyed the blood on his shirt. "Your wound—is it deep?"

He pulled back the torn cloth and inspected it. "Nay."

Clara bit her lip. "Eirwen's handiwork is ruined."

He was silent for a moment, then he sighed. "All things pass."

She could think of no reply. They sat for a time, not speaking, while the warmth of the brazier filled the room.

Finally, Owein gave a soft chuckle. "Ye used my lessons to good advantage in the tavern."

"You saw? I thought the trance had blinded you."

"Nay entirely. I saw the bastard take ye, and I saw your escape. Ye fought like a Celt lass."

Clara smiled. "I'll take that as a compliment."

" 'Twas meant as one."

"I'm not sure I deserve praise. I had little choice—I only did what I had to."

"That's called courage, lass."

Their eyes locked and held. It was true—she'd fought well, and survived. That alone brought satisfaction, but Owein's honest regard? It kindled a flame in her chest.

His gaze flicked over her. "Your hair . . ."

Clara's hand flew to her head. "Oh, no! I'd forgotten." She squeezed her eyes shut. "Do I look horrid?"

He laughed softly. "Ye could never look horrid."

"It was that man sitting next to us, the one who . . ." She swallowed. "He dragged me away. I had to do something."

"No doubt he regrets crossing ye. If he lives."

Clara inhaled sharply. "You think I killed him?"

"Ye might have."

The thought sickened her. Her face must have shown her distress, because Owein's voice turned soothing. "Ye did what ye had to, no more. And proud I am that ye did, for if ye had not we would be dead." He chuckled. "For a Roman merchant's daughter, ye have a fine hand with a blade."

Clara stared into her lap. She was no merchant's daughter, but a soldier's. Once they reached her father's villa, Owein would discover the deception. She should confess now. She opened her mouth, but the words stuck in her throat.

After a moment, she dared a glance at Owein. With a shiver of dread, she saw that his eyes had once again lost their focus. A third vision? But he was already so weak.

She moved to crouch beside him. "Owein? Can you hear me?"

He gave no response. He lifted his wounded arm and stared, unblinking, at the crimson stain on the white fabric.

"Blood," he whispered. "Why must I always see blood?"

He was barely breathing. Clara grasped his chin and urged him to look at her. "Owein."

His gaze skimmed past her and settled on a point beyond her right shoulder. His eyes were so intent that Clara turned and looked behind her. But there was nothing.

The breath left his lungs in a rush. He slumped sideways onto the floor and lay still.

Heart in her throat, Clara closed her hand on his fore-arm. Despite the room's warmth, his skin was cold as death.

Was this the payment the Horned God demanded?

Chapter Fourteen

The fog cleared slowly. When the last of the mist was gone, Owein found himself once again in the cozy roundhouse, gazing down on the pallet where his children lay.

A deep peace spread through him as he watched the innocents slumber. How long had it been since he'd felt such contentment? Not since he'd been a small lad, snuggled against his sister's side.

He turned. In the darkest part of the room lay another pallet he hadn't noticed before. He moved toward it, suddenly aware of the scent of lovemaking.

He approached the bed, his eyes fixed on the pale curve of a bare shoulder. A long skein of silver-blond hair veiled the curve of a creamy white breast.

Was this his future wife? The woman fated to be his destiny?

He stood and looked down at her, his emotions reeling. The woman stirred, rolling onto her back. Her countenance was fair. She had the look of a woman who had just been well loved. Her lips were red and pouting, her breasts full and round.

Her gray eyes fluttered open and her mouth curved. He felt as though he'd received a secret gift.

Lifting one hand, she reached for him. "Owein," she murmured. "Come to me. I await ye in Avalon."

"Owein?"

A woman's voice came from afar. The scent of springtime drifted with it. Both seemed familiar, but he couldn't remember why.

Hands grasped his shoulders. "Answer me!"

He tried to reply, but no words emerged. He floated in a warm pool of darkness, like a mother's womb.The warmth grew hotter and the current rougher, until he boiled in a cauldron.

The voice was fainter now. He could no longer make out the unknown woman's words. He drifted away, far away, into the darkness.

And then he felt her.

She was inside him, all around him. She was cool, like a night's breeze after a hot summer's day. She was mist in the valley, the dampness of the earth, the blessed rain that fell from the sky.

She knew him.

"Owein," she whispered urgently.

He frowned.

Emotion choked her voice. "I'm . . . I'm here. Come back to me."

He struggled to find her, fighting against the dark current of the spirit world. Three visions he'd had. After such a trial, could his soul ever return to his body?

It was Clara who found him, Clara who pulled him back. She was before him, showing the way. Beside him, lending her strength. Behind him, blocking the darkness with her Light.

She was in his arms.

Slowly, he began to understand his surroundings. The army watch station. He lay on his back, with Clara draped across him. Her rose petal sent surrounded him. Her forehead was pressed into the hollow of his neck. He felt moisture there, as if she were washing him clean with her tears.

He shifted, bringing her fully atop him, so the length of her body pressed against the length of his. His arms were so weak he could barely move her slight weight. She wriggled, helping him. His cock hardened against the cradle of her thighs.

She nuzzled his neck, planted a light trail of kisses along his jaw. It felt odd, feeling a woman's kiss against his shaved chin. She kissed his neck, and lower. The ties of his shirt came undone. Her lips pressed against his breastbone.

He groaned. She lifted her head and caught the sound with her mouth. She kissed him, deeply, snaking her tongue between his lips, threading her fingers through his hair.

"Lass . . ."

"Shh."

She kissed a path across his cheek. Her tongue grazed his ear, traveled down his neck to his shoulder. There was a scar there, a round depression where the metal tip of a flagellum had gouged his skin. She explored the mark with the tip of her tongue.

A bolt of shame shot through him. He inhaled sharply, his arms tightening around her. He wanted to throw her off, but he was too weak. His hand settled on her shorn head, his fingers spearing the short strands.

"Leave me, lass."

"My name is Clara. *Clara,* do you hear? And I will not leave you. You *need* me." She left the scar to kiss his chest.

He anchored her hips with his hands. Her *bare* hips. Like a man caught in a dream, he opened his eyes. Clara straddled him, her tunic unbelted and hiked to her waist. Deliberately, she caught his gaze. With excruciating slowness she lifted the garment over her head.

She was naked atop him. He could only stare. In the soft glow of the coals, she was more than beautiful. Her supple waist, her pink-tipped breasts, her dark, exotic eyes—aye, even her shorn hair. She was a goddess of the night—a moon spirit, perhaps—casting her Light upon him. It almost hurt to look at her.

Her fingers found the laces of his *braccas*. His blood surged hotly. Her palm closed on his flesh. He shuddered as a brutal stab of lust speared his gut. "What of your honor?" he gasped.

"I wish to give it to you."

"Your Roman father willna be pleased."

"I . . . I don't care about that. I love you, Owein. I want you to be my first lover."

Her expression was sober, her eyes soft and glittering with tears. The glow from the brazier danced over her face in shifting patterns. She slipped within his mind, but stayed hovering on the surface, far from the darkest parts of his soul. The sensation was almost bearable.

She smiled down at him. "You told me a Celt woman may choose her lover."

She kissed her way across his chest, laving first one flat nipple, then the other. Her mind undulated within his. If he hadn't been so weak from his visions, he might have stopped her. At least that was what he told himself.

His body tensed as she shifted backward. Her palm pressed the tip of his arousal. It surged into her hand. She tested his length with a virgin's touch, pressing far too lightly.

Every drop of resistance bled from Owein's mind. He felt himself sliding toward an unknown place. His grasp on her hips tightened. He wanted her desperately, but she was a virgin. He had to be sure she understood the risk.

"Clara," he said deliberately. Her name felt soft on his tongue. "Look at me."

She raised her head, her eyes wide and shining with sudden tears.

His breath came thickly. "If we do this, I might get ye with a child I couldna claim. What would ye do then?"

She stilled, and for one sickening instant Owein feared

she'd regained her senses. Then he felt her love blossom in his mind.

"I would hope he has your eyes," she said. "Your eyes, and your hair."

And Owein knew he was lost.

When she bent her head to his lips again, he didn't fight. How could he? She'd conquered him, broken through his resistance. When she offered her sweet mouth, he plundered it, taking every comfort she wished to give. When she arched her hips, he gripped her tightly, rocking her woman's center against his rigid shaft.

He skimmed his hands over her stomach, her waist, her breasts. Her skin was as soft as new petals. He drank in her dark eyes. She was so fine, so perfectly formed. She was delicacy and strength. Looking upon her filled his heart near to bursting.

Her fingers struggled with his shirt. "I want this off."

He managed to lift his torso enough so she could work the garments from his body. The sleeve of the linen shirt was sticky with blood—it tore away from his wound.

Clara gave a cry of dismay. "You're bleeding again."

" 'Tis nothing, lass."

"It's not noth—"

He rubbed a thumb across her nipple, distracting her. The ruse worked. Her breath hitched, and the words died on her lips. His hand skated down her torso, coming to rest on her hip. Her skin was perfect. So unlike his own scarred and mangled flesh.

He slid his fingers between her thighs.

She froze, her grip on his arm tightening painfully. He didn't care. She was slick with wanting him, and the knowledge caused his chest to expand. He teased her folds and felt her desire coil. The musk of her arousal mingled with her springtime scent.

He brushed his thumb across the swollen nub hidden in her curls. A tremor shot through her.

"Owein—"

She fit so easily in his embrace, as if she'd been fashioned just for him. His hands went to her hair, lifting and separating the shorn ends. He touched her cheeks, traced the line of her brows. "Ye are a beauty. But 'tis your strength that makes me want ye so."

She shook her head, but the hint of a smile curved her lips and her eyes sparkled with pleasure. Her hand sought his shaft. With a gentle touch, she guided him to the entrance of her body, only to pause, one hand braced on his chest. Her smile faded.

"Will it hurt?"

"The pain will pass quickly."

She bit her lower lip and nodded. Closing her eyes, she levered herself up and once again guided his shaft to her opening. Her touch was so light and hesitant Owein was sure he'd go mad before he could slide inside her. With an effort, he lay still.

She sank down on his shaft slowly. He flexed his hips, easing past her slick folds. When he encountered her maidenhead, he paused. He'd never had a virgin—he had no idea how best to proceed. Gently? Or would a hard thrust make the discomfort pass more quickly? He scanned her face, searching for a clue.

Her eyes were closed, her lips pressed firmly together. "That feels . . . strange."

"Strange," he muttered. Leaning forward, he caught the pebbled tip of her breast with his mouth. He suckled it, drawing a gasp of pleasure. At that same moment, he drew her hips down sharply, impaling her on his shaft.

She gave a strangled cry and instinctively tried to withdraw.

"Shh . . ." He clutched her to him, cradling the back of her head. "Stay still a moment, lass."

He felt her tears. "Clara," she muttered into his neck.

A rumble of laughter vibrated in his chest. "Clara," he agreed, smoothing her hair from her face. "Does it still hurt?"

"Not so much now."

He flexed his hips, stroking her intimately. "And this?"

She let out a moan. "By all the gods on Olympus, Owein! That feels . . ." He moved again and her words were lost in a moan.

His hands roamed her body, touching her breasts, sweeping over her waist, cupping her hips and arse. She was so delicate, so slight. And yet there was a vein of iron in her.

And magic. She was strong in the Light. He felt it flowing atop the surface of his mind. A wave of desire broke—a need for a deeper joining. But was the thought his own, or Clara's? He couldn't be sure. A frown creased his forehead as he remembered how she'd compelled him to leave the *mansio.* He'd been caught in a trance, bound like a slave, as he'd been all those years ago.

There had been no hope of escape . . .

Ropes burned his wrists.

Owein strained, twisting with savage strength. Pain shot up his arms, causing his shoulders to spasm. His ankles were lashed to the wooden frame as well, his legs splayed wide.

The slave master approached slowly. He snapped the wooden handle of the flagellum against the palm of his opposite hand, allowing Owein plenty of time to contemplate his fate. A slow, painful death, ordered to appease a woman's pride.

The rhythm of the flagellum commanded Owein's complete attention. The thongs swung in the sunlight, the sharpened bits of iron imbedded in the leather glinting. Cold sweat gathered on Owein's brow.

Thirty-nine lashes. Each would send dozens of jagged blades into his flesh.

A small crowd had gathered—mostly ragged, dirty slaves who kept their eyes cast downward. They'd been ordered to witness Owein's fate, but wouldn't take pleasure in it.

Aurelia would, though. She was there, in the front of the gathering, clinging to her husband's arm.

Owein captured her gaze. His hatred caused her smug expression to falter.

But only for an instant. She smiled again when the first blow fell.

Clara's breath hitched. Her voice vibrated with urgency. "Owein . . . where are you? What do you see? I can't—"

With a start, Owein came back to himself. Clara was sprawled atop him, her eyes shadowed with his memories. Her small hands gripped his shoulders with surprising strength. Belatedly, he realized he'd withdrawn almost completely from her body.

His lungs sucked air. Deliberately, he banished the memory of his flogging to the darkest recesses of his mind. He relaxed his arms, guiding Clara as she slid back down his shaft. Gathering her close, he eased her onto her back.

He rose above her. He could be that much a man, at least.

"Clara . . ." Her name was a prayer on his lips. He moved inside her, going deeper with each thrust. He would make her forget his lapse. Forget what she'd glimpsed of his shame.

If only he could forget as well.

She clutched his arms, her fingernails digging into his skin. This time, it was pleasure, not terror that gripped her. He could feel her inside his mind, battering the edges of his control.

His strokes quickened as he struggled to shore up his defenses. Her peak was near and his was not far behind. He dropped his head into the hollow of her shoulder, shuddering as the beginnings of his climax claimed him.

His fingers threaded her hair. He kissed her, taking her lips with bruising urgency. Her slender legs wrapped his hips. Her breath came in short gasps, her hands moving over him with frantic passion. Her touch was a cool, soothing brand on his hot skin.

She spoke in his mind. *Please, Owein, let me in. Let me share your darkness.*

Ah, lass . . .

Part of him wanted to push her away—another part, to accept her gift and lose himself within her Light forever. Helplessly, he thrust deeper as his peak came upon him. Her woman's passage clenched him like a hot fist. Stars exploded behind his eyes and his consciousness slipped.

He was inside her, and she within him.

Too close. He could not bear it.

He struggled to escape, even as the pleasure exploded.

Chapter Fifteen

If not for the soreness between her thighs, Clara might have thought she'd dreamed Owein's lovemaking. Half-dazed, she snuggled with her back to his chest. His lips brushed against her hair; his temple braid fell across her cheek in a soft caress. The weight of his muscular arm across her midsection felt pleasantly heavy. The coals in the brazier had gone dark, but she wasn't cold in the least. Sometime in the night she had pulled her cloak over the two of them.

So this was what it felt like to be loved by a man. She'd never dreamed it could be such bliss. Her body tingled with the memory of his hands, his mouth, his urgency. She could hear echoes of Owein's whispers—especially the sound of her name on his lips.

Her conscience was curiously silent. She'd given what her father had guarded so vigilantly—her virginity—to a wild barbarian. The thought should have appalled her. But it did not.

She eased onto her back. It was full daylight outside the watch station—hazy shafts of light pierced the gaps in the roof tiles, casting bright patches of sunlight on the floor and wall. For a moment, she wished the day away. But no—they were but a day's travel from her father's villa. She prayed the grail was there, as Owein had seen in his vision. She had to carry it to Father before it was too late.

She sat up, a sudden sick feeling in her stomach. The magic of the grail frightened her, but she would give anything to have her father well again. She loved him so. If he died, what would become of her?

If she refused to marry Valgus, he could use his guardianship to force her to marry him. Now that she knew what lovemaking could be, how could she bear that?

Her only hope lay in Father's recovery. Once he was well, she would appeal to his reason. Explain why she couldn't marry Valgus. Surely, she could make him understand that being a Senator's wife wasn't worth her happiness.

The warmth of the night deserted her. Troubled, she eased from Owein's side, and let her cloak fall from her shoulders. Groping for her tunic, she pulled it on quickly. Where were her girdle and sleeve pins? There. She fastened the pins and buckles with shaky fingers, then slid her feet into her boots.

The door groaned on its pegs when she opened it. Wrapping her cloak tightly about her, she stepped out into the daylight, blinking at the dazzle of the sunlight on the sea.

It took her a moment to realize she was not alone. A strange boy stood nearby, hands on his hips, watching her. Her eyes narrowed. Not a boy—a man. A man whose head was no higher than her breasts.

He had a grotesque melon of a head, accented by a bulbous nose. His torso was heavily muscled and nearly the proportion of a normal man's, but his legs and arms were thick and stumpy. He wore a mail shirt, a *gladius,* and a Legionary battle dagger, but no one could mistake him for a Roman soldier. His blond mustache and beard, shot with gray, were braided in the same primitive style Owein's had been.

Behind her, she heard Owein expel a mutter of astonishment. She turned slightly to look at him, while keeping the newcomer within her sight. Owein stood in the doorway to the watch station, dressed only in his *braccas.* With a start, Clara realized he was unarmed. As was she. Both their daggers had been lost in the fight at the *mansio.*

But while Owein was clearly amazed at the sight of the newcomer, he didn't seem concerned for their safety.

"Cormac," he said, shaking his head.

Clara started. Owein knew this gnome?

The little man inclined his head. "Well met, lad."

Owein snorted. "I canna imagine why I am surprised to meet ye here. Ye've ever had a talent for turning up in unexpected places."

The dwarf hooked his thumbs in his belt. "I thought ye dead." His eyes were bright. Clara realized with a start that they were wet with tears.

Owein looked very much like he wanted to embrace the small man, if he could figure a way to do it without dropping to his knees. Apparently he could not, for he made do with a nod. A succession of emotions, not all pleasant, flitted across his face.

"I'm very much alive, as ye can see."

Cormac's gaze darted to Clara, then back to Owein. He grinned, showing a row of crooked teeth. " 'Tis seven years since I last laid eyes on ye, Owein, but I'd nay have guessed ye'd change so much as to be plowing a Roman field. Ah, well. I suppose a woman's willingness overcomes her bloodline."

"Ye'd best watch your words," Owein cautioned.

Cormac shook his head. "Alive. By the Horned God, I'm glad to find it true. I looked for ye, ye know, after the battle."

The muscles in Owein's neck tensed. "I saw ye fall."

Cormac scoffed. "No Roman can keep me down. I gained my feet in time to retreat." His rough voice turned hoarse. "Ye were taken?"

Owein crossed his arms over his chest. "Aye."

"But escaped as well, I wager."

"After a time." A muscle ticked in Owein's jaw. "How long have ye been on my trail?"

"Since first light. Ye know how to unsettle a fine tavern, lad, that much I can say for ye. I arrived past midnight to find the place in an uproar. A man dead, even. When I got the full tale from the innkeeper, I knew the flame-headed Druid they spoke of had to be ye."

Owein cursed. "Are ye sure none followed ye?"

"Are ye daft? Ye frightened the stones from between their legs. They call ye demon, ye ken? Ye spurt fire from yer mouth and sever a man's cock with a lift of a finger. None of those cowards would seek ye out. Still," he added thoughtfully, "I wouldna pass that way again if I were ye."

"I dinna intend to," Owein muttered.

"Wait," Clara said suddenly. Both men looked toward her. She fixed her gaze on Cormac.

"You said you thought Owein was dead. Why would you suspect he was the Druid from the tavern?"

Cormac shifted. "Ah, well, perhaps I heard tell not so long ago that my kinsman was alive. That he was the holy man of the mountains whispered about in the alleys of Isca." He eyed Clara boldly. "Perhaps I even heard tell that the daughter of Sempronius Gracchus himself had run into the hills, seeking his aid."

Clara's lungs seized.

Owein's head whipped around. "Daughter of—" He stared. "Ye told me your father was a merchant."

Cormac snorted. "A merchant? A fine jest, that. Nay, this lass is Gracchus's daughter. I've seen her often enough in the market in Isca."

"I . . . I never saw you," Clara managed. She was all too aware of Owein's eyes upon her. Her knees went weak. She put a hand on the hut's stone wall, steadying herself.

Cormac gave her a gap-toothed grin. "Ah, well, when ye spy for a living, ye learn to be overlooked."

"Is it true?" Owein asked quietly. "Are ye Sempronius Gracchus's daughter?"

"I am." Clara raised her chin and braced herself for Owein's wrath. He said nothing. She shifted on her feet, wishing he would shout. Even if he were to blast her from here to Isca with his anger, it would be better than enduring his cold, unfeeling gaze.

"Might I ask, Owein," Cormac said mildly, "where ye are going with Gracchus's daughter?"

"I'm taking her home."

Cormac stroked his forefinger over his mustache. "Well, that's a fine thing, lad. Perhaps while yer in the city, ye might visit Rhiannon. Your sister's settled nearby, ye ken, with Lucius Aquila and his son."

Clara's head jerked up. The Celt healer was Owein's sister? No wonder he'd reacted to her name.

Owein regarded Cormac impassively. "I canna believe Lucius Aquila welcomes ye in his house. Ye tried very hard to kill him."

Cormac looked discomfited. "I'd nay be so foolish as to stand on that man's threshold. He's a hard one and his blacksmith son is no coward, either. I confine myself to greeting Rhiannon in the forum market. I canna say she is overjoyed to see me, but she's nay adverse to giving me food or coin. We are kin, after all."

"Of course," Owein said dryly.

"Ye should go to her, lad. She'd be glad to see ye alive. She's still your kin, for all she's given herself to a Roman."

Owein's gaze shuttered. "Nay. My sister has chosen a new life. 'Tis better if it doesn't include me."

Owein couldn't help flinching when Clara laid her hand on his shoulder. He only just managed to stop himself from flinging her away.

Cormac had faded into the forest to scout a trail to the city. Perhaps Owein should have taken on the task himself, to avoid being alone with Sempronius Gracchus's daughter. His anger was white hot, searing a hole in his chest.

"Dinna touch me, lass."

Clara snatched her hand away. "I want to explain."

"Ye needn't bother. Ye played me for a fool. A fine joke it was, too."

"No. It wasn't like that. I—" She reached for him again, but stopped just short of contact. Fear showed in her eyes. That was good, Owein told himself. Very good.

Then why did it rip at his soul?

He paced a few steps away. "Why did ye lie?"

"I should think the answer to that question is clear enough."

"I had the right to know the truth. I'm sure Aiden would nay have instructed ye to keep such a thing from me."

"No," she said hesitantly. "He urged me to tell all of it. But I was frightened. I knew full well Father's order had destroyed your village. Would you have promised to help me find my mother's cup if I'd told you why I wanted it?"

"Ye saw my village. Your father is a murderer."

"There was to be no bloodshed!"

"Blood soaked the ground," Owein spat out. "Innocent blood. 'Twas still wet when I arrived."

"What of the innocent Roman blood shed by Celt brigands?" Clara asked quietly. "A woman and her three daughters, used and murdered on the road from Isca to Maia. A merchant cart ambushed. Four young masonry apprentices hacked to pieces. The governor's own niece violated. Do you deny your clan gave aid to the savages who committed these crimes?"

Owein held himself very still. "If a kinsman came seeking food or care, we didna turn him away."

"What I told you before was true. The order to clear the hills came from the governor in Londinium. It was Father's hope that the brigands would be identified and punished. The other Celts were to be brought unharmed to Isca."

"To be sold as slaves."

"No. To live as freemen. As long as they surrendered peaceably."

Owein made a disbelieving sound in his throat. "What man comes along peaceably when his wife is snatched from his pallet in the dead of night? When his son is murdered and his daughter defiled before his eyes?"

"That cannot have been by my father's order."

"A commander is responsible for his men. I know the truth of what passed that night. I came too late, but not all were dead."

"The resettlement was supposed to be peaceful," Clara said quietly. "My father . . . he wasn't there. He couldn't have known."

Owein forced himself to unclench his fists. "He should have."

Tears swam in her dark eyes. "I am sorry."

The despair of that terrible day lodged like a stone in his chest. He'd gone to the circle of the Old Ones, seeking wisdom for the clan. When he returned, he found the village ravaged. But whether or not Gracchus sanctioned the attack, Owein knew Clara could hardly be held to blame. And yet the darkest corners of his soul could not absolve her completely. She was Roman. Perhaps that was all he needed to know.

Clara's voice intruded. "Why didn't you tell me Lucius Aquila's wife is your sister?"

Rhiannon. Did she think of him still? Or had her Roman stepson blotted Owein from his sister's memory?

"You should go home to her," Clara said softly.

"Nay."

"Why not? Rhiannon is the most loving person I've ever met. I know she would welcome you."

"I tried to kill her husband, lass."

"You are not seeking to kill him now," Clara pointed out. "And Lucius Aquila is not a vengeful man. Surely you can come to some understanding for Rhiannon's sake."

He shook his head. "The past canna be forgotten. Nor should it be."

"So," Cormac said. "Is it true Roman virgins beg to suckle barbarian cocks?"

Clara froze behind a screen of pines. She'd left Owein and Cormac, retreating into a copse to tend to her private needs. She returned to find them discussing her.

"I'm surprised ye dinna know the answer to that already," Owein replied. "Ye never used to have trouble luring women into your bed."

Cormac bristled. "I still don't, lad. But Roman virgins . . ." He shook his head. "They are locked up tighter than a Legionary pay vault." His voice grew throaty. "Gracchus's daughter—did she fall easily? Does she take ye in her mouth?"

"I willna answer that," Owein said.

Clara expelled the air that had stalled in her lungs.

Cormac laughed. "Ye were always a quiet one. Always gallant with the lasses."

They sat a moment in silence. Clara was about to make her presence known when Owein spoke. "Tribune Aurelius Valgus," he said slowly. "What can ye tell me of him?"

"Valgus? He's one of those patrician sons sent from Rome to peer over the shoulders of the true soldiers. Vain. Pompous. Frequents the baths and the barbershops. Enjoys whores, but often doesn't pay. His gambling debts are steep and his Senator father hasn't the coin to save him. Why do ye ask?"

"Gracchus has promised his daughter to Valgus as wife."

"Truly? I didna know. But aye, it makes sense. Gracchus is rich, but his bloodlines are mixed. It's no secret he'd like to buy his way into an influential patrician family." He laughed. "I hope Valgus doesna mind used goods."

"Have a care, man," Owein warned.

Cormac chuckled. "Ah, Owein, 'tis good to know ye are alive. I should have known sooner. By the gods, why did ye remain alone in the hills after Gracchus's purge? Ye should have come to the towns. If ye had, Rhys might have found ye."

"Rhys? Who is that?"

"The Bard of Avalon."

"Avalon? The Druid isle? But it was lost. Destroyed by the Romans years before my birth. The Holy Ones were slaughtered."

"Not all. Some fled to practice the ways of the Old Ones in secret. Cyric is descended from their line. Nine years ago, he gathered what was left of his family and returned to the sacred isle. Rhys is his grandson. The lad roams Britannia, gathering Celts touched by the Deep Magic. If they are willing, he brings them to Avalon. They are a clan of sorts—more than twenty souls, all Druids."

"I canna believe the Romans leave them in peace."

"The Romans dinna know of them. Cyric has cloaked Avalon with spells of protection."

"This Cyric is powerful?" Owein asked. "Does he wield the Deep Magic?"

"Nay. He considers the power of the gods too dangerous for mortals. He calls only the Light."

"Will it be enough to keep the Romans away, I wonder?"

"I dinna know," Cormac replied. "But I know there is a way to ensure Avalon's safety. The Lost Grail, smithed in Avalon and stolen during the Roman invasion, holds the power to safeguard the sacred isle." He paused. "I know ye seek the grail with Gracchus's daughter."

Owein made a sound of disbelief. "And how do ye know that?"

" 'Tis my trade to know," Cormac said modestly.

"The cup I seek was in Roman hands for many years. It might very well have been taken as spoils during the invasion of the west country." Owein exhaled. "It belongs in Druid hands. And that is where it soon will be."

Clara sucked in a breath. Was Owein's promise to her a

sham? Had he planned all along to steal the grail rather than allow her to take it to her father?

When Owein spoke again, his voice was hesitant. "Is there a young Druidess living on Avalon? A woman of rare beauty, with hair like a skein of shining silver?"

His words were like ice-tipped arrows flung into Clara's heart. A woman? What was this?

Cormac's reply was hoarse. "She's shown herself to ye already?"

"She exists?" Owein asked sharply.

"Aye," Cormac said in a choked voice. "Hers is a rare talent, far beyond the rest of the clan. With the Lost Grail in her hands, she would be more powerful still."

"She's the one who called the storms," Owein stated.

"She fears Cyric's Light willna be protection enough to shield Avalon. The Romans are scouting the Mendips, probing old silver mines. Should they move farther west, it will be hard to keep the sacred isle hidden."

"An awesome power indeed would be needed to counter the Second Legion."

Cormac swallowed. "With the Lost Grail in her hands, she will not fail. I am certain of it. Her magic is that strong."

"Then the Lost Grail shall be hers."

Chapter Sixteen

There was no doubt in Owein's mind: the Lost Grail belonged in Druid hands. Why then, did his guilt rise every time he looked at Clara?

She met his gaze boldly. He saw betrayal in her eyes, as if she'd guessed his scheme to return the grail to his people. Of course, he'd meant to take the grail after she'd used it to cure her father. Her *merchant* father, Owein thought savagely.

If anyone had a right to feel betrayed, it was he. Clara had fed him an outright lie. He'd lain with Sempronius Gracchus's daughter! He still couldn't force the notion into his mind.

They skirted the main road as they neared Isca, keeping to a sheltered foot trail. As the wilderness gave way to farms, Cormac forged ahead, saying he wanted to scout the outskirts of the city. Once he was gone, Clara turned to Owein, her eyes cold.

It occurred to him that he'd never seen her truly angry.

"You had no intention of helping me cure my father," she said tersely. "You meant to steal my mother's cup from the start."

"Aye," said Owein. "I meant to have the grail, but only after ye'd used it to heal your father. The father you claimed was a merchant."

"And now that you know the truth, you withdraw even that small bit of decency! You want my mother's cup for another woman. Some silver-haired Druidess."

Owein felt as if he'd been punched in the chest. "How do ye know that? Did ye use magic—"

"No magic," Clara said bitterly. "I heard you and Cormac plotting." Her eyes filled with tears. "I understand that you hate my father, but to condemn him to death so easily? How could you? You know how much I love him."

"The grail belongs to my people." Owein felt like the worst of beasts as he said it.

"You may have it. Just let me have it for Father first."

Owein's jaw set. "And where is his sickbed, lass? In the fortress?"

She wouldn't meet his gaze. "Yes."

"I canna follow you there."

"I'll bring the cup to you, once Father is well."

"Ye have no reason to keep your word," Owein said, his voice tight. "Once you disappear inside the fortress walls, ye'll be beyond my reach."

She laid a hand on his arm. "Please, Owein. I give you my word. Trust me in this."

His gaze locked with hers. When her tears began to fall, he knew he couldn't deny her request.

He nodded. "I'll speak to Cormac. We'll set a place and a time when ye'll bring the grail to us."

Her dark eyes lit with gratitude. Owein wondered that she didn't curse him again. He didn't deserve her thanks. But when Cormac returned from his scouting mission to Isca, he brought news that made Clara and Owein's bargain moot.

"Sempronius Gracchus is dead," the dwarf announced. "The city is abuzz with the news."

"No." Clara gasped her denial, her body flinching as if

from a blow. Without thinking, Owein put out a hand to steady her.

"When?" he asked Cormac.

The dwarf spat into a pile of dirty snow. "This morning."

"No," Clara repeated, her voice a whisper.

Her grief tore at Owein's conscience, even though he knew his decision to steal the grail had come too late to make a difference in Gracchus's decline. But he'd made the choice thinking Gracchus was still alive. The raw grief in Clara's voice only increased his guilt. No matter what kind of man Gracchus had been, no matter that his order had resulted in the death of Owein's adopted clan, one thing was clear—the Roman must have harbored a great love for his daughter, if she grieved his passing so keenly.

"Are . . . are you sure?" Clara asked in a small voice. "Perhaps there's been some mistake."

"No mistake, lass," Cormac said, not unkindly.

"I must go to him," she said, clutching her satchel to her stomach like a shield. "It was my task to close his eyes and place Charon's coin in his mouth. Who did those things in my stead?"

Her shoulders shook with silent tears. Against his better judgment, Owein pulled her close. He couldn't stop himself from smoothing his hand down her back.

She stiffened in his arms. "Don't pretend to regret my father's death. You wished for it often enough."

She disentangled herself from his embrace and paced a few steps away, still clutching her small satchel. A surge of protectiveness washed over Owein. Clara was alone now save for the man Gracchus had named as her husband and guardian. Valgus.

Owein could not allow that Roman dog to have her.

There had to be some way Owein could ensure Clara's happiness. He could never claim her, of course. His destiny lay with his own people, with the Druidess of his dreams.

The thought brought no joy. When he thought of love, he thought only of Clara. Clara, moving beneath him, gasping as she reached her peak. Clara speaking words of love. And yet, she was not his future, and he was not hers. How, then, was he to keep her safe?

The germ of an idea formed. He might leave Clara with Rhiannon. Thirteen years ago, Lucius Aquila had been a formidable army commander. Surely he was still man enough to protect Clara from Valgus. And Lucius's son, Marcus, had already offered her marriage. Owein knew little of Roman law, but surely, if Clara were to marry the blacksmith she would be beyond Valgus's reach.

He turned to Cormac. "Where is Tribune Valgus now? In the fortress?"

Cormac rocked back on his heels. "Nay, it seems he is not. He left some days ago. If any knows his whereabouts, I couldna discern it. Besides Gracchus's death, the only other news about town is talk of tomorrow's slave auction. The arena is bustling and traders are thick in the streets." He scratched his beard. "A fine diversion for our mission. With all the countryside crowded into the city, we'll be able to snatch the grail and flee."

" 'Tis a good plan." Owein's gaze strayed to Clara. With her father dead, she had no need of the grail. "I'll leave it to ye to carry the Lost Grail to Avalon," he told Cormac in a low voice.

Cormac's grizzled brows lifted. "And what of ye, lad?"

"I'll follow when I can. There's something I must do first."

Clara's father had envisioned an expansive estate. A high wall enclosed a sprawling two-story main house whose twin wings enclosed what was destined to be a formal garden. Several outbuildings had been planned—pig and sheep barns, a toolshed, a workhouse for curing leather and other such tasks. The foundations of these buildings were laid, but the walls remained unfinished.

The stable, however—an expansive structure built into the perimeter wall near the front gate—was complete. Clara's father, who had come up through the equestrian ranks, thought to breed horses on his retirement. Clara's eyes burned at the realization that he would never have that chance.

She couldn't imagine a world without her father in it. He might have been a hard man, but he'd never treated her with anything but love. If that love had blinded him to her strengths, she couldn't fault him. She clutched her satchel, wishing she could reach inside for her rose oil. But the vial was empty.

Owein would take the grail. Clara wasn't sure she cared. She'd always feared the cup's power, and in any case, she knew now that the grail belonged to his people. After he was gone, she would return to the fortress to meet her fate. She would refuse to wed Valgus, even petition the governor if necessary. Of course, Valgus had the power to make her life miserable, but she would deal with that. Perhaps, if she agreed never to marry at all, leaving him in control of her property, they could reach an understanding.

Cormac's arrival interrupted her dark musings. The dwarf had gone to scout the villa gates. "Valgus is in residence," he said. "The guard at the gates told me." He grinned. "He met with an unfortunate accident afterwards."

Clara swallowed a cry.

"He sent ye this gift," Cormac continued, handing the dead man's war belt to Owein. It held both sword and battle dagger.

"My thanks to him," Owein said, reaching for the weapons.

"Valgus has more men inside," Cormac continued. "But nay so many. Three, according to the poor bastard of a sentinel. And a cook as well. A guest is expected this night. A slave trader from town. Apparently, Valgus is heavily in debt to the man."

"Then we've come just in time," Owein said. "We'd best be in and out quickly." He turned to Clara. "Ye'll stay here, outside the gates." He shifted, peering intently at the villa, which was just visible over the top of the perimeter wall. "Describe the layout to me. Where is the room I seek?"

Clara obliged. Owein received the information with a nod. "Cormac and I will complete the task swiftly. Afterwards, ye'll go to the Aquila farm."

She couldn't hide her astonishment. "The Aquila farm? Then you've changed your mind about seeing your sister?"

The muscles in Owein's neck bunched. "Nay. I'll not be accompanying ye. Cormac will guide ye to the Aquilas, so ye may marry Lucius Aquila's son. If Rhiannon has had a hand in his upbringing, he is sure to be a fine man."

"Marry Marcus?" Clara shook her head. The notion seemed bizarre. "But . . . even if I wanted to—even if *Marcus* wanted to—Valgus would have to approve the match. He would never do it! By the terms of my father's will, my property goes to my husband when I marry. That's why Valgus is so eager to have me for himself."

"He'll nay get the chance, lass."

She eyed him. "What do you mean?"

"Ye will not have to go to him. Valgus will be dead before the night is out. I will make sure of that."

She stared at him, aghast. "You would commit murder for my sake?"

A muscle ticked in Owein's jaw. "By Cormac's report, 'tis no more than Valgus deserves. Once ye are free of him, ye may marry as ye will."

"No. I won't ever marry. Not after . . ." She looked away.

He lifted her chin with his knuckle, forcing her to meet his gaze. His eyes were blue and clear. "Ye *will* marry, lass. Ye will have a fine life."

"But—"

He touched her cheek. "Wait here for Cormac. When he arrives, make haste to my sister's home. Tell her . . ." He exhaled. "Tell her I am well, and that I hold her memory in my heart always."

And with that, he was gone.

* * *

The dead guard's sword was light in Owein's hand. He made his way through the deserted yard, skirting haphazard piles of bricks and tiles. Cormac followed on stealthy footsteps.

Full night had fallen. Lights streamed from the torches near the main entrance. The unfinished wings lay in darkness. Owein made for the farthest end of the north wing, where the windows hadn't yet received their grillwork.

"Stay here and keep watch," he told Cormac. "Give an owl's cry if anyone approaches."

The dwarf nodded once. Owein put his hand on the window's frame and lifted himself over the sill. It was a tight fit, and his sword belt clattered against the frame. Cormac uttered a soft oath as Owein dropped to the tiled floor in a crouch, listening.

All was silent. Carefully, he made his way down the passage, passing from chamber to chamber until he reached the main part of the house. Here, large rooms gave onto the long, columned hall. The floor was mosaic, the columns polished, and the walls painted with graceful figures that seemed real enough to step from the plaster. The windows fronting the courtyard glowed in the light of the flickering torches.

According to Clara's instruction, the receiving chamber bearing the war mural was off onto this passage. Voices drifted from the end of the hall, where a shaft of light spilled from an open door onto the hall's mosaic floor. Owein paused before a nearer door, which latched from the outside. He lifted the bar and swiftly stepped inside.

The room was empty.

Owein stared. Though the light was dim, there was no question in his mind that this was the chamber he sought. The war mural wrapped three sides of the room in grisly glory, just as his vision had shown. Even the artist's paints and brushes lay strewn about exactly as they'd been in his vision. The only thing missing was the sack of stolen treasure.

Had his vision been false? Or had Valgus moved the stolen loot in anticipation of the trader's arrival? Inhaling deeply, Owein closed his eyes and sent his mind searching.

The familiar ache sprung up behind his eyes.

He let his spirit roam free of his body, floating in a still world between sleep and waking. Muted pain beat at the edges of his mind, but he ignored it the best he could. With luck, the Horned God's price would be paid after Valgus was dead.

Dipping deeper into his trance, he moved back into the passageway, aware of his surroundings in a way that a waking man was not. Every noise was amplified, every movement clear.

He sensed each of the villa's inhabitants. Four men occupied a single chamber near the entry foyer. A woman shuffled about, muttering, a bit farther off, where Owein guessed the kitchen might be. And the Lost Grail . . .

He blinked through the pain in his head. An image of the grail rose clearly in his mind. The cup sat on a table in a dining chamber. On the couch behind it reclined a young, arrogantly handsome man with dark eyes and a clean-shaven chin. His lips moved, addressing his companion to the right, another Roman, but Owein couldn't make out his words. Two burly soldiers stood by the door.

The grail's power drew him. Stealthily, Owein moved toward the chamber occupied by Valgus and his guest, though he had no clear idea how he would liberate the grail from the dining table.

He paused before the door just as an owl's cry drifted from the courtyard.

An instant later, Clara entered his mind.

Owein and Cormac had barely disappeared through the gate when Clara heard hoofbeats, and the creak of a cart on the road.

She shrank into the shadows as the vehicle passed her hiding place, drawing her cloak about her shoulders and shivering from the cold. The cart had high sides and a top constructed of crossed saplings securely bound at the joints.

It was a slaver's cart, designed to transport human cargo. Two men rode the seatboard, one leaning back, the other handling the reins. Each wore a sword and dagger.

Dread burned Clara's gut. Owein would never have time to remove the grail from the villa before the slavers gained the gate. There were soldiers in the compound with Valgus—she was sure of it. Owein planned to kill Valgus, but it was likely he'd have to kill his guard first. And now, with the arrival of two more armed men, his task had just gotten more difficult.

She had to warn him.

Warily, she inched forward as the cart creaked to a halt. The driver gave a shout. When no answer came, he leaped to the ground. When he put a hand on the bars, the gate swung slowly inward.

"Bugger it all, Calidius," the man called to his companion. "No one's about." He strode through the gate. After a short interval he reappeared, swearing softly. "Valgus hasn't even left a stable hand to tend our horses."

Calidius's displeasure was evident. "I only hope he has the gold he owes me," he said as he swung down from the cart. His accent was far more refined than the first man's. "I've lost patience with his evasions."

"At least with Gracchus dead, his future losses shouldn't cause a problem," the other man remarked. He ambled to the horses and led them into the yard. "I hope he's brought Gracchus's cook. And a decent wine. We could be dining in the city rather than at this out-of-the-way hole."

"The tribune doesn't dare risk being seen in our company," Calidius informed him with an unpleasant laught. "Ah, well, I'll be sure to extract an extra *aureus* or two for our inconvenience."

The pair disappeared through the gate. The driver

stayed back with the horses, muttering under his breath as he bungled around in the stables. Calidius adjusted his sword belt and strode toward the villa's front door.

Clara stared after him, her heart pounding. She crept forward, keeping well within the dark shadow cast by the wall. As she slipped inside the gate, she reached out with her mind for Owein.

An owl gave a call.

In the next moment she found Owein. She was surprised to realize he was in a trance. With his concentration consumed by magic, it was an easy task to slip inside his mind.

His reaction was that of a sprinter catching his foot in a rut—a mental stumble, followed by a curse. His hot anger flooded her mind.

Get out.

He punctuated the command with a blast of magic. Their union was abruptly severed, leaving her gasping for air. She tried to enter again, but succeeded only in brushing the outer surface of his defenses. Try as she might, she couldn't go within.

But she had to warn him. She crept through the gate, her heart pounding. Where was he? She searched the gloom, but saw nothing.

A hint of movement at the edge of the unfinished north wing caught her eye. Cormac. Keeping to the shadow cast by the perimeter wall, she made her way toward the dwarf. He would need to know about the man Calidius had left in the stables.

As she scurried across the yard, the villa's front door opened. Valgus appeared, silhouetted by lamplight. Clara froze.

"Ho, Calidius, welcome." It seemed to Clara that Valgus's amity was forced.

"Valgus," Calidius said dryly. "If I were you, I would not leave my gate ajar to any stranger who takes a notion to visit."

Valgus frowned. "What do you mean, the gate was ajar? Where's my man?"

"Polishing his rod in the bushes, no doubt."

Valgus half turned in the doorway and shouted into the house. "Pullus! Get out here!"

A soldier appeared in the doorway. Valgus barked an order. The man gave a nod and left the building, heading toward the gate. Clara shrank farther into the shadow of the wall, hastening toward the place where she thought she'd seen Cormac.

There was no one there.

"By the Horned God's cock, where are ye, lad?"

Cormac's muttering came as if from far away, piercing the fog-world of Owein's vision. Owein ignored it, intent on his task.

Existing within both the dream world and the waking one was difficult, like viewing two scenes at once. He was aware of his body crouching in a darkened alcove off the main passageway. His spirit-mind was across the foyer, viewing the scene in the dining chamber. With Valgus and one of his guards gone to answer the front door, only the second guard remained.

The Lost Grail shone in the center of the table.

Go to the door, Owein urged the soldier. He spoke a Word of encouragement.

The man straightened and looked around, startled. When he saw nothing out of the ordinary, he shrugged and resumed his post. But a moment later, he frowned. Turning, he strode out the door.

Owein watched him join the others in the vestibule. Silently, his body moved to the dining chamber, rejoining his spirit mind.

The grail was more dazzling, more beautiful than he had imagined. For a full three heartbeats, he stared at it, almost afraid to extend his hand. Then a noise in the foyer roused him. Grasping the cup's base, he poured the wine it held into another vessel.

His arm tingled as he tucked the grail under his elbow. The magic tugged at his strength, causing him to stumble. Quickly, he righted himself and eased back into the hall.

He found Cormac at the near end of the unfinished north wing. The dwarf's avid gaze was fixed on the grail. "Ye've got it," he breathed.

The fog in Owein's head thinned. A dull ache sprang up behind his right eye. The grail was heavy in his arm, far beyond its true weight. "I told ye to remain in the yard."

"Ye took so long I feared ye'd been seen."

"Nay. Only delayed."

"Well, Valgus's guests have arrived," Cormac grunted, his eyes still riveted on the grail. He extended a hand. "Here. I'll carry it."

Owein hesitated, then nodded. The cup's magic drained his strength and worsened the ache in his head. And he had yet to confront Valgus.

"Take it," he said, "and dinna wait for me."

Cormac's hands closed on the grail. A shudder passed through him. "I'll carry it to her," he whispered. "Have no fear of that." He shoved the cup into his pack.

A guard appeared at the far end of the passageway, near the front entrance, where Valgus stood with the slaver and the second soldier.

"What is it, man?" the tribune demanded.

"Silus is dead, sir. His throat has been slit."

"By Pollux!" Valgus strode toward the door. The others followed.

Cormac tugged on his arm. "This way, lad. We'll go out the back. With any luck, there'll be a rear gate."

The dwarf led the way to a door at the back of the house. It gave onto a wide terrace. Owein stepped into the night air, his spirit-mind aware of angry voices in the front yard. Cormac paused. Owein extended his senses, searching for a rear gate.

He found Clara instead. Her worry batted like bird's wings at the edge of his mind. She feared for him. She wanted him to give up his plan to kill Valgus and flee.

It was an odd sensation, having someone frightened on his behalf.

Thank the Great Mother Owein didn't have to fear for her. Clara was safe outside the villa walls.

Chapter Seventeen

It was only by the purest of luck the soldiers didn't see her. When the pair rushed from the house, Clara was standing in the open, unprotected, with not so much as a stack of bricks to hide behind. Instinctively, she dropped into a crouch, hoping the night would be concealment enough. The nearest soldier scanned the yard, his gaze skimming past her.

Clara let out a sigh. She watched as the soldier turned his back on her and followed his companion to the gate. Seizing the opportunity, she darted for the unfinished north wing.

She pressed against the wall, her heart pounding. At the far end of the building, just around the corner, a brick stair led to a rear terrace. A door was there. Should she seek Owein inside the house? Or had he already found the grail and exited?

She approached the end of the wing and eased around the corner. A blur rushed at her, knocking her to the ground. Panic clogged her lungs. She balled her fist and struck out, blindly.

Her fist connected with flesh. A low voice uttered a curse. She punched again. Her knuckles collided with a nose.

Another curse. An iron grip closed on her wrist. "Will ye cease, lass?"

"Owein?"

His arm came around her, pulling her to her feet. "Aye, 'tis me." His tone was angry. "Can ye nay obey a simple order? I told ye to wait outside the gate."

"The slavers came." She looked up at him. "I tried to warn you through our connection, but you blocked me out."

Cormac's harsh whisper intruded. "Silence."

There was a shout from the front of the house. A dull clang, then muffled conversation.

"They've closed the front gate," Cormac muttered.

"Is there a back way out?" Owein asked Clara. His breath was labored, and his voice had a faraway quality. "A wooden gate, about half again the height of a man?"

Clara blinked. "Yes. Yes, there is. But most likely it will be locked."

"Show us. Lead the way. Quickly, now."

"All right." Stepping away from the house, Clara crossed the terrace and led the way down the steps."It's in the far corner of the new orchard." She shifted direction, cutting in a diagonal across the downward slope of the hill. Newly planted saplings were interspersed with a few old, grizzled trees.

Bare branches showed black against a charcoal sky. Clara slipped on a rut filled with ice, wrenching her ankle. Pain darted up her leg. She shoved herself back to her feet and pressed on.

The gate indeed was locked, but Owein didn't try to break through. "I'll not risk Valgus and the others hearing," he muttered. "Ye'll go over."

He bent, his hands closing about Clara's thighs, lifting her. The next instant her feet found purchase on his shoulder and she realized the top of the gate was within reach. She scrabbled to catch hold of it, but when she tried to heave herself upward, her arms wouldn't lift her weight.

"I can't—"

"Ye must," Owein muttered, grasping her ankles and lifting her higher. The top of the gate hit her midsection; she grabbed the stone wall to steady herself.

"Jump over, lass."

She peered at the ground on the other side of the gate. "Oh gods," she gasped. "It's too far."

Cormac, aided by Owein, scrabbled up beside her. "By the Horned God, woman, will ye cease whining and move? Ye'll be the death of us."

"It's nay so far," Owein said. "Swing over and drop your feet first."

The sound of the search drew closer. Owein's head swiveled toward it. "Go, lass. Now."

She positioned her body as Owein had instructed. Cormac gave her shoulders a shove.

"Oof—" She landed feet first, her legs crumpling beneath her. Her knees hit the snow hard, and for a moment Clara just sat, stunned. There was a thud and a spray of snow as Cormac landed beside her, his pack and sword flung to one side. The dwarf sprang up easily, righting his possessions and swatting the snow from his *braccas*.

Clara struggled to her feet. A heartbeat passed, then two, then the impact of what Owein had done hit her. "There's no way for him to get over. Not unless he breaks the lock."

"That he willna do," Cormac said. " 'Twould only draw the search to an open gate. He means to give us time to get away."

Clara stared at him. "But he'll be killed!"

Cormac looked down at his boots. "He's a Druid, lass, and a warrior besides. Dinna be so quick to dismiss him."

"He means to fight five men," Clara said furiously. "You should have stayed behind to help."

"Are ye daft? 'Twould be suicide."

She glowered at him. "Some fine kinsman you are."

"Ungrateful woman," Cormac muttered. Grasping her arm just above the elbow, he towed her away from the gate. "Owein's fighting for your freedom. Do ye mean for his efforts to be wasted? They will be if Valgus finds ye here on the road. Get going."

Clara tried to throw the dwarf off, but his grip was like iron. He hauled her, struggling, across the fields, bent on putting as much distance behind them as possible.

Not knowing what else to do, Clara closed her eyes and let her mind fly back to Owein. The trance still gripped him. It was a simple thing to slip past his defenses and into his mind.

Raw anger and rage boiled there. She heard the clang of iron on iron, felt pain erupt as a blow fell. Her stomach lurched, bile scouring her throat. The hatred that flowed through Owein's veins seeped into her mind, nearly suffocating her. He'd killed one guard and was bent on destroying another.

The man fell. Clara heard his scream. She felt Owein shift to face a third opponent.

The man lunged. Pain sliced through her. Her stomach dropped in a free fall. The ground rose up to meet her. No, that wasn't true, she was still on her feet, aware of Cormac dragging her across the snowy field. It was Owein's pain she felt; Owein's defeat. His trance was fading, yielding to the weakness that invariably followed a vision. He rolled to one side as his opponent closed in.

He would be killed. She couldn't allow it! She loved him too much to bear the thought he should be killed defending her.

Summoning all her strength, Clara offered it to him.

Owein blocked the flow of her power. *Nay. Get out.*

No. Let me help you!

He tried to cast her out. She resisted. She felt him fall, felt a heavy boot connect with his ribs. She could barely breathe, his pain was so great.

She expected a killing blow. It didn't come. Instead, she felt rough ropes bind Owein's upper arms behind his back. Next his ankles were bound and secured to the ropes on his arms. He lay with his face pressed into the cold mud, trussed like a pig, shame burning his mind.

"He's a brawny barbarian. A common brigand," she heard Valgus say, through Owein's senses. *"Fine for the arena. What will you give me for him?"*

"You want me to pay?" the man called Calidius replied, his tone incredulous. *"It was my man who brought him down!"*

A boot connected with Owein's temple. The next instant, Clara was cast out of his mind so violently that stars exploded behind her eyes.

She came back to her surroundings slowly, as if emerging from a tomb. Somehow, she was still on her feet.

Cormac's rough voice was in her ear. "This is where I leave ye. The Aquila farm is straight ahead."

Clara gripped his arm. "Owein isn't dead. I think . . . he's been taken by the slaver. We must go back—"

"Nay. I've done as much as Owein asked. Now, I . . . I've no choice but to go to *her.*" A grimace of pain crossed his face, and his breath came hard. "I have what she wants, ye see. I canna . . . resist . . . her call."

"Who?" asked Clara wildly. "What . . ." Her gaze snapped to his pack. A tingling awareness came over her. "The Lost Grail," she said quietly. "Then you did find it."

"Aye." He faded into the trees.

"No!" Clara cried. "Come back. I—"

But he was gone.

He'd been taken.

Again.

Owein breathed shallowly, lest his nostrils fill with mud. He lay with his face to the ground, his spine forced into an unnatural arch by his bonds. The slaver's man had tied him with savage pleasure, no doubt eager to exact revenge for the nick Owein's blade had dealt to his hip. Owein regretted he hadn't run the man through.

Clara's presence in his mind had distracted him. He'd stumbled, missing his mark. Then the fog of his trance had dissipated, bleeding the strength from his limbs. He'd had no chance after that.

Valgus went unharmed. Once again, Owein had failed, not even managing to end his own miserable life before falling to the enemy. He could not bear it. Not again.

He jerked against his bonds, but his efforts only drew a contemptuous laugh from the slaver's man. The trance had left him weak as a babe. A bellow of pure fury emerged from his lungs, but the cry did nothing but set Valgus chuckling.

Quick negotiations ensued. Dimly, Owein was aware that Valgus and the slaver—Calidius was his name—had reached an agreement. They would split the price Owein brought at the auction the next day.

A cart creaked past, one wheel coming within a handbreadth of Owein's head. Valgus laughed as a horse deposited a load of manure near Owein's chin.

A boot nudged his ribs, then kicked hard. Owein stifled a cry, rolling to one side. His shoulder sank into the pile of fetid muck the horse had left. Owein kept his breathing shallow, willing the contents of his stomach to stay out of his throat.

Calidius crouched beside him. Owein regarded his captor through slitted eyes. The man wore no beard and his clothing was fine. He gave a grunt of distaste as he grabbed a hank of Owein's hair. Unsheathing his dagger, he slid the point between Owein's lips, forcing his mouth open. Owein, helpless, could only glare.

"He's got all his teeth," Calidius said appraisingly. "He should bring a fair price. Perhaps as much as thirty *aurei.*"

"Good," Valgus grunted. "I'll have a man at the auction, watching. You'll be taking him now, I presume?"

"In a moment." Calidus bent over Owein, dagger in

hand. Grasping the end of Owein's temple braid, he jerked it taut. With a flick of his wrist, he severed it cleanly.

"Now he's ready," Calidius murmured, tossing the plait into the mud.

Marcus could not take his eyes from Clara Sempronia. He could hardly believe she was alive, let alone sitting on a bench in his home. Even bedraggled, with her hair shorn obscenely short, she was the most beautiful sight he'd ever seen.

He wanted to go to her. Comfort her. But he didn't. Even as he looked his fill, a single question turned round and round in his head.

Had she coupled with Rhiannon's Druid brother?

It certainly seemed that she might have. It had taken Rhiannon a full hour to calm Clara after she'd rung the gate bell. She'd fallen into the older woman's arms, sobbing out a story of Owein having been taken by slavers. She'd turned to Marcus, begging his help in freeing Rhiannon's brother.

Finally, she quieted. Breena stood at the cauldron, her young brow lined with worry as she prepared a calming draught of valerian and lavender. The strong scent of the herbs rose into the air, making Marcus's head swim.

Tears glistened on Clara's lashes. "Please, Marcus, you must rescue Owein. Tonight." Her voice was raw.

"Aye, Marcus, ye must." Rhiannon added her plea. "But ye canna think to fight Calidius. Take all the coin in the strongbox. Offer to buy Owein before tomorrow's auction."

"Aye," Aiden put in. "That would be the safest way to save the lad."

Marcus drew a deep breath and paced to the far end of the room. The tiles seemed unsteady under his feet. Thirteen years ago, in the north, he'd narrowly escaped a bloody fort attack only to be pitched into a far more horrible battle. Ignoring his father's order to hide, Marcus had crept to an eerie stone circle and huddled in the shadow of a towering oak while Owein, crazed with hatred and dark magic, had fought Lucius. Marcus's father had almost died that night.

Now Marcus was expected to save the Druid warrior who'd tried so hard to destroy his father? A Druid who, most probably, had taken the innocence of the woman Marcus loved? He stood very still, his body tight, his emotions churning in a dark, seething froth.

Rhiannon approached him with soft steps. He flinched when she laid a gentle hand on his shoulder.

"Please, Marcus. Do this for me. For the love I hold for ye."

Marcus didn't turn. "He nearly killed Father."

"True enough. But after, Owein came to realize how much I loved your father. He was the one who urged me to follow my heart and travel south with ye and Lucius." She moved in front of him, searching his face. "Please, Marcus. I beg ye."

Marcus's shoulders sagged. How could he refuse Rhiannon? She might not be his mother in truth, but her love and quiet strength had nurtured the man he was.

He covered her hand with his. "I will go. For you. But I warn you, we've not enough coin in the strongbox."

"I can help," Clara said. Shakily, she drew the strap of her satchel over her head.

Marcus took the bag, avoiding her gaze. His eyes widened when he saw its contents—not coin, but a tangle of gold and jewels, more than he'd ever seen in one place.

"Is it enough?" Clara asked anxiously.

"I should think so," Marcus said shortly. It was a small fortune.

He saddled his horse and set out for the Gracchus villa. A scant hour later, he returned home alone. Clara rushed to the door as he entered.

"I was too late," he told her. "The slavers have already taken him to the city."

Chapter Eighteen

Marcus was no stranger to the slave market. On the contrary, he was a regular customer. As a rule, his acquisitions were surly or terrified when purchased. Their emotions quickly shifted to disbelief, wariness, or gratitude when Marcus spoke the public words of manumission.

He wondered how Owein would react to freedom.

He approached the entrance to the pens, trying not to fidget with his toga. He hated the thing. A cold breeze whipped up his bare legs, making him wish for his *braccas*. But in the arena, he needed to stand with the other patricians. Looking the part aided his cause.

He'd never purchased a strong male in his prime; his family's precarious finances didn't permit such an extravagance. Even if they had, Marcus preferred to liberate the most desperate of the human chattel offered for sale. The women. The old. The babes.

With a regal nod, he slipped a copper *dupondius* to the slave guarding the carts. It was expected a serious buyer would want to inspect the day's offerings and take note of the lot in which certain slaves would be offered. Marcus would as soon have passed over this part of the proceedings. His stomach churned as he started down the first row of carts, searching for Owein.

The place stank. Some carts housed up to five or six unwashed bodies, huddled together in cold and despair on ill-smelling straw. Each cart contained two buckets, one for water, the other for sanitary needs. Often, it was impossible to distinguish between the two.

Misery permeated the air. Soft moans and loud sobs, the sniffling of the young ones and the prayers of the old. Almost all the captives were Celts. Some had been brought from the north, where the army skirmished along Hadrian's half-built Great Wall. Others had been caught in crime and sentenced to slavery. A few had sold themselves to satisfy their debts.

Striding ahead with grim purpose, Marcus located the aisle where the strong men were penned like beasts awaiting the games. He recognized his stepmother's brother immediately. The wild red-haired Celt was not the youth Marcus remembered, but his resemblance to Rhiannon was clear enough to Marcus's eye. He sprawled on the mucky floor of his cart, both arms raised, his wrists shackled to the sturdy oak bars over his head. His ankles were bound as well, to either side of the barred door. He wore only tattered, filthy *braccas.* Cuts and bruises covered his torso and face. One eyebrow was cut; blood dripped in a jagged line down the side of his face.

His eyes were closed, his breathing shallow. Marcus took advantage of the reprieve to note the lot number painted on a wooden sign leaning against the cart's wheel. Below the number was a description of the merchandise: *Male Celt. Outlaw. Free of disease. Strong back, good teeth.* There was more, but Marcus didn't have the stomach to read it.

"Owein."

The Druid opened his eyes but didn't otherwise move a muscle. The blue of his irises was intense, the exact color of

Breena's, Marcus realized with a start. But though Marcus and Breena had quarreled often enough, his sister's clear gaze had never held the pure hatred that Owein's did.

He resisted an urge to step back. He would not cower before this nightmare from his youth. He let a challenge show in his eyes.

Several heartbeats passed before recognition joined the animosity in Owein's expression. "Ye are Lucius Aquila's son," he said. His Latin was heavily accented.

"Yes." Though Marcus might have answered in Celtic, he did not.

"Ye have the look of him."

"I know." Stepping closer, Marcus catalogued Owein's injuries with the eye of a man whose stepmother was a healer. The Druid's limbs, at least, appeared to be sound. His cuts were superficial, though the one on his head had bled profusely. The faint imprint of a boot on his torso indicated bruised ribs at the least.

"Can you stand?" Marcus asked.

The question was met with a snort. "A fine joke, Roman."

"I mean, if your bonds were removed," Marcus snapped.

Owein regarded him steadily. "Why are ye here?"

"Surely you can guess. I am here at Rhiannon's request. And Clara's," he added after a pause.

An uncertain emotion flickered in Owein's eyes. "She is safe?"

"Yes. She waits with my stepmother and sister at the entrance to the arena."

Owein struggled, as if to rise, though such a gesture was futile. "What kind of man are ye to allow women near such a place?"

Marcus gave a snort. "Do you think I could have persuaded them to remain at the farm? They would have followed me even into the pens, if the guard had allowed it." He exhaled. "They'll not rest until I see you out of this place."

Owein's expression went blank. "Ye mean to buy me?"

"If your price isn't too high." It was a low blow, but Marcus found he couldn't resist delivering it.

Owein turned his head and spat. "Save your money, Roman. I'd sooner take a chance at the games than bow to ye as my master."

Marcus gritted his teeth. "I've no wish to be your master. Once I buy you, you'll be free."

Three men came to remove Owein from his cart.

He almost laughed at that. They treated him as if he were a bear, or a wildcat. They bound his arms behind him and stripped his *braccas* from his legs, leaving him naked in the chill air. They linked his ankles with a second rope.

When he moved forward, it was at a shuffle. One of the men picked up a placard leaning against the cart bearing Owein's description. A length of rope was attached; he looped it over Owein's head, positioning the sign on his chest.

Each slave for sale was similarly identified. The procession traversed the forum market and disappeared into the arena. Owein had been sold once before. But that had been in a small military camp, and the crowd had not been so large, nor so populated by enthusiastic civilians. Today Clara was in the throng. As were Rhiannon and her daughter. Owein tasted bile. Whatever he'd endured on that dark day long ago, this was far, far worse.

A man walked the row of slaves, flicking his whip, seemingly at random, clearly enjoying the encouraging shouts from the crowd. The lash fell across Owein's back. He arched in shock, but didn't cry out. He would not give his tormentor, nor the spectators, that satisfaction.

Fate drew him inexorably toward the arched portal leading to the arena. Clara was near. He could feel her as a soft flutter at the edges of his awareness. He doubted if she was conscious of him, for he'd locked the barrier of his mind against her as securely as the slaver's lackeys had bound his wrists and ankles. He would not allow her to enter his mind again.

The guard gave another flick of the whip. This time the lash caught Owein's hip. He sucked in a breath, stifling a cry.

At the entrance to the arena, the sign around his neck was replaced by a rope. The knot pulled tight as a handler jerked the leash. Owein recognized the man as Calidius's assistant, the one he'd tried to kill the night before. He held a slaver's flagellum, its multiple leather thongs knotted with sharp bits of metal. Owein stared at the instrument of torture, remembering. Sweat broke out on his brow.

Calidius's man hauled him toward the center of the arena, urging him forward with a lick of the lash. The crowd parted. Owein soon found himself shoved into a circle and prodded toward the stone block in the center. The patrons buzzed, crowding closer.

Calidius, flanked by a guard, stood at a podium nearby. The slave handler presented him with Owein's sign. Calidius made a show of perusing it.

"The next offering is a fine one," he pronounced.

"Looks like a wild beast!" cried a voice from the crowd.

"Look at that cock!" another said.

"He's so filthy, you can hardly see it!"

"Will you bathe him first, at least, Calidius?"

Though he knew it was fruitless, Owein struggled with his bonds, humiliation burning his throat. The bidders jeered, surging as close as the guards allowed. Those nearest were all men; behind, in the stands, the more idle spectators were of both sexes, though the women seemed only to be allowed in the higher levels.

For that, at least, Owein was thankful. The thought of Clara witnessing his shame at close quarters nauseated him. It was bad enough to know she was here, watching.

The whip licked between Owein's shoulder blades, forcing him to climb onto the auction stone. The tethers on his ankles made the maneuver difficult. He lifted his chin and fixed his gaze on the rim of blue sky that ringed the top level of the amphitheatre.

Calidius cleared his throat and read from the placard. "Lot fifty-four. Male Celt. Outlaw. Free of disease. Strong back, good teeth. Recommended for heavy labor or training in gladiatorial combat."

"But who will tame him for me?" someone called out. A laugh rippled through the crowd.

"A firm hand with the whip is all that's needed," Calidius professed. As if to punctuate this sentiment, his assistant applied the flagellum to Owein's shoulders. Owein hissed in pain. He lurched forward, nearly falling from the stone.

"See what I mean?" Calidius declared. "The bid opens at twelve gold *aurei.*"

"That's damn high," a portly man grumbled. Nevertheless, he raised his hand.

"Many thanks, Baldus. This one would be a fine addition to your gladiators, and would certainly draw a crowd to the arena. But what of the rest of you? I have twelve *aurei.* Do I hear fourteen?" A second bidder shouted his assent and the auction began in earnest, with several more men entering the fray.

None of them was Marcus Aquila.

Surely the blacksmith was present. Owein scanned the crowd, hating how his stomach soured at the thought that his enemy's son might have abandoned him. When he finally spied Marcus, standing within a knot of men on the far side of Calidius, his relief was acute. As was his shame.

Marcus was silent, seemingly intent on the bidding, though he made no offer himself. One by one, men dropped out, until only two bidders remained. The one called Baldus, who sought fodder for the games, and another, Flavius, a stout man with a booming voice. Marcus's brows drew together as they sparred, driving Owein's price higher.

Finally, Flavius shook his bald head. "Twenty-six gold *aurei!* Far too rich for my blood."

Calidius looked at Baldus. "Baldus holds at twenty-six, then. If there are no more—"

Marcus Aquila's voice rang out. "Twenty-seven."

Calidius turned in surprise. "Marcus Aquila? You wish to enter the bid at this late hour?"

Marcus inclined his head.

Baldus cursed. "The idiot blacksmith will free the brute, as he always does. Where's the sense in that? Aquila should be barred from the auctions."

"What I do with my property is surely no consideration of yours," Marcus replied coldly.

Baldus shot Marcus a look laced with contempt. He turned to the auctioneer. "Thirty-five *aurei.*"

The crowd gasped. Owein's gaze snapped to Marcus. The blacksmith's frown had deepened. Had the bid exceeded the contents of his purse?

Marcus's jaw set. "Thirty-six."

Baldus's eyes narrowed. "Thirty-eight."

"Thirty-nine."

"Forty."

Marcus's jaw looked as though it would snap. A deep inhale filled his chest.

"Fifty," he declared.

Baldus let out a bark. "Fifty aurei? For *that?*" He threw back his head and laughed, his gut jiggling heartily. "Can you believe it? Why, it's coin down the sewer!" He nodded to Calidius. "Let Aquila have the beast, with my blessing."

"Done," announced Calidius quickly. He looked like a man who'd stumbled across a gold mine. "Payment is due before possession," he told Marcus.

Marcus stepped to the podium. Opening a large leather satchel, he emptied the contents on its surface. Not only coin, but a pile of gold, silver, and gems.

Clara's jewelry.

"What's this?" Calidius said. "You know I accept only coin."

"The items here are worth more than fifty *aurei.*"

"I cannot be sure of that. And in any case, I will have the trouble of pricing and selling the pieces." He shook his head. "If you can't produce coin, I'll have to sell the brute to Baldus."

"No," Marcus said quickly. "I want him."

His hand hesitated only a scant moment before dropping to the hilt of the dagger sheathed at his belt. The blade slid smoothly from its sheath. Owein could see it was a stunning weapon, with intricate tracery and a tapered point. The hilt and pommel were inlaid with silver.

Calidius's guard reacted swiftly, drawing his sword and angling the tip toward Marcus's neck. "Drop your weapon."

Marcus met the guard's gaze squarely, making no move to obey. *By the Horned God!* Surely Lucius Aquila's son wasn't foolish enough to attack a slaver at auction? He would be dead in an instant.

Marcus flipped the dagger and offered it, hilt-first, to Calidius. "I trust this weapon is sufficient to complete the transaction."

Calidius's brows rose. He took hold of the weapon, his greed barely concealed. "Of your own make?"

"Of course." Marcus's voice sounded strained. "It's worth at least twenty-five *aurei.* Added to the coin and jewelry, there is more than enough value to purchase this slave."

"Include the scabbard as well, and I'll accept the deal."

Marcus hesitated only briefly before unbuckling his scabbard and placing it on the podium. Another work of art, the leather was tooled with a Celtic design, inlaid with silver. Owein could tell it pained the blacksmith to part with it.

A scroll was produced, which Marcus signed. He pressed his ring into the wax Calidius's man dripped at the bottom of the document. The transaction complete, Calidius rolled the papyrus and handed it to Marcus.

"Cut his ropes," Marcus said.

Calidius gave a swift shake of his head. "Not here in the arena. This one's dangerous."

"I've no doubt of that. All the same, I want him unbound. And since I've given up my dagger to you . . ."

"You'll get no refund if he runs," Calidius cautioned.

"I expect none."

"As you say. But I'll not endanger my customers." He nodded to Owein's handler. "Accompany Marcus Aquila and his slave to the forum market. Once there, you may cut the bonds."

"Yes, sir." The man gave a sharp tug on Owein's tether. Owein hadn't anticipated the move; his attention had been fixed on Aquila and Calidius. He stumbled off the auction block. He would have fallen if Marcus hadn't sprung forward to catch his arm. Their gazes met, briefly.

"Take your hands from me," he choked out, a tide of rage and helplessness rising hotly. Was Clara watching this humiliation? How would she bear to look at him, after seeing him paraded naked and sold like a beast?

Marcus stepped away. "Cut the ropes on this man's legs," he said. The guard looked at Calidius, who shrugged.

The relief Owein felt at having his legs unrestrained was overwhelming. And yet he hated that Marcus Aquila had been the one to grant that freedom.

"I'll take his tether as well," Marcus said.

The guard placed the end of the rope in Marcus's hand. Marcus's fist closed around it. Owein drew a sharp breath. Marcus looked up. His eyes met Owein's, assessing him.

Deliberately, Marcus let the rope drop. "Do not think to do anything that will upset Rhiannon," he warned in a low voice.

Owein jerked his head in a nod.

"Come."

Owein followed him from the arena, acutely aware of his nudity and the murmurings of the crowd. They passed into the forum market, where Calidius's man cut Owein's ropes. A small crowd gathered, gawking. Marcus tossed a coin to one of the venders and received a pair of *braccas,* worn but still serviceable. Owein jerked them on.

The spectacle hadn't ended. The crowd had an expectant air, and Marcus seemed to welcome the attention. Turning to the crowd, he pronounced the formal words of manumission.

"Before the people of Isca, I, Marcus Ulpius Aquila, citizen, declare this slave a free man. His name shall be entered in the city census. From this day forward, Owein of the Brigantes is a citizen of Rome."

A citizen of Rome? Owein stiffened. He couldn't imagine a worse insult.

His scowl must have revealed the sentiment, for Marcus sent him a quelling glance. He turned, facing Owein, but his words were spoken loudly, for the benefit of the crowd.

"Liber esto, amicus."

Be free, friend.

Pivoting sharply, Marcus strode away. Owein stared at his retreating form. After a moment's hesitation, he stalked after him. He caught up with Marcus in an area crowded with horses and carts. Marcus approached a pair of horses, patting them on the nose and speaking softly. He turned, propped his hip against the side of the cart, and folded his arms across his broad chest.

They stood for a moment, gazes locked in challenge. This was the man Clara would marry. The man who would share her bed and her life.

Owein had never hated anyone more.

"Where are the women?" he asked finally.

"It takes some time to make it down from the upper seating," Marcus replied in Celtic. "I expect they'll be here soon enough."

Owein stared. Until now, Marcus had spoken only in Latin, and Owein had assumed he didn't speak the Celt tongue. Few Romans did. But Marcus's last words had flowed in flawless Celtic. What was more, his accent was an echo of Owein's own northern lilt.

"Try," Marcus added crossly, "to exhibit at least a veneer of civility when they arrive."

"Dinna provoke me, man."

Marcus straightened. "Don't forget who spoke the public words of manumission."

Owein flexed his fingers, fighting his rage. He knew very well he was indebted to Marcus Aquila for his life and freedom. Perversely, he wanted nothing more than to smash his fist into the Roman's face.

Marcus's gaze snapped to a point behind Owein. "They are here," he murmured.

"Owein!"

Rhiannon. Owein turned, his heart constricting so tightly he feared it would stop beating. His sister was before him, running down the row of carts, all pretense of reserve abandoned. Clara and a young red-haired girl who could only be his sister's daughter were close behind her.

Owein couldn't make his feet move toward them. He stood, rooted to the ground, watching them come. Rhiannon reached him first. She made to throw her arms around him, but he caught her wrists and held her back.

"I'm covered in filth, little mama."

She tipped her head back and gazed up at him. She looked much as she did in his memories, save for a few lines about her eyes and mouth, and a strand or two of silver in her hair. Her amber eyes filled with tears. "Do ye think I care about a little dirt?"

"I care." He looked over her head. Clara had halted a few steps behind. Her expression was a question he didn't want to answer.

Rhiannon lifted a hand and riffled her fingers through his filthy hair, smoothing it back from his forehead. Her touch was soft, yet it went through his body like a blade. How many times had she soothed him this way, when he'd been a lad and she'd been the only mother he knew? He shut his eyes, tears burning behind his eyelids.

"Ye shouldn't have come to the arena," he said roughly.

"How could I stay away?"

"I'm nay worth the price Lucius Aquila's son paid."

"You're worth far more." She did fling her arms around him then, clutching him to her tightly. "Oh, Owein. I never thought to see ye again."

Owein gripped her shoulders. "Ye'll soil your dress."

But she wouldn't let him push her away. She clung to him all the tighter, her face pressed against his chest, her body shaking with sobs. Owein stood awkwardly, not wanting to embrace her for fear of dirtying her even more. But as her weeping continued, he found he could do nothing but enclose her in his arms. Looking over her head, he saw that Clara and Rhiannon's daughter were crying as well.

Marcus Aquila, however, was not.

"We're drawing an audience," he said curtly. "Let's remove this touching drama to the farm."

Owein let his hands fall to his sides.

"Placet."

As you say.

Chapter Nineteen

He was being an ass.

Marcus surveyed the scene before him with increasing self-disgust. Owein, freshly bathed and dressed in Lucius's spare *braccas* and shirt, occupied the chair by the hearth. The *braccas* were too short; they only just covered Owein's knees. Rhiannon fussed, bringing her brother a mug of *cervesia,* then remaining by his side while he drank.

Marcus found his stepmother's attentions profoundly irritating. The reaction shamed him. Was he so petty a man to begrudge Rhiannon's love for her brother? Or Breena's starry-eyed worship of the uncle she'd just met?

Perhaps the blame for Marcus's foul mood more properly rested upon the obvious fact that the woman he loved was enraptured with a Druid. Clara had hardly glanced away from Owein since he'd entered the room. Her gaze drank in the Celt's every movement—despite the fact that Owein hadn't addressed a single word to her, nor even, so far as Marcus could tell, glanced in her direction.

Owein was clearly uncomfortable in his sister's home. He'd refused to enter the indoor bathing rooms, insisting instead on washing outdoors in the frigid kitchen garden with a few rags and buckets of heated water. Even now, ensconced by the hearth, he sat stiffly. Marcus doubted Owein's rigid posture had anything to do with the salve Rhiannon was applying to the cuts on his back. No, Marcus suspected the wounds that pained Owein were far older.

Rhiannon's finger traced a puckered gouge on Owein's shoulder that could only have been made by a slaver's flagellum.

"When were ye taken?" she asked softly.

For a moment, Marcus thought Owein wouldn't answer. When he did, his tone was without inflection. "Seven winters past, in the north of Cambria. I . . . I dinna remember much of the battle."

Rhiannon's fingers stilled. "How long were ye . . . ?"

"Almost two years."

Rhiannon dipped her head, tears trickling down her cheeks. "If I had known . . ."

Owein covered her hand with his. "Dinna cry, little mama." He nodded across the table to Aiden. "The Great Mother sent this man to my aid."

The old Celt beamed. "Aye, my clan was blessed that day. Our people were glad to have a Wise One among us."

"It did ye little good in the end," Owein muttered.

An awkward silence ensued.

Owein lifted his gaze to Marcus. "I will repay my slave price, Roman."

It was an empty promise, and both men knew it. Owein could labor for years without earning the sum of fifty gold *aurei,* let alone the true value of Clara's jewelry and Marcus's dagger. To Marcus's credit, he just nodded. He found he hadn't the stomach to rip away Owein's last shred of dignity.

And yet, he wanted to. The lout could at least address him by name, rather than with the dubious title "Roman," pronounced with as much respect as the word "pig." An urge to sink a blade into the far wall struck hard. Marcus's hand was halfway to the hilt of his favorite dagger before he remembered he'd bartered it for Owein's freedom. He flexed his fingers, cursing under his breath.

Breena approached Owein, her head inclined shyly. She carried a bowl heaped with stew and chunks of bread. "Will ye eat, Uncle?"

"Aye, lass." Owein took the food, his mouth curving briefly.

Marcus's sister responded with her most dazzling smile. Owein's gaze lingered on the girl, his eyes narrowing when he saw Rhys's Druid pendant around her neck. Owein's gaze lifted to Breena's face. Marcus's frown deepened as the Druid's eyes lost their focus.

After a long moment, Owein gave a swift shake of his head and rubbed the bridge of his nose.

Rhiannon's gaze was troubled. "Are ye in pain, Owein? Is it—"

Owein's eyes were sober. "Your daughter has the Sight. What does your Roman husband think of that?"

Rhiannon bit her lip. "He doesn't know."

"Rhys wants to take me to the sacred isle," Breena put in. "To be trained in the ways of the Light."

Owein's brows lifted. "Rhys? The Druid Cormac told me of?"

Rhiannon nodded. "Rhys's grandfather, Cyric, wants Breena to foster on Avalon. He fears if she's not trained in the Light, her link to the Deep Magic could be turned to the Dark."

Owein's eyes were grave. "As Madog turned mine, all those years ago."

Rhiannon looked away. "Aye."

"And will your Roman husband give up his daughter to a band of Druids?"

"No," Marcus cut in. "He will not. And neither will I."

"Marcus, please. Let us nay speak of this now."

"You cannot avoid it forever, Mother."

Breena hastened to Marcus's side and put a hand on his

arm. "Marcus, Owein is here now. Perhaps . . . perhaps he can teach me."

Rhiannon turned hopeful eyes to her brother. "Ye are welcome here. Will ye stay, Owein?"

Owein looked into his bowl of stew. "I'm nay one to teach any of the Light. Also, I canna imagine Lucius Aquila would tolerate me in his house. I nearly killed him."

"I will handle Lucius," Rhiannon said quietly.

Privately, Marcus entertained doubts about that.

"Ye are my brother," Rhiannon continued. "Ye'll always have a home with me."

"I canna accept your offer," Owein said quietly. "I mean to be gone in the morning."

"Gone?" Clara, who until now had remained silent, half-rose from her seat. "Gone where?"

Owein met Clara's gaze fully for the first time since Marcus had taken him out of the arena. "Where I go is no concern of yours." His tone was almost brutal.

Clara paled.

Marcus could tolerate this travesty no longer. Abruptly, he strode across the room and held out his hand to Clara. He pitched his voice low, speaking in Latin. "Please. Walk with me. Outside, in the garden."

Clara looked toward Owein, who was staring so intently at his stew he might have been inspecting it for swimming insects. "All right," she said tightly.

She put her hand in his and his fingers closed around it.

Clara had left the house with her blacksmith.

The words that would have called her back had been on the tip of Owein's tongue. They'd gone unsaid. He could hardly bear to look at her, knowing what she'd witnessed in the arena. His shame was hard enough to bear before Rhiannon and her Roman son. Before Clara, his humiliation was complete. How she must pity him.

No man should be pitied by the woman he loved.

For he did love her. The realization struck him with all

the swiftness and fury of the slaver's whip. He loved her delicacy, her strength, her courage in the face of things far beyond her sheltered experience. But he could offer her no life, no future.

He could never dwell here, in her world. This Roman city burned a hole in his spirit. The arena and slave market, the press of bodies, the jumble of buildings piled atop one another—all these things were bad enough. But perhaps the worst was the high, somber walls of the fortress, declaring the might and supremacy of Rome. And the soldiers. They strode through the streets at every turn. He'd had a difficult time restraining his rage at the sight.

Valgus was one of those soldiers.

Owein had failed to kill the man. No doubt the snake had slithered back to his fortress, where Owein could never gain access. With Gracchus dead, Clara was in Valgus's power.

He raised his head and found Rhiannon watching him. Looking around, he realized he was alone with his sister. Breena had gone with Aiden to the kitchens just after Marcus and Clara had departed.

"What troubles ye so?" Rhiannon asked softly. "Your wounds?"

Owein shook his head and placed his half-empty bowl on the table. "Tell me," he asked. "What is needed to remove Valgus as Clara's guardian?"

Rhiannon's brows furrowed. "I'm not sure. Most likely a petition to the governor in Londinium, with a request to appoint another guardian in Valgus's stead."

"Would your husband agree to act as such?"

"I'm sure that Lucius would. He's in Londinium now. I could send him a message."

"Nay. Have Clara go to Londinium herself. Can ye spare Aquila's son to escort her?"

"Of course."

"Will ye see to it then? Have her leave as quickly as possible, in secret. Valgus didna see Clara at Gracchus's villa.

She's been gone from Isca for days—perhaps Valgus believes her lost, or dead. All the better if he does."

"Ye have the right of it." Rhiannon touched Owein's cheek. "But ye should take Clara to Londinium yourself."

"That I canna do," Owein said quietly.

Rhiannon said nothing, but the expression in her eyes told Owein he'd disappointed her. She wanted him to stay, become part of her world. Owein returned his attention to his stew, his heart hollow in his chest. He did not belong in her Roman house, no matter how warm the hearth, or how much he yearned for family. No matter how fiercely he wished he could be the civilized man Clara needed, he knew the task was beyond him.

Nay. He would leave in the morning, before his resolve weakened. He'd seen his future in Avalon. He would join with a silver-haired Druidess. Become the father of her children. He would live with others of his kind, in the wilderness, in whatever peace magic could provide.

A Roman farm could never be his home.

Clara tugged her hand from Marcus's as soon as she stepped from the hearth room. Her heart was pounding. Why had he sought her out? She slanted him a glance, but his dark eyes were fixed straight ahead. He said nothing as they passed under the covered walk and into the yard.

An air of hopelessness clung to the snow-shrouded garden. The trees were bare; the herbs drowned in graying slush. The thorny canes of the roses reminded her of death. Marcus didn't stop until he reached the fountain at the garden's center. Then he swung around and faced her, legs braced wide.

"You've lain with him," he said bluntly.

Whatever Clara had expected the bashful blacksmith to say, it hadn't been this. "Why do you think that?" she asked carefully.

"Because of the way you look at him. The pain in your

eyes." He ground his fist into his palm. "He pays you no notice at all! Why do you shame yourself before him?"

Clara stiffened her spine. "I cannot see how this is any concern of yours."

"I know of your father's will," Marcus said moodily. "It's all about town. He betrothed you to Valgus *in manu.*"

Clara nodded.

"You can't mean to marry Valgus. He's a man of dishonor."

"I've no wish to be his wife. But he's my guardian. I'll have to answer to him somehow."

"What if you were to walk away? Offer to leave the money and the property in his hands?"

"I would be destitute! Where would I go?"

Marcus drew a breath. "You would stay here. As my wife."

Clara's jaw slackened. "You're offering me marriage?"

"It shouldn't come as such a shock," he said irritably. "I offered for you once before."

He was not jesting. His jaw clenched with such force that Clara was afraid he might break a tooth. It occurred to her that behind the blacksmith's even-tempered façade lurked a depth of passion she'd not guessed at.

"Such an offer is a treasure, Marcus Aquila. Any woman would be proud to call you husband. But I cannot accept." She looked away. "You were right, a moment ago. Owein and I—"

"No," Marcus said quickly. "Don't tell me."

"But you asked if I had lain with him!"

"I shouldn't have. Clara, it makes no difference to me. My offer of marriage stands."

Clara shook her head. "You're far too noble, Marcus. I cannot accept you. I love Owein, and yes, I have lain with him."

Marcus swore.

"I'm sorry. Owein has my heart."

"He's not worthy of it," Marcus muttered.

Chapter Twenty

Rhys paused on silent feet, listening to the sounds of the night. He sensed an animal padding a short distance behind him. A wolf. The beast had made no move to attack. And yet, it remained close. Strange behavior for a wild creature.

Rhys's footsteps turned to the north. The wolf circled, forcing him back to the south. Back to Avalon. A sudden thought struck. Was the animal herding him?

He muttered an oath. This would not do. He'd come into the Mendip hills to search for Gwen. Now this wolf was forcing him to retrace his steps.

Hefin flew to and fro above him, wings flapping in agitation. Three times the merlin had rushed the wolf, talons extended menacingly. The animal had snarled and snapped its jaws, once even coming away with a tail feather between its teeth. After that, Hefin kept his distance.

This farce could not go on. Rhys pivoted to face the direction where he believed the wolf to be lurking. He spread his legs and flexed his knees, his palm resting lightly on the pommel of his dagger. If this animal wanted a confrontation, so be it.

"Come out," he commanded. He was not sure his attempt at communication would work—he was most gifted in sensing the knowledge of birds, not the intentions of four-footed creatures. Still, he could try.

"Step into the moonlight, where I can see ye."

To his amazement, the wolf obeyed.

The beast was a female, with a silver-gray coat and dark markings around its eyes. It didn't take a threatening stance, as Rhys had expected. Instead, it went down on its haunches and laid its head on its paws. Rhys could have sworn the animal was bidding him draw near.

His hand dropped from his dagger. He paced a few steps closer, then, when the wolf made no threatening move, he stepped closer still and dropped into a crouch.

"What is it ye want of me, friend?"

The wolf raised its muzzle, gave a brief yip, then turned and bounded off. A moment later, it paused and looked back. Rhys rubbed the stubble on his jaw, bemused. The wolf meant for him to follow.

He did. When the animal plunged into the water, close to the raft Rhys had left hidden in a clump of reeds, Rhys followed. The she-wolf paddled toward the sacred isle, though not to the hidden dock near the village. Bemused, Rhys poled his craft to the far side of Avalon's smaller hill. The wolf emerged from the swamp, shaking its coat. Rhys leaped off the raft and pulled it onto the shore.

Above, Hefin screeched disapprovingly. The wolf padded forward into a bright patch of moonlight. It halted to nose a hollow in a rotting stump, as if trying to pull something out. Hunkering down beside the animal, Rhys peered inside.

The dull gleam of aged silver caught his eye. He extended an unsteady hand into the cavity and drew forth a pendant. For a long moment, he just stared at the pattern on its face: the mark of the Druids of Avalon, the same design Rhys bore on his chest.

Rhys's heart nearly seized. This was Gwen's pendant.

She'd worn it since the day of their mother's death, had duplicated its pattern in her forge, crafting similar pendants for the women of Avalon. Never had he seen her without it—it was too old and powerful, and far too dear to her. The sister he'd once known would never have tossed it aside. Unless . . .

He shoved his arm into the hollow and pulled out a wad of damp fabric. He recognized the tunic as Gwen's. His gut twisted. Was his sister dead, or taken by a slaver? Or was there some other explanation?

His attention snapped to the wolf. The beast had brought him to this place for a reason. Tentatively, he reached out with his mind, as he so often did with Hefin. But if the wolf held knowledge of Gwen in its primitive brain, Rhys couldn't discern it. And yet . . .

"Show me," he said softly.

The wolf inclined its head and thumped its tail once, then turned and started picking its way up the slope. Rhys looped the pendant's chain around his neck and followed. The animal set a swift pace, disappearing beyond a turn in the trail. Rhys hastened after it. Finally, it paused. At first Rhys saw nothing out of place. But then he sensed the tingle of magic. Dark magic. His eyes adjusted, picking out a subtle cleft in the hillside. The form of a rough shelter was just visible.

A grunting akin to the song made by rutting pigs drifted from the makeshift hut. A man moaned; a woman gave a sharp cry.

The wolf stood motionless, hackles raised. Rhys knew a rush of sickening dread. Time and again, his sister had refused Cyric's instruction to take a husband. Rhys had believed Gwen defied their grandfather because she wasn't yet ready to give her body to a man. Had he been wrong?

Had Gwen truly fallen from the Light?

"What in the name of the Horned God himself are ye doing out here, lad?"

Aiden's complaint drifted into the loft where Owein lay on his stomach, atop a wool blanket spread on a heap of straw. The open cuts left by the slaver's lash made it difficult to stretch out on his back, as was his usual habit. His head ached. The image of Clara placing her small hand in Marcus Aquila's large one was vivid in his mind.

He shoved himself up on his hands and knees, wincing as his bruised ribs protested. Rhiannon had bandaged his torso, clucking and scolding as she wound the strips of linen tightly. It had almost seemed as though he'd gone back in time, with his sister tending him after some youthful mishap. Until he looked up and saw Clara's hopeful eyes, watching him.

Crouching, he peered over the edge of the loft. Aiden stood below, leaning heavily on a stout oak walking stick. "Answer me!" Aiden's thin voice was surprisingly vehement. "What are ye doing in this sheep barn?"

"I could be asking ye the same question, old man. Ye should be abed."

Aiden shook his staff. "Come down here, Wise One. I mean to speak with ye."

Owein snorted at the title. Half the time, he didn't know if Aiden pronounced it in reverence or in jest. There was no use in trying to send Aiden away. Owein knew his grandfather by marriage well enough to realize the man would have his way.

It had been much the same when he'd offered Eirwen as Owein's bride.

"Lower your voice, old man," he said as he descended the ladder. "You're disturbing the sheep."

"Hmph," Aiden replied, blinking as Owein presented himself. A fat ewe bleated, crowding her lambs into a corner.

Owein's swift gaze took in Aiden's bent form. The old Celt's complexion had yellowed and his beard was far whiter than Owein remembered. The misshapen bruise on his forehead was a mottled purple. His throat suddenly felt full. Despite his jesting, he'd never truly thought of Aiden as old. In the hills, the man had been hale and sturdy.

Owein had been more than surprised to see Aiden in Rhiannon's kitchen. His sister's tale of Valgus's brutality and Marcus Aquila's quick action filled Owein with helpless rage. The old man's life and freedom were further debts to Marcus Aquila that Owein would never repay.

"Are ye truly well?" Owein asked.

"My bones ache. But that's nothing remarkable for a man of my years." Aiden scratched his beard. "Though I can tell ye, lad, the beating Valgus gave me didna help in the least. 'Twas my fortune young Aquila was there. If he hadna been, no doubt I'd be dead."

"Aye, Aquila," Owein muttered.

"He's a good man. Solid and true. He should have yer gratitude. Ye'd be fodder for the festival games if he hadna bought ye."

Owein's jaw twitched. "I ken that well enough."

"Here," Aiden said, drawing a crumpled scroll from within his shirt. "Marcus bade me give this to ye."

The papyrus bore a few lines of writing in a bold hand. Marcus had affixed his seal at the bottom.

"It's your letter of manumission," Aiden told him. He patted his chest. "I have my own right here. We are Roman citizens, lad. No one may call us slave again."

Owein took the paper, rolled it tightly, and shoved it into the waist of his *braccas*. Why was freedom such a heavy burden?

"I thank ye." He turned to climb back into the loft.

" 'Tis young Aquila ye should be thanking," Aiden called after him.

Owein grunted.

The old man produced a long sigh. "I ask again—what are ye doin' out here, lad?"

Owein halted with one foot on the ladder. "Seeking rest."

"Rhiannon has a bed for ye in the house."

"I'll nay sleep in a Roman home."

"And yet a Roman barn suffices?"

Owein sighed. "Spit it out, old man. What brings ye here?"

Aiden gave him a long look. "Go to her, lad."

"Who?"

"Ye know verra well."

Owein pressed two fingers against the sudden sharp pain above his right eye. "Ye should never have sent her to me. Sempronius Gracchus's daughter! What were ye thinking? Had ye forgotten Eirwen entirely?"

Aiden stiffened, and Owein immediately regretted his words. "I didna mean—"

"Nay, dinna explain. I know what ye are feeling. Eirwen was a fine lass. I canna tell ye how deeply I grieved for her. I was so bent with pain I wished I might die. Then the Roman commander claimed me from his men's spoils, along with old Myrna, and Blayne, with his lame leg. All those who would have been disposed of by the slavers." He gripped the knot on the top of his staff. "I learned that Gracchus wasna the monster I thought him to be. A hard man, to be sure, but nay a cruel one. Our duties were light, and we were well fed. Even so, I walked in darkness. I wouldna eat for grief of Eirwen. I weakened so much that I took to my pallet. 'Twas Clara's love that saved me. In her, I recovered some of what I lost with Eirwen's death."

"The Roman lass has an innocent spirit."

"She is strong in the Light. I see the Deep Magic shining about her, with none of its darkness. And yet, she knew nothing of her power. She believed the magic rested solely within the grail."

"Ye believe it does not?"

"The Lost Grail holds great power, 'tis true, but 'tis hidden to most. When Clara touches the cup, its Light flows like a wellspring. I knew ye would want to know of it."

" 'Twas a difficult road ye set her on. She nearly died before she reached me." Owein regarded the older man moodily. "Why would ye do such a thing?"

"The gods sent a sign. The morning after the thief emptied the dining chamber of its treasures, a raven and a dove drank together from the courtyard fountain. I knew to send Clara to ye."

"Ye make no sense."

"Do ye nay understand? Ye and Clara must hold the grail together."

"Ye are daft. The grail must return to its makers. My kinsman carries it to Avalon."

"Avalon," Aiden said softly. "There is discord on the sacred isle. The silver-haired lad—Rhys—'tis nay within his power to bring harmony. Light wars against Dark. If the Lost Grail falls to the wrong side, what then?"

Owein frowned.

"If the Deep Magic of the grail is called by one owned by darkness, there will be destruction. The guilty will die, perhaps, but the good as well. Would ye doom all of Isca? What of your sister's family? What of the other Celts who have mixed their blood and their lives with the Romans? I once thought we could live apart from the Romans, Owein. But now I'm nay so sure. We are becoming one people. When misfortune befalls one, the other suffers."

Owein hesitated. "What would ye have me do?"

"Sempronius Gracchus is dead. There is nothing to hold Clara in Isca. She has the Deep Magic within her. She must go with ye to Avalon. To the grail."

"Bring a patrician Roman woman into a circle of Druids? Have ye lost your wits?" He exhaled. "They wouldna receive her, if indeed they let her live at all. Even if I did subscribe to such a foolish plan, I am sure Clara would nay go with me."

"What makes ye think that?"

Owein dragged a hand across his face. "Marcus Aquila wants her. She told me once she wasn't adverse to his suit, but her father turned him away because of his trade. As you say, Aquila's a fine man, and a Roman. He'll protect Clara far better than I could."

Aiden only shook his head. "I wouldna be so certain of that, lad."

"Tell me, Clara, do ye love my brother?"

Clara started at the sound of Rhiannon's soft voice. She hadn't heard the healer enter—it was well past midnight and the house was silent. She turned from the fire to see Rhiannon standing in the doorway.

"Is it so obvious?"

Rhiannon moved into the room. Her expression was sad, and the smile that touched her lips was fleeting. "As obvious as Marcus's love for ye."

Clara let out a breath. "There was a time when I would have welcomed Marcus's attentions, if my father had allowed it. But that was before . . ."

Rhiannon sank onto the bench at Clara's side. "Love doesn't always choose the safest path. I, of all people, know that."

Clara eyed the older woman curiously. She knew little of Rhiannon's union with her Roman husband. "Was it . . . difficult for you and Lucius Aquila?"

Rhiannon gave a soft laugh. "Difficult is far too mild a word. Lucius and I met when I put an arrow in his arse on the battlefield."

"You fought in battle?" Clara could hardly believe it. Rhiannon wasn't large and robust like many Celt women. She stood barely taller than Clara.

"I fought to protect Owein. He was but a lad, and my whole world. I only wish . . ."

"What?" asked Clara when Rhiannon's voice trailed off.

She shook her head. "It doesn't signify now. It was so long ago, and he has changed so much." She sighed. "There is much of the Dark in him."

"Yes." A sudden chill skittered through Clara's body.

She remembered all too well the violence churning in Owein's soul.

"Will ye draw back, then? Give up on your love?"

Rhiannon's gentle words caused Clara's eyes to burn. "I should. He doesn't want me."

"I dinna believe that. I see how his attention follows ye, even if his eyes do not."

Clara dashed a tear from her cheek. "I've tried so many ways to reach him. He blocks every one."

"There is always a path," Rhiannon said. "Ye have only to find it."

Rhys crept toward the sound of human rutting, sloughing through a sea of reluctance and disgust. His loathing sprang only partly from the fear of discovering his sister inside the makeshift shelter. Another measure of his aversion sprang from the dark magic encircling the place. A spell had been woven into the fabric of the forest, akin to the spell Cyric had wrought on Avalon. The magic was so strong, it had sunk into the very soil beneath his feet.

The she-wolf crouched on its haunches a good distance behind him. Hefin circled above, also keeping his distance. Rhys felt the pulse of dark magic with every step. His blood pounded in his veins and his stomach sickened. He maneuvered near a gap in the walls and peered through. The hut was small, occupied by little more than a dirt hearth, a table, and a pallet. A makeshift lamp—no more than smoldering tallow-soaked rags in a wooden bowl—cast an uneven glow.

The hearth was cold. Rhys was glad it was so when he saw what lay in it. Long white bones that could only have come from a human body lay stacked with oak branches and squares of peat. More human bones decorated the wall. A skull graced the center of the table. Beside it was a gleaming cup of crystal and silver, polished but clearly old. Etched on its bowl was the triple spiral and quartered circle that was the mark of the Druids of Avalon.

Rhys drew a sharp breath. The Lost Grail had found its way home.

A man and a woman writhed naked on the pallet. Gwen faced away from Rhys, her long silver hair streaming down her back. The man she rode was the dwarf, Cormac.

Rhys thought he would lose the contents of his stomach.

The woman shifted, her head dropping back. Her long fingernails scraped long red lines on Cormac's chest. Cormac responded with a groan, jabbing his hips upward. In that instant, Rhys realized two things: first, that the dwarf's stunted arms and legs were spread, tied to stout posts set in the ground.

Second, that the woman atop Cormac was not Gwendolyn.

Rhys's rush of relief was soon supplanted by shock. He blinked, not trusting his senses. The whore riding the dwarf was his gentle cousin, Blodwen.

But not Blodwen as Rhys knew her. Nay, this was Blodwen as she'd once been, beautiful and unscarred. The gray of her hair had reverted to the silver-blond it had been before the Roman soldiers had used her. Her shoulders were unbent, her figure supple and lithe.

It was an illusion, Rhys realized. Glamour set in place and held by magic.

Rhys set his hand on a stone to steady himself. He and all the Druids of Avalon—Cyric included!—had believed Blodwen's magic destroyed by the torture she'd suffered as a girl.

They had been wrong.

Blodwen screamed her release, her body convulsing. A dark red glow sprang up about her, as if she were consumed by flames. It was all Rhys could do to hold himself steady as his cousin rose to her feet. She stood with legs spread wide, straddling her captive lover.

Cormac groaned. "By the Horned God's mercy, woman! Dinna leave me wanting." He arched his hips in supplication, struggling against his bonds.

Rhys stared with horrified fascination at the dwarf's cock. Huge, red, and engorged, the quivering red staff was grotesquely long and thick. By the gods! How could any woman take such a member into her body?

Blodwen looked down at him, a smile playing on her lips. Fiery energy crackled along her limbs. "I'll leave ye as hard as I like."

Cormac's face went purple. "Bitch! Untie me now!"

Blodwen pouted. "Nay. I'll have need of ye again soon, and the more painful your lust, the more power I draw from it. Ye'll remain as ye are."

Cormac swore, straining fruitlessly against the ropes binding his limbs. "Ye'll live to regret this, whore."

Blodwen bent at the waist and took Cormac's balls in her hands. Rhys winced as she twisted the sacs, wrenching a scream from the dwarf's throat. Immediately, she crouched, taking the large head of his cock into her mouth. Within seconds, Cormac was moaning and pleading for release.

She didn't grant it. Padding on silent feet, she approached the table and leaned over the grail, peering into its bowl. A line appeared between her brows.

She was scrying, Rhys realized with a start. Did Blodwen possess the Sight as well as glamour and the power to alter the fabric of the forest? Had she also manipulated the elements in calling the storm, and cursed Cyric's health? Such a combination of powers was far beyond what Rhys had believed possible, save in the tales of the Old Ones.

His brows drew together. If Blodwen possessed such great magic, and used it so freely, the price for her own strength should have been high. But she betrayed no glimmer of weakness. Nay, on the contrary, it seemed to Rhys his cousin's vigor was greater than he'd ever seen it. Was the Lost Grail responsible for the difference? Or did her dark coupling with the dwarf replenish her strength?

Blodwen looked up from the cup and smiled down at Cormac, who lay groaning. "The King is in Isca, at the home of his sister. I've shown him his reward and he is eager to claim it. His Roman bitch believes she can hold him, but she'll find soon enough that she cannot. Owein will be my consort. He'll lie at my feet in your place."

Cormac rasped a harsh breath. "The lad will nay satisfy ye as I do. His cock is but a twig compared with my thick branch. Your pleasure will be nothing. Your magic will die. Ye need *me,* woman. Not him."

Blodwen gave him a pitying look. "Surely ye canna believe that. Aye, yours was the cock that woke my power, but in the end, your wand is attached to a man with no magic."

She dipped a finger in the grail. "Owein is a Druid, and claimed by the Horned God. His grandmother was the last of the great Celtic Queens. When I join with him in the Lost Land, my power will know no bounds. Storms will rise. The Roman fortress will fall."

Her lips twisted. "Those who used me so cruelly will die. And in Avalon—no more will my own people pity me." She gave a soft laugh. "Indeed, with Isca in ruins, Cyric and Gwendolyn dead, and the grail of my foremothers in my hands, no one shall deny me my place as High Druidess of Avalon."

Chapter Twenty-one

How Rhys managed to stumble from Blodwen's lair without revealing himself to her, he didn't know. Tears blinded his eyes; he poled his raft from Avalon's shore with shaking hands. His gentle cousin had embraced the Dark. She meant to kill Gwendolyn! He couldn't believe it was true. And yet he'd heard it with his own ears.

The Mendips loomed above Rhys before he realized he'd approached them with a purpose. Once again, he'd followed the paddling she-wolf. The beast emerged from the swamp, barely pausing before it scurried up a steep, bare slope riddled with crevices and depressions. Rhys scrambled in its wake. The wolf halted before a tall, narrow crevice and gave a low growl.

"What do ye mean? Is Gwen in this cave?"

For Rhys was sure the wolf was Gwen's companion, as Hefin was his own.

The wolf gave a yip. Rhys fumbled in his shoulder pack, drawing forth flint, tinder, and a thin reed dipped in tallow. It took three tries, but at last his trembling fingers sparked a flame. Armed with the meager light, Rhys entered the cave.

The stench of darkness and evil assaulted him. A dark spell guarded this place. Rhys's stomach rolled. Dropping to a crouch, he forced himself to advance. The flame flickered weakly. Somewhere beyond its illumination he heard the drip of water.

After a short time, he could go no farther, though the path was clear. An unnatural force held his limbs in check. He strained his eyes into the darkness. Was that a hint of movement?

"Gwen?"

Silence reigned, broken only by the steady pulse of dripping water. Then a whisper bled into his mind.

Rhys? Brother?

Rhys's heart slammed against his ribs. "Gwen?"

A weak chuckle echoed through his brain. *Have ye found another who can speak to your spirit?*

Hesitantly, he formed his next words silently, as he'd done so often when he and Gwen were children. *We've not conversed this way since . . .*

The first flow of my moonblood.

Aye.

Ye were angry that I became a woman while ye were still a lad.

I didna begrudge ye, Rhys protested. *Ye were the one who drew away. After that day, ye no longer spoke in my mind.*

Gwen's thoughts whispered in his brain. *The silence was nay my choice. My power had turned to the Deep Magic.*

Then it's true. Ye've defied Cyric's teachings. Touched the Deep Magic. Touched the Dark.

He could feel Gwen's bitterness. *Ye believe that of me?*

I dinna know what to believe! Ye shirk your duty to the clan, vanishing into the swamps, giving no explanation, covering your trail with magic . . .

I've no choice. When the Deep Magic calls, I canna resist it. But I haven't turned to the Dark, as Blodwen has . . .

Rhys's hand shook, making the candlelight quiver on the walls of the cave. *Ye know of Blodwen?*

Aye, I sought to stop her, but she was cunning. She waited until I was trapped by my own magic, then sprang her snare.

Rhys frowned. *What do ye mean, trapped by your own magic?*

His only answer was the dripping silence of the cave. Again, he tried to go forward, only to be repulsed.

"Gwen. Where are ye?"

A faint sound, soft footsteps, echoed from the darkness. *If I show myself, ye must promise secrecy.*

"I'll not aid a Dark purpose."

I would not ask that of ye.

Rhys swallowed. "Then I'll give a brother's promise."

The footsteps grew closer. He frowned. They were too light and silent to be the steps of a woman.

A she-wolf stepped into the light. The animal was haggard and wasted, its coat wet and matted with blood on one flank. Its legs trembled, then folded into a crouch. Its silver gaze sought Rhys.

Rhys stared at the animal, the fine hairs on his nape rising. Nay. It could not be . . .

Do ye nay know me, brother?

He nearly lost his grip on the taper. "Gwen?"

The wolf dipped its head.

He stared, his jaw slack, his mind stunned beyond belief. Aye, he'd heard tales of Old Ones who could alter their human forms, but such Deep Magic had been long lost in the mists of time. No Druid in a thousand years had touched it.

"What enchantment is this?" he whispered. "Have ye sold your soul to learn it?"

Nay, Rhys. 'Tis part of me. I had but to answer the call of the Deep Magic.

"Little wonder ye hid this power from Cyric."

Aye, he would have forbidden it, and that I couldna bear. When the Deep Magic compels, I must obey.

"And the she-wolf who led me here?"

Ardra is my companion. As Hefin is yours.

A cold hand touched the back of Rhys's neck.

Rhys, does our grandfather still live? Or has he succumbed to Blodwen's darkness?

"He lives, but for how much longer I canna say."

Ye must find a way to release me from this enchantment. With our power joined, we may have a chance. We can call the Deep Magic together.

"Cyric willna allow it."

We have no choice. Blodwen seeks the Lost Grail. She means to use it in darkness, to avenge herself on those who stole her innocence. If she finds it—

" 'Tis too late," Rhys said softly. "The Lost Grail is in Blodwen's hands."

Then we must take it. When she raises the grail in darkness, the Deep Magic will rise. She believes she can control it, but I tell ye, Rhys, she cannot. She will destroy far more than her enemies. She will destroy Avalon itself.

The wolf that was Gwen struggled to its feet and lurched forward, only to fall to the ground in a heap. Rhys strained to reach his sister. He spoke a Word, called every bit of his magic. But try as he might, he could not break through Blodwen's spell.

"It's no use. I am not strong enough."

Rhys, ye must break through this spell! I must get free. Ye dinna understand the secret of the grail. He felt her desperation deepen. *Only a Daughter of the Lady can call the power of the grail.*

Rhys stared. "Truly? Are ye sure?"

Aye. Mother told me the secret before she died. If ye cannot free me, all is lost. If Blodwen uses the grail to call dark magic, I alone possess the power and the birthright to stop her.

"Nay," Rhys whispered, stunned. According to old Aiden, Clara Sempronia had touched the magic of the grail. Could it be that the grail was her birthright as well?

"Gwen," Rhys said shakily. "Dinna lose faith. Ye are nay alone in this. I believe . . . I believe there may be another Daughter."

* * *

Clara's heart pounded. Rhiannon's encouragement had given her hope enough to make the journey across the frozen garden. But as she slipped through the door of the sheep barn, her resolve faltered. Owein hated the Roman world so thoroughly that he would not even sleep under his beloved sister's roof. What hope did Clara have of convincing him to stay in Isca?

She stood motionless in the sliver of moonlight that spilled past the edge of the plank door. The barn smelled of hay and wet wool. She wrinkled her nose. Not long ago, she would have thought the odor rank and groped for her rose oil. But now she took comfort in the animals' warmth and peace.

The deep rise and fall of Owein's breath drifted from the loft. After so many nights spent lying beside him, the rhythm was almost as familiar as her own heartbeat. She pictured him sprawled on the hay, a formidable figure even in sleep. Tiny bird wings fluttered in her belly. It took all her resolve to force her sluggish feet to the base of the ladder.

She climbed. The ladder's rungs were rough under her hands. A sharp splinter slid into her flesh. She bit her lip rather than cry out.

Owein was stretched out on his stomach atop a checkered blanket. A shard of moonlight fell across his splayed legs. Clara paused, breathless. Even sleeping, even scarred, he was beautiful.

Creeping forward as silently as she could, she knelt beside him. He didn't stir.

His bent arms pillowed his cheek. She studied his profile, taking in the auburn stubble covering his chin. His hair was mussed, curling this way and that, with a bit of hay tangled in it. Gently, she tugged the stalk from the auburn strands.

There was a slight chill in the loft despite the heat of the animals below. Clara hesitated, then lay down on the blanket beside Owein, warming herself, wondering again how his body could hold such flames within. Propping herself on one elbow, she let her gaze roam over his body. He wore no shirt—only the bandages Rhiannon had wrapped around his torso.

In the darkness, Clara could just make out the angry cuts of the slaver's whip across his shoulders, glossed with healing salve. The aroma of the herbs, combined with Owein's own clean masculine scent, set her senses spinning. Deep inside, Clara felt the wanting begin.

Her instinct was to reach for him with her mind as she'd done so many times before. But he would not want that. So she simply leaned into him and kissed an angry welt on his shoulder.

A ripple passed through his body. He tensed, his breath running shallow. He lay still for a moment, then, slowly, rolled onto his side and propped his head in his hand.

She held his gaze and said nothing.

His expression veiled his thoughts. She felt an urge to leap to her feet and run, but she quelled it. She started to reach for him, then let her hand fall to the blanket. "Are you . . . well?"

He gave a short laugh. "Aye, well enough, lass."

Tears formed in her eyes. "Clara."

He smudged the moisture from her cheek with his thumb. "Clara," he agreed softly, his lips quirking.

His expression grew intent, the dark heat of his eyes drawing her in. But it didn't last. His gaze dropped.

"Did Aquila's son ask for your hand?"

Clara's lips parted. "How did you know?"

"Ye told me once of his interest. 'Tis easy enough to see it hadn't dimmed."

"It has now," Clara said.

"I dinna understand."

"I refused Marcus's proposal. I . . . I told him I love you."

She held her breath, hoping Owein would echo her sentiment. But as the moments spun out and he made no response, her heart sank into her stomach. Perhaps Rhiannon had been wrong. Perhaps Owein didn't care for her at all. Was she the worst of fools, following him into a hayloft like a wanton?

And yet, he owed her some answers. "You're afraid of my power," she said quietly. "You have been from the first. Is that why you refused to teach me?"

"Lass—"

"You needn't fear me, Owein. I want only to help you release the darkness in your past. But you won't let me."

He crushed a stalk of hay between his fingers. "I heard a Roman tale once. Or perhaps it was a story from the Greeks. 'Twas of a man lost at sea for many years."

"Ulysses?"

"Aye, I believe so. He met a temptress, a woman whose song lured sailors to crash their ships on her rocky shore. They died in ecstasy, the siren's voice echoing in their ears. All their yearning to possess her was for naught, for she was beyond their reach." He crumpled the hay in his fist. "So it is with us. Ye are beyond my reach. Wanting ye will destroy me."

"Because I am Roman?"

"At first, I would have given that as the reason. But the rift between us is much wider than the circumstances of our births. Ye have so much Light inside. I would taint ye with my darkness. I could not live with that."

"Then renounce your darkness. Let it go." Her voice shook. "I know you've endured much, but—"

"Ye know little of it, lass. Nor would I ever wish ye to know more."

"But I want to know," she whispered. "Please. Tell me."

He rose so abruptly he nearly smacked his head on a roof rafter. "I can tell ye this—I was a quarry slave. My job was hauling stone from the pit to the loading yard. Every day without end until I thought I would go mad. The food was rancid, barely enough to keep me alive. Each night, my shackles were fastened to an iron ring. Each morning, I grieved death hadna come while I slept."

He leaned one hand on the rafter, his head bent. Clara longed to go to him, to reach for him with both her body and her mind. But she sensed she wouldn't be welcomed.

"I escaped," he said, "more than once. Each time I was whipped. And the last time . . . have ye seen a flagellum, lass? 'Tis a most effective tool."

Tears stung Clara's eyes.

"They bound my limbs," he said evenly. "Stretched my arms and legs taut on a wooden frame. At first, I tried not to cry out as the lashes fell. But as the flogging went on, I found that vow impossible to keep."

"Oh, Owein." Tears spilled down her cheeks. "I wish I could take it all from you."

"Ye cannot." He shook his head. "That's why ye must leave."

"But—I know you want me."

He made an impatient motion. "That means nothing. Any man who breathes would want ye."

She moved close, drawn by his pain. "But I don't want any man. I want you. I love you, Owein."

"Lass . . ."

She leaned forward and covered his mouth with hers. "Clara," she said against his lips. She skimmed her palm over his arm, his waist. After a brief hesitation, she slid her hand between them and cupped his phallus through the soft wool of his *braccas.* "My name," she said, "is Clara."

He held himself very still. "Have ye gone from virgin to siren, then?"

"You've only yourself to thank if I have." She kissed him again. "Lie with me, Owein."

He broke contact with a muffled curse. He pressed his forehead against hers, his breathing ragged. His hand closed on her upper arm. He didn't draw her closer, but neither did he push her away.

" 'Twould nay be right."

"Why not? You told me Celt lasses may choose their lovers. Why can I not choose you?"

"Ye are nay a Celt lass."

"Perhaps not, but there's no one left to guard my virtue. My father is dead."

His grip gentled. "I am sorry for that."

She searched his gaze. "Are you truly? Even after what he did to your village?"

Owein let out a long breath. "Your father was a soldier discharging his duty. If that put him at odds with my people, 'tis no fault of yours. I dinna hate ye for it. I mourn your loss, because you loved him."

Clara's eyes stung. "Thank you," she whispered. She sensed Owein's will softening. Perhaps, if she kept her mind separate from his, he wouldn't feel the need to push her away.

She wrapped her arms around his neck and pressed her breasts against his chest. Her thighs cradled his erect phallus. A small moan escaped her lips.

She kissed him, her tongue running along the seam of his mouth. When his lips didn't part, she kissed her way along his jaw, down his neck. The pulse at the base of his throat pounded a rapid beat.

She pressed a hot kiss upon it. She trailed her fingers down his bare chest and stomach, and lower, searching for the laces of his *braccas*. His phallus strained against the ties.

Heat lapped her loins in exquisite waves. An ache quickly spread through her belly to her chest, making it difficult to draw breath. Swiftly, she loosened the ties at his waist and slid her hands inside his *braccas,* over his bare hips.

"Stop, lass." But he made no move to enforce his command. His voice was strained.

A husky, seductive laugh emerged from her throat. She hardly recognized the sound as her own—she had never before imagined herself in the role of siren. She tugged apart his *braccas*, freeing his phallus. It sprang hot and heavy into her hand. The joy of touching him in this intimate way moved her deeply.

She peered at his face. His features were rigid, as if carved from granite. His blue eyes were indigo in the darkness, the ring of color almost consumed by its black center.

She began a slow stroke of his phallus, base to tip, moving the silken heat of his skin over the iron-hard muscle beneath. He sucked in a breath. His hand cupped the back of her head, drawing it to his chest. She kissed the bare skin above his bandages, tasting salt.

"Lass . . ."

"Clara."

He let out a groan. "Clara . . . ye must stop this madness."

She let her mouth drift lower. Dropping to her knees, she skimmed her lips past the linen bandage to brush his bare belly. His taste intoxicated her. "I want madness, Owein. And I want you. All of you. The light and the darkness."

He groaned again, tightening his grip on her hair past the threshold of comfort. She didn't care. She wanted to take him inside her. Consume him, feel his pleasure and his pain. She wanted to know the vulnerable part of him that showed only when their minds and bodies were joined. She wanted to kiss his scars, those on his skin and those in his heart. Heal him with her love.

She could do it, if he would only let her.

He wanted to bury himself inside her.

He wanted to mark her as his. Love her so thoroughly that she would never be free to love another. The temptation was overwhelming, but Owein fought it with all his strength. For he couldn't take Clara without offering his own surrender.

And that he could not do. He had no place in her world, and despite Aiden's entreaties, Clara had no place in his. Owein's destiny lay with the Druids of Avalon, with the silver-haired woman of his visions.

Clara trapped him with her dark, luminous gaze. Giving a siren's smile, she dipped her head and slowly, deliberately kissed the tip of his arousal.

By the stones and the sky! With a groan he hauled her to her feet, holding her apart from him with rigid arms. Cool air flowed between their bodies. He released her and stepped back, shaken.

She was wearing one of Rhiannon's tunics, a colorful garment of homespun wool. In it, she looked almost like a Celt lass.

"Go back to the house," he bit off. "Return to your soft bedchamber."

"Come with me."

"I dinna belong there."

"You hardly belong in a sheep barn!"

"It matters not. I'll soon be gone."

Her voice rose a note. "You don't have to go anywhere. Rhiannon wants you to stay. You could make a home with your sister's family. And with me."

"Ye would bind your life to a freed slave?"

"I would bind my life to *you.* No matter that Valgus would never give his permission. I would gladly abandon my father's fortune to be with you."

What would it be like to have Clara as his wife? Wake with her beside him each morning? Watch her belly grow round with his child? It was a vision of a false future. He closed his eyes, willing it to pass.

"Ye canna give up your life and property for one such as me. Go with Marcus Aquila to Londinium. Have my sister's husband plead your case before the governor. If ye must have a guardian, Lucius Aquila would be a benign one."

She regarded him seriously. "I will do that if you stand by me. You are a citizen now. If my petition is successful, we could marry. Rhiannon would welcome us—"

"I canna live where Romans are thicker than trees in a forest." Silently, he begged her to understand. "I need to dwell among my own kind."

Her eyes flashed with hurt, making him feel like the lowest swine. "You mean to go to Avalon?"

"Aye."

She drew a breath. "I . . . I would go with you."

He dragged a hand through his hair. "To an outlawed Druid enclave? Do ye think they allow Roman women in their midst?"

"Roman or not, I have magic. I want to learn to use it. If you won't teach me, perhaps there are others in Avalon who will."

"And perhaps there are some in Avalon who would as soon kill ye as risk bringing the Roman army down on their heads! Put it out of your mind."

A chill wind gusted, whistling through the cracks in the barn walls. A sudden dart of pain pierced Owein's right eye. He drew a sharp breath.

Nay. Not a vision. Not now.

Clara shivered, her eyes going dark with fear. "Did you feel that?" She peered at him more closely. "Owein. What is it? You look . . ."

He tried to focus on her face, but her features were distorted. Wisps of fog blurred into gray.

Her voice came as a whisper. "A vision?"

"Aye." He licked lips gone suddenly dry. "Leave me. Now."

"No. Not when—"

"Leave me."

His temple throbbed. He rubbed his eyes with his fist, trying to clear his fogged sight.

He felt her hand on his arm, her fear beating at the edges of his mind. "Let me help you. Let me share this with you."

"Nay. Ye dinna understand what ye ask."

The wind blew again, an icy blast of frigid air that seemed to come from nowhere. More fog swirled in his vision. Clara's frightened voice faded as something coalesced out of the mist.

Blood.

Pouring in trickles and rivulets, gathering in streams,

coursing thickly through channels gouged like wounds in the frozen ground. Human bodies, dead and bloated, snagged on the matted reeds. Putrid fish and the remains of a black-crested lapwing floated in the willows. Corruption oozed through the air, waves of stench more palpable than a rolling fog.

A limp form floated past. A dark-haired corpse, its face hidden. Owein waded toward it, muck dragging at his limbs. He heaved the body onto its back.

Clara's sightless eyes stared up at him.

A roar of anguish rose in Owein's throat. Pain exploded in his head.

And then the vision vanished, scattered by Light.

"Owein!"

Clara grasped Owein's shoulders and shook with all her might. He'd gone still and pale as death. Instinctively, she cast her mind into his, flooding him with Light.

He started, his eyes jerking open to lock with hers for one long, suspended moment. Then, with an oath, he pushed her away and rolled onto his hands and knees. He knelt, head hanging and arms rigid, for what seemed a long time.

"Owein?"

She stroked back the curls that had fallen into his face. His hot forehead seared her fingers. She gentled her voice, her lips brushing his ear. "Have you come back?" She pressed a kiss to his temple. "Don't worry. I'm here. I won't leave you."

A shudder wracked his body. She leaned into him, her arm about him, trying to encircle all of his broad torso. Her strength and love flowed freely along their mental connection.

"Lass." His voice was raw. "Ye dinna understand. 'Tis beyond my strength to protect ye from what is inside me."

The wind howled, shrieking through the barn. A sheep bleated in fear. "Then don't," she whispered. "Let me in."

Arms shaking, he shoved himself off his knees and out of her embrace. He tried to stand, but the effort was beyond him. Dropping back to a crouch, he let his head drop. "Leave me."

The hay rustled under Clara's knees as she crept toward him, approaching as if he were a wild beast or a rabid dog. He didn't fend her off. Perhaps he couldn't.

She laid a hand on his head. "Owein."

"Ye shouldna have come here."

"But I did. I'm not leaving you, Owein. Not like this. You need me."

He looked up. "I need no one."

It was a lie. She could see it in his eyes. He was drowning in need, suffocating with want. And yet, he wouldn't act on his desires. He feared she couldn't survive his darkness.

But she could. She knew it. It would be terrifying, but she would do it. For him.

She drew him into her arms and he didn't resist. She knelt with his cheek pillowed between her breasts, her arms cradling him as she would a child.

"Please Owein. Let me help you."

"Nay. Ye dinna understand the darkness that can rise from the Deep Magic. It's strong within me. I fear . . ." He swallowed. "I fear it will break ye, Clara, and that I could not bear."

"I'm not so fragile. You should know that by now."

He opened his mouth. She didn't want to hear the words that would drive her away. She sought his lips, kissing him deeply, with all her love.

With a sigh, he relented. His arms wrapped around her torso, melding their bodies. Sinking back on the blanket, she urged him to cover her with his body.

She throbbed with need; she yearned to feel him inside. His mind responded to her desire. He allowed her to sink below the surface, letting her feel the first layers of his darkness. Allowed her to feel his sorrows and shames, as if they'd been part of her own experience.

She was far from the darkest corners of his soul, but even so, the raw emotion she touched caused her to recoil. For the first time, she sensed the true depth of Owein's darkness. His hatred for her people was so deep and festering it sickened her.

Bile seared a pathway up her throat. Her courage faltered. Her hands, which had been stroking the back of his neck, stilled.

He tensed. "Now do ye understand, lass?"

She drew a breath. "I . . . I think I do."

Closing her eyes, she drew him close and pressed her forehead to his. Putrid, suffocating darkness rushed toward her. Hatred—but that wasn't all. She recognized despair as well—a hopelessness so empty, so bereft, that her body shook with the force of it. She gasped, digging her fingernails into his arms.

She allowed the darkness to seep into her own mind.

He jerked his head back. "Nay, ye musn't—"

Tears spilled from her eyes. "Oh, Owein, how do you bear it?"

His breath came hard. "I bear it because I must."

He gazed at her, his expression gentling. He brought one forefinger up to trace the line of her lower lip. She caught it in her teeth, holding it gently while running the tip of her tongue over the pad of his finger.

Surprise flared in his eyes. He stared at her, transfixed. She turned her head into his palm and kissed it. Wrapping her arms about him, she brought him down atop her.

Hesitantly, as if he feared she would break, he ran a hand up her leg, lifting the hem of her borrowed tunic as he went. With a small smile she lent aid to his cause, shifting her hips and wriggling the fabric over her head. He watched, bemused, as she emerged naked from the cocoon of soft wool.

He touched the shorn ends of her hair. "Are ye sure, lass?"

"Yes." She arched into him, her fingers already shoving his *braccas* over his hips. The garment soon found its way into the hay. He moved over her once again, dipping his head and drawing the tip of her breast into his mouth. She gasped her pleasure, tangling her fingers in his hair, holding him in place.

He kissed a line to her other breast and lavished it with the same attention as the first. He trailed his tongue down her torso, circling the indentation of her navel. Her legs parted, her essence seeking his heat and love. His pain called to her, but she forced herself to stay on the surface of his mind. She sensed that if she went deeper, he would turn her away.

He nuzzled the curls between her thighs, his tongue delving into the slick folds. She gasped. Never had she imagined this! She clutched the blanket, bunching the fabric in her fists. His callused palms skimmed the soft skin of her hips and bottom, lifting her, opening her to his ministrations.

When he had her gasping, calling his name, he kissed his way back up her body. "Ye are so sweet," he murmured. "Like honey. Like springtime. Ah, lass . . ."

"Clara." She smiled, letting her love shine in her eyes.

His blue eyes darkened. "Clara."

She shifted beneath him, wrapping her fingers around his phallus, pleased with her own boldness. When she squeezed the blunt tip, he let out a guttural groan.

She guided him into her body. The air left her lungs as he entered on one long, thick slide. Holding himself above her, he fixed his eyes on her face as he began thrusting. She rose to meet him, hips undulating in a rhythm that was gentle at first, then frantic. Closing her eyes, she reached for him with her mind, sending out Light. It lapped at the edges of his darkness.

His control slipped. A thread of panic followed, even as his pleasure rose. She moved deeper into his mind, soothing his fright. She sought his Dark center, though the reality of his pain terrified her. She could heal him. She knew she could.

But at the same moment she touched his darkness, he slipped a hand between them, touching that hidden nub that was the center of her pleasure. Sensation flashed, scattering her concentration. He stroked again, circling the tight bud, then plucking it gently.

"Oh, Owein." Helplessly, she shuddered her release, her legs convulsing around his hips. "My beloved."

"Clara." He drove into her, urging her to a new ecstasy. She thrashed against him. His hands clamped on her hips, steadying her as he plunged again and again into the haven of her body.

"It's too much. I can't . . ."

Her body stiffened. He smothered her astonished cry with his mouth, drinking it in like a dying man. Her inner muscles clenched around him. His phallus went rigid, as hard as any rock. He emptied himself within her, pumping his hips as his seed entered her womb.

It seemed a long time before his trembling arms relaxed and he collapsed beside her. He lay with his forehead buried in the crook of her neck. She lifted a hand to thread her fingers through his hair. She wished they could stay this way always, just the two of them, alone, with no past or future to haunt them. His arm tightened, as if he were as reluctant as she to let the moment pass. But already the bliss was fading.

She shivered. He eased gently from her arms and retrieved her tunic. He returned and wrapped it about her. She snuggled into the soft wool.

"Owein?" she whispered, not opening her eyes.

"Aye, lass?"

"I love you."

He exhaled. "Ye shouldn't."

Her voice came as if from the edge of a dream. "You're right, of course, but I do anyway. And . . . I never want to stop."

Owein propped himself on one arm, watching the play of soft moonlight on Clara's face. Her breathing lengthened and deepened. When he was sure she was asleep, he slid carefully away.

Shame washed through him. He'd taken far more from her than he could ever give in return.

When morning found him gone, she would hate him for it.

Chapter Twenty-two

The ocean churned like the Great Mother's cauldron.

A dark line of clouds advanced from the west, blotting the blue from the sky. A dingy collection of mud and wattle huts huddled on the shore, doors and shutters drawn tight against the coming maelstrom. Ferryboats and rafts bobbed like corks against the pier.

No sane man would attempt a crossing in such surf. And yet, Rhys had no choice. The more he thought on it, the more he was certain it was true. Clara Sempronia had called the power of the Lost Grail. She had to be a Daughter of the Lady. With Gwen trapped, she alone could repel Blodwen's evil.

The Lost Grail had been fashioned by the twin Daughters of the Lady. One of these Daughters was the foremother of Rhys, Gwen, and Blodwen, the other had been thought dead. Rhys now believed that after escaping with the grail, the second Daughter had found a home with the Romans. Clara, with her ability to call the grail's magic, must be the second Daughter's descendant.

Clara had the power to take the grail from Blodwen. And

yet . . . she was Roman, with no training in Druidry. That fact troubled Rhys deeply. Without knowledge of the Words and spells of the Old Ones, Clara might crumple before Blodwen's magic.

Rhys banished the thought to a corner of his mind. His first task was to find Clara. Once he secured her promise of aid, he would formulate a plan.

He pounded on the door of a ramshackle dwelling, the wind whipping his hair about his face. The dark sky had begun to spit sleet, but the full brunt of the storm was some hours off. Hefin rose with a squawk, settling atop the frozen eaves. Rhys pounded again with the side of his fist. "Angus! Are ye there, man?"

"Who be asking?"

"Rhys, the bard."

A latch inside the hut lifted and the door was pulled wide. Rhys stumbled over the threshold, into the arms of a grizzled fisherman. "Rhys!" Angus exclaimed. "What're ye doing about on such a foul morning?"

"I need passage across the channel to Isca. Now."

Angus plucked his graying beard. "Ye've lost yer wits, lad, to be sure. No boatman would chance a crossing in this storm."

"Ye've rowed in foul weather before."

"When I was younger, perhaps, with no one but meself to mind." He gave a nervous glance toward the corner of the hut's single room, where a dour-faced woman sat suckling a babe.

Rhys stifled a curse. He'd forgotten Angus's young wife had so recently given him a son. He gave the new mother a swift bow.

The woman remained unsmiling. " 'Tis an ill wind that blows. 'Tis magic, nay?"

At Rhys's nod, Angus shivered. "I canna be taking ye to Isca. Nay this day. Perhaps on the morrow . . ."

"The morrow will be too late," Rhys said, turning toward

the door. "My thanks. I'll seek out Vaughn. He'll accommodate me."

Angus exchanged a glance with his wife. "Vaughn willna be rowing ye anywhere. He died a sennight past." He cleared his throat. "Stay here, lad. I'll row out when the storm lifts."

"I thank ye, Angus, but nay. I'll seek another boatman."

But a short time later, Rhys's stomach was seething as violently as the ocean. No man was willing to take to the sea in such weather. In all honesty, he couldn't blame them.

Rhys eyed the vessels pitching against the wharf. Did he dare borrow a boat? Nay, his skills as a seaman were negligible. It would be suicide to row on his own. Despite the time it would add to the journey, he would have to take the land route.

He turned his face to the coast road. At least the wind was at his back, he thought grimly.

Hefin glided above him, shadowing Rhys's steady jog. As the village receded, the merlin darted ahead. Rhys pushed to quicken his stride. With luck, he would arrive in Isca the following evening. He prayed Clara was still at the Aquila farm. But what of Owein? Even now he might be traveling to Avalon. If the Druid fell into Blodwen's snare, what destruction would follow?

His legs pounded on the path, skirting treacherous patches of ice. Rhys slowed, his eyes scanning the ground. An injury now would be disastrous.

Intent on picking out hazards, Rhys didn't see Hefin dive until the merlin was full upon him. The raptor descended in a flurry of wings, sinking its talons into the fleshy muscle between Rhys's shoulder and neck. Rhys stumbled, his feet flying out from under him as his boot hit an icy patch. He went down with a cry. It was a moment before he gathered his wits.

Hefin fluttered gracefully to the ground in front of him—far enough, Rhys noted sourly, to avoid his master's grasp. Rhys rubbed his smarting shoulder and glared at the bird. "What in the name of the Great Mother was that for?"

The animal cocked its head to one side and let out a squawk. Waddling like a chicken, it ventured a few steps closer.

Rhys stared at it intently. "What is it, friend?"

With a flap of its wings, the merlin lifted into the air, then settled back down again. In the back of Rhys's mind, an idea formed, born of Hefin's instincts.

Fly.

The bird tilted its head. Its small, dark eye blinked.

Another picture formed. Gwen, as a wolf. The figure morphed into a merlin. The bird rose into the sky, joining another of its kind.

The bottom dropped out of Rhys's stomach. "Ye want me to change? Impossible. Friend, I haven't the power my sister commands. I never had."

Another image flashed into Rhys's mind. The sun's rays, rising over the horizon.

Rhys blinked, confusion racing through him. Could it be? Was it possible the power of the Old Ones rose inside him, as it had in Gwen?

A single idea sprang into Rhys's mind.

Try.

He stood on shaking legs. "It's forbidden to call the Deep Magic. I canna go against Cyric's—"

Hefin cut him off with a screech.

Rhys stared at the bird. Call the Deep Magic? As Gwen had? Did he dare?

The long road to Isca rose in his mind. Two days' hard travel, even without the storm breaking over him. Two days while Gwen remained trapped and wounded. Two days while Blodwen lured Owein into the Lost Lands.

How could he *not* call the Deep Magic?

"All right," he heard himself say softly. "I will try." Doing his utmost to ignore the tremor radiating through his limbs, he spread his arms wide.

What would it mean to release his humanity—to change into a dumb beast and lift into the sky, where no man had the right to soar? Terror gripped him as another thought occurred. What if he succeeded in changing, but not in returning to human form? Would he lose the thoughts and emotions that made him a man, becoming a beast in truth? Or would his man's soul be trapped within an animal's body?

Had Gwen felt the same fears, the first time she'd turned? Rhys wished his sister were by his side now, to offer advice as she so often had when they were young. She'd always been the first to assault any challenge. Never had he thought he'd be called upon to save her.

With an effort, he calmed his fears. His lips parted, the syllables of an ancient chant emerging from his throat. It was a prayer of the Old Ones, a song that expressed the wonder of all the creation of the Great Mother and her consort, the Horned God. For did not the Deep Magic flow in every corner of their world? Did the Mother not join with the God in birthing every facet of existence? All came from the God and Goddess, therefore all was one. He only prayed the Great Mother would shield him from the shadows of her creation.

The chant ended, leaving his mind clear and silent. In the absence of thought, his senses opened fully. He heard the hiss of the wind, felt the sting of sleet. The smell of winter's decay and the salt tang from the nearby sea greeted his nostrils.

Hefin's feathers ruffled. The merlin sent an image into Rhys's mind: the countryside and sea spread out like a blanket, as a bird in flight might see it. Had any man ever beheld such a view? Avalon appeared as two bumps surrounded by glassy swamps. The treetops were a blanket of greenery. The ocean's waves were tiny tufts of white on an expanse of gray-blue.

Was it truly possible Rhys might see these things with his own eyes? He gazed at Hefin. The merlin had come to him unbidden. Had it chosen him because it sensed a kindred spirit?

Taking a deep breath, he shut his eyes. In his mind's eye he held the picture of a merlin. Slowly, he approached, sinking his consciousness within the image.

At first, all he felt was a slight tingling. It began in his feet, as if some power had emerged from the earth. It radiated up his legs, into his torso, along his arms. It ended in his fingertips and the crown of his head. The sensation was odd, as if he stood on the membrane of an enormous, vibrating drum.

"Great Mother," he prayed. "Grant me this gift for the good of the Light."

At once the tingling intensified. The very marrow of his being throbbed.

Pain seared his body. His bones twisted from within. There was a crackling, popping sound, as sinew and flesh contracted. Panic clogged Rhys's lungs, but he could force no cry from his lips. The world spun dizzily.

His skin was afire, stretched tight over bone and muscle. He fell, writhing, to the frozen ground.

When at last the agony faded, he dared not move. His body felt different. His heart fluttered in his chest, its beat fast and light. When he opened his eyes, the sea and shore sprang at him in sharp relief. Colors were muted, but the details! He saw every ripple of sand, every swell of the waves, every feather on a tern's wing.

The slap of the sea on the shore echoed painfully in his ears. He could hear every whisper of the sea grasses, and even the scurrying feet of a mouse as it burrowed in the sand.

Movement arrested his attention. With a flurry of brown feathers, Hefin dropped into view. Rhys scrambled backward, his heart racing. The merlin had grown huge! Rhys stared as the creature tilted its head and regarded him solemnly.

Slowly, understanding crept over him. Hefin hadn't grown to the size of a man; it was Rhys who had shrunk. Experimentally, he extended his arms. They were no longer human limbs, but wings.

He stood on clawed feet, his talons flexing on the snow-covered rock. He swayed, trying to get the feel of this new body. His clothes were lying in a crumpled heap. If a traveler came upon them, what would he think?

His human mind seemed intact, thanks be to the Great Mother. Yet he had a merlin's mind as well. Cool and ruthless, born of the Deep Magic. Rhys felt the pull of that force. It was a power that existed outside of time. It had come into being long before man had conceived his weak notions of good and evil. He drew almost close enough to touch it, then, gasping, wrenched away. With an effort, he turned his attention to his new body, ruffling and settling his feathers. It was a strange sensation.

Hefin spread his wings and brought them down with a great rush of air. Effortlessly, the merlin rose into the air to perch on the low branch of an elm.

Rhys imitated the movement. It took three tries, and an ignoble tumble, but at last he gained the low branch. From there Hefin rose to the treetops. Rhys followed, only just snagging a thin, swaying limb. The storm's vanguard winds whipped around him. The world below spun crazily.

Haste.

The idea had come from Hefin. Rhys opened his beak to reply, but managed only a screech. When Hefin flapped into the air, Rhys opened his wings and followed. He rose, hovering above the sea.

Something like laughter spread through him. He was flying! He did a loop, reveling in his incredible skill. Flying! It was a miracle.

Hefin screeched a warning. Rhys, in the middle of a gleeful spin, didn't respond. A crosswind struck him like a blow. The sensation was akin to being toppled by a violent wave. Rhys scrabbled to gain control, working the air currents as he would a turbulent surf, to no avail. He couldn't get the rhythm of his new wings. The sea rushed at him.

It was only by the merest chance that he righted himself before smashing into the churning water. Chastened, he steadied himself with a slow beat of his wings before rising to meet Hefin.

Isca, he told the bird.

The merlin gave a squawk and turned to the northeast.

Even the heat of the forge couldn't loosen the angry knot in Marcus's stomach. Clara hadn't so much as glanced behind her as she entered the sheep barn last night. Had she no pride, to seek out a man who spurned her? He hefted his hammer and brought it down with all his might on the anvil. The force of the blow traveled up his arm.

He stared sourly at the new dagger blade he'd nearly split in two. Ruined. Disgusted, he dropped the piece into a trough of sand. Abandoning the furnace, he strode to his worktable and gathered three of his best throwing daggers. Not even pausing to remove his blacksmith's apron, he headed for the door.

Dawn had broken reluctantly. A stiff wind blew and dark clouds piled on the horizon. The sweat of the forge turned to ice on his skin. Marcus frowned. Another storm. Was it driven by Druidry? By Owein, as Rhys had suspected? Or was another force at work? He closed his eyes and tried to feel the magic.

Nothing.

"Pollux," Marcus muttered. Despite the storm, despite the magic, all he could think of was Clara's rejection. And for what? So she could couple in the hay with a Druid who would soon be gone? For Marcus was sure Owein meant to leave for Avalon. He would want to practice his sorcerer's arts with his own kind.

The thought of Druids gathering in the swamplands created a burning sensation in the pit of Marcus's stomach. It didn't matter that Rhys insisted Avalon served only the Light. Marcus did not believe it. Power was seductive. There would always be those who would convince themselves the good they sought could only be achieved through evil.

He unlocked the yard gate, leaving it open a crack behind him. Leaving the farmhouse compound, he strode across a stubbled wheat field, angling toward the forest and the clearing beyond, where his practice targets—stumps and slabs of wood set at various heights and distances—awaited.

His first throw hit his target dead center. He gripped the hilt of the second knife, closing one eye to judge his aim. A sudden thought rose: what if Clara carried Owein's child? If the Druid did not claim the babe, was Marcus willing to do so?

The second blade missed its mark, glancing off the edge of the target. He scowled, muttering darkly.

"Marcus?"

He looked up to find Breena beside him. He hadn't heard her approach, but that was no surprise. The wind was far from silent and his sister could move like a wraith.

"Is there a problem at the house?" he asked, frowning.

"Nay." She seemed nervous, her fingers twisting together—a gesture she rarely made.

She looked so distressed that Marcus's heart skipped a beat. "Is it . . . did you have one of your nightmares?" Had she touched on some darkness she couldn't face?

"Nay," she said, not meeting his gaze. "I thought . . . I thought to ask your advice."

His brows raised. "On what subject?"

"It's Rhys. I feel so strange when I'm near him. Hot and cold at once. I think . . . I think I love him. But I don't know if he feels the same."

Marcus let out a breath. No magic, just a girl's infatuation. "Of course Rhys doesn't love you. At least, not in that way. He's nearly twice your age."

"It's not uncommon for older men to marry younger women."

"Maybe not, but you're only a girl." Marcus shook his head. "Rhys is a man, Bree, and you know nothing of men. You have no idea what they—"

She pressed her lips into a thin line. "I know you and Rhys visit the tavern wenches."

Marcus started. "You do?"

"Aye. And once, last summer, when you were short on coin, you shared a woman between you." She scowled. "You should be careful what you discuss in the fields when you think no one is listening."

"By Jupiter, Bree! Have you no decency?"

"Not where spying on my brother is concerned," she said, but her attempt at levity didn't reach her eyes. She looked skyward, troubled. Then she gave a gasp.

"Look, Marcus! Two merlins. Above the western field."

"*Two* merlins?" Marcus followed her outstretched finger. Sure enough, two birds circled. But it wasn't possible one could be Rhys's falcon. The creature always flew alone.

"They fly before the storm," Breena said.

The pair dropped low, circling the forest beyond the edge of the clearing. Marcus watched them, his brow furrowing. Something was wrong with one of the birds. Its flight was erratic, dipping and jerking awkwardly. Its companion circled, almost as if offering encouragement or instruction.

Marcus dismissed the fanciful notion. His artist's imagination, as always, churned with fantasy. No feathered conversation was going on overhead. One merlin was sick, or injured, that was all. He rubbed his eyes, trying to get a firmer grip on himself.

Breena's breath caught. "Marcus—look!"

The wounded falcon had dipped low, leaving its companion to rise on an updraft. The bird hovered just above the trees at the far edge of the clearing, wings spread, head angled downward as if assessing the hardness of the ground. An instant later, it dropped like a rock and disappeared.

Breena gasped and ran toward it.

"Bree, come back!" Marcus might as well have tried to command the wind. Swearing, he jogged after her, his boots crunching the frozen stubble. His forge apron, heavy with tools, bounced at his waist.

Breena disappeared into the trees. Marcus found her kneeling beside the fallen raptor, her hand outstretched and trembling. The bird thrashed, its left wing limp. When Breena shifted closer, it let out a shrill squawk.

The merlin overhead screeched a warning.

"Don't touch it," Marcus warned, grabbing Bree's arm and jerking her back. "Its mate may attack, and you can't help in any case." He groped for his remaining dagger. "I'll kill it and be done with it."

"No!" Breena twisted violently. "You don't understand. I have to help him."

An icy gust of wind blasted through the trees. Overhead, a limb gave an ominous crack. Marcus glanced up, then dragged Breena clear of the brittle branch.

"It's not safe here in the woods. And it's freezing besides. Let's go back."

"No. Let me go."

"When you're safe in the house."

The merlin flopped on its side. Breena clawed at Marcus's arm, to no avail. She tried a kick to his knee, but he blocked it with his thigh.

"Marcus," she said, her voice pleading. "Please."

He turned, prepared to drag his sister away bodily if that was what it took to get her out of harm's way.

"Marcus," she whispered again, her voice strangled. "Look."

He turned back to scold her, but the words died in his throat.

The merlin was changing.

Panic surged within him, sharp and urgent. Little good it

did—Marcus's legs were rooted to the ground, his hand frozen on Breena's arm. His mind, trapped inside his unresponsive body, screamed at him, urging him to flee, but he could not. He could only stare in horror as impossible sorcery unfolded before him.

The merlin twisted on the ground. Elongated. Its bones snapped, a truly awful sound. Under the creature's covering of feathers, its body grew. Then the feathers smoothed into skin. The bird's head rounded, its curved beak smoothing into nose and lips. Clawed feet grew human toes. Wings stretched into arms.

The raptor's cries faded, leaving only the low moan of a man.

"No," Marcus whispered. He staggered back a step, dragging Breena with him. *"No."*

Breena's voice trembled. "I tried to tell you."

"It cannot be." Horror burgeoned inside him, until he feared his chest would burst. "It can *not* be."

It cannot be. The phrase was a hammer on the anvil of his skull. His stomach roiled. He wanted desperately to look away, but he could not. He could only stare as, with a flash of light, Rhys shook off the last vestiges of his animal form.

Never, in all his dark nightmares, had Marcus dared to dream something so ghastly.

Rhys sat before him, legs splayed, arms upon his knees, head bowed, his breath coming in sharp spurts. A shudder wracked his body. With an abrupt motion, he rolled onto his hands and knees and emptied the contents of his stomach onto the ground.

It was only then Marcus realized the Druid was naked.

He thrust Breena behind him. With a groan, Rhys knelt back on his haunches, cradling his left elbow.

"Rhys," Breena breathed.

Rhys's head jerked up, his gaze locking with Marcus's.

"Cover yourself," Marcus said sharply.

Rhys's eyes flicked to Breena and widened. His cheeks

flooded with color. Keeping one hand firmly on Breena, Marcus untied his forge apron with the other hand and tossed it to Rhys.

"Here."

Rhys caught the apron, tools and all, with his injured arm. The weight caused his elbow to twist. He paled, sweat appearing on his forehead, but he said nothing as he tied the garment awkwardly about his waist. Slowly, he rose to his feet. With a screech, Hefin dove through the branches to land on his shoulder.

Breena tried to go to him. Did the girl have no sense at all? Marcus stopped her forward motion. "Stay back. You don't know what this . . ." He swallowed. "This *man* might do."

"It's Rhys, Marcus! He would never hurt us!"

"That's true," Rhys said quietly, his gaze never wavering from Marcus's face. "I bring ye no harm."

"No harm? You changed from bird to man before my eyes! What are you? A spirit? A demon?"

"I'm a man," Rhys said quietly. "No more or less than you."

"Something more, I'm thinking." Marcus stared at Hefin, perched on Rhys's shoulder. The creature's black eye regarded him unblinkingly. Was the bird a Druid as well? "At best, you're a sorcerer. At worst . . ." Marcus didn't want to consider the worst. "You're not welcome here."

The first darts of sleet stung Marcus's cheek. Hefin ruffled his wing feathers and settled, talons flexing on Rhys's bare shoulders. Marcus wondered how the silver-haired Celt managed to look so regal standing nearly naked in the winter dawn. The frigid wind was fierce, but Rhys paid it no notice.

"I mean no harm," Rhys repeated. "Indeed, I've come seeking help. I'll be gone once she agrees to come with me."

Marcus felt Breena's quick intake of breath. "You're not taking my sister anywhere," he said, his tone deadly.

"I've not come for Breena."

"Then who?"

"The Roman woman. The one who sought the Lost Grail."

"Clara?" Marcus sucked in a breath. "For what purpose?"

"She must accompany me to the sacred isle."

Marcus regarded Rhys with distrust. "You would bring a Roman to Avalon? I cannot believe that."

"I'll explain to Clara."

"If you think I'll allow you near her—"

"Marcus," Breena interrupted. "You cannot presume to speak for Clara!"

Marcus set his jaw. "Very well." He renewed his grip on Breena's arm. "I'll take you to her." Pivoting, he set out for home.

He'd not gone two paces before Rhys called him back. "Marcus?"

He stopped and turned. "What?"

The Druid spread his arms wide. "Might I first trouble ye for some clothes?"

Clara sat at Rhiannon's table, crumbling a crust of bread. Owein's sister had ordered her to eat, so she'd dutifully chewed a mouthful of leftover stew. A cup filled with steaming liquid sat at her elbow, but Clara suspected it would take much more than a potion of herbs to warm her.

Owein was gone.

She cradled the cup with numb fingers, searching her heart for a flicker of emotion. Curiously, she felt little. The pain and guilt of her father's death, which had been so all-consuming the night before, was only a dim ache. Since the sickening moment she'd awakened alone in the cold barn loft, her body had been encased by ice. It was as if she stood outside herself, gazing at some unknown woman sitting in her chair. The woman's face was drawn and pale, her eyes blank, her movements tiny and weak.

The intimate places of Clara's body ached from Owein's lovemaking. What if she carried his babe? Valgus would never allow her to keep the child. She splayed a hand on her flat stomach. She would abandon her inheritance rather than give up Owein's babe.

She stared into her cup. Last night, she'd been sure that Owein loved her. She'd seen it in his mind, felt it in the reverent way he'd worshipped her body. He thought he protected her by keeping her away from his memories. She shivered, feeling again his nausea, his rush of despair and humiliation. His hatred of those who had hurt him.

She'd backed away from the worst of his darkness. If she had tried harder to heal Owein's pain, would he be at her side now?

Rhiannon looked up from her cauldron, twin lines of worry etched in the center of her forehead. "Dinna blame yourself for Owein's departure, Clara."

Owein's sister had spoken in Latin, so Clara responded in kind. But the words felt thick and heavy on her tongue, so unlike the lilting language she'd whispered to Owein last night. "You've been very kind."

"You brought my brother to me. I can never repay you for that."

"But now he's gone again. Nothing has changed."

"I know he's alive. That means everything."

Clara gripped her cup. The brew's fragrance was pleasing, but she couldn't bring herself to take a sip. "Owein was alone in the mountains for so long. He needs a family. If I hadn't been here, he might have stayed with you."

Rhiannon left her cauldron to sit in the chair opposite Clara. "Why do you say that?"

"It was my love that drove him away."

"Or his love for you."

A sliver of pain slid through a crack in Clara's frozen heart. "Do you think he loves me? I hoped so, but now . . ."

Rhiannon reached across the table and squeezed Clara's forearm. "He does. I'm sure of it." The furrows in her brow deepened. "But there's darkness inside him . . ."

"He won't let me touch it. I—" She broke off as the door opened.

Marcus entered the hearth room, steering Breena in front of him. The girl's expression was furious; she flounced away as soon as she passed the threshold. Marcus stepped to one side, allowing a second man to enter.

Clara's eyes widened. The newcomer was a Celt, tall and lanky. He was dressed oddly, in a shirt far too baggy and *braccas* far too short for his frame. His hair was unlike any Clara had ever seen—it fell in silver-blond waves to his shoulders. His gray eyes were weary—indeed, his entire body seemed to strum with the same fatigue Owein endured after one of his visions. One arm hung limply at his side.

Nevertheless, his eyes were alert. He scanned the room quickly, his gaze passing over Rhiannon to settle on Clara. She read a wary hope in his expression. She shifted in her seat, unnerved.

"Rhys," Rhiannon said, standing. "What are ye doing here? Are ye injured?"

He glanced down at his arm, as if he'd forgotten it pained him. " 'Tis but a strain, I think."

Rhiannon's gaze darted to Breena. "Have ye come—"

Breena cut in. "It's not me he—"

"Hold your tongue for once," muttered Marcus. "Where is Owein?" he asked, ignoring Breena's huff of annoyance.

"Gone," Clara said, standing. "To Avalon." Her voice sounded hoarse.

Rhys swore under his breath. "To Blodwen," he said grimly. "My cousin. It was she who spoke the curse that sickened our grandfather."

Rhiannon started. "Ye were nay aware of evil in your midst?"

Rhys reddened. "One of our number suspected. My twin, Gwendolyn. Blodwen has imprisoned her." He swallowed. "My cousin has gained the Lost Grail."

"From Cormac?" Clara asked.

"Aye. The dwarf is caught in Blodwen's web. But she seeks yet another victim. A King born of the ancient line of Celtic queens, who will join with her in darkness. The man she wants as her consort possesses a strong link to the Deep Magic."

"Owein," Rhiannon whispered.

"Aye. Blodwen has set a trap for him. If he succumbs to it, I dinna know what darkness will follow."

"I know," Breena murmured. She winced, rubbing the bridge of her nose. Her voice grew thin, her eyes unfocused. "I See . . . the seas rising. The earth shaking. The fortress reduced to rubble. A Dark Queen rises, a Dark King at her side. They hold the Lost Grail. It's filled with blood . . ."

She gasped, bending double. Rhiannon was at her daughter's side in a heartbeat, arms encircling her torso. Rhys watched with troubled eyes as the healer eased the shuddering girl onto a bench by the hearth. Clara sensed he wanted to go to Breena, but something held him back. Was it Marcus, who stood so grimly with his muscular arms crossed against his chest?

Rhys turned to Clara. To her surprise, he moved close and took her hand, prying her fingers from the edge of the table.

"I need your help, cousin."

His touch was warm and comforting. She studied their joined hands, then looked up as the meaning of his words penetrated her brain. "Cousin? What do you mean? I'm no Celt."

"Nay," Rhys conceded. "But I believe we share a common ancestor. Long ago, before the Romans marched on the west country, a ship from the East was wrecked on the shores of Avalon. All died save one woman, heavy with child. No one ever learned her name—they called her simply, 'The Lady.' "

"Who was she?"

"The disciple of an Eastern prophet executed by the Romans. A band of his followers feared for their lives. They fled by sea, meaning to land in Gaul, but a storm blew them north to Avalon. The Druids living there took the woman in. She told them of her master, a man who led people to the Light.

"The Lady carried a plain wooden cup that had once held the prophet's blood. The Deep Magic was strong in the vessel. Any who drank from it were cured of illness. Soon after, the Lady was delivered of twin daughters. When the girls were but infants, their mother disappeared into the swamps. Her body was never found."

"How terrible," Clara murmured.

"The Daughters remained in Avalon. When they grew, it was found that they possessed a link to the Deep Magic. The clan decided the Daughters should be trained in the ways of the Old Ones. They were schooled in magic and learned the art of smithcraft. As young women, they encased their mother's wooden cup with silver and crystal, adding the magic of the Old Ones to the power of the Lady's prophet." Rhys met Clara's gaze. "Their cup is the one ye once held. The Lost Grail of Avalon."

"But I don't understand," Clara said. "If the grail was made in Avalon, how did it come into my grandmother's hands?"

"When the Legions marched on the west, I believe one Daughter escaped with the grail and found a home among the Romans. That Daughter is your ancestor, Clara."

"And her sister?"

"My own foremother." Rhys inclined his head. "We are kin."

Clara's head grew light. She was kin to Druids? "It's impossible," she whispered.

"Nay. Gwen, my sister, entrusted me with the grail's secret. Only a Daughter of the Lady may call its power. One such Daughter is Blodwen. Gwen is another. And then, there is you." Rhys's fingers tightened on hers. "Ye feel the Deep Magic, do ye not?"

"Yes. I wanted to learn more, but Owein refused to teach me."

"I'll try to teach ye what ye need to know, if ye will agree to oppose Blodwen. Will ye come with me to Avalon, Clara?"

To wrest the grail from the hands of a sorceress? The thought made her ill. But if Owein were walking into a trap . . .

"I'll come," she said quietly.

"Think hard before ye consent. 'Twill nay be an easy task to claim the Lost Grail." He exhaled sharply. "Blodwen's power is strong. She's taken it from a dark source that does not demand her strength in payment." With brief words Rhys painted a nauseating picture of Blodwen's foul use of Cormac, the dwarf. "I cannot lie to ye," he finished. "This endeavor may cost your life."

"And . . . if I don't try?"

"Blodwen seeks revenge for a grievous wrong done to her in her youth. And I find I canna condemn her for her hatred of the soldiers who used her so cruelly. But in her mind the blame has spread to include all Romans, and indeed, all Celts who have made peace with Rome." He gave a troubled glance toward Breena, who still sat huddled on the bench with Rhiannon. "I believe Breena has Seen a shadow of Blodwen's intent."

The wind wailed, rattling the shutters.

"I will go," Clara repeated.

Rhys's shoulders sagged. "Thank the Great Mother. We'll leave within the hour."

"Are you well enough?" Rhiannon asked, her face lined with worry. "Your arm—"

"It's fine," Rhys said abruptly. His eyes darted to where Marcus leaned against the doorjamb, his expression hard, his fingers stroking the hilt of his dagger. "Marcus, may I trouble ye for provisions? And a pair of swift horses?"

Marcus's gaze passed to Clara, then to Breena, then back

to Rhys. He muttered a soft curse under his breath. "On one condition," he said. "And there will be no argument."

"What is that?" Rhys asked cautiously.

"I'm going with you."

Clara had never ridden a horse. Her father hadn't allowed it.

She clung to the reins, terrified, her head bowed to keep the worst of the sleet from driving into her eyes. The gray mare pitched like a boat, chafing her thighs. She was thankful for the ancient pair of Marcus's *braccas* Rhiannon had insisted she wear under her tunic. She fully expected the creature to bolt, but as the day faded into night it became apparent her mare was interested in nothing but following Rhys's mount. Marcus brought up the rear, his anger so hot Clara could almost feel it singeing her cloak.

Marcus hadn't wanted her to risk herself, but what choice did she have? If Owein was heading into a trap set by a crazed Druidess, Clara could hardly refuse her aid. And then there had been Breena's vision. She shuddered. She couldn't sit in Isca, waiting for a Dark storm to consume the city.

Instead, she rode to meet it.

The journey was rough, even on horseback. Clara thought of Owein, on foot. Would they reach Avalon before him? She closed her eyes and searched for him. The attempt proved useless.

Rhys spent a good portion of the ride by Clara's side, asking about her link to the Deep Magic and answering her questions about Druidry. She learned that to touch her magic, she needed a clear mind. At Rhys's bidding, she practiced emptying her mind of thoughts as she rode. It was not an easy task.

Both the God and the Goddess were of the Deep Magic, Rhys explained. A Druid could choose to follow his deity either in Light or in darkness, or with a combination of both. "My grandfather," he said, "will not allow darkness on Avalon. He follows only the Light. This was the teaching brought by the Lady from the East—harm none, even for good purposes. Forgive every hurt, even those inflicted by your enemy."

"That seems a hard road to follow," Clara said.

"It is." Rhys hesitated, then sighed. "After Blodwen was abused, her father, Padrig, wanted to take vengeance. Cyric refused. He does not allow the use of Deep Magic, even for justice, because it makes one vulnerable to darkness. Instead of retribution, Cyric advised forgiveness. Padrig bowed to his brother's will, and it seemed Blodwen did, too. But I know now she never found the Light's peace. How could she, with her magic and beauty gone, and pity in every glance that came her way?" He shook his head. "The path of the Light is a hard one, Clara. I canna say for certain that I agree with all Cyric's decisions."

Clara frowned. "It seems so complex. I'm not sure what you expect me to do. How am I to face Blodwen and gain the grail when I know so little?"

Rhys shifted in his saddle. "Ye have only to follow my lead. I'll not let ye fall. Blodwen means to join with Owein in the Lost Land. We must go there and prevent it."

"The Lost Land? What is that?"

"The Lost Land is the place that separates Annwyn, the realm of the gods, from the realm of men. Only those with a strong link to the Deep Magic may enter."

Clara swallowed. "Once we are there, what then?"

"I dinna know, precisely. We will seek the wisdom of the Great Mother. She will guide us."

His words did little to comfort Clara. How was she to face a sorceress, when she had so little knowledge of her own magic? If only Owein had been willing to teach her more.

With nightfall, the sleet changed to snow. Clara teetered in her saddle, jerking awake just in time to keep herself from falling.

Marcus rode up alongside her and grabbed her reins.

"This is lunacy," he shouted ahead to Rhys. "It's too dark to go on. Clara needs rest."

Rhys half-turned in his saddle. "There's no time."

"It'll do you no good if she falls ill," Marcus retorted. "To say nothing of the horses."

Above them, a raptor shrieked. Clara looked skyward and recognized the merlin she'd seen on Rhys's arm just before they'd left the Aquila farm. It had flown off to the west, and she'd not seen it again until now.

The bird called a second time, swooping low. Rhys's mare reared. Rhys settled the beast and dismounted. Striding a short distance away, he raised his arm. The merlin landed.

Clara watched the tall Celt as he murmured soothing words to the bird. It cocked its head and lifted its wings in response.

"It almost looks as if they're speaking," she said out loud.

A muscle in Marcus's jaw twitched. "They are. It's part of Rhys's sorcery."

Clara's eyes widened. "What a wonder," she murmured.

"A foul twist of nature, to my mind," Marcus replied.

Rhys raised his arm and Hefin took wing. When he turned toward them, his eyes were troubled. "We have no time to rest," he said. "Owein approaches Avalon."

Chapter Twenty-three

Owein moved silently through the swamplands. Avalon lay before him, a black mound against the night sky, curtained by snowfall. He frowned. He felt no call from the high slope of the sacred isle, where it was said its magic was most powerful. Instead, the far side of Avalon's smaller hill beckoned.

The ache between his eyes intensified, but it didn't occur to Owein that he might turn back. A vision guided him. The gray-eyed Druidess of his dream, the woman destined to become the mother of his babes. Her silver tresses streamed about her body like waves of light. A simple white tunic accented her lush breasts and hips.

Slender arms lifted. She held the Lost Grail.

"Beloved," she whispered. "Come to me."

Beloved.

Clara had uttered the same endearment—had it been only the night before? For a shuddering instant, Owein could do nothing but remember the softness of her skin as she pressed her body to his. When he breathed, her rose scent lingered. Her murmurs and sighs echoed in his ears. And when she'd reached her peak . . .

He muttered a curse, shaking his head to clear it. Clara was not for him; she would marry Marcus Aquila, a man who was part of her own world. Owein's destiny lay in Avalon.

He raised his eyes, searching for signs of life. Was that a shimmer of light? The flicker dazzled his eyes. The ache in his head intensified.

I can soothe the pain, a voice whispered in his mind. *Ye need never feel it again. Come home and I will show ye.*

Come home.

Was there such a place?

He pushed Clara's image into the darkest corner of his mind and turned his face to the hillside.

Mist shrouded Avalon.

The tempest that had blown most of the day had calmed in the night, and the fallen snow seemed to insulate rather than chill. Marcus didn't take much comfort in the storm's changing character. The silence of the swamps was too deep. Though he couldn't feel any magic, he knew it was abroad.

His gaze sought his companions. Clara's face was pale and drawn, while Rhys's jaw seemed chiseled from stone. Marcus calmed his own nerves by muttering every curse he knew—in Latin, in Celtic, and even a few in Greek—under his breath.

The moon filtered through the thinning clouds, casting an otherworldly glow over the swamps. The tip of Avalon rode above the mist; its base was swathed in fog. Rhys halted at the water's edge. Marcus dismounted silently and searched for a place where the horses could cross. The water's surface was strewn with ice and floating debris, but at least it was calm.

Finding a rocky outcropping that promised firmer footing, Marcus swung back into his saddle. The horses advanced slowly, placing each hoof with care. As the mist closed in, Rhys's mare shied to the left, nearly pitching him into the water.

"Ye might train your beasts better," Rhys muttered to Marcus.

"Ye might learn to handle a Roman saddle," Marcus retorted.

Rhys grumbled a reply.

Paradoxically, the trading of insults eased the knot in Marcus's stomach. He and Rhys had often sparred in this manner during the long years of their friendship, and Rhys's lack of horsemanship had been a frequent topic of discussion. The Druid's skill was sufficient to keep his seat while the animals forded the swamp, however.

They emerged onto a small beach littered with rafts and small log boats. Rhys quickly dismounted, tethering the lead horse to a tree branch.

"Come," Rhys said to Clara, indicating what might have been a path, had it been visible through the fog.

Marcus exchanged a glance with Clara and started forward. Rhys held up a hand, halting Marcus's progress. His gaze didn't quite reach Marcus's as he said, "Only Clara may advance. I've already overstepped Cyric's rules by bringing a Roman this far. Ye may not come farther."

Marcus scowled. "Clara is Roman."

"Clara is a Daughter of the Lady. You are not."

Marcus crossed his arms over his chest. "It makes no difference. I go where she goes."

" 'Tis nay possible. There are wards and protective spells. One with no magic cannot climb the sacred hill."

Ignoring him, Marcus pushed past Rhys and started up the path. He'd not gone far when his limbs grew heavy and the air in his lungs thickened. He struggled, trying to take the next step up the mountain.

He could not do it.

"Ye canna go farther. 'Tis useless to try. The spell was wrought by Cyric."

Marcus managed one more step before dropping to one knee, chest heaving. "I am enchanted, then?"

"Nay. Simply . . . discouraged."

With an effort, Marcus gained his feet. He looked at Clara. She seemed to have no difficulty walking the path. "You don't have to go," Marcus told her. "I'll take you back to Isca whenever you say the word."

She touched his arm. "Please understand, Marcus."

Marcus searched her gaze. "Do you love him that much?"

"Yes."

He exhaled, and nodded once. "I'll be here, with the horses, until . . . until I know you have no more need of me."

He watched her disappear into the mist. The next moment, the ground beneath his feet trembled slightly. He thought at first he'd imagined it, until the horses whinnied in distress.

He went to comfort them.

A subtle tremor shook the island, vibrating the soles of Clara's feet. Deep Magic pulsed beneath her, in the earth. Above, the snow swirled angrily, the wind whipping her cloak about her and reaching with icy fingers to dance upon her spine. The grail was near—she could feel the tug of its magic on her heart.

The path Rhys followed led through a deserted village. "All gone," he muttered. "They'll be near the summit, at the stone that marks the entrance to the Lost Land."

Rhys climbed, weaving a series of switchbacks around the hill. Clara paused a moment, then followed.

The Druids of Avalon were gathered around a blazing bonfire that occupied the space between a round hut and a smooth white boulder. They numbered twenty in all, including a few children. She quickly scanned their faces. "Owein is not here," she murmured to Rhys.

"Nay," he said. "I didna expect him to be."

"But then why did we come—"

Her question died as a tall, dark-haired Druid stepped forward. A hunched old woman advanced at his side, her ancient face shadowed and drawn. The man's eyes flicked over Clara. Anger burned there.

"Ye've brought an enemy to the sacred isle?" he demanded of Rhys. "As Cyric lies dying? Have ye lost all reason?"

Hefin chose that moment to dive, barely missing the Druid's head. The man flinched, his arms flying up in protection. Rhys called the merlin's name. The bird settled itself on its master's forearm, blinking solemnly.

"Clara is no enemy, Padrig. She is a Daughter of the Lady."

Padrig's eyes narrowed on Clara. A skitter of dread raced down her spine. "Impossible. She is Roman."

"She's passed Cyric's wards unharmed. She's held the Lost Grail and called its magic. Now she will pass into the Lost Land and reclaim the grail from the traitor."

"Gwendolyn," Padrig said bitterly.

"Nay, not Gwen." Rhys met the older man's gaze squarely. "Blodwen."

Padrig snorted. "My daughter? She canna enter the Lost Land, and well ye know it. She has no magic."

"Blodwen has rediscovered her power," Rhys said quietly. "She's pledged it to the service of darkness, to avenge those who abused her. The soldiers Cyric did not pursue. In striking them down, she cares not if innocents suffer."

Padrig's face drained of color. "Blodwen wouldna do such a thing. She is a gentle soul!"

"Even a gentle soul may turn to darkness when the pain is great enough," Rhys said. His expression was bleak; his tone laced with sorrow. "Blodwen is a Daughter of the Lady. Her power is great. She called the ill winds and pronounced the Words that sickened Cyric. When Gwen suspected her wrongdoing, Blodwen imprisoned her by magic."

There were murmurs all around. " 'Tis a lie!" Padrig spat.

"Nay, Uncle. Blodwen has gained the Lost Grail. Now she uses her power to call the Druid Owein, of the line of Queen Cartimandua. She means to join with him in the Lost Land, sealing her mastery of the world."

The old woman at Padrig's side spoke for the first time. "Your charge is most serious. What proof do ye offer?"

"The proof of my own eyes, Mared." Briefly, Rhys told how Blodwen had used Cormac to regain her power. Padrig's countenance turned ill. Mared's eyes saddened.

"Clara is a Daughter of the Lady," Rhys repeated. "The Great Mother will allow her passage to the Lost Land."

Mared nodded. "It will be as the Goddess wishes. The Roman woman may attempt to enter. But ye must stay at her side."

"I mean to." Rhys guided Clara to the stone. Standing beside her, he raised his hand and spoke a single syllable. The guttural incantation vibrated in Clara's skull.

Clara stared at the rock in bewilderment. The light from the fire danced over its face, illuminating its ridges and valleys. "I . . . don't understand."

"I've spoken the Word of entrance. Do as I do," he added, placing his hand on the stone.

As if in a trance, Clara mimicked his action. Despite the cold night, the rock felt warm. "It's a door, then? You will move it aside?"

"Nay."

"Then how—?"

"Look inside yourself, Clara. Ye'll find the answer there."

She splayed both hands over the stone. Her eyelids drifted closed. Her mind opened, searching for guidance.

She found Owein.

He was nearby.

I'm coming to you, she thought. *Wait for me.*

There was no reply. Had he even heard?

Drawing a breath, she reached for him. As she did, her hands sank into the stone. The company of Druids gave up a collective gasp.

Her eyes flew open. Her arms had sunk into the rock. It was a strange sight. Her flesh was enveloped in heat, but the sensation was not painful. Before her, she felt Owein's presence. At her side, Rhys stood, his fingers still splayed on the white rock.

He met her gaze, frowning.

"What . . . what does this mean?" Clara whispered.

"It means," he said quietly. "That the Great Mother requires ye to enter the Lost Land alone."

A touch, like a cool hand on his heated brow, alighted on Owein's mind. He halted, confused. There could be only one source of that sensation.

Clara.

But how could that be? He'd left her safe at the Aquila farm with a storm closing in. Surely she couldn't have followed him to Avalon.

He hesitated, wondering if he should go back to investigate. But the urge to advance was strong. A light glimmered in the cleft of the hillside. Thoughts of Clara faded as a surge of magic carried him forward. The silver-haired Druidess awaited.

He followed a narrow and winding trail. The light grew brighter, until its source became clear. The glow emanated from a smooth white rock wedged between two darker boulders, amid the ruin of a rough hut. Drawn to the stone, Owein halted before it.

Come to me, beloved.

Frowning, he placed his palm on the smooth, cool surface.

There was a pulling sensation, as if his body were being sucked forward. A rush of noise in his ears, a flash of pain, and then all was silent. He opened his eyes, blinking.

He stood in a village yard, in the center of a cluster of roundhouses surrounded by a high palisade wall. He faced the door of a solid-looking dwelling with mud walls and a high cone-shaped thatched roof. The home from his dreams? Hesitating only a second, he strode forward and pulled open the door.

The silver-haired woman stood at the hearth, stirring her cauldron. His gaze roamed, taking in chairs, a loom, a table, and a wide bed pallet. Shelves were filled with crockery, bundles of herbs dangled from the rafters, a wreath hung over the door.

His attention returned to the Druidess. If Owein had thought her beautiful in his dreams, he'd had but a glimpse of the loveliness that confronted him now. She was tall and regal, with lush breasts, narrow waist, and full hips, all clad in white. Silver-blond hair streamed over her shoulders.

Her magic surrounded him but didn't intrude on his mind. It was wholly unlike Clara's intimate touch, yet the effect was similar. The pain behind his eyes faded and his strength grew.

And yet . . . something didn't feel quite right.

He hesitated, brows drawing together as he tried to understand. The woman moved gracefully to the far side of the room. Her back to him, she lifted a cloth draped over a shelf and removed what was beneath it. Turning with arms extended, she offered it to him.

The Lost Grail. He could feel the vessel's power, calling him. The woman's lush red lips curved in a smile.

"Welcome, Owein."

He inclined his head. "Ye know my name. Will ye tell me yours?"

"Blodwen," she said. "I am a Daughter of the Lady. As ye are a son of queens." She lifted the grail. "I thank ye. The Lost Grail came to me from your hands through your kinsman, Cormac."

"The dwarf is nearby?"

"Nay. He has gone."

He swept his arm to one side, encompassing the dwelling. "And this place?" he asked. "What is it? 'Tis nay the world of men, that much I know. I stood before the stone in the hillside, then found myself here. 'Tis a shadow of the future, I am thinking."

"Aye. The Lost Land shows us a vision of things to come." Her lashes fluttered, her eyes cast downward, a smile playing about her lips. "This is our home, Owein. The one we will have in our future." She sent a glance to the pallet behind her, where two tousled heads, one fair, one russet, peeked from the coverlet. "These are our children."

Owein's chest constricted. A family. *His* family.

"Ye will be my husband, and I your wife." She lifted the Lost Grail. The motion caused her tunic to slip, revealing a milky-white shoulder.

"Come. Ye must be weary after your long journey. Drink from my cup, and lie with me on our pallet."

She tilted the cup, revealing its contents.

Blood.

Marcus kept a wary eye on the path Rhys and Clara had taken. With night falling, he didn't relish the thought of being left alone in this place of sorcery. What if one of the Druids came down to the shore? What manner of curse would they put on him?

He paced uneasily. He'd built a small fire, but the wood was damp, and he was afraid the scent would bring trouble. Still, he couldn't bear to sit alone in the dark, jumping every time the wind rustled the reeds.

The horses picked up his mood, shifting and whinnying nervously. A sudden splash had him pivoting quickly. He'd thought any danger would come from the island, but perhaps he'd been mistaken. The swamp could very well be enchanted, too. He strained to see the black water. Did some beast lurk in its depths?

Another splash. The light of his fire was reflected back as two silver points of light. Marcus froze.

A form coalesced on the shore. Silver like the mist, it seemed to drift before becoming completely real. Marcus tensed, his breath all but gone, as an enormous gray she-wolf advanced on silent feet, head and tail held low.

The horses shied, twisting their tethers. Marcus stood his ground, eyes trained on the animal before him. His fingers found the hilt of his dagger, flexing almost imperceptibly. If the beast sprang, he would throw. But not before. He could not kill such a beautiful creature unless he was compelled to it.

The wolf halted a short distance away. A trickle of sweat rolled down the side of Marcus's face. His hands were clammy; his grip on his dagger was slipping. But he dared not shift to adjust the weapon.

A soft footstep sounded behind him. By Pollux! Marcus kept his gaze fixed on the wolf and eased back in his stance, preparing to meet whatever new peril had sprung up behind him.

"Marcus . . ."

Rhys.

"Where's Clara?"

"She's gone after Owein."

"Alone?"

"Aye."

He muttered a curse.

"I wasn't permitted to follow," Rhys said quietly. "I tried, but . . ." His gaze fixed on the wolf.

The creature inclined its head, as if in greeting.

Rhys tensed. "Trouble?"

Marcus was uncertain whether Rhys addressed him or the wolf.

The beast answered with a low growl. Its ears slanted forward; its tail lowered. Marcus raised his dagger.

"Nay, Marcus. Leave her be."

"And be mauled? Not likely."

"This she-wolf willna harm ye. She brings me . . . news."

Somehow, that pronouncement didn't make Marcus feel any calmer.

Several silent moments passed. Some understanding

seemed to flash between the wolf and Rhys. Then the creature turned and slipped back into the water.

Marcus let out a long breath. "Thank Jupiter. It's going."

"We must follow." Rhys's voice was tight.

"Follow a wolf into the night? That's beyond idiocy."

Rhys was already moving toward the horses. Marcus sheathed his dagger and hurried to stop him. "The mounts are already spooked. They'll never follow a wolf."

"Then we'll take a boat," Rhys said, changing course. "I only pray we arrive quickly enough."

"Arrive where? Quickly enough for what?"

Rhys didn't answer. After a brief hesitation, Marcus sheathed his dagger and took a burning branch from his fire. Rhys shoved a log boat into the water and looked back at him. Marcus swallowed his misgivings and climbed in.

The wolf swam into the falling snow. Rhys dipped a paddle in the water, propelling the boat after it.

"Do you have any idea where the beast is leading us?" Marcus asked after a time.

"To Gwendolyn."

"Your twin?"

"Aye."

"And . . . you say the beast told you to hurry?"

"Aye."

Marcus steeled himself. "Is the wolf a Druid as well? A human in wolf form?"

"Nay. 'Tis but a wolf. But only a fool would ignore the wisdom of our animal brothers."

"Are you calling me a fool?" Marcus asked sharply.

Rhys exhaled. "Marcus Aquila, I would call ye nothing but friend, if ye would allow it."

Marcus remained silent as Rhys paddled across the swamp. The Mendips neared, rising above them like sleeping giants. When they ran aground, Marcus handed the torch to Rhys, then sprang to the shore to haul the boat from the water.

Rhys was already scrabbling up a long slope within the

cleft of two hillocks, following the wolf. Marcus strode after him, ignoring the instinct that urged him to dive back into the swamp. Had he lost his mind completely? Whatever magic Rhys was rushing toward, Marcus wanted no part of it.

The Celt halted at a crevice in the rocky wall of the hillside, holding the light high. The wolf bared its teeth in a snarl, pacing before the narrow opening.

Dread prickled up Marcus's spine. "Is your sister here?"

Rhys nodded. "Trapped by Blodwen's spell. I tried to free her, but my cousin's magic was too strong. Now, perhaps, with her attention drawn to other matters . . ." He raised his hand toward the cave, palm flat, fingers spread. "I may be able to weaken the spell."

Marcus groped for his dagger, though he knew the gesture was futile. "Enough to free her?"

Rhys glanced at him. "With your help."

Marcus peered into the depths of the crevice, but saw nothing. Heard nothing save the steady drip of water. "Are you sure she's still there?"

The wolf gave a low growl.

"Aye," Rhys said simply.

"You really understand that animal," Marcus said uneasily. "Can you speak with any beast?"

Rhys hesitated before answering. "My talent is the magic of the forest. I receive impressions from many animals, but I converse most easily with Hefin, and now with this wolf." He paused. "Hefin is my companion, as ye know. And this wolf . . . this wolf is Gwen's."

Marcus had an uneasy feeling Rhys was trying to tell him more than he wanted to say out loud. The realization made Marcus fervently wish for his bedchamber in Isca.

"Are you telling me that your sister can . . . change?" He choked on the word.

"To wolf form," Rhys said quietly. "As I shift into a merlin."

Instinctively, Marcus eased back, down the slope.

"Dinna leave. Please. I need your help."

Panic squeezed Marcus's lungs. "My help is nothing. I have no magic. I want no part of this.

Rhys offered the torch to Marcus. "My power isn't strong enough to bring down Blodwen's enchantment entirely. But I believe I can bend it enough so ye may pass. Please. Gwen is injured. Help me save her."

Marcus looked into Rhys's eyes. Where he might have seen a Druid, he saw only a friend. He drew a breath and willed the panic inside him to ease.

"What must I do?"

"I'll weaken the spell as much as I can. Ye must enter the cave and bring Gwen out."

"You want me to walk though a sorceress's spell?" Marcus would rather have pierced his palm with an iron poker.

"For the sake of the friendship we once shared."

"We share it still," Marcus muttered. "I'll go. But . . ." He could barely speak the words. "What . . . form . . . is Gwen in?"

"She was a wolf when last I saw her."

Marcus swallowed and adjusted his damp grip on the torch. "All right."

Lifting both hands, Rhys closed his eyes and began a chant. Marcus blinked. A shimmering light surrounded Rhys's head, as if the air vibrated with magic. His syllables were low and guttural; the words—if words they were—blended in one long, unbroken phrase. The sound made Marcus slightly nauseous.

Sick with dread, Marcus stepped into the cave. The narrow crevice compelled him to turn sideways to enter, thrusting the torch before him. Shadows lurched on the walls. A bead of sweat rolled into his eye. Cursing, he swiped at it.

Drawing a breath, he advanced, Rhys's chant fading like a dream as he moved farther and farther into the mountain. The sloping floor was slick with ice, forcing him to place his steps with care. The descent should have been easy, but the deeper he went into the cave the more his limbs dragged, until Marcus felt as though he were swimming through honey.

His brain felt muddled. Why was he in this place? Why did he not turn back? He clawed through the muck in his brain, trying frantically to remember.

A soft whine sounded. A wolf.

The animal was his goal, though at the moment, Marcus couldn't quite remember why. But he knew with a certainty that it was imperative he reach the creature. He moved toward the sound, each step becoming more difficult than the one before. Now it felt as though he were moving through molten rock. The cave's air, thick and dark, congealed in his lungs.

The ceiling slanted low, forcing him into a crouch. The sputtering flame of his torch licked the rocks. Had he reached the inner limit of the passage? Just when he thought he could go no further, he stepped into a small cavern.

Here, the enchantment seemed less. He raised the torch. The meager flame cast a lurching shadow on the walls. The dark form approached.

A wolf.

The beast's silver fur was wet and ragged. Its head lowered. A growl emerged from the beast's throat, setting Marcus's heart pounding. Could this feral creature truly be a woman in animal form? The notion seemed too fantastic—too horrific—to contemplate.

He took a hesitant step, prompting another snarl from his quarry. Was the fire responsible for the beast's reaction? Moving slowly so as not to prompt an attack, Marcus wedged the sputtering torch into a split in the cavern wall.

He stepped away from the light. The she-wolf turned with him, revealing a streak of blood on her flank. Marcus broke out in a cold sweat. Only an idiot would approach a wounded predator.

The wolf snarled. Marcus lowered himself into a crouch, attempting to appear less threatening. The feeble ruse seemed to work; the rumble in the wolf's throat ceased.

The animal went still. It was close enough that Marcus could gaze into its eyes. The irises were gray, like Rhys's. Was it his imagination, or did they hold a spark of intelligence?

"I've come to help," he said hoarsely.

The wolf regarded him, unblinking.

He held out one hand. "Rhys sent me."

The animal's head came up. Was that a glimmer of hope in its eyes? "Follow me and I'll take you to him."

The wolf hesitated, then stalked toward Marcus, head low, hackles raised. Marcus dared not do so much as breathe. His hand seemed miles away from the hilt of his dagger. But what did that matter? He couldn't throw his blade at this beast.

The wolf's paws scrabbled on a patch of ice. Before Marcus could react, it collapsed. With a shudder, it closed its eyes and lay still.

"No!" Marcus sprang forward. Kneeling, he pressed a hand to the beast's flank. The wolf stirred, emitting a groan that seemed almost human. Without stopping to consider the wisdom of his actions, Marcus scooped the animal into his arms.

He'd taken no more than a step when the wolf began to change.

At first, Marcus thought it a trick of the dying torchlight. The wolf's silver fur shimmered. He tightened his hold on the animal as its fur smoothed, then disappeared, leaving bare skin. The long muzzle softened and shifted, the details resolving into a woman's face. Ears shrank, cheekbones arched, lips formed. The wolf's body elongated, and for a moment what Marcus held in his arms was neither woman nor beast. A brilliant burst of light forced his eyes closed. Flashes of silver danced on the insides of his eyelids.

The sensation of the burden changed. Where once his arms had cradled wet fur, now he felt the touch of damp human skin. A whisper of hair tickled the inside of his elbow. A soft breast rose and fell against his chest.

He opened his eyes.

A woman lay naked in his arms. Her face shone deathly pale in the erratic light of the sputtering torch. Her features were a more delicate version of Rhys's regal countenance—strong and fine, with high arching brows and cheekbones. Long, silver-blond hair cascaded over Marcus's forearm in tangles. Her breasts were full, her belly softly rounded, her legs long and firm.

Marcus swallowed. Hard.

Pale eyelashes fluttered, revealing gray eyes like the wolf's. But these eyes belonged to a woman, not a beast.

They widened slightly at the sight of him. "Who—?"

A moan cut off her words. She twisted, her arm moving to reveal a gash in her side. The wound was red and ugly, with puckered edges that oozed white corruption. Clearly, the injury had gone days without tending.

Marcus muttered a curse. She needed a healer, quickly.

At that moment, the torch spat sparks and died, leaving him in utter blackness. Heart pounding, Marcus pivoted toward the exit, his arms tightening on his burden. Moving carefully, he reached the cavern wall and groped in the direction he thought—hoped—would lead to the passageway.

He found it. He ducked through the low portal, cursing as his head thumped against stone. He moved toward the mouth of the cave, climbing the twisted path. After what seemed an interminable amount of time, he heard Rhys chanting hoarsely, an edge of desperation in his voice.

He gained the entrance, stumbling. Snow swirled around him. The wind had strengthened fiercely—it hit him with an icy blast. Marcus went down on his knees, cradling Gwen's head as he fell. Primitive emotion passed through him. This woman would not—would *never*—come to injury at his hands.

Rhys was beside him in a heartbeat, already stripping off his cloak. He wrapped it around Gwen's still form. Then he fished a silver pendant from around his neck and slipped its chain over Gwen's head. "Is she—"

"Alive," Marcus gasped. He could feel the Druidess's

blood moving and pulsing as if it were his own. "But she's wounded—"

Rhys made a sound deep in his throat. "We must take her to Mared."

"Is she your healer?"

"Aye."

Marcus had already gained his feet. Rhys moved to take his sister, but Marcus found he could not bear to let her go. "I'll carry her," he muttered, looking up to challenge Rhys's protest.

But Rhys only stepped back and nodded.

Clara could feel Owein's presence within the Lost Land. He wasn't far away, but he was cloaked in darkness. Not the same darkness that enveloped Clara—pure and cool—but a heated blackness that spewed the stomach-heaving stench of sulfur.

She moved toward it. Into it. Each breath seared her throat, set fire to her lungs. Calming her mind as Rhys had taught her, she reached inside to touch her Light. She summoned a barrier of brilliance, wrapping it around her in a mantle of protection. Her next breath came easier.

She reached for Owein, calling his name in her mind. She received no answer. She moved forward—to what, she had no idea. She could see nothing beyond the sphere of her own Light. She moved again, seeking him.

She passed through the arched opening to find herself in the center of a Celt village. A cluster of roundhouses nestled within stout palisade walls. The scene was peaceful enough, and yet, Clara felt a wrongness about it. A darkness.

Owein? Where are you?

There was no answer.

But she sensed his essence, white and black swirling together. Dark magic surrounded him, surging, enveloping, seeking to absorb the bright part of him.

Clara threw her mind forward, desperate to reach him in

time. Once darkness blotted out Owein's Light, he would be lost.

Ruby liquid rippled in the bowl of the Lost Grail.

"Blood," Owein said thickly.

Blodwen laughed. With a delicate motion, she lifted the cup and extended it to him. "Nay. 'Tis but wine."

"A Roman drink."

"A symbol of our triumph over the enemy. Drink, Owein, and the Deep Magic will come to our aid. Together, we will drive the Romans from the west."

He shook his head. "I've seen more violence than I can bear. I want no more. I wish only a peaceful home." His gaze dropped to the babes, sleeping curled like pups. "Children."

Blodwen's beautiful countenance darkened. "The Lost Land shows the future—but 'tis a future unfulfilled if we dinna fight for it. Do ye think the Romans will suffer us to live in peace? Do ye think they will leave our son alive, our daughter untouched?"

"I will protect them."

Her voice seethed with anger. "I tell ye, ye willna be able to, as long as the Legions remain. They are defilers. They willna rest until every Celt man is dead, and every Celt woman planted with their foul seed."

She lifted the grail. "We can drive the Romans back to Gaul. We can live in peace, raise our children without fear. The power of the Lost Grail will aid us."

Owein gazed at the grail. Red liquid sloshed in its bowl. *Too thick to be wine,* he thought.

It was blood.

But perhaps blood was fitting.

He took the cup in his hands.

Chapter Twenty-four

A cry reverberated in Owein's skull.

No!

Clara. His head lifted in stunned surprise. She was here, within the Lost Land. Swiftly, he blocked her entry into his mind. He could ill afford the distraction such a union would bring.

A sharp knife of pain stabbed Owein's right eye. The Lost Grail vibrated in his hands, sending shocks through his palms and up his arms. The ruby surface of its liquid fractured into a thousand glistening fragments.

He could not look away from the cup. The reflections on the surface of the blood called to him. He sank his mind into the vague images and emerged into a scene of horror.

Isca lay in ruins, the great stone wall of its fortress tossed about like so many pebbles. A dark sky above the city crackled with lightning. The wind churned the sea into a froth.

Flames crackled against the turbulent sky. The city burned, sending smoke and ash pouring into the heavens. Celts and Roman alike streamed from the broken walls like ants, piling fruitlessly on the upper slopes of the city. The raging sea had flooded the flatlands surrounding the city. There was no route of escape.

He tore his eyes away. Blodwen stood calmly before him, her gray gaze watchful.

"Ye cannot bring this about," he said, shaken. "No Druid's power is so great."

"I assure ye, mine is." She dipped her finger into the cup, stirring. "Drink, Owein. Drink, so that we may save our people."

"Nay. This cup is meant for healing. It's essence is Light. Not destruction."

"It matters not. The Lost Grail is a path to the Deep Magic of the gods. We will wield it together as King and Queen."

"No human should be so bold as to claim a place among the gods."

"We will. It is my destiny. And my revenge."

"Revenge?"

"Aye. Revenge on those who took my innocence. My magic. Romans," she spat. "They savaged me until I begged for death. Then they cut me while they laughed. Afterwards, even my own father couldn't bear to look at me. And my uncle? He wouldna allow my kin to pursue the monsters who harmed me."

Owein frowned. "I dinna understand."

Tears glittered in her eyes. For an instant, her expression crumpled into vulnerability. Then her eyes hardened and her jaw set. "I will show ye," she said, her voice flat. "And then ye will know."

Light shimmered about her face, then faded, taking her beauty with it. Owein realized Blodwen's sweet countenance had been an illusion. With her magic withdrawn, her true face was a hideous mass of scars, created by the cut and slice of a blade. The largest gash extended in a diagonal from one cheekbone to her jaw, catching the corner of her mouth. There were numerous other, smaller cuts.

Owein's stomach turned. No one—man, woman, or beast—should ever be used thus.

"Who did this?" he asked, his voice deadly soft.

"Soldiers from the fortress at Isca. They left me for dead, but Cyric forbade my father's vengeance. 'Revenge is nay the way of the Light,' he said." Her laugh was hollow. "If that is so, what use is Light? There is far more justice in darkness."

"So ye would destroy the fortress and city now, to avenge this wrong?"

" 'Tis my right."

"And the innocents? What of them?"

Her face contorted. "There are no innocents in Isca. Only Romans."

"Many Celts dwell there as well."

"Traitors."

"Nay. Kinsmen." Owein's own kin. "Perhaps they dinna live the life of our ancestors, but neither do they live the life of Rome. Many Romans have changed as well, learning Celt ways." His voice lowered. "I willna have ye harm them, Blodwen."

Anger flared in her eyes. Her scars vanished, once again cloaked with illusion. Power crackled about her like red lightning.

"Ye refuse your aid?"

Owein regarded her steadily. "Aye."

" 'Tis nay your own will speaking. 'Tis the Roman witch. She's placed a foul enchantment upon ye."

"Ye are mistaken. I speak for myself."

"I'm nay such a fool to believe that! She stalks ye like a wolf! She is close, seeking to turn ye from me. That, I canna allow."

She raised one hand. A stream of red light flashed past Owein's shoulder. He spun about in time to see Clara pitching through the doorway. She landed on her hands and knees near the hearth.

* * *

"Clara!"

Owein's voice. Clara looked up, dazed. One moment, she'd been standing before the door of a hut. The next instant, a violent force had pulled her through the portal and cast her on the hard ground.

"Owein?" He was here, before her, standing on the other side of a blazing fire. He held her mother's cup. The ancient silver shone dully in his hands.

A shadow fell over her. "On your feet, bitch."

Clara looked up, dazed. The silver-haired beauty standing over her could only be Blodwen. Magic poured from her in waves of heat. Not a steady hearth flame like Owein's power, but an angry, raging wildfire that carried a stench of burned flesh. Sick, putrid hate singed the edges of Clara's mind. She shrank back with a cry.

"Ye willna hurt her." Owein had moved to stand between Clara and the Druidess. Clara sensed his fear for her, well hidden behind his hard expression.

"I shall do as I wish," Blodwen replied. She lifted one hand and uttered a Word.

Burning pain exploded in Clara's chest. She wrapped her arms around her torso, bending double. Owein cried out, springing toward her, only to be brought up short by Blodwen's magic as Clara gasped for breath.

"Stop this," Owein said tersely.

"Drink. If ye do not . . ." She nodded at Clara.

Clara's throat constricted, as if a searing hand had closed on her neck. She clawed at it, desperate for air. But there was nothing to grab onto, no fingers to pry away. Darkness blotted the edges of her vision.

"Nay." Owein raised his hand, fingers spread. He spoke a Word. The sound reverberated against the walls of the hut, and for an instant, the tightness in Clara's throat eased. She managed a single gulp of air before her windpipe squeezed again.

And she understood that however strong Owein's magic, it was no match for Blodwen's.

Owein grabbed for Clara. His hand grasped only air. It was as if she'd faded back, out of touch. Try as he might, he couldn't reach her. Red liquid sloshed in the grail, spilling over the sides, streaking his fingers.

Clara's choked whisper pleaded in his mind. *Owein . . .*

Blodwen smiled. "Ye canna reach her, Owein. Not unless I allow it."

He cursed. "Stop this. She's done no wrong."

"She was born a Roman. That is enough."

"Release her."

Blodwen nodded to the Lost Grail. "Perhaps. After ye drink."

Clara slumped to the floor and lay still. Owein kept his eyes fixed on the uneven rise and fall of her chest.

"Would ye condemn her, Owein?" Blodwen said, her voice softly taunting. "I could snuff out her life with one finger." She laughed, her silver hair rippling about her shoulders. Had he ever thought her beautiful? In his dream, her darkness had been masked.

"Ye would pay a steep price for that," Owein said softly. "The gods would demand it."

"Do ye nay understand? For me, there is no payment. My magic comes from within. Not from the gods."

He stared at her. " 'Tis pure folly to think that."

"Nay. 'Tis the truth. I have become a goddess. I would make ye my god consort. Drink of the wine, and ye will understand."

His eyes warred with hers, then his gaze dropped to the red liquid that trembled in the grail. The sweet, iron tang of it assaulted his nostrils. "This is not wine."

She held up one slender arm, wrist turned outward. A thin, red line slashed across the white skin. She laughed. "Aye, ye speak the truth. 'Tis blood. My own."

Revulsion rolled through him. "Ye are insane."

" 'Tis the world that has gone insane. I have discovered the secrets of the Old Ones. They knew the path to the Lost Land, and from there the road to Annwyn, where the gods dwell. I will follow them. With ye." She extended her forefinger to Clara. "Drink, Owein, or I will kill her."

Clara gasped, struggling for air. He couldn't let her die here, at his feet. Reluctantly, Owein brought the Lost Grail to his lips. Its silver rim was warm. Alive.

A whisper of Clara's consciousness brushed his mind. *No, Owein! You cannot obey her.*

I must. For you.

No. I think . . . I think there is another way.

Owein went still. Blodwen's eyes narrowed, watching him.

How?

He felt Clara's hesitation. *Open your mind. Fully. I . . . I will channel the power of the Lost Grail through you.*

My darkness—

It will not stop me. Please, Owein.

"My patience grows thin," Blodwen said harshly. "Drink."

Clara pressed deeper into Owein's mind. With a deliberate breath, he steeled himself for her intrusion. Could she survive it? He didn't know. Yet he had no choice but to let her try.

He lowered his defenses. Showed her the path to darkness. Felt her fear as she approached.

He lowered the grail and met Blodwen's gaze squarely. "I will not drink."

"Ye dare defy me?"

"Aye, I dare."

A rough Word emerged from the back of Blodwen's throat. The sound struck Owein like the blow of a battle sword. Pain exploded behind his eyes. A thick, gray smoke enveloped him, agony running like shards of glass through his veins. Blodwen was forcing this torture upon him, and Clara—she was there, sharing it with him. Panic spilled into his gut. His fingers tightened convulsively on the grail. Against his will, his hand moved. Slowly, the rim of the cup rose to press once more to his lips.

Victory flared in Blodwen's eyes. "Drink."

He could all but taste her blood on his tongue. He spoke the most powerful Word he knew, but it had no effect. His magic could not overcome her strength.

She might defeat him, but he would not go willingly. His anger surged, his darkness rising to meet hers. He would give his life to destroy whatever part of her power he could.

But he would not risk Clara.

Leave me, he told her.

No. Her Light blazed in his consciousness. He sensed her fear, of him and the grail, and of Blodwen's dark might. Yet she didn't falter. *Let me in. Let me go deeper.*

He hung, suspended on the knife's edge of his pride. She didn't know what she asked. How could he expose the torture of his past to her Light? She would feel it as he had, know every moment of his pain and despair. She would experience his rage, be consumed by his darkness. Her Light would fade.

He would die a thousand deaths to prevent that. And yet, she would die unless he took the chance that she could prevail. How could he deny her that possibility? It was all they had.

If she were destroyed, the guilt would be his, forever. He should have seen through Blodwen's trap. He should have known the vision the Druidess had sent him was false. When had he ever had a vision of peace and hope? Of love?

All Owein could See was blood.

In the end, there was no choice to make. With a sigh, he yielded, opening his mind completely.

In a heartbeat, Clara surged to the center of his being, seeking the blackest part of his soul. Illumination fell on his darkest memory.

Powerless, he hung suspended as Clara's Light shone on Eirwen's bloodied body. Owein was on his knees at her side, his cheek pressed against her swollen belly. Just days before, the promise of new life had stirred under his palms. Now there was only death. Owein's child would never be born.

He felt Clara's touch, absorbing his despair. She gasped as it seared her, but somehow, she welcomed the pain. Accepted it.

Accepted *him.*

The darkness Owein had so jealously guarded began to melt. Its power dissolved into nothingness. Like a wave of brightness crashing on a brilliant shore, Light took its place.

With all his being, Owein aligned himself with Clara. He felt his power flowing with hers. It flashed through his body, traveled down his arms, blazed through his fingertips, into the Lost Grail.

The cup was still pressed to his lips. Owein lowered the vessel easily, holding it at arm's length.

A frown creased Blodwen's delicate brow. "How—"

With a deliberate motion, he upended the cup and poured its contents onto the hearth.

Blood splashed into the fire, hissing.

"No!" Blodwen's fury came swiftly. Pain hammered into Owein's skull. He felt Clara's cry as the full impact of it surged through their mental connection.

He felt Clara's recoil. He reached for her with his mind. *Dinna fight. Resistance will only make the pain worse.*

He felt Clara's fear, then her acquiescence. Her psyche bowed, letting Blodwen's fury wash through her. Waves of pain hammered them both. Hatred. Shame. Degradation. How well Owein understood all Blodwen had endured. But where Owein had sought to contain his darkness, Blodwen had flung hers far and wide.

The putrid stink of her malice clogged Owein's lungs. The Druidess's soul was like a rotting carcass, crawling with maggots. The dark perverted pleasures that had unleashed her power were revealed. Her wounded soul struck with the claws of a dark beast, leaving a path of flames.

Clara lay motionless by the hearth. Owein felt his strength drain, sapped by Blodwen's fury. He struggled to stay upright in the face of her fury. Would the Druidess's rage destroy them all?

Look into the grail.

At Clara's urging, Owein's gaze dropped. Tilting the grail, he looked into the bowl. The mark inside gleamed, streaked with blood.

The triple spiral in the center of the pattern began to turn. The circle about it glowed white, its four quarters resolving into the shape of a cross. The vines encircled all, binding the Deep Magic. A shaft of Light arced from the cup, blinding him.

A single Word, spoken by Clara, reverberated in his mind.

Peace.

Chapter Twenty-five

Slowly, Clara became aware of her body pressed to a bed of cold stone. As she lay, not moving, a tremor passed through the rock. A shower of pebbles splattered all around.

A hand clutched her arm. "Clara."

Arms lifted her to a sitting position. Looking up, she met Owein's troubled gaze. Behind his head, a rocky dome glittered with crystals. A thousand streams of light cast an eerie glow all around.

She rubbed her eyes. "Where . . . where are we?"

He gave a swift shake of his head. "I dinna know. A cave, of a sort. But nay one of the human world. I think we are still in the Lost Land."

Clara shoved herself upright, battling a rush of vertigo. "Blodwen . . ."

"There."

She swallowed a gasp. The Druidess lay on her back, face pale, arms outstretched. Her face was a mass of scars, her hair thin and gray. Despite the evil Blodwen had plotted, Clara felt her chest clutch in pity.

Owein crouched, testing the pulse at her throat. "She lives."

The earth trembled again, loosing a rain of debris from the cave ceiling. Owein hunched over the Druidess, protecting her scarred face. A chunk of rock fell, striking him on the shoulder.

"We must flee," Owein said.

Clara looked around. As far as she could tell, the cavern had no exit. "How?"

Owein slid his arms under Blodwen. Clara could tell by the strain around his eyes that the effort pushed him to the limit of his strength. She understood why. The magic they shared had drained her of strength as well. Her limbs felt like rubber. Her stomach boiled with nausea. When she swung her head around, the walls of the cave spun.

Another rumble. She covered her head as a shower of stones fell. When it passed, she met Owein's gaze. "Which way?"

He scanned the cavern. "There," he said suddenly. "The white stone."

"Yes. It's like the stone on Avalon's high slope." Scrambling to her feet, she started toward it.

"Wait. The grail. Do ye see it?"

Clara looked about. "No."

"Find it. Quickly."

She made a circuit of the cavern, scanning the debris. Closing her eyes, she let her senses expand, seeking a hint of the grail's magic. But she felt nothing.

The ground trembled and shook.

"Watch out!" Owein cried.

She pitched to one side, barely avoiding a falling chunk of the cavern's ceiling. Owein shifted Blodwen over one shoulder and grabbed Clara's wrist.

"Forget the grail," he muttered. "The gods want us gone."

He yanked her toward the white stone. They fell through together, sound and sensation streaking past in a blur. It took Clara a moment or two before she realized she lay sprawled in the deep snow collected within the cleft of a hill. She lifted her head. Owein crouched nearby, with Blodwen motionless beside him.

She frowned up at Owein. "What is this place?"

"The far side of Avalon, in the underbelly of the low hill."

She pushed herself up, her eyes lighting on a white stone partially buried by a rockslide. "But I entered the Lost Land on the high slope. Could this be a second entrance?"

"Aye, so it would seem."

"And the grail remains within. The cup is lost again."

"Perhaps nay completely," Owein said, nodding.

Clara followed his gaze. A spring bubbled from beneath the white stone. It flowed in gentle rivulets, snaking through the snow. She frowned, leaning closer. The stream was tinted red.

Owein's expression was one of wonder. " 'Tis like a vision I had," he said softly. "The vision that led me to you."

"Is it . . . blood?" Clara whispered.

Owein dipped one hand in the stream. "Nay. Water. I can feel its magic. A gift of the grail, I am thinking."

Clara let out a breath. "Perhaps so."

Blodwen stirred, groaning. A tremor ran through her body. Owein went to the Druidess. Her eyes fluttered open, staring blankly. Clara wondered how much the Druidess remembered of her fury. Indeed, she wondered if Blodwen remembered her own name.

"We must take her to the village," Clara said. "To Rhys."

Owein looked up sharply. "The wandering Druid Cormac spoke of? Was it he who brought ye here?"

"Yes. He and Marcus—"

He went stiff. "Marcus Aquila?"

"Yes."

"That Roman accompanied ye to Avalon? And the Druids didna strike him down?"

"No."

"The lad has stones," Owein muttered. "Ye could do far worse than marry him."

The words sliced like a knife inserted between her ribs. Clara had seen the deepest part of Owein's soul. She'd seen his longings, knew his heart.

As he knew hers. Why, then, did he push her away?

Chapter Twenty-six

Rhys clasped Gwendolyn's cold hand, hardly daring to take his eyes from her face. He hardly recognized his sister, she was so haggard and still. His heart clenched. His twin might have died if Marcus Aquila hadn't helped save her.

"Are ye sure she will recover?" he asked Mared.

The old healer fixed him with a disgruntled look. "Do ye doubt my word, Rhys?"

"Nay, of course not," he said hastily. "I only wondered . . . shouldn't she have awakened by now?"

"Her wounds are deep."

"The gash on her side looks much better."

"Gwendolyn's worst hurt is not that of the flesh. Her spirit was injured far more deeply." Mared placed her hand on his arm. "She will recover. But she has been touched by dark magic, Rhys. The effects will linger long after she wakes."

Rhys sighed. He'd never known Mared to be mistaken. What aftereffects of Blodwen's magic might Gwen experience? Would she share her suffering with him? A hollow feeling in Rhys's chest told him Gwen might once again draw away.

He turned to Cyric. The Druid Master lay on a pallet beside his granddaughter, his breath rasping peacefully. The sound was sweet music to Rhys's ears. When Clara and Owein had overcome Blodwen's darkness, the enchantment weighing Rhys's grandfather had begun to dissipate. Rhys sent a prayer of thanks to the Great Mother. He'd not been ready to lose Cyric.

"And Blodwen?" he asked Mared quietly. He couldn't help feeling guilt for the hurt his cousin had inflicted. He and Blodwen had been raised together. Rhys had been devastated when she'd been maimed, yet he'd never suspected the darkness she harbored. Perhaps if he had, he might have been able to turn her from the path she'd chosen.

Mared rose. "Attend me outside, Rhys."

Rhys replaced Gwen's hand on her pallet and covered it with her blanket. Rising, he followed the healer out of the hut.

"We must speak of Blodwen," Mared said once they'd reached the village common.

"How does she fare?" His cousin had been unconscious when Owein had carried her into the village. Padrig had been distraught, and was even now on the high slope, pouring out his pain to the Great Mother. Mared had attended Blodwen, tight-lipped, in a hut on the edge of the village.

"She's awakened. Her body, at least, is strong. But her magic is gone. Darkness has left her spirit in ashes." She turned grave eyes on Rhys. "Ye know as well as I do judgment must be passed. With both Cyric and Gwen ill, that task falls to ye."

Rhys had expected this. "And if I dinna wish to pass it?"

Mared's expression remained firm. " 'Tis hard, I know. But the law must be fulfilled."

Rhys stared out over the swamps. "I canna condemn her. Nor would Cyric want me to. He ever preaches forgiveness."

"She canna stay in Avalon, Rhys. The clan willna have it."

"Are ye certain her power is gone? It's nay merely hidden, like before?"

"I am certain. She's an empty husk."

Rhys sighed. Looking up, he spied Hefin perched at the peak of a cone-shaped roof. He stared at the merlin for several moments, then turned back to Mared. "Blodwen will leave the sacred isle. Today. Give her what provisions she can carry and tell her to journey across the swamps." He swallowed. " 'Twill be her task to make a life for herself in the Roman towns."

" 'Tis almost a death sentence. Blodwen knows no Latin. Her scarred face will bring nothing but stares and curses. Perhaps," Mared said quietly, "she would prefer death."

"Perhaps so," Rhys answered quietly. "But I willna pass that judgment."

Clara brought a meal of barley bread and mutton to Marcus. Sitting on a log near the docks, he spoke little as he consumed the food. When he was done, he sat with his elbows propped on his spread knees and avoided her gaze.

His mare grazed nearby, its saddle cinched and ready for a rider. Marcus meant to leave, and soon.

"Mared says Cyric has improved greatly," Clara told him. "Gwendolyn is out of danger as well."

Marcus's eyes flashed with a dark emotion she didn't understand. "That is good."

"Cyric has chosen Gwen as his successor," Clara went on. "Can you believe it? A woman as leader of Avalon?"

Marcus scowled darkly. "They will not let me near her."

"No." Mared had been adamant. Marcus was not allowed in the village, no matter that he had saved Gwen's life. Rhys had bowed to the healer's authority, drawing

Marcus's ire. It seemed Cyric's rules were not to be bent, even for a friend.

"Give Aiden my love when you reach Isca," Clara said, for want of anything else.

Marcus rose. "I will." He paused, examining her. "Are you sure you don't want to return with me?"

Clara shook her head. "With my father dead, there is nothing for me in the city, save more trouble with Valgus. Your father may take my petition to Londinium. If he's successful, you'll have all the more funds to spend at the slave auctions."

Marcus's dark eyes were troubled. "You'll have a hard life here."

"It's my choice."

He hesitated, then nodded. Rising to his feet, he enclosed her in an embrace. His touch was that of a brother, or a close friend. "I'll leave the spare horses for your use."

She smiled. "Thank you."

He touched her cheek. "I hope you'll be happy here."

"I hope so, too."

He swung into the saddle and was off, fording the swamp without a backward glance.

The soft moan drifted over the moor like the sigh of a lost spirit. Cormac drew up short and tilted his head, listening. The sound came again, a clear, haunting cry of despair. 'Twas a woman's voice.

Deliberately, Cormac set to whistling.

He shifted the pack on his shoulders, wincing a bit when the strap rubbed against the open wound on his wrist. The lament came again, louder. He gritted his teeth. Why should Blodwen's desolation scratch at him like a fevered cat? He should be greeting her suffering with shouts of joy.

And yet he wasn't.

"I'm a swiving idiot," he muttered to the deserted landscape. "I should be overjoyed that at last the Horned God favors me. 'Tis long past time, I say."

Circling, he found her tracks easily enough. They showed an erratic gait and an uncertain path. He should leave her to her fate. After all, he owed her nothing.

And yet, he couldn't.

Curse him for a fool, but there it was. Muttering under his breath, he followed her trail to an outcrop of rocks overlooking the sea. He found her huddled in the lee of a large boulder, knees drawn up tight to her chest. Her hair hung in limp shanks, and her white robe was dirty and ragged.

She looked utterly harmless. Still, he approached with caution. Despite Rhys's assurances, he couldn't quite believe her magic was gone. She'd bested him more times than he could count. He'd not be played the fool now.

She didn't raise her head as he approached. He halted, gazing down at her. 'Twas a novel feeling, looking down at a lass. Most often, Cormac stood eye-level with a woman's teats.

"Well met, Blodwen."

Her chin jerked up, her gray eyes widening with fear. The sight of her nearly made him stagger backward. He'd forgotten how ugly she was without the glamour.

Her scars whitened as blood rushed into the surrounding skin. Her tongue darted out, licking her chapped lips.

"Cormac."

Instinctively, he flinched, anticipating a blast of magic. It never came. He shifted, lowering his pack to the ground with a thud. "Your magic is truly gone, then?"

She nodded.

He grinned and took a step closer. She shrank back against the stone, as if trying to become one with it. Seeing Blodwen cower spun his head faster than a mug of strong ale. He felt his cock twitch.

A slow smile spread over his face. "I believe," he said, "that I prefer ye this way."

She cast her eyes downward.

Cormac caught her chin in his hand and forced it up. "Look at me when I speak to ye, woman."

She trembled like moor grass in the wind. Her gray eyes blinked up at him, huge with fear. "Y-yes, Cormac."

His cock hardened, lengthening against his thigh.

"I have nothing left." She licked her lips. "The magic is gone."

"Even when I do this?" Cormac's hand drifted downward, covering her breast. He palmed her roughly. She gasped and arched into his hand.

He felt no surge of magic. Saw no crackle of red about her body. Felt no urge to drop to his knees and pleasure her.

He could walk away if he wished. Leave her.

The knowledge made him bold. He tweaked her nipple, earning a throaty moan. She stared up at him, her face flushed with arousal.

He flashed her a grin and bent to open his pack.

She bit her lip. "Do ye have food?"

"Are ye hungry?"

"Aye."

He clucked his tongue against the roof of his mouth. " 'Tis a pity 'tis nay time for a meal."

He withdrew a coiled length of rope from his pack.

Blodwen's eyes grew as wide as two moons.

They were beautiful eyes, Cormac thought, despite the fact they occupied a face covered with scars. But what did he care for scars, anyway? Scars didn't affect a woman's ability to take a man's cock in her mouth, nor did they hinder the spreading of her thighs.

He grabbed Blodwen's wrist and tied the rope about it. The other end he looped about his hand. "Ye'll come with me," he told her. "Do what I say and ye'll keep a full belly."

She nodded.

He stood, whistling a jaunty melody, some bawdy tune

he'd once heard. If he remembered correctly, the song concerned a farmer, his wife—and a very thick carrot.

He chuckled as he led Blodwen down the trail.

She came willingly. Cormac squared his shoulders. A man could get used to such an obedient wench.

Indeed he could.

Chapter Twenty-seven

"I thank ye," the tall, silver-haired Druid said, inclining his head. "Ye have returned the Lost Grail to Avalon."

Owein shifted, uncomfortable with Rhys's gratitude. " 'Twas nay I who brought the cup to the sacred isle. Nor is the cup in the hands of the Druids of Avalon. The grail is lost once more."

Rhys shook his head. "Hidden, perhaps, but nay lost. The red spring flows from the earth where the grail is buried. Mared senses healing magic in the water."

"As do I," Clara said. "I'm glad my mother's cup has returned to the place where it was made."

"There's a place for ye here as well. Both of ye. Will ye remain?"

Owein shifted. A home, away from the Romans, among his own kind. It was what he'd dreamed of for so long. But for Clara? He looked around the village complex, seeing it through her eyes: a haphazard arrangement of mud and wattle huts, huddled together on a windy slope. Sheep and pigs roamed freely in the common area enclosed by the palisade wall. The women here were sturdy and tall, with faces weathered beyond their years. They were no strangers to hard labor. Indeed, with only twenty or so in the village, every pair of hands was needed for weaving, tending crops, cooking, making clothes, hunting, fishing, herb-gathering . . . the list went on and on.

Try as he might, he could not picture Clara living such a hard life. She was so delicate and fine. It was far more likely the fat sow nuzzling the ground would sprout wings and fly to the rooftops. What was worse, Owein had a feeling that during the frequent visits Clara had paid to the docks in the last few days, Marcus Aquila had told her the same thing.

Rhys was watching him, waiting for an answer. Owein searched the Druid's gray eyes. He sensed a friend, a man whose loyalty never wavered. How long had it been since Owein had counted such a man as kin? He inclined his head. "I would be honored to remain in Avalon."

Rhys clapped a hand on Owein's shoulder, his smile broad and welcoming. "I am glad of it." He turned to Clara. "And will the Daughter stay as well?"

Owein felt Clara's eyes upon him. "I will," she said.

He met her gaze squarely, with raised eyebrows. "What of your fortune in Isca?"

"What of it? Without my father, it means little. I plan to send a petition to the governor, requesting Lucius Aquila be appointed my guardian. If it's successful, I'll give all my property to Marcus Aquila."

Marcus Aquila. Owein's gut twisted. He hated the way Clara's voice grew soft whenever she uttered the man's name. If Marcus had agreed to accept Clara's property, did he not expect to get Clara in the bargain?

"Marcus will use my inheritance to free slaves," Clara said to Rhys, who nodded. "But I will remain in Avalon."

Clara caught Owein's gaze. She regarded him steadily, her brows raised in challenge.

"Excuse us," Owein said shortly to Rhys. At the Druid's nod, he took Clara's elbow and drew her toward the sheep pens.

She wrinkled her nose at the smell. At one time, Owein might have laughed at her expression of disgust. Now he said only, "The stench will be much worse in the summer."

She set her jaw. "I'll get used to it."

"There are no hot baths in Avalon," Owein continued. "No rose oil. No slave lads to keep the furnace stoked so the heated air may warm your toes. There are no Roman cooks, no wheat bread, no spices. If ye want water, ye must haul it from the spring."

Clara's expression hardened. "You speak as if you don't want me to stay."

Owein rubbed the back of his neck. " 'Tis nay what I want that matters. For all my power of Sight, I canna see ye living here."

"You think I'm not strong enough."

"Nay. I know well enough that ye have a spine of hardened iron. But ye weren't raised to this kind of life, Clara. I canna believe ye'll be happy."

"You think I'd be happy in Isca? Without you?"

"I think ye would forget me, in time." He sighed. "Marcus Aquila is far more suited to ye than I am. He sits on the docks, waiting to take you home."

"No. He left this morning."

Owein frowned. "That canna be true. He wants ye."

"Maybe once he thought he did, but not now. He's gone, and as you can see, I am here. I mean to stay, Owein. And I thought . . . I hoped you wanted me here."

He shifted, not daring to meet her eyes. "I canna believe ye would give up all the comforts of a Roman life for one such as me. Not after ye saw all my shame. All my darkness."

"Oh, Owein." She reached out to him. Touched his chin, where the red stubble had begun to thicken. But his beard didn't seem to bother her as it once had.

"How could I condemn you for your darkness?" she said. "You endured so much, and yet you never lost your honor, never struck out at the innocent as Blodwen did." Her fingertips brushed his lips. "And besides, you're not the only reason I wish to stay in Avalon. I want to stay for myself, too. For my magic."

A tendril of hope unfurled in Owein's chest. If Clara truly wished to stay in Avalon, who was he to drive her away? The gods knew he wanted her at his side. Perhaps it was time to let the last of his darkness go.

And accept happiness in its place.

He caught her hand, halting her exploration of his jawline. Turning it in his, he pressed a kiss on her open palm.

She smiled and sighed, relaxing into his body. He drew her in tightly, his arm wrapping around her. She fit so perfectly beside him.

He let out a long breath. "I thank ye."

She looked up. "For what?"

"For pursuing me into Blodwen's trap. I could nay have stopped her madness without ye, lass."

"Clara," she said with a mock scowl. "How many times must I tell you?"

Easing away, he took her hands in his. "Clara," he agreed softly. "How I love ye."

He brought her hands to his lips. Without releasing her gaze, he caught the tip of one forefinger in his mouth and suckled it.

Her breath caught. He turned his head, rubbing his new beard against her palm.

"That prickles," she said.

"Think how it would feel on the tender skin between your thighs," he whispered.

She went still, her breath catching. Surreptitiously, she darted a glance right and left, as if assessing the villagers milling about the yard. One or two were watching their conversation with undisguised interest, Owein noted with some amusement. He'd lived alone for so long, he'd all but forgotten that privacy was not an aspect of village life.

Clara went up on tiptoe, wrapping her arms about his neck. Her lips brushed his ear. "Is there a hut free, do you think?" she whispered. "I want to show you how eager I am to be your wife."

He raised his brows. "Are ye offering me marriage, then, lass?"

Clara smiled, her eyes sparking with mischief. "Celt women choose their own husbands. If I'm to live here in Avalon, shouldn't I uphold the custom?" Her gaze softened. "I ask you now, Owein of Avalon—will you join hands with me before the clan?"

Owein chuckled, bending his head to whisper his answer against her lips.

"Aye, lass, I'll take your hand. And I'll give ye my heart in return."

Epilogue

A silver menagerie graced the shelf above Marcus's worktable. A fawn with long, uncertain legs. A bear, clawing the air. An owl, solemn and silent. A squirrel . . . a hare . . . an eagle, all fashioned by Marcus's hand from scraps of silver left over from more lucrative commissions.

He turned his newest creation this way and that, scrutinizing it for flaws. He saw none. The creature was so real he half-expected it to leap off his palm. It was quite possibly the finest figurine he'd ever created.

It was a she-wolf.

The animal regarded him with silent gray eyes. He'd sculpted them exactly as he remembered them—solemn and wide, with a magic that could look through a man's soul. They were shadowed eyes. Eyes that had seen more than they could bear.

A sudden chill overtook him.

He glanced toward the furnace, where a half-finished plow blade awaited. The coals had cooled while he'd sat dawdling. Pushing to his feet, he placed the she-wolf on the shelf with the other forest creatures.

Perhaps now his memories of Gwendolyn would fade.

HISTORICAL NOTE

Over twenty years ago, while traveling in England on my honeymoon, I visited Glastonbury, once known as the mystical island of Avalon. In the years since the Druids, Avalon's surrounding swamps have given way to flat, fertile farmland, but the sacred island still resonates with magic and legend.

The Chalice Well, also known as the Goddess Well, is one of these legends. Originally a sacred pagan spring, the waters of the Chalice Well are tinged a deep red. The scientific explanation for this phenomenon stresses the high iron content of the water. A more lyrical tale—and one which I much prefer—suggests the red waters flow from the Holy Grail, which lies buried beneath the well.

I hope you enjoyed my fantasy of how the Grail found a home under the hills of Avalon. For more Grail legends and Celtic trivia, as well as free short stories, giveaways and prizes, please visit my Web site at www.joynash.com.